# Sisters
## *of the*
# Confederacy

# Books by Lauraine Snelling

*Hawaiian Sunrise*

## A SECRET REFUGE

*Daughter of Twin Oaks    Sisters of the Confederacy*
*The Long Way Home*

## RED RIVER OF THE NORTH

*An Untamed Land    The Reapers' Song*
*A New Day Rising    Tender Mercies*
*A Land to Call Home    Blessing in Disguise*

## RETURN TO RED RIVER

*A Dream to Follow*

## HIGH HURDLES

*Olympic Dreams    Close Quarters*
*DJ's Challenge    Moving Up*
*Setting the Pace    Letting Go*
*Out of the Blue    Raising the Bar*
*Storm Clouds    Class Act*

## GOLDEN FILLY SERIES

*The Race    Shadow Over San Mateo*
*Eagle's Wings    Out of the Mist*
*Go for the Glory    Second Wind*
*Kentucky Dreamer    Close Call*
*Call for Courage    The Winner's Circle*

# LAURAINE SNELLING

# Sisters *of the* Confederacy

BETHANYHOUSE
PUBLISHERS
MINNEAPOLIS, MINNESOTA

*Sisters of the Confederacy*
Copyright © 2000
Lauraine Snelling

Cover by Dan Thornberg

Published by Bethany House Publishers
A Ministry of Bethany Fellowship International
11400 Hampshire Avenue South
Bloomington, Minnesota 55438
www.bethanyhouse.com

Printed in the United States of America by
Bethany Press International, Bloomington, Minnesota 55438

---

**Library of Congress Cataloging-in-Publication Data**

Snelling, Lauraine.
    Sisters of the Confederacy / by Lauraine Snelling.
        p.   cm. — (A secret refuge ; 2)
     ISBN 1–55661–840–9 (pbk.)
     1. United States—History—Civil War, 1861–1865—Fiction.  2. Overland journeys to the Pacific—Fiction.  3. Women abolitionists—Fiction.  4. Women pioneers—Fiction.  5. Sisters—Fiction.  I. Title.
PS3569.N39 S57    2000
813'.54—dc21                                     00–010798

---

To the Sharons in my life.
You encourage me, push me, love me,
make me laugh, make my life richer as my friends.
Thanks, and may God bless you
even more richly than you bless me.

LAURAINE SNELLING is an award-winning author of over twenty-five books, including fiction and nonfiction for adults and young adults. Besides writing both books and articles, she teaches at writers' conferences across the country. She and her husband, Wayne, have two grown sons and four granddogs, and they make their home in California.

# CHAPTER ONE

"Hey, boy, lemme see that horse of yours."

Marse Jesse Highwood, in reality Jesselynn, turned at the shout. A blue-clad soldier, his belly protruding between dark suspenders and hanging over the waistband of his blue britches, waved at her, letting her know whom he was accosting. As she turned her mare and drew closer, she could see a scar starting below his left eye and disappearing into a fox red beard. His eyes, the faded blue of a Yankee shirt washed too many times, glittered beneath bushy eyebrows. Sergeant stripes on the shirt sleeve made Jesse sit straighter.

"Yes, suh?" She kept her gaze below his chin.

"What you doin' with such a fine horse? Don't you know we need every horse we can git for the Union army?"

"Old Sunny here, suh, why she just near to foal and might would die with heavy ridin'. My daddy rode her home from the war so he could get well again and go back to fight. He say she need rest, jus' like him."

"What army was he with?"

*Oh, drat, my mouth's got me in trouble again. Who would he have fought with on the Union side? As if he would have fought for the Union, but* . . . She wracked her mind for the name of a Union general, all the while knowing her daddy fought in the legislature to keep the Union before he was forced to put on a Confederate uniform and go off to be killed. "With Kirby Smith, suh." She knew this man couldn't be from Tennessee, his accent was more mountain than Northern. Even so,

7

her answer was a gamble. At least he had called her "boy."

"Good outfit." He walked around the mare, who was obviously heavy with foal. The only reason Jesselynn rode her instead of one of the stallions was because of the influx of blue army men in Springfield. She should have tied her outside of town and walked in.

But then, leaving a horse in the care of a young black man left them both open for thievery. Slave traders or horse traders—neither much cared if their new possession was free before they caught them. If only she hadn't felt the need to check on Aunt Agatha, who'd been living in Springfield since her husband, Hiram, was killed in the early days of the war. But with the death of her housemate, Agatha needed family.

"Be on your way, then. And greet your daddy for me. He musta took a lot of abuse from his neighbors if he went north to fight."

"Yes, suh, he surely did. Why they nigh to burned our barn one night, they was so fired up." *Shut your mouth and get on out of here.* Jesselynn touched one finger to the brim of her droopy felt hat and nudged Sunshine on up the street.

"You got any other horses out to home?"

His call sent shivers up her back. "No, suh, you done took them all." That part at least was true. There were no more horses at home in Kentucky. She had the remaining stallions and mares with her in a cave southwest of town.

One good thing, she'd sure enough learned to lie well. Just tripped right off her tongue, they did. Dealing with the guilt was something else. All those years hearing the Scriptures at her mother's knee made her detest lying. But keeping everyone alive was more important. Why in the world was a Union sergeant lurking on the back streets like this? Their encampment was north of town. An area she wisely stayed away from—far away from.

When her heartbeat returned to normal, she patted the mare's shoulder and straightened her own. "That was one close call, old girl. This is the last time I bring you to town." *Or any of our other horses.* But Aunt Agatha most likely needed more wood by now. In the saddlebags she carried a rabbit Benjamin had snared. She hoped her aunt would volunteer to repay her with some of the vegetables stored in her root cellar. The two old ladies had raised a fine garden and kept enough hens to sell a few eggs.

Now, with Lettie gone, Agatha lived alone in a borrowed house.

A house that looked as if it would fall down if one kicked a porch post. Jesselynn rode on past the hingeless gate, now tied in place with hemp rope, and into the shed-roofed barn. The barn had been built with stalls for horses and a bay to store a buggy. The stalls had gone the way of firewood, and who knew what happened to the buggy. Most likely it was sold early on for supplies. Now only a few laying hens clucked and scratched in the dusty corners.

Jesselynn tied the mare to one of the posts and, after loosening the saddle girth, swung the saddlebags over her shoulder and headed for the house. Off to her left the remains of a garden long ago harvested appeared to be sprouting new cabbage from the stalks. A row of greens had shot up new growth too. Jesselynn ducked under the clothesline and crossed the muddy soil to check on the green leaves that looked so bright against the bleached cornstalks. Each time she came, she'd been cutting more of the garden refuse for the hens. If they had some fencing, they could build a run from the barn to the garden and let the hens help themselves.

Had her aunt even been outside to see this bit of bounty?

Back at the door she dragged her boots across the scraper set into the step, trying to remove the mud from the garden. Not hearing anyone moving around, she knocked and waited.

No answer. Had Aunt Agatha gone somewhere? If so, where?

She pounded on the door, rattling the frame as she did so. She should have brought Meshach along to make necessary repairs.

Still no answer. She turned the knob and pushed open the door, sticking her head in to call for her aunt again before she entered. Removing a hat that looked as if some rodent had been nibbling the brim, she ran her fingers through hair that had recently been darkened by walnut-husk dye and shorn by Ophelia, formerly one of her father's slaves and now freed along with the rest of them. Ophelia had cut only men's hair before, but since Jesselynn was acting that part, short was best, and ragged didn't hurt.

Since the shearing had happened the night before, Jesse was still trying to get used to it. Would she ever be able to have long hair again and regain her place in the world of women? Did she even want to?

She brushed mud and horsehair off her britches. Her apparel was always a bone of contention between her and her aunt. At least if her clothes were clean, maybe the old lady wouldn't huff so stridently.

"Aunt Agatha?" Jesselynn laid the rabbit carcass that she had skinned and wrapped in brown paper on the table and traipsed through the house, checking every room in case her aunt had fallen or something. No one was about.

Surely she hadn't left that long ago and would be back soon. The stove was still warm, and embers glowed in the firebox. Jesselynn added a few more sticks of wood and filled a pot with water from the reservoir. Taking a knife from the drawer, she cut up the rabbit and put the pieces in the heating water. She found an onion in the pantry, chopped and added it, along with salt and pepper, and set the lid on the kettle.

Now, how else could she make herself useful?

Nothing was out of place. Each tabletop was dust free. Her aunt's Bible lay on the whatnot table by her chair, the bookmark set in the New Testament. Jesselynn flipped open the pages and read the words of 2 Corinthians 1, shaking her head. The Lord of comfort had been remarkably absent from her life in the last months. Of course her saying—nay, screaming—"I want nothing to do with you. You don't bother me, and I won't come sniveling to you" might have something to do with that. She shivered in the chilly house, though it wasn't cold. Life just wasn't what she had dreamed it to be, all because of that wicked war.

She gritted her teeth and returned to the kitchen. Perhaps she should start bread.

She combed the pantry, but the empty shelves told their own story. Her aunt had not had money to put in supplies. And Jesselynn had nothing to give to her. She and her band were living hand to mouth as it was. Surely she could put flour and sugar and such on the account at the store.

Hearing feet scraping at the back door, she returned to the kitchen to check on the stewing rabbit and moved the kettle to the back to slow down the boiling.

"Ah, Jesselynn, how good to see you."

The humph at the end had to do with Jesselynn's clothing, but as Jesse had no intention of donning the petticoats and skirts her aunt had dragged out of the clothes press, she ignored it. "Brought you a rabbit snared just this morning," she said, greeting her aunt. At five foot seven, Jesselynn was tall for a young woman, and when she hugged her diminutive aunt, shock bolted from mind to heart.

Her aunt had lost more weight. Pleasantly rounded when Jesselynn first arrived in Springfield back in November, Aunt Agatha no longer filled out her waist, and the skirt had been taken in. Bones poked through the shawl she wore around her shoulders, and the skin of her face hung in folds under her chin.

"How long since you've eaten?" Nothing like getting directly to the point.

Agatha pulled herself upright, and starch returned to her backbone. "I had an egg for breakfast, thank you."

"And bread?"

Agatha turned away to lift the pot lid and stir the cooking rabbit. "Never you mind, young lady. I have my fruits and vegetables in the cellar, and—"

"What if you traded some of your stores for the things you can't grow? Surely there must be a merchant willing to trade."

"There might be."

Jesselynn waited, but her aunt continued stirring the pot. *How can I help you if I don't know what's wrong?* Like a whop up the side of her head, she suddenly realized the problem. Agatha couldn't get them there. Had even a basket become too heavy for her to carry? Of course, she wouldn't ask for help. But surely someone going by in a wagon could take her few tradable things to the store.

As her mother had always quoted, "Pride goeth before a fall." And her aunt was certainly long on pride. Somehow Jesse wasn't surprised. *Must be a family trait.*

How could she phrase her question so she wouldn't get lambasted for interfering? "If . . . if you'd like me to, I could carry some cabbages and carrots to the store for you, on my horse, that is."

"That would be right nice. I reckon I can spare a few of each."

"What about one of those barrels of apples I saw down there?"

"Need a wagon for that."

"True, but the next time Meshach comes in, we could manage it."

"All right, but you must take some of the things with you too. I'm sure you could use them."

"I will. Now, what would you like me to bring back?"

"Oh, flour, sugar, lard—"

"Beans?"

"No. Got plenty of them. How I would dearly love a cup of tea."

"You have dried beans?"

"Of course. Leather britches and dried shelled. You take a basket on down to the cellar and bring us up a potato or two and a mess of leather britches along with carrots and a turnip. Then fill a gunnysack to take to the store." With every word, Agatha's energy returned and her voice resumed more of its normal commanding air.

With all that food in store, why was the old lady fading away as she appeared to be? Was she ailing and not mentioning it?

"Oh, and go by the post office too, if you would. Just think how pleasant dinner would be if we heard from Richmond."

Jesselynn hadn't planned on staying for dinner, but what could she say? She took a gunnysack from a hook by the back door and went out around the house to the cellar doors. She shoved up the rusty hatch and, bending over, pulled one of the angled doors upright to lean it against the post set for that express purpose. "I bet she can't even open these doors. I should have thought of that and brought more into the house for her. Can't believe she's growing weak so quickly." Jesselynn continued muttering as she made her way down the six rock steps onto the dirt floor of the cellar. While the flat rocks laid a path to the bins, water from the winter rains had been seeping in already and turned most of the floor to mush. Someone at least had had the foresight to build the bins on raised dirt and put logs beneath the apple barrels. The bags of snap beans dried whole with two on a stem to resemble britches and the other dried vegetables hung from nails pounded into the floor joists above.

Aunt Agatha might be frail looking now, but she and her friend Lettie Copsewald had worked like Trojans during the summer and fall to get all this set by. Jesselynn chose an assortment of carrots, turnips, parsnips, and rutabagas, plus some potatoes and two heads of cabbage for her bag for the store, then placed some of each in the basket for upstairs. She'd get more to take out to the cave when she returned from her errands.

The clouds hung sullen gray as she mounted Sunshine for the ride to the store. She might be better walking, but time was running out if she was to be back to camp by dark. The new cave they had located after leaving the one where Dunlivey found them was south and west of Springfield, several miles farther from town. Not anywhere near as convenient as the first had been, especially if they needed to walk in all the time now.

The mule had been more of a loss than she'd anticipated.

With thoughts chasing through her mind like dogs after cats, she still remembered to stay off the main streets. No sense letting herself in for more trouble, although that hadn't helped earlier. *"Greet your father for me."* Not likely. Her snort made Sunshine flick her ears and pick up the pace.

Once at the store, she wasted a couple of minutes talking with Lawrence Dummont, the proprietor. "Just as I thought," Jesselynn said, expelling a sigh that had been building for some time. "So you're saying my aunt could put it on account if she wanted to?"

"I wouldn't let that dear old lady starve. What kind of a man do you think I am?"

Jesselynn blinked at the "dear old lady."

"'Specially after all she's been through. But without her or someone telling me, how was I to know?"

"You have a point there, Mr. Dummont." Jesselynn set her sack of produce on the counter. "So you would be willing to trade, then?"

"Of course." He opened the bag, peered in, and set it to the side, nodding at Jesselynn. "Now, what can I git you?"

Jesselynn gave him her list and waited while he measured things out. She ambled around the store looking longingly at the boots, the bolts of cloth, the ready-made pants and shirts for the two little boys in camp, her brother Thaddeus Joshua—or Joshwa, as he said it— and Sammy, the baby they'd found beside a dead slave woman. Wouldn't Ophelia love that bolt of red-and-white check cotton? But they'd have to get by. She fingered the money in her pocket.

At the counter as she was putting her supplies back in the tow sack, she remembered to ask, "Could you use a barrel of apples?"

"Sure enough. Those soldiers love to come buy apples, or anything fresh for that matter. According to them, army food gets pretty monotonous."

"Well, at least they get enough to fill their bellies. You wouldn't know anyone who had a gallon or so of milk for sale?"

"Not right offhand. You might ask at the farms outside of town." He wrote some numbers in his ledger. "Now you tell Miz Highwood to come in anytime. She has all the credit she needs right here on the books."

"Thank you kindly, Mr. Dummont. I'll find a way to pay you somehow."

"Don't make you no nevermind. Between God and Miz Dummont, I'd suffer in both lives if I didn't help out where I could."

Jesselynn debated leaving her horse tied beside the store but decided that was more dangerous than riding her the two blocks to the post office.

The city bustled with what looked to Jesselynn like twice as much wagon traffic as usual, army personnel and the civilians who accompanied their menfolk in the army. If nothing else, the war was a boon to places like Springfield, bringing increased business on all sides. Unless, of course, a battle was fought over it.

Jesselynn trotted up the steps and inside the brick building with a sign reading *United States Post Office*. She crossed to the counter, her heels clicking on the marble floor. "Good day. Do you have any mail for Mrs. Hiram Highwood or Master Jesse Highwood?"

"Let me see." The man with the green eyeshade and arm bands holding back the sleeves of his white shirt turned and sorted through the boxes along the wall. He returned with three envelopes. "One for Miz Highwood and two for you. You are Jesse Highwood, right?"

"Yes, sir. Thank you, sir." Jesselynn looked at the handwriting on her two letters and could have jumped for joy. One from her sister Louisa in Richmond and one from Lucinda, the head of the household help at Twin Oaks. Cavendar Dunlivey had lied when he said slavers got all those left at Twin Oaks. No longer could she call her people slaves, since she herself had signed the manumission papers in her father's name, but what other title could she give them? Perhaps if Lucinda and the others were still on the home place, Dunlivey had also lied about burning the farm to the ground. Letters from home! No longer did she notice the lowering gray clouds.

Not even attempting to hide her smile, she tucked the letters in her shirt pocket and mounted her horse. No sense loitering here in plain view while she read the letters. She could do that at the house. "Come on, Sunshine, let's hustle on back."

———

"A letter for you," Jesse called to Aunt Agatha when she entered the kitchen.

"Coming." The answer floated down from upstairs.

Jesselynn moved the teakettle to the hottest part of the stove. She picked up the lid on the stewpot and savored the fragrance of rabbit stew. The wild roots and herbs they'd been using at the cave in no way measured up to good garden fare.

"Where's your teapot?" she asked as Agatha entered the kitchen, several pieces of clothing slung over her arm.

Agatha pointed to a high shelf in the cupboard and laid the garments across the back of a chair. Bright pink spots on her cheeks, most likely from the exertion of bending over trunks or boxes, made her look more like herself. "Why?"

"Because Mr. Dummont included a packet of tea with the groceries. He said you must be in terrible need of a cup of tea by now." A little fib to make her aunt feel better paled against the lies she was forced to tell on a regular basis.

"Oh, he is such a good man." Agatha gazed at the brown paper packet with shining eyes.

*Then why are you so tied in knots about asking for flour and other things you can't live without?* But Jesselynn kept the thought to herself and slit open the letter from Lucinda.

> *Dear Marse Jesse,*
> *I am sorry I did not write before, but things have been very bad here. Dey burned de house and barns right after you left and cotched many of de field hands to sell to de slavers. Some of us got out and hid in de woods for weeks, too 'fraid to come out. Dere no place to dry de t'bacca, but we go ask Marse Marsh if we can use his barn. He say yes, so if dere be some crop, he sell it for us. When you come home, Marse Jesse? We made a shack out of logs so we be out of de rain. Joseph hurt him back. You write us by Marse Marsh. He bring it here. God bless you. Come home soon.*
> *Lucinda*

Jesselynn closed her eyes. So Dunlivey *had* burned Twin Oaks and sold most of the freed slaves. Her gorge rose, threatening to choke her.

She opened her eyes to see her aunt staring at the sheet of paper she held, her face as stark white as the letter.

# CHAPTER TWO

"Aunt, what is it? What is wrong?"

Agatha waved the paper and blinked her eyes as if she were having trouble seeing.

Jesselynn dropped to her knees beside her aunt and took the lady's shaking hands in her own. They were icy and quivering like cottonwood leaves in the breeze. "Please tell me. What is wrong?"

The old woman seemed to shrink within herself right before Jesselynn's eyes, aging years in moments. She handed Jesselynn the letter, mouthing words but unable to speak.

Was she having a fit? Jesselynn had once seen an old man sink to the ground and start twitching, then go slack, one side of his face looking like candle wax in the heat as it melted to one side.

Agatha pointed to the paper. "Read it," she croaked.

Jesselynn scanned the precise legal writing, then went back to read the entire letter. Her heart took up a staccato beat. "They can't just throw you out!"

"But of course they can. I thought dear Lettie had paid the taxes last year, but obviously she didn't. I hold no title to the house since she died. I just lived here at the gracious invitation from a friend to a widow in dire straits. And even if I did have the title, I have no money for taxes. Appears to me I shall be homeless before the robins nest."

Jesselynn studied her aunt. The woman was not complaining, just stating facts as she saw them, and at the moment, Jesse saw no other alternative either. "Is there someone else you can live with?"

Aunt Agatha shrugged, a brief motion that barely raised her thin shoulders. "I shall ask around. I am strong. I can be a good companion to someone who is more advanced in years than I."

*Strong? It wouldn't need a brisk breeze to blow you over.* Had her aunt no idea that she had slipped so far downhill in the last few weeks? Did she never look in a mirror? What had she done with a disposition more than slightly verging on that of a sergeant or a general, a woman sure of her place in Southern semiaristocracy? Had it slid away with the disappearing flesh?

*War! And man's ego! They are responsible for this. Both Father and Uncle Hiram thought they could help save the South. Now their families have to pay for their gallantry by being left with nothing. Aunt Agatha should be able to go to Twin Oaks, where relatives would take her in. But her relatives are no longer there. They're now hoping to be taken in themselves. It's always the war! The horrid war!* She had to clamp her teeth together to keep the anger from spewing forth.

Jesselynn folded the paper and inserted it back in the envelope. "Perhaps the new owner would let you continue to live here."

"Perhaps. If I were able to pay for the privilege. But look around. This place is falling down around its posts. The roof leaks. The walls are riddled with vermin and dry rot. The best thing to do is burn or bury it." Her face sagged, sorrow seeping out of her pores. "Not like our home place. Ah, Jesselynn, Oakfield was beautiful. Much like Twin Oaks, since Hiram always thought of that as home." Her eyes sharpened. "But the dirty deserters stole what horses we had left, burned our farm, and even knocked over Hiram's gravestone. There was nothin' left."

*Except the slaves you sold like they were cattle.* Jesselynn still couldn't understand her aunt doing such a thing. Why, she could no more have sold Twin Oaks's slaves than cut off her right hand. That was why she had freed them all before she left home, not that it saved those Dunlivey had caught after burning Twin Oaks. Burning seemed to be a favorite tool of ruffians, deserters, and Yankee soldiers. That and lynching.

The thought made her shudder. Benjamin had come so close to being hanged. The freed slaves she had with her were more her family now than her two sisters whom she'd sent to Richmond to keep safe.

Danger and hardship had a tendency to draw folks close together no matter what color their skin.

*You'll have to invite Aunt Agatha to come west with you.* The thought, more like her mother speaking across the reaches between heaven and earth, made her catch her breath. No. No way would she take this weak and trembling woman with them, nor the whaleboned one she'd known when they arrived in Springfield in November. Either way, there was no room in the wagon for Aunt Agatha.

"I need to be going so I can get back to the cave before dark."

Agatha nodded. "Make sure you get yourself plenty of the store from the cellar. Hate to see any of it go to waste." She motioned toward the stove. "I wouldn't turn down any meat you might want to bring in. And wood."

"I'll see to it, Aunt Agatha. But with all the soldiers in town, using the horses to pull the wagon is taking a big chance. Since the mule was stolen . . ." She shrugged. "After coming all this way, I sure don't want to lose them now."

"No, no. Of course not." The older woman traced the outline of the envelope lying on the table. "Think I'll ask Mr. Dummont at the store if he would like to come by and help himself. That would allow me to purchase more of the things I need. Unless I find another place to live, of course. I would want to take some with me."

"I reckon." Jesselynn lifted her coat from the hook on the wall. "I'll be back when I can. You take care now, you hear?"

"Oh, I will. Give that little Thaddeus a kiss for me. I sure do want to see that baby before he's a grown man." Agatha tipped her head sideways to make it easy for Jesselynn to drop a kiss on her cheek.

"I'll try to bring him in. One day Meshach may come and bring you back to our camp. If you would like to visit, that is." Jesselynn could hear her mother extending an invitation in the same tone of voice. What on earth was the matter with her for even suggesting such a thing?

"We'll see." The arch of her eyebrow was more reminiscent of the *real* Aunt Agatha than anything else Jesselynn had seen since she arrived.

With two tow sacks full of vegetables, both dried and fresh, and apples on top for the pure joy of eating, she headed on out of town, keeping a sharp lookout for any more soldiers. Perhaps they were all back at camp by now. If that were the case, then she or Meshach should come and go just about twilight. She'd heard from home. Remembering made the ride seem like minutes. Carrie married. Zachary still alive. Life went on even here.

Darkness hid the land by the time she drew near to the cave. She whistled the three notes they'd agreed upon for a signal, and when one answered, she rode down the bank to where the mouth of the cave was fairly well hidden by a trio of maple trees and brush. They had stumbled on it quite by accident. Of course Meshach said God had led them to their new home, but she had only nodded. Benjamin found it when he'd skidded down the bank on the way to the creek that meandered along the bottom of the hollow. Ridges and hollows, as the locals called the terrain, the Ozark Mountains without any peaks.

"What take you so long?" Meshach met her at the cave entrance. A big man in every way, long legs, broad shoulders, hands big enough to hoist a tobacco hogshead yet gentle enough to comfort little Sammy who clung to his leg like a bloodsucker. Meshach bent down and swung the toddler up to his shoulder. Since they'd found Sammy, he had learned to walk. He was perhaps too weak before, but it didn't take him long to totter after Thaddeus once his legs grew strong enough. Sammy tangled his little fingers in Meshach's kinky black hair, the better to hold on. Meshach had the little one's leg in a firm grip should he start to topple off.

Jesselynn swung to the ground and untied the tow sacks, so heavy that one was beginning to fray at the bottom. "Here. This should help our larder, and we each get a big red apple for dessert."

"Good. Daniel done brung in another deer. 'Phelia settin' strips to dry already. Fried liver for supper." He flinched as the little one on his shoulder yanked on a handful of hair.

"Where's Thaddeus?"

"Down de creek with Daniel, fishin'. Benjamin still grazin' de horses."

"Good." They each picked up a sack and started for the cave. At the same time Meshach swung Sammy down from his shoulder and under his arm like a tied-off sack of grain. Meshach's hair grazed the roof within the cave, but he had to duck to enter. With the horses roped off at the back where the ceiling was higher and the fire kept burning near the front, they were safe from wild animals as well as the elements. Curious humans were another matter; thus, they took great care not to make visible trails to the cave and the surrounding area.

"Oh, Meshach, Ophelia, I got so excited about the apples I almost forgot to tell you. We have a letter from Lucinda and one from Louisa, which I forgot to read to Aunt Agatha. For shame."

"Glory be to God. Dey's safe." Meshach spoke as reverently as if they were in front of the altar in church.

Ophelia clasped her hands to her chest and rocked back and forth. "Thank you, Jesus. Thank you, Jesus." She opened her eyes again and shook her head. "You read to us right now?"

"You don't want to wait for the others?"

"Kin read it again. Dat man lied to us."

"If you mean Dunlivey, not quite." Even the mention of his name made her stomach churn. Cavendar Dunlivey had been pure evil wearing men's britches. At least she hoped and prayed he was gone. When they left him gutshot in the clearing, she'd promised to send a doctor back, and Meshach had done so, but there had been no word of his demise. But no one lived being gutshot.

Without a miracle.

The vivid memory brought burning anger. She hoped he'd died a very slow and extremely painful death. A quick death was far too merciful for the likes of him. Her mother would say she had to forgive Dunlivey in spite of the atrocities he had committed. But she wasn't ready to grant forgiveness to a man who could do such awful things. Would she ever?

As she read the letters in the light of the fire, she kept one ear tuned for the jabbering of one little boy and the teasing of the two young black men who cared for the "young marse."

"Praise de Lawd, Marse Zachary still alive and gettin' well. And Missy Carrie Mae done got married." Tears coursing down her cheeks, Ophelia used Meshach's broad chest for a towel.

*Tell me these people don't care for us as much as we care for them. They are not my slaves, but my family.* Jesselynn wiped the tears from her own eyes and sniffed. She still had a brother—not a whole one, but a live one nevertheless. Restoring Twin Oaks would be up to him. Saving the Thoroughbreds was even more important to her now. They had to have something left to start over with.

Hearing the fluted call of a mockingbird, Meshach loosened his hold on Ophelia and stepped to the mouth of the cave to answer.

Within moments Thaddeus tore into the cave, a string of two small fish hanging from one hand. "I catch fish. See, Jesse, my fish."

Jesselynn held them up and glanced over to see a look of delight on Benjamin's face.

"He done caught dem hisself." He laid a hand on Thaddeus's curly head. "He be good fisherman."

"Those are some fish." She reached over, grabbed Thaddeus around his middle, and pulled him right into her arms so she could hug and kiss him. He made a face and wriggled to escape.

"Show 'Phelia."

"Good fish. Good boy." Ophelia admired his two fish and glanced up to see the string that Daniel held. "Oh, hallelujah days! We have fish and fried potatoes for supper."

"And cooked cabbage with onion and a bit of dried venison." Jesselynn wrapped her arms around her middle. "My belly is dancing up and down."

"Read to dem." Meshach had to shout to be heard above the chatter.

"We got two letters today, finally one from Lucinda and one from Louisa. Which do you want first?"

"Lucinda," the two said in unison.

Jesselynn read the letter again amid tears and cries of "praise de Lawd" and "thank you, Jesus" as if no one had heard it before.

"Dey's alive." Benjamin cleared his throat and turned away to wipe his eyes. "Smoke bad in here."

"I know." Jesselynn ducked to hide her smile. Why shouldn't he cry? The rest of them surely had been.

"Someone still live at Twin Oaks." Daniel spoke reverently, much like Meshach had. While the buildings were gone, their family was still there, at least part of them.

"Read de next one—please."

Jesselynn did so, receiving many of the same reactions. Who could accept it all? Such wonderful news in both missives!

"De Lawd giveth and de Lawd taketh away, blessed be de name of de Lawd." Meshach's deep, rich voice rolled around the cave almost like music.

As the others agreed, Jesselynn wanted to cover her ears. The Lord did too much taking, far as she was concerned. "To think Louisa had been caring for this poor soldier, not knowing that he was really her brother, and now he's back at Aunt Sylvania's along with other wounded." She shook her head. "Amazing."

"De Lawd's doing." Meshach managed to have the last word.

Supper that night was a grand affair, and when she brought out the apples for dessert, the only sound to be heard in the cave was the crunch of teeth into crisp apples and the slurping of juice.

"Ah, me. That some supper. We save de liver for tomorrow."

"With more potatoes." Jesselynn never would have dreamed she could be so ecstatic over apples and potatoes.

Jane Ellen, another one of the additions to her family since the trip began, started getting the boys ready for bed. While she still spoke little, she no longer had to be fed and walked, as she had after her brother's death. Now she took on her share, helping Ophelia with the cooking and the smoking of meat. She had volunteered to take over tanning the hides so they would have one hide for a blanket and the other to make moccasins for Daniel and the two little ones. Thaddeus had outgrown his boots and now wore thong-laced foot coverings, more makeshift than moccasin. She'd make his with the hair side in and an extra pad for the sole. That should keep Thaddeus's feet warm. They were fortunate the winter had been mild so far.

They all heard the noise at the same time and froze to listen better. Benjamin faded out the opening of the cave like a wisp of smoke.

# CHAPTER THREE

Richmond, Virginia
Early January 1863

The men were arguing again.

To keep from eavesdropping, Louisa Highwood strolled between the rosebushes in her aunt Sylvania's garden, the garden she and her wounded men from the army hospital had brought back into its former beauty. Golden daffodils nodded a greeting, and primroses glowed under the magnolia as though an artist had dabbed his brush in bright yellows, reds, and pinks, then spattered the colors in happy profusion. Red and pink azaleas bordered the fence and the house, inviting her to cut a bouquet or two for the rooms inside, which she did, filling the flat basket she carried for just that purpose.

Cutting and arranging flowers always brought her a time of peace. As usual, the Lord met her there too.

*I know you know where he is. I just wish you would give me some indication. If my lieutenant is alive, please bring him back. If he's already gone home to be with you . . .* The tears blurred the branch of azalea, so she snipped thin air, grazing her finger enough she was sure she'd see blood. "That was close." She blinked and sniffed, settling her clippers in the basket in order to blow her nose on the hanky she always carried in her apron pocket.

The crinkle of paper reminded her that Lieutenant Gilbert Lessling's last letter lay hidden close at hand. Reading the letter brought his face vividly to her and made praying for him easier. If she could see him so clearly, he surely must still be on this earth.

At least that's what she told herself. She sniffed again and, putting the hanky back in her pocket, smoothed the white apron over her sky blue dimity dress. Gilbert had said he liked her in blue. It brought out the blue of her eyes and made her hair look even more golden. Since Gilbert rarely spent a portion of his few words on compliments, she hoarded every one of them.

"Miss Louisa, breakfast ready."

"I'm coming." She cut a couple more branches and with a last sigh turned back to the house. Since her brother Zachary had come home, he forbade her volunteering on the ward at the hospital, so her day stretched long in front of her. Thinking of his stubbornness tightened her jaw. "I'll have it out with him again. Just because we have three extra men here doesn't mean I don't have time for those poor miserable men at the hospital. Such selfishness. Mama would take a willow switch to him if she were here."

"You say sumpin', Miss Louisa?" Abby looked up from forking ham slices onto a platter.

"Just muttering." Louisa set her basket on the bench and, picking up the full bucket of water, poured some into another. Then sticking the branches in water, she wiped her hands on her apron. "There, that'll hold them until I get back to fill the vases. Let me take that in, and you bring the rest of the food."

She bumped the swinging door to the dining room open with her backside and entered the room where four recovering Confederate soldiers cut off their discussion as if blowing out a candle, even to the smoke still rising on the air.

One more reason to want to tear into her brother. Before he came home, she'd been privy to whatever discussions had gone on in this house, and there'd been plenty. "Carry on, gentlemen. My ears aren't that tender." Instead of slamming the platter down, which was what she felt like doing, she set it gently and with a pleasant smile. The fury she would reserve for Zachary. Holy fury seemed appropriate at the moment.

"And a fine good morning to you too, dear Louisa." Zachary Highwood winked at her with his remaining eye, an act made even more a caricature by the scar that ran from above his eyebrow, under the black patch worn to cover the missing eye, and down to his jaw. Only a man made of pure dash could carry off such an act—and Zachary did. While she wanted to rant and rave, as usual he made her laugh.

The sound released the other men from their frozen stances, and chuckles made their way around the table.

"Now, that's much better." Aunt Sylvania, in a gray morning dress and a lace cap on her head, set the silver coffeepot in front of her place and took her seat. "Who would like to say the grace this morning?" She smiled at each of the men. "Sergeant Blackstone, it must be about your turn."

Louisa bowed her head, the desire to see the flush running up the good sergeant's neck nearly irresistible. He had come so far in the last weeks that soon he would be ready for discharge. To this point at least, none of those missing a limb had been sent back to battle, not that they weren't willing, if not ready.

"Bless us oh Lord for these gifts we are about to receive, in thy precious name amen." The words ran together in his mumbled haste.

The amen echoed around the table, and they each reached for the platter nearest them to pass on to the next.

Louisa, sitting next to her brother, who still liked to tease her about calling herself *Missus* Zachary Highwood, since that was the only way she could work at the hospital, delivered a quick kick to his ankle. *That ought to get his attention.* She'd learned the practice years earlier at the family table at Twin Oaks.

If she hadn't been watching, she would have missed his flinch. His chuckle said he knew what was bothering her.

"No, you cannot return to work at the hospital." He hid his remark behind the biscuit basket.

"Whyever not?" She kept her smile in place and spoke through her teeth, another skill from long ago when they didn't want their mother to know what was going on.

"You know why not." He did the same.

"Zachary, dear, would you please pass the ham?" Aunt Sylvania arched an eyebrow.

Had she figured out their little trick? Louisa turned to the silent man on her other side. "Would you like me to cut your meat? Just this time, of course." Trying to save face for those missing a hand until they got the hang of it had become her specialty. She kept her whisper low.

His brief nod was her only answer. She had yet to get him to converse with her, but she didn't let a tide of silence stop her.

"The garden is beautiful this morning, Lieutenant Jones. Those pansies you transplanted yesterday were all smiling up at me." While she chatted, she buttered a biscuit, spread honey on it, and cut up the slice of ham. "I surely do appreciate all the work you fellows are doing out there. Miss Julie next door is hoping y'all will come on over to her house and get at the weeds there. Shame how our gardens have nearly gone wild since the war. I'm hoping to get the potatoes and peas in the ground today. Wouldn't fresh peas be the perfect thing?"

She felt like a ninny running on like that, but she had learned that the tone of her voice and her ready smile accomplished far more than silences and frowns. These men needed a taste of home, and she aimed to supply it.

With breakfast finished, they spent the next hour exercising injured muscles, retraining the remaining limbs, or applying new dressings, all the while listening to *The Merchant of Venice* being read by none other than Aunt Sylvania herself.

"I have work to do here today, so I'll not join you in the garden." Zachary stopped at her shoulder as she gathered up her supplies. He'd grown adept at using one crutch now that he had fashioned a short peg to strap to the remaining stump of his right leg. Even though the stump came up raw at times, he refused to hop and hobble any longer.

"I'll be back." She smiled brightly for the benefit of the others.

"I'm sure you will."

Once she had the men teaming up to plant or dig, she headed back to the house, smiling at Reuben, who had set one of the men to stirring the sheets boiling over the outside fire. The laundry was never ending, just like the cooking and cleaning.

"I'm on my way to church," Aunt Sylvania said, pulling on her much-darned gloves. "I do wish you would come. There are never enough hands to roll bandages or sew uniforms." She set her hat at the proper angle and picked up her basket.

"Perhaps later." They both knew those words were a fabrication. Louisa had chosen to attend the Friends Church, much to her aunt's consternation. "Where is Zachary?"

"At his desk."

"Have a good gossip while you work." She kissed her aunt's cheek, closing the front door behind her. As if caring for the men the way they did wasn't enough. She stopped in the arched doorway to watch her brother laboriously writing a letter with his left hand. While his penmanship was at least legible now, she knew how he hated the ink blots that at times disfigured the pages. Who could he be writing to with such intensity?

"The answer is no," Zachary said before Louisa could even ask the question.

"But, Zachary . . ." She clenched both hands and teeth.

"It is bad enough that you are working like a fishwife here." He set the quill down and capped the ink.

"Who are you writing to?" Changing the subject might help.

"A friend."

His short answer did more to arouse her curiosity than anything else.

"Oh? Male or female?" She stopped behind him, trying to get a peek at the salutation. He covered it with his arm, leaning back nonchalantly as if the covering was not intentional.

She knew differently.

"Actually, dear wife, it's none of your business." The emphasis on *wife* warned her someone was behind her. She dropped a kiss on the top of his head for good measure.

"I'd write it for you if you asked nicely." Keeping a hand on his shoulder, she turned enough to see a strange man standing in the archway she'd so recently vacated. "Can I help you, sir?"

"No." Zachary answered for the man. "He came to see me. Could you bring us some lemonade, please, dear?" At the same time Zachary gestured to the chair by the desk. "Have a seat, soldier."

"Of course, *darling*. I'll be right back." He'd already drunk enough lemonade to float a ship was her thought as she left the room. Once out of sight, she paused long enough to hear one word—morphine.

# CHAPTER FOUR

## Springfield, Missouri

"Sojers on de road."

"Blue or gray?" Jesselynn knew when they took this cave so near the Wire Road that there could be problems, but no other caves they'd seen had been so perfectly fitted for their needs.

"Confederate."

Benjamin, at twenty years old, had seen war before when he'd accompanied Jesselynn's father, Major Joshua Highwood, off to battle. Thanks to Benjamin's fortitude, he had brought the major home to die. He'd become their scout, since he could move through a thicket like a puff of smoke and run for miles without dropping.

"Many sojers. All on horses. With light cannon."

"Oh, Lord, if they attack the garrison at Springfield, what will happen to Aunt Agatha? Her house isn't four blocks from the camp, since they took over the middle of the town."

"Plenty bluebellies dere. Many guns." Meshach had often been looking for work and gotten to know the town pretty well. "Dey marchin' all de time."

"Dey ask we want to join up." Benjamin shook his head, the light of laughter in his eyes caught by the firelight. "I'se done wid de war."

"I wish we *all* were done 'wid de war.' " Jesselynn couldn't resist teasing him. She and Benjamin had grown up together. He had been a member of the household staff. When he went off to war with her father, sorrow struck her almost as badly as when her brothers had gone. The stories she'd heard of the ways some Southern planters mistreated their slaves bore no relation to the way her father had run Twin Oaks.

*So what do I do about Aunt Agatha?* Jesselynn looked around the cave. The boys and Jane Ellen were sound asleep against the wall nearest the fire. The six horses were roped off in the rear of the cave. A long, low fire lay between a tunnel of racks full of drying venison, and a salted haunch hung just above the racks to smoke as a ham. Meshach had used vines to tie cut saplings and branches together into shelves for their few household things, and their foodstuffs were stored in the wooden boxes they'd brought from Twin Oaks. The wagon was hidden in a thicket up on the edge of the ridge. Pegs driven into cracks in the limestone walls held the harnesses and other tack.

There was just no more room.

And Aunt Agatha was an old woman, an opinionated old woman.

"You want I should go see to the road again?" Benjamin hunkered down beside her.

Jesselynn shook her head. "No sense to it. Since the mouth of our cave faces east, there's no chance of someone seeing our light. Least not from the road. And a scout might just happen upon you. They'd shoot you for spyin'."

"Dey not catch me." His tone carried no hint of bravado, just stated a simple fact.

While Jesselynn believed him, she wasn't about to take a chance. "Someone will have to go check on Aunt Agatha in the morning." She had a pretty good idea who that *someone* was going to be.

———

A snort from one of the horses woke her from a dream-riddled sleep that had caused her to miss out on any rest. She sat up, listening so hard her breathing seemed louder than a windstorm. Nothing. One of the men mumbled in his sleep. Someone else snored gently. Normal night sounds. Soundlessly she laid aside her quilt, picked up her boots from under the edge of her bedding, and, carrying them, made her way to the mouth of the cave. Overhead the stars hung close in an azure velvet sky, but off to the east, the sky had lightened only enough to be noticeable.

She sucked in a breath of air not redolent with drying meat and horse dung and sat down on a rock to pull on her boots. Even the birds had yet to realize the new day was almost upon them. Quiet and solitude, two things that had been seriously lacking from her life for some time. She struck off to relieve herself and gather wood on the way back. They were having to range farther and farther for wood for the fires, since they'd now been in this cave nigh onto two months.

Time they looked for another. They had to take the horses farther to pasture too. If only she dared start for Independence now while the roads were still firm. Once the spring rains began, they wouldn't make anywhere near ten miles a day. But if they left now, they'd have to find someplace to live out there until the wagon trains heading west started forming up. From what she'd heard, caves like those around this area were next to nonexistent. About like their money.

Besides, she couldn't start until after the mares foaled and the babies grew strong enough to handle the trip.

As the sky lightened, the birds took up their chorus. A cardinal sang his lovely aria, and a jay scolded her for trespassing. Off in the distance a dog barked. If an army the size Benjamin saw had passed through, the morning woods had little to say about it. Surely if Springfield was under attack, they would hear the guns, at least from up on the ridge.

She checked Daniel's snare line, tied two dead rabbits to her belt, and kept on walking. How were they to get enough money for the journey? Selling Chess would break Thaddy's heart, but the horse was fully recovered now from his gunshot wound and would bring them over a hundred dollars, maybe even as much as a hundred fifty. She'd hoped to use him to help pull the wagon and ease up on the mares awhile, then sell him in Independence.

Picking up wood as she went, she circled back to the cave, dragging a couple of big branches she'd lashed together and overlaid with other wood on the top. The downed tree she'd located would make up quite a stack of firewood.

Meshach met her at the cave's entrance. "You all right?"

"Just woke up and couldn't go back to sleep." She dropped her load. "I found a downed tree that looks to be good and dry but not yet rotted." She pointed to the southeast. "Over there. I can locate it again."

Not that the woods were impenetrable. Up on the ridges lay prairie with the trees in the hollows and along the creeks and lakes. At this time of year, instead of green, the land wore an orange garment of grasses, dead clinging leaves, and underbrush. The rising sun gilded the edges and lightened the tree trunks on the eastern face, darkening the bark on the other. Staring south she thought about Sergeant Barnabas White, the Confederate soldier they'd nursed back to health so he could return to his home in Arkansas. He was minus part of a leg but hale otherwise.

He'd promised to write. But there'd been no letters from Arkansas, so it was a good thing she'd not given her heart away a second time. The first time seemed so long ago, in another lifetime, another world. Now thoughts of John Follett were more a friendly haze than a heart-tearing ache.

The morning seemed ripe for reflection.

"I take de horses for to drink and to graze." Meshach stretched, the muscles bulging under the fabric of his shirt. "Den go to town. Check on work and Miss Agatha?"

"Have you eaten?"

"Got me biscuits and dried deer. Be enough." He patted his pocket.

Jesselynn untied the two rabbits from her belt. "I checked the snares." She held them up by their ears. "You take these in to Aunt Agatha. I'll gut them first. Bring back the skins." Relief that Meshach had volunteered to go to town made her want to tap her feet and whistle a tune. While she set about dressing the rabbits, Meshach went into the cave and returned with two horses. Ahab, their oldest Thoroughbred stallion, snorted and pranced in the brisk air. No matter how matted and dirty they kept him, when he stood at attention like this, there was no doubt of his lineage.

Jesselynn sighed. Good breeding showed no matter what. Within moments Meshach had all six horses attached to a long line so that one man could lead them and set off down the hill to the creek.

Silence settled around Jesselynn again. She swiftly gutted the two rabbits and, tying their back feet together, hung them over a tree limb to keep them out of the dirt. The entrails she threw off into a thicket for the wild critters to eat. No sense wasting them.

The children were still sleeping, but Ophelia had cornmeal sizzling in a skillet over the coals. She'd made up the mush the night before and set it to cool in a pan, then sliced it for frying. From the looks of it, she'd mixed in meat of some kind. The other pan held the four smaller fish. Daniel and Benjamin were just cleaning their plates.

"Looks good. We haven't had fried mush for too long."

"Din't have no cornmeal." Ophelia used her apron as a potholder and pulled one of the frying pans back to cooler coals. "You ready for eatin'?"

"Yes, thank you."

Benjamin and Daniel cuffed each other on the way out of the cave, their laughter echoing a friendly sound, like home.

"Jesse?" The sleepy voice came from the pallets. "I got to go."

"I'll take you." Jane Ellen rolled to her feet, shook out her shift, and reached down for Thaddeus's hand. Since her brother had died from bad lungs and she'd finally returned to the real world from wandering lost somewhere in her mind, she pretty much took care of the two boys. Their antics seemed to help her through her grieving.

"I want Jesse."

"Come here, baby, and give me a hug, then you go on with Jane Ellen. I've already been outside, and I'm fixin' to eat right about now."

"Not baby. Sammy baby." Thaddeus rubbed his eyes with his fists as barefooted he crossed the sandy floor of the cave. Jesselynn gave him a quick hug and a peck on the cheek because his squirming meant he needed to go *now*. Jane Ellen swooped him up in her arms and trotted with him, giggles and all, out the entrance.

The quiet of the cave let Jesse's thoughts take over again. *What do I do about Aunt Agatha?* She took her plate and wandered to the cave mouth, listening for gunfire. She heard only normal sounds. While her mind said that was good, her heart cautioned that something was going to happen. Not if, but *when*.

As soon as she finished eating and Daniel and Benjamin had brought in a stockpile of cut wood, Jesselynn sent Benjamin off to scout Wire Road and on north toward the town of Springfield. Ozark lay closer, but the post office and her aunt were in Springfield.

"Now, you be careful. Don't take any chances, you hear?"

He nodded. "You wants me to see 'bout Miz Highwood?"

"No, just find out what you can. Meshach will go in later." But it all depended on whether or not there had been a battle. Not knowing kept her stomach roiling.

Daniel went fishing and setting a trotline, Jane Ellen entertained the little ones, and Jesselynn and Ophelia sliced more strips of the venison and hung them to dry. While she sharpened her knife, Jesselynn tried to figure out when and where the troops would attack. And why now? Did the Confederates hope to take over Missouri? Why couldn't they just stay down in Arkansas?

But when Benjamin returned with reports of seeing nothing but that plenty of soldiers had passed, she took in a deep breath and decided everyone should stay at the cave. If only she knew what was happening!

As the next day passed, they could feel the temperature dropping by the hour. Everyone pitched in to sew rabbit skins together for warm shirts, mittens, and moccasins for the two little boys. Jane Ellen was another matter. Taking the softest deerskins, Jesselynn fashioned them into a jerkin that reached her knees. Meshach and Ophelia stitched more skins into over-the-knee moccasins, wrapped with a thong for the young woman.

Jane Ellen put on her new clothes and turned in place, running her hands down the soft leather. "I never had nothin' so purty in all my life. You sure this is for me?" Her eyes and face shone like a mirror reflecting the sun.

"Doesn't look like it would fit anyone else." Jesselynn pulled a rabbit-skin shirt over Thaddeus's head. "Okay, little man, how does that feel?"

"Warm." He rubbed his cheek on the fur-side-up collar. "Soft." He flung his arms around Jesselynn's neck. "Thank you."

"Why, you are most welcome. And who's been teaching you to say thank you?" *You should have been, you ninny. What kind of manners is he growing up with? Mother would be so ashamed.*

Thaddy pointed at Jane Ellen, who stood clenching her hands together.

"I don' mean to be fo'ard or nothin'."

"Jane Ellen, I am so truly grateful for all the things you do around here. Why, child, what would we do without you?" Jesselynn knew she sounded exactly like her mother. Not that that was a bad thing, but it caught her by surprise nonetheless.

Two days later they heard cannon fire to the north of them.

# CHAPTER FIVE

"Where you goin'?" Meshach gripped the reins under Chess's bit.

"I've got to see if Aunt Agatha is all right."

"You can't go now. Dey's still shootin'."

Jesselynn slumped forward in her saddle. She couldn't help but recognize the wisdom of his words, but she had the terrible feeling her aunt was in trouble and needed her.

"We go together on toward dark so we can sneak into de town."

*But what if she is wounded and there's no one to help her?* Jesselynn dismounted, feeling guilt like the weight of the heavens pressing her down. So many to take care of. How would she stand it if Aunt Agatha was forced to join them in the cave earlier than either dreamed?

Within herself she cursed the war and the men who thought war so glorious, including her brothers. Her father had done everything he could to keep Kentucky out of it, but hotter heads than his had prevailed.

The thought of the western prairies and Oregon was becoming more practical all the time. And more real. What started as Meshach's dream was rapidly becoming hers. Anything to get away from battles and skirmishes and soldiers of either gray or blue. If she never saw another uniform, it would be far too soon.

"Is Chess trained to harness yet?"

"Some. You want we take him and Dulcie to pull de wagon?"

"I think so." Jesselynn rubbed her forehead. "I don't know what I want." With her monthlies upon her again, she felt like crawling under her quilt and pulling it over her head. None of this thinking and worrying. She shivered in a blast of cold air blown from the north through the hollow, turning it into a wind tunnel.

The wind also brought the sound of artillery fire. She flinched every time a cannon fired. If they could hear the reports this far away, what was it like in town? One of the four small forts built throughout the city was only a few blocks from Agatha's home. Who was firing? Union or Confederate howitzers or both? While she'd never been in an area under siege, she'd seen the aftermath.

"Jesse. Up." Thaddeus reached his arms high as he begged. When she paid him no nevermind, distracted by another volley, he tugged on her pants leg.

Acting on habit and paying no attention to her actions, she swung him up into her arms and rocked from side to side. "Can anyone live through all that?"

"Jesse." Thaddeus swung to the side to look directly in her face, and when that didn't work, he put his hands on both her cheeks and turned her face his way.

"Stop that." She jerked away but melted instantly when his round blue eyes swam with tears. "Sorry, baby. Jesse is thinking of something else."

"Guns go boom."

"Yes, that they do." *And people die, and houses and stores are destroyed. Why can't they go fight out in the woods instead of in a town?* She had heard stories of how the fashionable people from Washington and other cities had taken picnic baskets out to sit on the bluffs and watch the fighting down below. In some cases retreating soldiers ran right over the spectators.

Sometime later Benjamin returned from a scouting trip, and after standing by the fire to warm himself for a bit, he turned to Meshach. "I found somethin' real interestin'."

"What you find?" Meshach kept working the deer hide, softening it so they could make clothing from it.

"Tracks of our mule."

Jesselynn looked up from her stitching. "Where?"

" 'Bout three miles south. I follow, cotch up, and watch. Dey got five niggers in chains."

"Slave traders!" Jesselynn hissed the word with pure venom. "The ones who beat Daniel."

"But why dey beat 'im and den try to lynch 'im?"

"Pure stupid mean, like Dunlivey. That's why." *What if these are Dunlivey's men? The ones who deserted him?* Jesselynn let her thoughts take off on this trail. Having the mule back would be a godsend. But having five extra mouths to feed would be tantamount to disaster.

"We get dem. I takes care of movin' dem on." Meshach looked up from studying his clasped hands. Sitting on the other side of the fire, his eyes shone white in the gloom.

"But they'll come lookin' for them."

"Maybe not."

"You'd . . ." Jesselynn gulped. Shooting in self-defense was one thing. Looking to murder was another. Yet how many people had this band murdered, lynched, or burned out? "But the Bible says, 'Thou shalt not kill.'"

"Bible also say, 'eye for an eye.'"

Here she was arguing with Meshach, using the Bible, all the while trying to convince herself that God didn't really matter. Or at least that He didn't care what happened in this brutal mess of man's own making. She shook her head. "I'll go with you."

"No." Meshach motioned to the two sleeping boys, to Jane Ellen and Ophelia. "Someone need take care of dem."

Jesselynn knew he meant if the three men didn't come back. The thought gave her a raging case of dry mouth. She set her sewing aside, rose, and got a drink out of the bucket of water. Standing, sipping the cold water, she studied the big black man across the cave. Gentle was always her first thought of him. She thought she knew him through and through.

"When?"

"Tonight."

"But you said we would go for Aunt Agatha." She was the mistress. She had to take control here.

"Yes. First town, den we go."

*Five fugitive slaves and Aunt Agatha?* But then, Aunt Agatha might be just fine, mostly frightened out of her wits by the shelling but cooking meals and reading her Bible, and . . . Jesselynn thought longingly of that quilt again. And her silent surrender to its comfort.

What if they didn't come back? What would she do?

"We come back, Marse Jesse. Don' you fear."

She shoved her hands in her pockets. "That's what Father said too, and Zachary and Adam and John and every other man I know. Meshach, they will do their living best to kill you. Don't doubt that for a minute."

"Not if dey don' hear us comin'." His words fell in a silence punctuated by Ophelia's sniffling and a log breaking in the fire. Sparks flew upward. Meshach stood. "I get de wagon ready. We start soon."

With cut firewood loaded in the wagon bed, they set off for town under gray skies and a chilling wind. They would either leave the firewood off for Aunt Agatha or take it to Mr. Dummont at the store in exchange for grain for the two mares. The closer the time for foaling, the better feeding they needed.

Jesselynn pulled her wool coat tighter around her shoulders. Now if she'd only made herself a cap of the deerskin, the wind wouldn't penetrate clear to her bones. They could see smoke on the horizon as soon as they topped the last ridge to the prairie.

As they drew closer, Jesselynn shuddered. From here it looked as if the entire town was afire. Surely they wouldn't torch Springfield. But within a mile or so, they could see the fires were separate, not a massive conflagration.

When Meshach drove into a yard that had a large open barn, she looked at him with questions jumping faster than her words.

"What . . ."

He held up a hand. "We be safe here. We walk rest of de way."

"Oh. How do you know—?" Again her question was cut off by that same hand now guiding the horses into the dark barn. He wrapped the reins around the brake handle and stepped to the ground. While he tied the horses to a post, Jesselynn stood and stamped her feet, willing feeling back into them before she tried the descent.

"Don't we need to ask, to tell . . ."

He shook his head and strode on ahead of her. She dogtrotted to catch up to his long strides.

"Meshach, wait!"

"Sorry, Marse Jesse. I got to thinkin' 'bout dem slavers, and I get so mad I want to go after dem now."

He slowed to her speed, even though she knew she walked fast. And thinking of Aunt Agatha leant wings to her feet anyway. They walked around a hole in the street caused by an exploding cannon-ball. One of the houses a block from her aunt's was burned to the ground and still smoldering. A dog lay dead in the street. An old man and a woman stood crying in front of a house now minus half a roof.

Jesselynn broke into a jog. "Please, God, please, God." She had no idea what she was saying. All she could think about was Aunt Agatha. Agatha lying dead under a tumble of rafters. Agatha bleeding with no one to bandage her.

They stopped in front of the house. Several windows had been shot out, and the brick chimney now lay in a pile of bricks. And while other homes were starting to light lamps and candles against the graying dusk, not a glimmer showed in the black eyes of the sagging house.

"Aunt Agatha?" Jesselynn pushed open the back door. "Agatha, where are you?" She listened for an answer that never came. She rushed through the house, checking the rooms downstairs while Meshach took the second floor.

"Nothin'." They met at the foot of the staircase.

"Me either. Where could she be?"

"Someone take her in? Big hole in de roof. Cannonball go through de wall too. Bad time when rain or storm come."

"You check that way, and I'll go this way." Jesselynn pointed up the street. "And we meet back here in just a few minutes."

She pounded on doors, but no one would or could answer. Where were all the people who lived on this street? Were they in hiding, afraid to answer? Had the soldiers rounded up all the citizens of Springfield? She darted out of one picket gate and ran to the next house. Looking over her shoulder, she saw Meshach heading back for Aunt Agatha's, so she turned and ran back.

"Dey's in de church two blocks dat way." He pointed toward the west.

As they jogged down a side street, he added, "De reverend put out a call for all who were hurt or dere houses shelled to come to de church. De people bring food and keep warm dere."

But Agatha wasn't at the church. And no one claimed to have seen her.

"I'm sorry," the pastor said. "If she arrives, I will tell her you are looking for her. Ah, did you check the cellar? Many of the older people around here hid in the cellar and barricaded the door."

"Thank you, no, I didn't think of the cellar, but we hollered loud enough to wake the dead."

Jesselynn and Meshach trotted back to the house. "I'll get a candle, and you see if you can open that door."

Jesselynn found a candle but not a spill to light it, and the fire had long since gone out. She dropped the candle on the table in disgust and hurried back outside.

"De door locked from inside." Meshach stood and, puffing slightly, put his hands on his hips. "Call her. Say who you are."

*What if she hid in the cellar like a cat that crawls away to die? Father would never forgive me for not taking better care of his sister.* Jesselynn leaned over the door. "Aunt Agatha, it's me, Marse Jesse, your nephew." She knew those words, if anything, would bring her aunt out of hiding, if she were able. "Aunt Agatha, can you hear me? Are you hurt?"

"Jesselynn?" The weak voice brought tears of gratitude flowing down Jesselynn's cheeks.

"Yes, Aunt, it's me. Can you unlock the door?"

"Who's with you?"

"Meshach has come to help. Just open the door now, hear?"

They listened to the scratch and thud of a board being removed from the brackets on the underside of the doors.

"There."

Meshach pulled up on the edge of the door and laid it back, then the other one.

Aunt Agatha's face glowed white in the dimness. Jesselynn clattered down the stone steps and took her aunt in her arms. "Come, let's get you out of here. You must be freezing. You are shivering."

"I carry her?"

"I can walk, thank you." The spice back in her voice made Jesselynn smile at Meshach and receive one in return. Spice was good.

A silence lay over the town, the sound of no shooting or yelling almost as loud as the battle. Smoke hung in the air, smelling both of burning wood and gunpowder. The wind of earlier had died with the falling of the sun, even though the cloud cover prevented them from seeing a sunset. A child wailed in a house somewhere near them.

Agatha used the railing to pull herself up the remaining steps.

"How bad is the damage to the house? I heard a terrible crash some hours ago."

"Cannonball knock over de chimbley. Big hole in roof and one wall. Rain come in some bad."

They entered the dark house, following Agatha, who had no need to feel her way.

"Then I shall have to sleep in the parlor." She crossed to the stove and rattled the grate. "If you would light the stove, Jesselynn, I will put supper on to heat."

"But you have no chimney."

"Surely the stovepipe works. Start it and we shall see how it draws."

"Aunt Agatha, I think you should come with us. We have the wagon near here, and you can bring a few of your things."

"Pshaw. Reckon I will remain here until they force me to leave." She returned from the pantry with the pot Jesselynn had started the rabbit stew in. "Not a lot here, but we can make do."

"Aunt, you aren't listenin' to me. You would be safe with us in the cave."

"Ain't never lived in a cave and don't intend to start now." She glared at Jesselynn. "Now you goin' to start that stove, or am I goin' to have to do it myself?"

"The army may come through here and force everyone to evacuate tomorrow." Jesselynn found a live coal in the ashes and shaved small curls off a pitch-pine log from the woodbox. When that began to smolder, she blew on it gently until a tiny flame flared bright. Adding more bits, she had the fire burning merrily within a matter of minutes. She added a couple of pieces of split wood and set the lids back in place, adjusting the damper for maximum draw.

Meshach cleared his throat from his place by the door. While it wasn't full dark yet, it was getting close.

What could she do, short of manhandling the old woman out to the wagon and tying her down?

# CHAPTER SIX

## Richmond, Virginia

"Where you goin'?"

"Out." Louisa adjusted her hat in the hall mirror. A glance at her brother lounging against the newel post made her clamp her teeth against further information. Two could play the secrecy game.

"When you comin' back?"

She turned, blew him a kiss, and patted his cheek. "When I get here." She could hear him fuming as she sailed out the front door and knew he watched her, so after latching the gate, she turned right instead of left. She'd have to make a detour around the blocks to get back to the hospital, but if the men needed morphine, she would get it for them. She'd go right to the top and ask the general where she could obtain some. The last time she'd been to the apothecary, he'd shaken his head. Laudanum would have to do. All the morphine was going to the troops.

A breeze kicked up as she neared the hospital from the opposite direction. She looked up to see the high clouds of a few minutes earlier lowering and threading together. Rain might be in the offing. She hurried up the brick steps and pulled open the heavy front door. The miasma of pain and stench greeted her before she could take one step over the threshold. She'd been away from it just long enough to have forgotten how terrible it really was.

"Why, Miz Highwood, how good to see you." One of the doctors stopped on his way down the stairs. "We surely do miss you around here, but perhaps you are doing more good with the men you are caring for. I, for one, am grateful for the efforts of your family and friends, let me tell you."

"Thank you, Doctor. We'll have room for two new ones in the next couple of weeks, I think." No matter how she wanted to return to her mission here, she would not whine and whimper. They expected her to be home caring for her husband and the others. "Is the general in?"

"Up in his office." The doctor indicated the third floor.

"Thank you." She felt like gagging as she mounted the steps. Someone screamed; others moaned. Things hadn't changed a bit.

The general's adjutant sat at the desk in the hall. That hadn't changed either, except that the young man in the uniform wasn't someone she recognized. *Bother. How long had the other been gone?*

"Good afternoon, ma'am. How can I be of service?"

She glanced down to see a newly lettered nameplate. "Ah, yes, Mr. Bromley. My name is Louisa Highwood, and I would like to see the general for a few moments."

"And your business, ma'am?" He halted in a brief motion to stand.

"I . . . ah . . . I need to see him on a matter of medications, for some of his men, those staying with us at my aunt's house." At the confused look he sent her, she knew he had no idea what she was talking about. "Just tell him Mrs. Highwood is here." *Surely he'll see me. He can't have forgotten.*

The young man returned instantly and held the door open for her. "The general will see you now."

Louisa walked through the door as the general came around the end of his desk, hand outstretched. "Good of you to see me, sir."

"Ah, child, if you only knew what delight your smiling face brings to this old heart of mine. We do miss you around here. We most certainly do." While he spoke he pulled out a chair and ushered her to it. "Sit and let me just look at you."

She sat as he'd asked and folded her hands in her lap. Dust motes danced in the sun streaming in from the window, making her wonder if the storm had blown the other way or just held off. Finally, in place of squirming, she smiled and leaned slightly forward. "I have come to ask a favor of you."

"Anything I can do for you, just ask. I owe you so much for all your service here. But before you continue, first tell me how that husband of yours is doing."

"Just fine, General. He is able to get around well with one crutch and makes a joke out of stumping around on the peg he fashioned for his missing foot." She didn't tell him of the dark times when Zachary withdrew and refused to come out until he had "his demons under control," as he put it. "He helps the others when he can and makes sure they all realize they are still in the army."

"We now have other homes opened up to us, thanks to your willingness to start the ball rolling. The men who convalesce in private homes do much better than those here. If only we had a hundred women like you."

Louisa could feel the heat surge up to her hairline. "Thank you, sir." She took a deep breath and leaped in before he could say something else to embarrass her. "I heard my br—er—husband mention . . ." She looked up to catch a twinkle in his eye. *Had he caught her gaffe?*

The surgeon general leaned forward, hands clasped on the desk in front of him. "That is all right, Miss Highwood." The emphasis on the *Miss* let her know that he knew.

"When did you figure out my little charade?"

"Not long after you took your brother home with you. Someone, I don't remember who, had known him from before. When we bragged about our Missus Louisa Highwood, he set us straight." His face sobered. "You know I never would have let an unmarried young woman work here like you did."

"I know that. Living that lie was one of the hardest things I've ever done." Louisa took her turn to lean forward. "But I had to do something more than sew and knit. I just had to."

"I understand. But if the favor is to come back here to help us, I would have to say no."

"I realize that, but that's not it. Zachary mentioned morphine, and while I tried to get some at the apothecary, he said none was available. If one of my men needs morphine, I knew to come straight here for it."

The general shook his head. "I'm sorry, my dear, but I'd give my right arm for it myself. What little bit comes in is used on the frontlines. We resort to whiskey here—get the men as drunk as possible before surgery. There's no morphine to be had south of the Mason and Dixon Line."

"I see."

"I wish I could help you. I wish I could help my men." He shook his head. "Short of hijacking a Northern train, I fear . . ." He stared into her eyes. "Now, don't you go getting any wild-headed ideas, young lady."

Louisa stared down at her lap. *Calm down, heart. We must think this through before going off half-cocked.* She raised her gaze back to the man behind the desk, using her eyelashes to their best advantage. Appearing young and innocent was not difficult. "No, sir, but I do have one more question."

"Yes?"

"Ah . . ." She tried to cut off the dream. "Have you heard anything more about Lieutenant Lessling? Was his body found in that train wreck?"

The general sighed and shook his head. "No, but then many were beyond identifying."

"And you are sure he was on that train?" *Dare I even hope?*

"No, I cannot say for absolute truth he was on that train. But he never reached home. His sister wrote and asked about him, and we've not found him in any of our hospitals."

"Could he be a prisoner of war?" She could scarcely get the words out, the thought was so terrible. But better that than dead. At least that way there was a chance of seeing him again someday.

The general came around the desk to take her hand. "My dear Miss Louisa, I cannot hold out false hope for you. Gilbert was a fine young man and an outstanding soldier. I'm sure that if he were alive, we would hear. Somehow, we would have heard."

Louisa turned from the compassion in his gaze to stare out the window. Sunbeams no longer danced. Instead, deepening gray filled the window. Was that thunder she heard?

"I . . . I better go before I get soaked. Thank you for your time."

"You're welcome. Greet your brother for me." He walked her to the door.

She stopped before leaving. "But there is morphine available in the North, correct?"

"I imagine. For those who have the money. Anything can be bought if one has the money and the resources." He laid a hand on her shoulder. "But don't you go getting any farfetched ideas, young lady. You are too valuable for the Southern cause right where you are, helping our men to heal."

"Yes, sir. Good day." She fetched a half curtsey and, after flashing him a smile, added, "You come on over for dinner one day and visit with your men. It would do them a world of good."

"Thank you. I'll do that."

She kept her feet to the ladylike walk her aunt would be so proud of and made her way down the stairs, out into the blustery wind.

"If there is morphine to be found, I will find it." Her vow met with a thunder roll. Lightning flashed a few seconds later as she bent against the wind to hurry home.

"Dere's mail." Abby, nearly dancing with anticipation, met Louisa at the door.

"From Jesselynn. Oh, praise be to God." Louisa sat down on the stairs without even shedding her shawl. Opening the envelope, she unfolded the thin sheet of paper and read swiftly.

"Oh my, things aren't what she'd planned. They are still living in a cave near Springfield, but they are all well. Here, let me read this part.

> 'Christmas made me so homesick for Twin Oaks I thought I might fall weeping and melt into a puddle, nevermore to suffer like this. We fashioned gifts for Thaddeus and Sammy, but all I could think of was the festivities of home: the house decorated with cedar boughs; the tree lit with candles; our singing at the church and at home; Lucinda carrying in the Christmas goose, all roasted to crackling brown; and pecan pie. My mouth waters at the thought. But worst of all, no mother or father to wish us Merry Christmas.'"

Louisa stopped reading to wipe the tears from her eyes with one finger. "Ah, me. We had such a merrier Christmas here." She glanced up to the ceiling. "And at least we were warm and dry with enough to eat and a roof over our heads. Lord, forgive me for taking so many things for granted."

"Me too." Abby used her apron to wipe her eyes. "Dem poor chilluns."

Louisa sniffed and returned to the letter.

> "'Forgive me, dearest sister, for sounding so gloomy, but

I have one more thing to say, and then I shall write of livelier things. I have decided that if God does indeed exist, He no longer can stomach what men are doing to one another and has withdrawn from the affairs of men. I will no longer pray or read that book of His, because doing so is a waste of precious time.' "

Louisa shut her eyes. "Ah, Abby, we must pray for her. Pray without ceasing. One thing that has always been a comfort to me is that my brothers and sisters have all accepted Jesus Christ as their Savior, and no matter how far apart we are in this life, we shall be together again in heaven. I know Mama and Daddy are waiting for us, and that one day we shall all go home."

"And in heaven, dere is no white nor black, no slave nor free, but we shall stand before de Lawd, all his chilluns together." Abby blew her nose. "Is dere more?"

"A little." Louisa took up the paper again.

" 'Greet my dear brother and sister. I am grateful to know you are all safe. Thaddeus is growing faster than we can keep him in clothes, and Sammy too. Jane Ellen has taken over the care of those two, and I believe caring for someone else is bringing her back to herself. We all send our love. I am sorry this letter has been so dreary, but I cannot talk of these things with the others. Please forgive me.

Your loving sister,
Jesselynn

P.S. I almost signed this Jesse, but I have to have one place where I can be Jesselynn, a woman, daughter, sister, and friend. JH

P.P.S. I should just tear this up and not mail it, but paper is too precious for such waste. JH' "

Louisa folded the letter and slid it back into the envelope. "The war. Always the war."

"I best get to fixin' de supper. Reuben done bought a chicken at de market. He say meat gettin' scarcer ever day."

Louisa knew that feeding the extra men was causing distress with her aunt's finances, but what else could they do? "Then we'll have to make it stretch for two meals. Add lots of vegetables and extra dumplin's. That bread I smell will have to fill up any holes." She pushed herself to her feet and hung her shawl on the coat-tree by the newel post. "Let me change my clothes, and I'll be down to help."

As she climbed the stairs, her mind roamed back to her discussion with the general at the hospital. *Lord, what do we do? Oh, Father, please take care of my dear confused sister. Bring her back to you so she can be comforted. Please, Lord, let us all make it through this terrible war and get back together.* God had done miracles before, but would He do this one?

# CHAPTER SEVEN

## Springfield, Missouri

"I should have *made* her come."

"How? Tie her up?" Meshach clucked the horses to a faster pace. Darkness hugged them round about.

Jesselynn felt at any turn they might meet something terrible, like those three renegades with the chained slaves. *People kill for horses, to protect themselves, or to avenge another. Some kill for pure pleasure, like Dunlivey.* Everything evil she measured against the Dunlivey scale. Would killing the slave runners make Meshach and the others murderers? How would they live with that? Or was killing different for men? She knew now that she would kill to protect her family. And she would have killed to protect Twin Oaks. She knew that for certain. She withdrew into the hood created by the blanket Aunt Agatha had pressed upon her. In payment for her stubbornness perhaps? So many things to think about. Had the war loosed some evil monster across the land that gave people the right, or the need, or the desire to kill? Or was the monster always buried beneath the surface, waiting for the opportunity to raise its filthy head and be loosed?

Had Meshach ever killed anyone before? That thought made her slant a look his way, but the dark was so profound she saw only a blurred hulk. Yet she was close enough to him on the wagon seat to feel his warmth through the blanket.

Was killing animals for their food and clothing making it possible for him to kill another human being?

Suddenly she thought of the wood they had brought to town.

The wagon was light again, the wood gone. "What happened to the wood?"

"Left in de barn."

"Why? Do you know those people well?"

"Good 'nough. Dey need wood."

"Did they pay you?"

"No, suh."

*Leave it alone.* Jesselynn ignored the voice of reason. "But why them?"

"Dey be Quakers."

"Oh." *And that is my answer? After all, I didn't cut the wood, but . . .* Like the sun coming up right now in the west, the truth hit her. Quakers were often part of the underground for carrying escaped slaves north to freedom. She started to ask another question but clamped her lips before the words passed them. If they freed those captive slaves tonight, they would most likely go to that house. The wood was Meshach's way of helping out.

"Meshach, did you ever think of leaving Twin Oaks, of running away?"

"Thought about it, but dat my home. Marse was good to me. Teached me to read and write, teached me a trade, and let me keep my own money. I owe him."

"But now?"

"Now I make sure him daughter and son be safe. Den I farm my own land, land I homestead so it be free like me."

His voice rang in the darkness, so sure, so proud. Not the Meshach she had known all her life, but a man who understood the difference between slave and free and would never go back.

*No wonder he wants to free those poor wretches in irons.* "I'll go with you."

"No, someone need take care of de others."

Meshach whistled their signal, and as soon as it was returned, he drove the wagon into the thicket and unhitched the horses to lead them out the other side. Jesselynn gathered up the stores Agatha had pressed upon them and followed him down the steep slope to the cave.

The three black men, none of them smiling now, took one of the rifles and the pistol and the cold chisel to break the chains if they didn't get a key, then disappeared out the mouth of the cave. Ophelia ran after them for one more hug and kiss from Meshach, then returned to the fire to sit rocking with her arms around her middle. With the children already asleep, Jesselynn stoked a small part of the fire higher so she could have light to sew. She didn't try to make conversation.

Ophelia knew as well as she what the men planned to do—and the danger inherent in the scheme. At any word she might shatter into sobbing little bits and slip down onto the sandy floor.

After a while her mutterings penetrated Jesselynn's own chambers of fear and horror.

"Lawd, Lawd. Jesus, Son of God, have mercy. Lawd, Lawd." She repeated the words without seeming to even draw a breath.

Jesselynn gritted her teeth. The singsong seeped into her bones and reverberated there, ringing clear like a crystal glass struck by a spoon. Rising and falling, now intelligible, now not. If they brought her comfort, Jesselynn didn't see it. She wanted to scream at the woman to stop.

She wanted to run after the men and plead with them to come back.

She kept on stitching.

Once she went and stood at the mouth of the cave, listening, straining to hear over hollows and ridges to a camp somewhere south. It was not so far away that they'd taken the horses, but it was out of hearing range. She should have forced Meshach to take the traders in to the law in Springfield. That was the proper thing to do.

But trafficking in slaves wasn't illegal in Missouri. All the scum had to say was they caught these runaways and were taking them back to their masters. They might even have papers to show that they were hunting certain escaped slaves. And besides, how would she *force* Meshach to do anything?

She rubbed her arms to warm them and returned to the fire, trying to ignore Ophelia's haunting song without end.

She caught herself nodding off after stoking the fire more times than she cared to count, so she decided to skin and cut up the rabbits she'd forgotten to take to Aunt Agatha and set them to frying. The fragrance of sizzling meat overlaid the smell of horse droppings. Even though Daniel cleaned the cave floor every day, the smell could still get a bit strong.

One of the horses snorted. Jesselynn leaped to her feet and

ducked under the rope to clamp a hand over Ahab's quivering nostrils. If there was someone out there and they heard a horse whinny, sure to heaven they'd come looking. She looked longingly at the rifle leaning against the wall of the cave.

" 'Phelia." She tried again, hissing louder, not wanting her voice to carry beyond the fire. " 'Phelia, hush and get the gun."

Ophelia rocked again, then rose and drifted across the sand to pick up the rifle. She held it barrel down and brought it to Jesselynn.

"Here, you guard the horses. Do not let Ahab whinny. He's heard something." Shifting places, she took the rifle and ran to the mouth of the cave, hugging the shadowed wall. Not that much of the firelight showed beyond the slight bend anyway. But shadows would show with so little light. She stopped just inside the overhang, holding her breath to hear anything untoward.

The two-tone whistle came. She grabbed the wall to keep from falling when her knees started to buckle. Jerking herself upright, she took two steps outside to whistle back. It took her three attempts before she could work up enough spit to wet her lips and whistle.

The rattle of iron chains preceded the arrival. Horses snorted. Meshach led one horse with a scarecrow on its back. Two other horses and Roman, their mule, carried two riders each. Leave it to Meshach to put the others ahead of his own need.

Daniel slid off the back of one of the horses and came to stand in front of Jesselynn. "Dey de mens what beat me up." The narrowing of his eyes as he spoke said more than his words.

"One of dem's Dunlivey's partner." Meshach helped the first of his charges down from the horse, a young woman who clutched Meshach's jacket over her bare breasts. If there were welts on her back to match those on her legs, it was no wonder her eyes wore a wild-animal look.

"You're sure?"

Meshach nodded. "I never forget dat face."

Jesselynn took in a deep breath as she saw the open sores on legs gone stick thin from lack of food and eyes of men too afraid to hope. None of them looked as if they could have gone a step farther.

"Supper is ready." Ophelia was dishing up plates as the new people straggled into the cave and sank down around the fire, holding their hands to the heat. Tears ran down the woman's face.

Looking at them, Jesselynn knew they couldn't send them to that house in town without first getting them stronger. They definitely needed a bigger cave—now! It was a good thing Aunt Agatha hadn't come home with them.

With hardly a word, the newly freed slaves collapsed around the fire as soon as they finished eating. They didn't ask for blankets. They didn't ask for anything. They fell as if a giant puppeteer had cut their strings.

As Jesselynn crawled into her quilt, so exhausted she could barely fold the top over her shoulders, she heard Ophelia crooning, this time a song of praise, and Meshach comforting her with a gentle rumbling voice. Between the two of them, they soothed Jesselynn into a deep sleep.

Daniel and Benjamin took turns standing watch.

———

"How are we going to feed all these mouths?" Jesselynn asked Meshach in the morning as they stood outside the cave. Their guests had yet to stir.

"Go hunting. Cut wood for Marse Dummont for store supplies. Won't be long before dey ready to travel again."

"And clothe them?" Jesselynn had already decided to cut up the blanket from Agatha to make shirts for the men. Their bare feet were crusted with chilblains, and some of the sores looked gangrenous to her. The cruelty of the slavers made her turn cold inside. How could one man treat another this way?

"We share what God gave us." His simple answer made her snap back.

"Looks to me like we work backbreaking hard for every small thing that we have."

"We not like dem slavers." Another simple answer, this one making guilt wash her face white.

"Thank G-G—heavens for that."

"I do."

Jesselynn threw her hands in the air and let them drop. How was she to reason with this man?

"Dey work when dey have de strength. Maybe weak now, but a day or two of belly being full and dey strength come back."

"I surely do hope so."

"Better to pray so."

Jesselynn had started back into the cave but spun around to point a finger in Meshach's direction. "You go too far, Meshach, into what is not your business."

But Meshach only looked at her. With what? Pity? Jesselynn spun away again and strode on into the cave. Daniel had the horses out to water and graze already, and even the horses walking out hadn't awakened the newcomers. Were they still alive, or had they died during the night?

She knew the answer to that, since she'd already watched them breathe to make certain they needn't dig more graves. Ophelia smiled at her, nodded a good morning, and handed her the long-handled wooden spoon to stir the mush laced with chopped bits of dried venison. The rabbit stew last night had disappeared within minutes.

The boys woke up, and Jane Ellen took them outside for their morning duty, both staring openmouthed at the floor crowded with slumbering bodies. They kept quiet only by a strict glare from Jesselynn. Sammy had his thumb in his round mouth and stared back over Jane Ellen's shoulder.

As Jesselynn stirred the pot, she studied the tangled mass of limbs. Three of the men were the same deep black as Meshach, with kinky hair cut so short it appeared to have recently been shaved. The lighter-skinned male still wore signs of boyhood, his shoulders not much wider than his waist and long of leg and arm, as though he had yet to grow into them. His face in repose would be beautiful once the bruises healed. One eye was swollen shut, one ear cut and bloodied, and the side of his face had a long scrape that looked as if he'd been dragged along the ground.

The woman definitely had white blood and, once her lashes healed, would be comely. It looked as if a whip had taken a chunk of flesh from beside her eye. So close she came to losing it. From what appeared to be blood on her shredded skirt, Jesselynn suspected the men had raped her more than once.

*If they weren't already dead, I'd kill them myself.* The thought made her stop stirring for a moment. She knew it was true. No one should ever be treated as these poor souls had been.

One of the men opened his eyes and looked around. He rolled his head to the side as if he didn't remember coming here during the night. He lifted his shackle-free hands and looked down at his feet. "Thank you, Jesus," he whispered. "And you, Mi-Marse." His brow wrinkled as if not sure which she was. "Kin I go outside?"

"Yes, of course, but stay right near. We have to be cautious so we are not found out."

He pushed himself to his feet and staggered a bit before getting his balance, then limped outside, bracing himself on the wall with one hand. One by one the others followed except for the woman, who had yet to move. The men returned with Meshach herding them.

"Breakfast ready?"

"Yes. Call Jane Ellen and the boys."

"Dey wid Phelia down at de creek. Sammy hate him face washed."

"In that cold water, I don't blame him." Jesselynn filled wooden trenchers with the mush and the men dug in with their fingers. When she handed them each a hot biscuit, one stared at it as though he'd seen gold.

"Thankee, suh." The others chorused their appreciation, emptied their trenchers, and eyed the kettle.

"As soon as the others eat, you can have the rest." She chose to chew on a piece of dried venison. The sight of their hunger turned her off mush.

While the family ate, she laid a hand on the sleeping woman's cheek. Sure enough, she had a fever, and her breathing seemed labored. Jesselynn set Ophelia to boiling up some willow bark tea, and taking warm water and a cloth, she washed the woman's face, shoulders, and arms. In one hand she found clenched a bit of meat from supper the night before.

"What is her name?" She looked to the men who now seemed much more lively.

"Sarah. Dey already have her befo' me," the light-skinned youth answered, and the others nodded.

"Has she been sick long?"

"Him kick her in belly. She lose baby."

Jesselynn didn't want to know who *him* was. Once more she was grateful her men had done what they felt necessary.

"When did that happen?"

"Two, three days ago." At least the boy knew that many numbers.

"She too sick to walk, so we stay in one camp," one of the other men added.

Jesselynn and Ophelia exchanged glances and set to making

things better for poor beaten Sarah. They fixed a pallet for her, bathed her, and dipped broth from a kettle simmering with the rabbits Daniel had caught in his snares. Her eyes fluttered open one moment, and a smile lit her face. She drank the broth and fell right back to sleep. They set Jane Ellen to tending the sick woman, and Jesselynn took the boys outside to play while the sun shone. The air crackled with cold, and frost still glittered near trees in the shade.

"They bad sick?" Thaddeus shook his head. "Jesse, you fix." He looked up at her with eyes full of trust as he took her hand. "Find catepiwar?"

"Sorry, Thaddy—"

"Joshwa," he corrected her absently as he moved leaves around, looking for fuzzy caterpillars.

"All right, Joshwa. The caterpillars have all gone to sleep for the winter in cocoons so they can become butterflies next summer."

"Butterflies?" He looked all around as if expecting them to flutter by.

"No, not now. Next summer."

"Want butterflies."

"Sorry." She chuckled at the look of intensity with which he glared at her. She shook her head. "I can't help it. Many animals and insects go to sleep for the winter."

He planted his fists on his hips and with legs spread looked so like his dead father that she caught her breath. He was Joshwa all right. They'd named him perfectly.

"Here, let's build a house with these sticks. Help me stack them for the walls, like a cabin." She set the sticks on top of each other to form a log cabin. What she wouldn't give for one right now. But to care for all these, it would have to be huge.

Thaddy had the walls several sticks up when Sammy stepped right in the middle of it. With a howl, Thaddy shoved Sammy smack on his rear. Sammy responded with a louder howl. Meshach scooped both boys up under his arms and strode down the hill with them, threatening to dump them both in the ice-cold creek if they didn't hush.

Jesselynn got to her feet and dusted her hands off on her britches. They'd not heard any more artillery fire, so maybe the battle ended the day before. She could hear the boys still giggling. She'd have to talk with Thaddeus about his temper. Stopping, she counted out the days. Why, he had a birthday in a few weeks. He would be three. "Little Marse," as Meshach called him, should have a present of some sort for his birthday. Her mind flipped back to Twin Oaks. Birthdays had always been important celebrations in their family. Lucinda would bake a three-layer frosted cake. Lighter than air were Lucinda's cakes.

Jesselynn's mouth watered at the memory. Would she ever taste one of Lucinda's lemon cakes again? She dusted her hands and returned to the cave for her writing materials. While everyone was busy elsewhere, now was a good time to answer the precious letters. They could take them to the post office next time she went to Aunt Agatha's.

By the time she finished, the sun rode close to its zenith and Ophelia was calling her name.

"She gettin' weaker not stronger."

Jesselynn knelt by the sick woman. "She lost too much blood, I imagine. Poor thing. Come now, Sarah, you must try to drink more broth." She held a cup to the woman's mouth and propped up her head with the other hand.

Sarah drank three or four swallows, then tipped her head away.

"No will to live." Jane Ellen wrung out another cloth and laid it over the sick woman's forehead.

"I know. Can't say as I blame her."

The men filed into the cave again as if they were still chained together and sat in a row by the fire. They'd given their names, but Jesselynn still had no idea who was who, other than the boy and Sarah.

That night Meshach gathered the fugitives around him and laid out his plan. They would go to the house in Springfield in the night. There, others would take them north to freedom. "But first you get strong enough for de trip."

Jesselynn brought over the two shirts she'd made from the blanket. "Sorry, the other isn't done yet. I have more piecing to do on it."

The biggest man, Moses, brushed the nap of the shirt with a reverent hand. "I neber had such a good shirt."

"Put it on." She mimicked pulling it over her head. "That should help keep you warm. Now if only we had something for your feet."

Ophelia had given them all hot water to wash with and then bandaged the sores that needed it. With the new shirts on, they looked almost human again, instead of like refuse left by the road-side.

———————

"Marse Jesse?" The voice woke her in the middle of the night. "Yes?"

"I think Sarah done gone home to be with the Lord." Jane Ellen's voice was muffled with tears. "I tried to keep her alive, Marse Jesse, I tried."

"I know. You did all you could." After checking to make sure the woman had truly left this world, Jesselynn covered the black woman's face with the blanket. Rage at the cruelty of it all boiled red before her eyes.

Fighting tears herself, Jesselynn gathered Jane Ellen into her arms and rocked her until she slept. Glancing up, she saw one of the men watching her with a puzzled look.

*Ah, if you only knew the whole story. What did it matter if they suspected she was Miss instead of Marse?*

# CHAPTER EIGHT

*Did they bury those men? The ones they . . .* Jesselynn slammed the door of her mind.

"De Lawd giveth and de Lawd taketh away. Blessed be de name of de Lawd." Meshach raised his voice on the last words at the gravesite of Sarah. They didn't even have a last name for the poor woman, only an idea of how terribly she'd been treated during the final days of her life.

Before she came to them.

Jesselynn made herself stay at the service, for politeness if nothing else. While Jane Ellen had tears running down her cheeks, none of the others had had time to much care about the deceased. Was death becoming such a commonplace thing that she couldn't even summon up sadness? All the regret stemmed from not being able to save her.

"We'll go tonight," Meshach said as they walked back up the slope to the cave.

"I'll come too. That way if we are stopped, I can say I'm taking my slaves in to work on my aunt's house. No one can argue with that, and that's what we will do if followed." For a change, Meshach didn't argue with her. She had hoped he would see the reason in her plan.

He'd spent the day breaking two of the new horses to the harness so they could leave the Thoroughbreds safe in the cave. Neither of the mares should be working now, and they surely didn't want to use the stallions. The filly was getting big and heavy enough to train, but Jesselynn hated to break her to harness before the saddle. Chess and Roman had a kicking contest while out to pasture. They'd have to learn to get along, that was all.

"I loaded the wagon with wood too. Best we take some tools along if we be workin' on de house." His raised eyebrow told her he was teasing her.

"Good idea. I reckon we'll look right proper."

By afternoon the temperature was dropping again after two fairly warm days. Jesselynn took the two remaining deer hides and wrapped the men's feet. Daniel had given the younger man his deerskin shirt, saying he could always make another. They shot deer aplenty.

The shirt he now wore of Meshach's looked like a tent on his slender frame.

Thaddeus pointed at Daniel and giggled, setting Sammy off, which made Jane Ellen smile and the freed slaves actually laugh. Never had the cave heard such ringing laughter.

Jesselynn wished she could laugh. Lately it seemed that as tears had dried up, so had her laughter, blowing away like puffs of a dandelion. What if they were caught? Would her story hold up? Of course it would. It sounded perfectly plausible. But what if someone acted suspicious? Could she trust these men to carry out the deception if needed?

She was getting plenty of practice in shutting off disturbing questions. As her mother always said, *"One step at a time."* Of course she had added something like *"God only lights the way ahead one step at a time."* But Jesselynn was trying to ignore that last part.

Frost was already coating the ground when they hitched up the team and started off. The two-hour trip to town seemed to go on forever because they couldn't see the landmarks. A sickle moon hung low in the west by the time the lights of Springfield came into view. Many houses were dark already, either the folks gone to bed or the house damaged too badly in the battle to use.

Since the Quaker house was close to the edge of town, Jesselynn halted the wagon under an oak tree that would have been good shade in the summer. Tonight its naked branches rattled in the rising wind.

"Now follow me like I said." Meshach spoke softly. Within seconds they all disappeared into an alley running along the backs of the houses. Jesselynn gave them a few minutes head start and then drove her wagon on up the street, turning at the corner to pass the Quaker house. As she drew even with the barn, Meshach climbed back aboard the wagon, and they continued on until they reached Dummont's store. Quickly they unloaded the wood, stacking it behind the building. Jesselynn stuck a note into the doorframe telling who left the wood, and they headed back out of town.

They'd driven for some time before Jesselynn said, "Now I feel I can breathe again." She slapped the reins, and the horses picked up a fast trot. If they loped, the wagon might fall apart for sure. By the time they arrived back at the ridge, the moon had set and clouds hid the stars.

"Snow." Meshach shivered as he unhooked the traces. "No one be able to track dem back to here, and dey not know de way."

Jesselynn knew he meant if someone forced the black men to talk, they wouldn't be able to tell where they'd been. For all they knew they'd been north or east of Springfield, from the roundabout way they entered town. And snow would cover any trails that had built up around the camp. Now if only they could figure out what to do with all the extra horses until they could be sold. Even with putting them farther back in the cave, feeding and watering them took more effort.

But selling them would bring in the money they so desperately needed, and the Union army was always looking for horses. Now they could keep Chess longer.

"God do provide," Meshach said with a grin and a pat on her shoulder. Jesselynn tried to ignore him, but his joy was as catching as a yawn. She caught herself whistling under her breath as she went about her chores.

---

They woke in the morning to a drift of snow halfway into the cave and to their own shivering, even though the fire had been kept going all night.

"Now I wish we had those extra deer hides to stretch across that opening." Jesselynn shook her head. "And to keep us warm." To think she'd gone to sleep dreaming of selling the extra horses today and bringing home bacon and lard, even eggs and peppermint candy for the boys of all sizes. And coffee. How wonderful a cup of coffee would taste on a cold morning like this.

The storm settled in and howled around the cave for the next two days. It let up, then returned with a vengeance. Meshach built a partial wall at the cave mouth to keep out the worst of the wind and cold. While they took most of the horses down to the creek to drink, Jesselynn chose to melt snow for the mares. She didn't want them slipping and sliding going down the hill as the others had.

She doled out the oats, wishing she had some for the others when Ahab nickered for a treat too.

"Sorry, old son, but the mamas need this worse than you."

That's something else she would buy—oats for the horses and hay if she could find some.

On the good days, Daniel and Benjamin each brought in a deer, and Meshach stretched the hides over a bar at the top and hung another at the bottom so his swinging door could be pushed aside when they took the horses out.

The cave instantly felt warmer, though darker.

"Good thing we got de horses. Dey help keep us warm."

"I wonder how Aunt Agatha is. With that hole in her roof..." Jesselynn shook her head. "Stubborn old woman." *Runs in the family*, giggled her inner voice. But the concern for Aunt Agatha wouldn't leave her alone. She went to sleep with it and woke up with it.

As soon as the snow stopped coming down and started melting, she decided to head for Springfield. They couldn't take the wagon yet, but they could take the horses into the army encampment and offer to sell them to the Union soldiers. If the Confederates were in charge, she'd sell them there if they would pay her in gold.

She gathered some of the dried venison for Aunt Agatha, along with the day's catch of rabbits, but as she got ready, she thought more and more about the Confederates having taken Springfield. They would conscript the horses, pay her in Confederate dollars, and wish her well. She knew that as well as she knew her own name. Only the Yankees had gold.

"Meshach, do you think the folks that own the barn we kept the wagon in would mind if we tied some horses there for a while?"

"Dey not mind. Why?"

"Can't take them in if the Confederates are in power."

He nodded. "I take Roman, you ride Chess?"

She nodded. No sense trying to go alone. "We can stop at Dummont's and pick up supplies too." Knowing they had a credit at the store took another load off her mind. She refused to let her mind play with the money they would get for the horses. Still seemed like blood money to her, but caring for her people was more important to her than mourning three men who took delight in destroying others. She had yet to ask Meshach what had actually happened that night, and most likely she never would.

Sometimes there was safety in not knowing.

White waves crested across the prairie, blown in drifts by a determined wind that even now tugged at their hats and tried to blow holes in their coats. Had it not been for the wind, the day would have been right balmy after the blizzards of the last days. She squinted against sun so bright off the snow, her eyes watered. Even the brim of her hat, pulled down low to shield her face, failed to protect her.

The horses worked up a sweat before they'd gone more than a mile and were blowing hard after plowing through a section of belly-deep snow, too soft to have a crust. By the time they got to town, she and Meshach had to dismount and stamp their feet to get the circulation flowing again. The United States flag snapping in the wind over the fort let them know who was in charge. The Confederate attack had been repulsed, so they could take the horses right in.

Snow had cleaned the town up, hiding the shell holes, trash, and dirt. White roofs with smoke coming from chimneys, capped fences, and a snowman here and there said Springfield had gone back to life as usual. The main streets were fast becoming mudholes as wagons and horses traversed the town.

A sentry stopped them at the edge of the parade grounds.

"Can you tell me where to find the quartermaster?"

"What for?"

"We have some horses for sale." She nodded to the three on lead lines.

"Then you'd want to see Cap'n Maddock. He's in charge." The man pointed to a two-story house that had been commandeered by the army. A platoon of soldiers, rifles on their shoulders, marched back and forth across the field at the command of a hard-voiced officer. Smoke rose from chimneys of sod and wood buildings alike. To the side was a corral and low barn, the stables. And a line of wash flapping in the wind proclaimed the presence of the laundry.

Jesselynn nodded and turned to her right. Trotting up the block, she saw enlisted men shoveling snow from walks, women in heavy wool shawls with market baskets on their arms, and a plethora of horses and riders coming and going, many of them to and from the big house. She handed Meshach the lead rein and flipped Chess's reins over the hitching rail to the side of the iron-fenced yard.

Two enlisted men, buttons gleaming gold in the sunlight, stood on either side of the fan-lighted front door.

"I came to see Captain Maddock. I have some horses to show him."

"Second floor on your right. The private then will see you up."

"Thank you." She entered the interior, dim after the brightness outside, and stood for a moment to let her eyes grow accustomed.

"Your name, boy?" The cherry-cheeked man behind the desk in the entry barked at her. He didn't look old enough to shave yet, let alone wear a uniform.

"Jesse Highwood, suh. I come to see Captain Maddock."

"State your business."

"I have three horses to sell."

"Only three?"

"Yes, suh." She felt like saluting and resisted the temptation to give any further information. Benjamin had reminded her of that before they left the cave.

"Jones, take him up."

She straightened her shoulders and sucked in a breath of courage as he opened the dark walnut door.

"Young man to see you about some horses, sir."

"Show him in."

When Jesselynn stood before the desk, she removed her hat and clutched it in front of her. The officer finished what he was writing and looked up at her. "You have horses for sale?"

"Yes, suh. Three."

"Where'd you get them?"

"Found 'em loose in the woods."

"You didn't rustle them, did you?"

"No, suh!" Again she clamped her lips against embroidering her story. After all, they *had* found them in the woods, hard used like the blacks.

"I'll give you a hundred dollars for each one if they prove up sound."

She shook her head. "No, suh, mah daddy tan mah hide if I sells them so cheap."

"A hundred twenty-five."

Another shake of her head. "Hundred fifty. In gold."

"I can't go that high. Hundred forty, and that's my last offer, unless you'll take a hundred sixty a head, in paper?"

Jesselynn didn't have to debate on that. "Gold."

"In gold it is." He turned to the young man standing just inside the door. "Jones, go out and check to make sure these animals are sound."

"I wouldn't bring you a lame horse."

"Others have tried." He pulled out a drawer, drew out a bag that clanked when he set it on the desk top, and began filling out a requisition form. "Name?"

She gave him the information he asked for—and nothing extra.

"Can you read or write?"

"Yes, suh."

"Good, then sign here."

Jesselynn read quickly through the form and signed her name at the bottom. Jones reentered the room as she finished.

"A bit on the thin side, sir, but no limping, no obvious problems."

"Good. Because if I find out one isn't sound . . ." He let a silence stretch. "Why, then we come after the seller."

"Yes, suh." Oh, how she ached to tell him what to do with his gold, but they needed it too badly. Those three horses were the fare for their journey west and feed for both man and beast in the cave. While the officer didn't look as if he'd ever missed a meal, she now knew what real hunger felt like.

She counted carefully along with him as he set the gold out in stacks of fives. Eight stacks plus two, four hundred and twenty dollars. At least he didn't try to short her. She hadn't seen so much money at one time in far too long.

"If you *find* any more horses loose in the woods, come see me again. You drive a hard bargain, young man. Your daddy should be proud of you."

"Thank you, suh." She took the two leather pouches of gold, wishing she had brought the saddlebags up to hold it.

"Sure you wouldn't just as soon have some of that in paper?"

"No, suh."

Outside at the horses, she handed Meshach one of the bags and put the other in her saddlebag, at the same time looking around to see if anyone was watching them. People had been killed for a lot less than what they now carried.

Stopping at the store, they bought two sacks of oats, coffee, sugar, peppermint sticks, and a dozen eggs to go along with the bacon.

"We'll have to come back with the wagon for the rest we need."

"Be glad to deliver if you'd like." Mr. Dummont gave her the change from one ten-dollar gold piece.

"Thanks, but I need to visit Aunt Agatha." She handed him another gold piece. "Hold this for her account."

"I'll do that."

"We might have to walk partway, with all this load." She swung atop Chess, and they headed for Aunt Agatha's house, twin sacks of coffee and tea, along with cheese and other frivolities she knew were needed. Sharing the bounty was half the fun. "Meshach, do you want to give the Quakers one of these gold pieces, or maybe two?"

"Dat be right good of you." His smile made the snow glitter dim.

She planned on giving each of the men a gold piece but not right now. If someone stopped them and they had a ten-dollar gold piece, they'd be thrown in jail for robbery or worse. When they put the horses in the shed at Aunt Agatha's, she gave Meshach two coins.

The first thing she noticed was that no smoke rose from the chimney. Had Agatha run out of wood? No, the stack by the back door attested to that. Where could she be? After a perfunctory knock, she and Meshach entered a room nearly as cold as the outside.

"Aunt Agatha!" Calling her name, they searched every room. No one there, alive or dead. Where could she be now?

# CHAPTER NINE

## Richmond, Virginia

"I'm coming. I'm coming."

"I gets it, Miss Louisa." Abby came trotting from the kitchen.

Louisa jumped the last step of the walnut stairs and crossed to the front door. "Thanks, but I'm right here." Who could be calling at this time of the morning? Swinging the door open, she broke into a delighted grin. "Why, Carrie Mae, you don't have to ring the bell. You used to live here."

"I know, but Jefferson likes me to be proper, so I'm practicin' every chance I get." The two sisters exchanged hugs and entered the parlor arm in arm. While Carrie Mae was the youngest of the three sisters, she looked older due to her deep green velvet traveling suit, including her hat with a matching feather that swept over one shoulder.

"Don't you look lovely." Louisa ignored a slight twinge of jealousy and stepped back to admire her sister's outfit. "Jefferson must be doing well."

"Oh, he is the best husband." Carrie Mae clasped her gloved hands to her bosom. "He works so hard but never is too tired to attend a rout or dinner or even a ball. I wish you would come with us sometime." She leaned forward with a wide smile. "Why, we were even invited to Mary Chestnut's for tea. Such stimulatin' conversation."

Louisa smiled and patted her sister's shoulder. "You know things like that have never been my style." *Let alone I have no gowns to wear to formal do's, no shoes, nor*... She left off the self-pity and guided her sister to a chair. "Now, which would you like—tea or coffee?"

"Oh, tea, thank you. Where's Aunt Sylvania?"

"Gone to church to help the ladies." Louisa hurried down the hall to the kitchen to order refreshments. On the way, she glanced in a mirror and made a face. Her hair needed pinning up, and she wore one of her older house dresses. Forcing men to move limbs that had near frozen in place didn't take a fashion plate. "Could you make tea, please, Abby, and I do hope there are some of your good molasses cookies left." She'd used them as bribes for the men.

"I fixes somethin'. Lawsy sakes, she sure do look purty."

"That she does. I wonder if she and Jefferson"—Louisa put a twist on her brother-in-law's name—"would take one of our wounded soldiers into their home?" She knew the question was catty. Jefferson believed he was doing his part for the South by helping in the legislature, and he demanded that his wife look and act the part of a successful lawyer's wife.

Carrie Mae had always loved dressing up.

Hurrying back down the hall, Louisa remembered the letter. "Oh, sister, I have a wonderful surprise for you. Be right back."

"What is it?"

Louisa ignored the question and dashed up the stairs to her room. The letter from Jesselynn lay in her writing case, along with a partially written answer. Letter in hand, she danced down the stairs again, waving the envelope gaily.

"A letter? From whom?" Light dawned. "From Jesselynn. Oh, don't tease me. Read it, or better yet, let me read it myself."

Louisa handed her the envelope and took her own chair, the better to watch her sister's expressive face. Just as they had for each one she'd read the letter to, tears sprang instantly to her sister's eyes.

"Oh no. I had no idea things were so bad. I ... I guess I thought they were safe in town or something." She returned to her reading. "Ah, and I have so much. Louisa, I feel guilty for ... for ..."

"For being safe and warm and ..."

"And our Christmas was wonderful. Jefferson's family spoiled me rotten." She laid the letter in her lap. "Is there nothin' we can do?"

"Pray for her. Oh, Carrie Mae, we must pray for the things she needs but more so for the rescue of her soul."

"God will never let her go."

"I know." But Louisa also knew of soldiers who died cursing the Lord they had worshiped as boys.

Carrie Mae put the letter back in the envelope. "I will write to her tonight." She thought a moment. "No, we have a dinner to attend tonight. But I will pray for her, and I will write tomorrow. Where do we send the letter?"

"To the post office in Springfield. She got our other letters there."

During the silence, Louisa glanced around the room. The pallets for two of their recovering men lay stacked against one wall. Their extra clothing was folded in a neat pile on a chair. A pipe and tobacco pouch resided on a whatnot table. While the men were very neat, still there was always what could be called clutter around.

There had been no clutter at Carrie Mae's home, a flat downtown near the courthouse.

"I see you still have your soldiers here." Carrie Mae pulled off her gloves and laid them in her reticule.

"Yes, as soon as one is ready to go home, we'd have two to take his place, had we room for them. One thing we don't lack is wounded soldiers." Did she dare to tell her of the idea that had been brewing since she saw the general at the hospital?

She didn't. "So tell me the news."

Carrie Mae studied her hands clasped in her lap, then looked up to send her sister a smile of pure joy. "The best news of all, short of the war ending, is that I am in the family way."

"Oh, how wonderful." Louisa fell to her knees at her sister's side, taking her hands. "That truly is the most marvelous news. When will the baby be born?"

"August, near as we can figure."

"Have you seen a doctor?"

"No. Whatever for? I've been askin' some of the other wives about a midwife, though. I always thought when I had a baby, Mama and Lucinda would be there to care for me. And Daddy would be walkin' the floor with my husband."

"Most likely passing the whiskey and telling tall tales in Daddy's office." Louisa sat back on her heels. "Are you feeling all right?"

"So far. Just some queasiness in the mornin'." Carrie Mae took Louisa's hands in hers and rubbed the backs with her thumbs. "Ah, Louisa, I want Jesselynn here. I want to tell her my good news, and the three of us can sew baby things together. She would knit me a sweater. You know her knitting is so much better than mine."

"And a hat and booties. Soakers and a little dress so cunning..." Louisa fought the lump that clogged her throat and caused her eyes to burn. She sniffed and blinked. "There could be a miracle, you know, and the war end so she can come home."

"But her last letter said they are headin' west." Carrie Mae shook her head slowly, as though hope had died. "We're never goin' to see them again. I just know it." Tears trembled on her lashes; then one meandered down her cheek. "Some days I miss Mama so bad I could just..."

They sniffed together, and Louisa pulled a handkerchief out of her apron pocket. She dried her sister's eyes before wiping her own.

"But we go on."

Carrie Mae looked deep into her sister's eyes, as if searching for something. Louisa knew not what. Carrie Mae clenched her lower lip between her teeth. A whisper came, faint and drenched in fear. "Mama died in childbirth."

"Oh, baby sister." Louisa gathered Carrie Mae into her arms. "You are young and strong and healthy, just right for child bearing. You will do real fine, and then we'll have a baby to fuss over."

"A baby?" Abby set the tea tray down with a rattle. "You gonna have a baby, Miss Carrie Mae?" Her face shone with joy.

Carrie Mae nodded, dashed an errant tear away, and smiled with trembling lips.

"Oh, lawsy me. We gonna have a baby. I better gits to hemmin' diapers. We ain't had no baby in dis family in too many years. Wait till Miss Sylvania hears dis. She be over de moon wi' joy." Abby left the room, chuckling as she went.

"Have you written to Jesselynn yet?"

"No, I wanted to tell you first." She accepted the cup of tea Louisa poured. "Jefferson said we must look for a house now. Our flat is too small for a baby and a mammy. Wouldn't Lucinda love to mother another Highwood baby?"

"That she would." Louisa nibbled a cookie after dunking it in her tea.

"You think she would come if I sent for her?"

Louisa stopped chewing. "Why, Carrie Mae Steadly, that is the most wonderful idea anyone has had in ages. Of course, you might have to send someone for her. Can you think of her taking the train here all by herself?"

"I wish Aunt Sylvania would get home."

"Not till late afternoon. She takes her lunch with her, and they work most of the day." Louisa stopped and let the thoughts flow. "Oh, I have the best idea."

"What?" Carrie Mae leaned forward. "Tell me."

"Well, it has nothin' to do with you, but what if I taught my wounded soldiers to knit and sew? They could help with the war effort that way and would most likely feel like they are doing something useful."

"Men sewing and knitting. Louisa Highwood, have you lost your mind?"

"Wait till Zachary hears *this* idea." The words made her chuckle. *Along with the other one. Things are likely to get pretty lively around here.*

# CHAPTER TEN

## Springfield, Missouri

"I can't leave without knowing where she is!"

"Need be home before dark."

"Meshach, I know that!" She felt like screaming. What could have happened to Agatha? Somewhere from the far reaches of her memory, she heard her father saying, *"That aggravating Agatha, I swain . . ."* Jesselynn now understood why. Couldn't she have at least left a note?

"The post office!" Jesselynn spun on her heel and darted out the door, Meshach right behind her. Sure enough, there was a letter addressed to Master Jesse Highwood from Mrs. Hiram Highwood. Jesselynn tore it open and read swiftly. "She's taken a position with an elderly couple over on Sunshine Street." She looked back to the postmaster. "Could you please tell me where that is?"

He gave her directions, and they left as fast as they'd come.

She literally threw herself off the horse and ran up the walk to a house in much better shape than the one Agatha previously had been in. At least the roof appeared to be in one piece. This area of town didn't seem to have suffered any damage from the battle. Again a two-story house, this one painted white with green shutters. Three shallow steps led up to a porch with heavy pillars that stretched across the entire front of the house.

Jesselynn knocked on the carved oak door with an oval glass center.

Aunt Agatha parted the lace curtain and, peering out, smiled and opened the door. "I knew you would find me." She hugged her niece and patted her shoulder. "When the Reverend said these old folks needed some help, why, I knew it was an answer to prayer. Since none of the things in that house of Lettie's were my own, I just packed my bag and came right on over. I was goin' to sell all the food in the basement to Mr. Dummont, but I knew you could use some of it and perhaps would bring some over here for us, as well."

Jesselynn had never heard her aunt run on so. But then she hadn't known her all that long either.

"Would you like to meet the dears?" Agatha took her arm and pulled her toward the kitchen.

"No, I think not, not today. We have to get on home. I just wanted to make sure you were all right. You've even been haunting my dreams in that drafty, old falling-down house."

"Are you sure? You can't stay even for a cup of tea?"

Jesselynn nodded and extricated herself from her aunt's grasp. She patted the liver-spotted hand. "Do you have any money of your own with you?"

Agatha pulled herself upright and managed somehow to look down her nose at her niece, who was a good four inches taller than she.

"Now, don't go gettin' all het up. We're family, and I feel responsible. I sold some horses today. . . ."

"Not the Thoroughbreds?" Agatha gave "aghast" a new meaning.

"No, no. Some we found after a battle in the woods. We healed them up and sold them to the army." She dug in her pocket and pulled out several silver dollars and a ten-dollar gold piece. "Here, just in case you need it."

"No. I will not take money from you when I don't need it." She stared at the coins on the outstretched palm, picked out two dollars, and closed Jesselynn's fingers back over the rest. "I know you mean well, dear Jesse . . ." At Jesselynn's raised eyebrow she cut off the further syllable. "But I am just fine here."

"All right, but if you need anything, you also have a credit at Dummont's store. Keep that in mind, and if you need to get ahold of me, well, you did it." She kissed her aunt's cheek and opened the door. "Take care now, you hear?"

"That's just what your daddy always said when he left. Bless his heart. And yours too."

Jesselynn stepped back out on the porch, so grateful she didn't have to come in with the wagon and carry her aunt out to the cave that she could have leaped the picket fence.

She filled Meshach in on the news as they rode out of town, both of them keeping an eye out for anyone who might be following them. If the captain suspected they had more horses, he might send someone after them.

"Dat old woman goin' to come west, you just watch."

"She's fine where she is." *Oh, I hope so. I do not need anyone else to cart along.*

Meshach gave her that wise smile he wore when he was absolutely sure about something. Her mother had sometimes said she felt Meshach had a bit of the prophet in him, that it would most likely come out more as he grew older. There had been times when he had foreseen something, but Jesselynn had pooh-poohed his predictions. The thought of Aunt Agatha in a wagon heading west didn't bear thinking about.

They circled round and came to the cave from a different direction, even though their earlier tracks led directly to their entrance. Meshach whistled, received an answer, and down the slope they went. The boys ran to greet them when they led the horse and mule into the cave.

"Gone long time." Thaddeus held his arms high to be picked up. Jesselynn hugged him and settled him in the saddle. Had he been much taller, he wouldn't have fit; the ceiling was that low. "Good Chess." He leaned forward and patted the horse's shoulder.

Jesselynn led him back to the horse corral, as they called it, and swung her brother to the ground so she could unsaddle. "Do you hear that?" She cocked her head as if listening closely.

"What?" Thaddeus looked around.

"That sound?" She pretended to listen again. At the puzzled look he gave her, she said, "That little voice callin' your name. Hear it? Thaddeus." She made her voice soft and whispery.

He wrinkled his brow trying so hard to hear.

Jesselynn glanced up to see the big grin on Meshach's face.

"I hears it." He leaned close to the saddlebag behind the saddle. "From in dere."

Thaddeus clapped his hands. "Me see."

Jesselynn lifted the flap on the leather bag and peered inside. "Sure enough. There he is."

"Me see!"

Jesselynn reached inside her saddlebag and brought out the sack of peppermint sticks. Instead of just two, she'd bought one for every one of them. "Here. You hand them out."

Thaddeus did that, his chest swelling enough to pop his buttons if he'd had any. He went to each person around the cave and gravely gave them a red-and-white peppermint candy stick, accepted their thanks, then plunked himself down by the fire to suck on his own. He patted the rock beside him. "Jesse, you sit here."

"I will." She pulled out the sack of coffee beans and gave them to Ophelia, who inhaled the fragrance and closed her eyes in delight. The rest of the food things she set down on the bench of lashed branches Meshach had made during the days of confinement. "That ought to make things easier for a while."

Sammy, candy stick in mouth, sat down beside Thaddeus and held out his candy in a sandy fist. "Good."

Jesselynn debated where to store the gold coins. She was not concerned that one of her people would steal them, but she wanted them safe in case they were attacked. And so they didn't get scattered. The storage boxes were too obvious a place. Finally she kept out one coin and rolled the two leather bags containing the rest in a scrap of leftover deerskin, then set the packet under a rock in the horse corral, off to the side above the ground by a foot or so. When satisfied, she showed the hidden place to Meshach in case something happened to her.

The snow melted within a week, setting the creek to frothing fury so that Daniel and Benjamin had to be careful when letting the horses drink. No longer could they stand in the shallows and drink contentedly. The bank sometimes gave way, and all they needed was for one of the mares to be injured.

Jesselynn checked them daily as their bags swelled and their bellies sagged. "Make sure you hold them tight so they can't take off somewhere to drop those foals," she admonished the men. Benjamin, who'd worked with the horses since he was a small child, gave her a wide, slow smile.

"Yes, Marse."

Jesselynn rolled her eyes and laughed. "Sorry. But we can't afford to lose a baby. Those two are the foundation for the herd after the war. If only we could do something about foaling stalls. We have to separate the mares out. Ahab could get feisty and hurt one of them."

"If we need stalls, we make stalls." Meshach beckoned to the two younger men. "Now we cut posts." Within a week they had sunk posts as far as the floor of the cave permitted and run rails to the walls. While the stalls weren't airy and roomy like those at Twin Oaks, they would be adequate. Next he chopped down an oak tree and split off withes to make two oaken buckets. When he set Daniel to cutting thin withes for baskets, Ophelia wandered around in a happy daze for hours before she began to weave an oaken basket.

Benjamin bagged two deer, so they stretched the new hides over the doorway and brought the weathered ones in to tan.

The next morning Jesselynn was trying to get ready to leave for town when Jane Ellen asked, "Where's Sammy?"

"I don't know." Jesselynn dropped the harness and glanced around the cave. Since the day had dawned clear, the open door let in some extra light, but not a lot. "Thaddeus, where's Sammy?"

The little boy looked up from his building sticks. "Don't know."

Ophelia ran to the mouth of the cave. "Sammy! You get on in here."

Jesselynn joined her, cupping her hands around her mouth. "Sammy!" She called his name twice and shook her head. "Surely he didn't toddle off. He wouldn't leave Thaddeus."

"Then where he be?" Ophelia dashed away the tears already forming. "He can't be gone. Sammy!"

Jesselynn reentered the cave. Could he have crawled back under the covers? She thought for a moment. No. Jane Ellen had gone hunting for wood and leaves by herself this time. Could Sammy have followed her?

"S-a-m-m-y." Ophelia's voice sounded fainter.

"Here."

Jesselynn spun away from the stores and glanced around the dim room. No little black boy. "Sammy?"

"Here."

"Thaddeus, do you see Sammy?"

Thaddeus looked up from his building and glanced around the area. "Over there." He went back to building his cabin.

Jesselynn swallowed. He'd pointed to the horses. She bent down, and her heart took an extra beat. There sat Sammy under Dulcie.

"Sammy, don't move. Just stay right where you are. Thaddeus, go call Ophelia. Now." She eased her way over to the horses. "Thank God, he's not under Roman," she whispered. "Easy, girl, now don't get restless here." She laid a hand on the mare's shoulder. Sunshine shifted, turning to see if Jesselynn had the feed bucket with her. She bumped Dulcie, and the mare laid her ears back.

"Easy." *One kick and he could be dead. God, hold the animals steady, please.* With one hand on the mare's halter, she reached under with the other and grabbed Sammy's arm. He let out a howl, Dulcie backed up, and Jesselynn had the little boy tucked under her arm. "Sammy, I could paddle your behind till you won't sit down for a week." She slipped under the bar holding the horses back and plunked him down on the rock by the fire. "You know better than to go in with the horses. Shame on you!" The finger she shook in his tear-streaming face moved of its own accord. Her heart had yet to settle to a regular rhythm.

Ophelia ran in and snatched the baby up in her arms, raining kisses on his cheeks and hair.

"He needs a switchin' so's he won't do that again."

"Yes, suh, Marse Jesse, I do dat." She turned the little one end for end and walloped him three times. Sammy screamed, Ophelia sobbed, and Thaddeus came running in.

"No, don't hit Sammy. No." He grabbed around Ophelia's leg and hung on. Sammy clung around her neck.

Jesselynn headed for the cave entrance. If she stayed she might laugh at the scene going on. Leave it to Thaddeus to protect his friend. But if she laughed, she might start crying, and if she did that, she might never stop. Once she'd walked off some of the fear and anger, she remembered what she'd done. *So I prayed. That was only in an emergency, mind you. I don't want anything to do with a God who allows war and guerrilla bands and slave traders and little boys almost getting stomped, and . . .* She sniffed back the tears. *So I'm sorry I said anythin'. I won't do it again, you hear?* She propped herself against a rock, thanks to knees that felt ready to give way, and sighed, the kind of sigh that takes the starch out of shoulders and neck and belly. "But thank you anyway."

Sammy still sniffed occasionally when she returned to the cave. Thaddeus glared at her.

"Thank you for savin' the little scamp." Ophelia had a three-foot rawhide string tied around Sammy's wrist and her ankle. "He don' go nowhere now."

"Good idea. At least until Jane Ellen comes back. I'm taking the wagon to town to clear out Agatha's cellar. Think on what you need while I harness the team." *Where I'll store it all, I have no idea, but I know we'll use it.*

————

Sometime later Jesselynn dusted off her hands after loading the wagon at Aunt Agatha's. Keeping some apples out, she took the barrel over to the store and had Dummont credit it to her account.

"There's wood outside the back door of the house and in the shed. You could get that, too, and put it against her account."

"She ain't used any of what you left last time. I feel strange having all this credit built up like this."

"Don't worry. I need a small keg of molasses and ten sacks of oats, if you have them."

"I do. Anything else?"

Jesselynn pulled out her shopping list. She'd drawn around the little boys' feet and the big ones' too. "We need boots in all these sizes, heavy pants for two men, and some yardage. You selling any knittin' wool? My ma would sure like some wool for knittin' stockings." She breathed a sigh of relief. Almost trapped herself there.

Mr. Dummont's face fairly glowed as he set her order on the counter. "Now, how many yards and what kind of material?"

Jesselynn contemplated her list as if she didn't know what the females of the group rightly wanted. "Ah, black wool for britches and some pretty cotton for my sister." She studied the list again, trying to look confused like a very young man might over women's things. "Hard to read her writing. That's three yards wool and four cotton, I guess. While you finish up getting it all in order, I'm taking some stuff over to Aunt Agatha. Be back soon."

But when she drove up to the new house and knocked on the door, a bent-over old man answered. "They's gone to the church," he said in a weak voice after she introduced herself and her errand. "But you can unload the things in the coach house there. We don't have horses any longer."

"Thank you, sir, and please tell Aunt that I was by."

She unloaded the last of the vegetables, both dried and fresh, although some of it looked a bit shriveled now. By keeping the root crops, other than the potatoes, covered with sand, the vegetables had retained their moisture and flavor. Her mind flashed back to Twin Oaks. All they had put by gone up in flames. And the larder had been massive, though they left all the root crops in the ground and covered the rows with straw to dig out when needed. Surely her people were able to dig those to help keep them going. If only she could figure a way to send some of her gold to them.

Back at the store she helped Dummont load the wagon, then drove off for the cave. They should be set now for the next month or so. On her way home she thought back to her habit of praying in an emergency. She'd gotten over a lot in the last months. She could get over that habit too.

---

Rain brought in the month of February, rain in never-ceasing sheets of silver that turned the hills to mud and the creek to a roaring river. No longer did they water the horses near the cave but took them up the hollow to another calmer place. Finding grazing took much of the day for Daniel or Benjamin. The hay Jesselynn managed to buy from a farmer and bring back in the wagon could only be fed to the mares, since they were being kept inside. Besides finding wood, bringing in dry leaves for bedding the stalls was a major part of Jane Ellen's and Thaddeus's day.

"We've got to find another cave," Jesselynn said one night after supper. "We've stripped the area around here bare."

"But we set up for the foalin' here." Benjamin looked toward the back of the cave where the two mares occupied their own stalls, the others dozing in the corral.

"I know that. But any day now we'll have foals, and we can carry them in the wagon if it is too far. I don't know what else to do."

"Spring come soon," Meshach reminded her.

"Not soon enough." Jesselynn laid aside her knitting and rubbed her upper arms. The cold damp was almost worse than the snow and blizzard. This cold ate right into one's bones and belly.

"You want I should take Roman and go lookin' tomorrow?" Benjamin asked.

"No, you stay here and let Daniel go." She glanced over in time to see the younger man look down at the floor as if studying something of supreme importance. She knew since his beating that he rarely headed far from the cave by himself, but she hadn't brought it up. They'd punished the culprits, but there were others as bad or worse. "How about if I go with you?" She surprised herself with her suggestion. She hadn't left the cave for more than brief forays for days. She hated to be gone from the mares. Too much was riding on their progeny.

Besides, like a cat, she hated to get wet. The look of gratitude he sent her warmed her heart even if her hands were freezing.

"Best we wait till it dry out some." Meshach offered his opinion, not looking up from the wood he was smoothing with a deer antler. "I found more pasture a mile or so across another ridge. Take horses there tomorrow."

Jesselynn nodded. Another reprieve.

She checked the mares one last time before going to bed. Dulcie showed the beginning signs of coming birth. She shifted from one front foot to the other and turned her head to nip at her sides. "Easy girl, you've done this often enough to know what's happening." She laid a hand on the mare's side and again on her flank and waited. Sure enough, a contraction rolled through, not hard yet but beginning.

"You s'pose they remember from time to time like women do?" Strange to be having a conversation with Meshach about something so . . . so natural but not usually discussed between a man and a woman. But then, it was not so strange considering all they had been through. This would hopefully be a peaceful and easy time.

"Don' know. But dis mare, she be one fine mama. You go sleep. I call you."

Jesselynn yawned and leaned her forehead against the mare's neck. "Don't let me sleep through it."

"I won't." He settled himself in the corner of the stall. "You get de scissors and a strip of rawhide to tie off de cord. I catch dis baby"—he held up his cupped hands—"right here."

Jesselynn chuckled softly as she spread her quilt on the warm sand by the fire. One of the horses coughed, another shifted, and one filled the cave with the sharp scent of fresh droppings. All the others slept while the firelight flickered on the cave walls.

If only they could stay here. This cave had become home. The next might not be near as nice. She could hear Dulcie shifting in the crackling leaves of her stall.

Fear sneaked in, in spite of her best efforts. What if Dulcie had trouble birthing? What if the foal was breech? *What ifs* beat against her skull as she fell into a sleep made restless with nightmares.

# CHAPTER ELEVEN

February 1863

"What a beauty." Jesselynn held up the burning brand so she could see better.

"She is dat." Meshach scrubbed the foal, still wet from the birthing sack, with a handful of clean leaves and a piece of soft deerskin. He'd already cleaned its nostrils and wiped its eyes and ears. The baby pulled her head away and tried to get her twiggy legs underneath her. Dulcie nosed her baby and licked her face. Back on her feet and hardly having broken a sweat, the mare drank some warm water with molasses in it and now was encouraging her daughter to get on her feet.

Both Meshach and Jesselynn stayed back out of the way and watched the age-old process unfold. The baby's legs did more folding than unfolding. Forelegs straight out in front of her, she bobbled from side to side, then pushed with her haunches and dug a trail in the floor with her nose. Shaking her head, she lay panting, then tried again. This time she made it halfway up before getting side heavy and crashing back down with a groan, if the little noise she made could be called that.

Dulcie nosed her again, making soft mother sounds that were easy for even the humans to understand. Her daughter didn't seem to speak the language yet. She lay flat out on her side panting.

"Should we help her?"

"Not yet. Just watch."

Suddenly the filly raised her head, rolled up on her belly, and threw herself to her feet, all four legs outstretched to brace her, nose down as if to get one more point of balance.

Jesselynn gave a sigh of delight and relief. Joseph used to say that the best ones were on their feet within an hour, and surely this one was. She'd need plenty of heart to make it to Oregon Territory. Or back to Twin Oaks if the war happened to be over in the next couple of months.

Step by tottering step, the foal made it to her mother's bag and found a teat to nurse. Her bitty brush of a tail ticked back and forth, marking perfect time like the metronome that used to keep Jesselynn in agony at the piano.

"Glad that's over." She checked on Sunshine, who slept placidly in the corner after having observed the foal's arrival. Then taking her journal out, she wrote the date and approximate time of the baby's birth, along with any other information she could think of. Compared to the foaling stalls at Twin Oaks, this one was mighty rough, but it served the purpose. Now to keep the foal healthy, dry being the first order of need. And getting her dam enough water, hay, and grain—all necessary, but not all available. Closing the book, she recapped her ink bottle and wrapped the journal back in its oilskin cloth. Her father would be proud. Dulcie was one of his favorites. Just a shame she didn't throw a colt.

---

Thaddeus was ecstatic in the morning. Filly was his new word for the day, and if he said it once, he said it a thousand times. When he strayed into the stall, Meshach grabbed him by the back of the britches and hauled him out between the railings.

"Stay out of there," he reprimanded.

Thaddeus nodded. From then on, he sat with his elbows on the lower rail and reached in to touch the filly whenever she came near enough. When she lay down for a snooze in the corner near him, he nearly climbed in to sleep with her. Instead, he stroked her neck and sang his own little song to the sleeping baby.

"He a horseman through and through." Meshach and Jesselynn sat nearby too, just in case Dulcie decided she didn't want the boy baby petting *her* baby. But Dulcie slept in her corner, flat out, as hard as her offspring.

"Now look, Thaddeus Joshua Highwood, you stay out of that

stall, and I mean it. No reaching so far over the bars that you are more in than out."

His lower lip came out, his eyes slit. Jesselynn could tell she was in for a full-blown Highwood tantrum, so she did the same, including hands on hips. She stuck her face down into his. "And if you let out one scream, I am going to turn you over my knee and give you a walloping like you never had before. Hear me?" She didn't shout, but they could have heard her across two ridges if it weren't raining outside.

Nose to nose, the two stood for a long second before Thaddeus had a remarkable change of mind and smiled sweetly.

"Yes."

"Yes, what?"

"Yes me not go in stall."

"Sammy neither?" She'd already discovered she had a devious small brother when one day she found Sammy getting him a biscuit he'd been told he couldn't have.

Again he shook his head.

"Good. You want to play button, button?" At his nod, she pointed to the pile of small branches that needed breaking and stacking for kindling. "As soon as you finish your chores." He started to stick his lip out, thought better of it, and began breaking sticks. Jesselynn looked up to see Ophelia laughing to herself. She shook her head and went back to her sewing. Jane Ellen sat against a log, drawing one of the deerskins back and forth across a ridged stone to soften the leather. She too hid a chuckle. Thaddeus had tried to boss her around more than once, just as he had the others. Little Highwood banty rooster.

Sunshine foaled two nights later with a little longer on the delivery side but produced a strong colt for the labor. He was on his feet even faster than the filly, some pounds larger and heavier boned.

"He goin' be a fast one. Look at dem legs and chest. He take after him daddy for sure."

"Both of these are by Ahab. Shame we don't have another bloodline."

"We got Domino. You watch. He throw good colts too. Breed him to the filly. That be good match."

Jesselynn watched the colt nursing for the second time. Including Chess, they now had eight horses and one mule. Quite a herd when you thought about it. Also quite a bunch to keep hidden—and fed.

And with the sodden morass of the prairies, they wouldn't be able to leave anytime soon. She'd have to buy more hay but not from the same farmer. What kind of an excuse could she use this time? New to the area worked before. Victim of a barn burning? Now that might be an idea. There had been plenty of fighting going on in the area. The memory of a well-filled, sweet-smelling hayloft in the barn at Twin Oaks stabbed at her.

*I've got to quit thinking about the past.* True words, but not so easily put into practice. Once the door opened, other memories stepped through. The big house, her mother braiding her hair, her father sitting at his desk with cigar smoke curling around his head. All four of the children playing croquet, riding Ahab for morning workouts, the smell of the cookhouse when Lucinda had supper cooking.

Her eyes misted and she sniffed. "God, I hate the war." Clenching her teeth and feeling the rage that shot clear to her fingertips chased the memories back behind closed doors. She locked those doors in her mind and tried to make wise decisions regarding those in her care. Hay for the mares, pasture for the rest of the horses, a new cave to call home until they could head west. And what to do about Aunt Agatha?

Ophelia gave her a wide berth, sensing that Jesselynn bordered on breaking into rage or tears—she wasn't sure which. Any more than Jesselynn herself was. Even the little boys stayed away from her, Thaddeus standing with his thumb and forefinger in his mouth, staring at her, then averting his eyes when she glanced his way.

She sewed with a vengeance, stabbing the needle into the fabric as if her life depended on finishing the pair of pants in an hour. Jane Ellen alternately sat beside her, her fingers busy with softening the hide, her smile offering comfort, or she took the boys to the mouth of the cave to dig in the dirt.

The problem with sewing was it left her mind free to wander in the maze.

———

Three days later they were no closer to moving.

"Rode ev'ry ridge and holler within five miles of here. Many caves but all too small." Benjamin stood near the fire to dry off. Even his deerskin jacket was soaked clear through.

Jesselynn stared at the jacket. If she oiled it, the rain would run off. Why hadn't she thought of that before? "When your shirt is dry, let's rub some grease in it. You won't get so wet that way."

Benjamin looked at her as if she'd walked off and left her mind behind.

"Dat mean we look farther." Meshach looked up from the rabbit skins he was pulling over the stretchers he'd made from stiff branches. Soon he'd have enough skins tanned for someone to sew another garment. Ophelia needed something warmer, as did Meshach himself.

———

"I'm goin' to town." Jesselynn made the announcement the next morning.

"In de rain?" Meshach dropped an armload of wood on the pile.

"It looks to be lettin' up." She stuck her head out far enough to see lightening in the east and even overhead. Surely the drizzle would let up. At least it wasn't pouring. The feeling that she would explode if she had to spend one more day in the dark cave had only intensified. "I'll ride Chess and take Roman to pack some things home, er back." She hated calling the cave home. She waved a hand to cut off Meshach's offer to go along. "No. This way I can bring back four sacks of grain on Roman. Ophelia, what do you need? Or want?"

Ophelia looked at her, questions wrinkling her broad brow.

"I know. We need to save every cent we have for the trip west, but . . ." Somehow, maybe if she spent some of the hoard, she thought she might feel better. So many things they needed—clothes, lamps, even candles would be a wonderfully welcome addition to the dark cave.

"We gonna need horseshoes before we go to Independence." Meshach held up his knife, the blade so shortened by sharpening it could hardly be called a knife any longer. "And this. Goin' have to tar de wagon too. And grease de wheels. I sets de rims before we go."

"We need the wagon for most of those things, though."

"I know. We just got to think of dem."

So many things they had taken for granted at home. Beeswax for candles or tallow. Even though they'd had fat deer here, all the tallow had been used for frying. Shame they hadn't shot a bear. Bear grease worked wonders for boots and waterproofing things. What she wouldn't give for a cup of steaming tea. The coffee was gone again, even though Ophelia had toasted oats and ground them with the coffee beans to make them last longer.

Sammy had a runny nose and a cough, so maybe horehound syrup could stop that.

"We need salt and cornmeal." Since they'd had molasses, the mush had disappeared more readily. While she'd bought the molasses for the mares, they had all enjoyed it.

Jesselynn strode to push back the deer-hide door and check the weather. Sure enough, there was a patch of blue sky up above, but the sun was still under the clouds.

"I get de horses for you." Meshach headed out to where Daniel was grazing the horses. Benjamin was off hunting.

Jesselynn tucked the fresh rabbit and a bundle of dried venison into her saddlebags. Even if Aunt Agatha lived in a decent house now, they might appreciate fresh meat.

"Me go?" Thaddeus clung to her leg.

"No, not this time. Someday." She looked around, trying to think if they had anything else to trade at the store. She ignored his sad look and sat down to replace her moccasins with boots. Lacing them, she broke a lace. "Ophelia, could you please hand me a rawhide string?" She pulled out the remaining shoelace and, reaching to the side, dropped it in Thaddeus's hand. "Now you can tie something together."

The frown turned to a grin. "Tie Sammy."

"No." But Jesselynn had to smile. How like a little boy. She reached over, took the string, and tied it around his wrist. "Now you go play, or you can stack kindling."

By the time she left, the sun had managed to break through the cloud cover. But if she'd thought it muddy at the cave, when she saw the streets of Springfield, she almost wished for the cave again. Mud-weighted wagon wheels, mud-covered horses. She felt as though gray mud weighed down her shoulders. The burden was getting to be too much.

# CHAPTER TWELVE

## Richmond, Virginia

"Aunt Sylvania, don't we have a relative in Washington?"

"Why, yes, your cousin Arlington Logan, twice removed on my mother's side. Why, I haven't heard about him in years. He was studyin' to be a doctor, as I recall."

Louisa felt her heart pick up the pace. *So which side of the war is he on?* "A doctor?" She set the baby sweater she was knitting in her lap. Fine yellow yarn was such a treat after all the natural wool for men's socks.

"He must be . . . let's see . . ." Sylvania closed her eyes to remember better. "Why, he must be in his early forties by now. I think he married into the Weintraubs of Washington. I didn't have much contact with him after his mother passed away. Fine woman, his mother."

Louisa kept perfectly still, not wanting to interrupt her aunt's memories. Something in it might be important. She heard the front door open and close. Zachary must be home again. He'd been at a meeting, the likes of which he'd refused to share with her, no matter how hard she had badgered him.

"Good evening, Aunt. Sorry I am so late."

Louisa glared at him, receiving a raised eyebrow in return. He bent and kissed his aunt's cheek.

"Yes, dear boy, I am glad to see you home." Sylvania patted his hand. "You remember talk of your cousin Arlington up in Washington?"

Louisa laid down the baby sweater and picked up a sock to continue her knitting as if she hadn't a care in the world.

"A bit. What brought him to mind?"

"Ah, might you like a cup of tea? Abby baked some of her lemon cookies just for you. Shame you weren't here for supper to make her happy." Louisa hoped the barb might distract him.

Like his father before him, once on a scent, he refused to be distracted. "Arlington, hmm."

"Louisa was asking if we didn't have relatives in Washington. Mercy me, I think we have relatives clear across the South, not that Washington is any longer a part of the South." She shook her head. "This war, such a horror."

Zachary turned toward his sister so he could question her with his good eye.

Louisa watched him from under her lashes, keeping her head down enough that he couldn't see. Her needles sang a tune of speed. "Drat!" She stopped, leaned closer to the lamplight, and took out three stitches to pick up one that had dropped.

"Louisa."

"In a moment. You don't want some soldier to get a blister because of a knot in his stocking heel, do you?"

"No, of course not." Zachary sat in the chair that seemed to have become his in the weeks he'd been ambulatory. He rubbed his leg where the leather straps and buckles sometimes dug into his flesh. "Do we have any more lamb's wool?"

"Not that I know of, dear. I'll ask Abby," Aunt Sylvania replied, returning to her knitting. The cry for warm woolen stockings was great in the damp and cold of the winter, and most women toted their knitting with them to pick up at any free moment.

Louisa could smell the cigar smoke from several of the men gathered out on the back veranda smoking and most likely discussing either the war events or their dreams of home. She wished her brother would go join them. She glanced at him again. He seemed to be settling in for the duration.

When Abby brought a tray with teacups and teapot and a platter of cookies, he thanked her and helped himself. The scent of narcissus wafted in the half-opened window, the breeze billowing the lace curtains. Louisa shivered and got up to close the window. While the day had been mild for February, evening was bringing back the chill.

She crossed the room and kissed her aunt. "Think I'll go finish

Jesselynn's letter with our good news. Do you have a message for her?"

"Just tell her I am praying that our Father will keep them all safe and bring us all back together one day."

"I will. Good night, dear." She knew if she could get up the stairs, Zachary most likely wouldn't try to question her tonight.

"So soon? Here, I have something I'd like to show you." He heaved himself to his foot, and short of running away, she was trapped. The thought of stealing his crutch almost made her laugh. Now, wouldn't *that* be a trick?

Waiting for him to get moving forward gave her time to finish her cup of tea and set it back on the tray. Then taking another cookie, she followed his no-longer-stumping gait down the hall. When he wanted to, he could move fairly swiftly. Shutting the door behind them, he turned to her.

"All right. Now what are you up to?"

He knew her too well. *Nothing* would not work. She sent up a *help* prayer and took a seat on the horsehair settee. She could hear her mother's voice, the slow drawl emphasizing her wisdom all the more. *"Honesty is the best policy."*

"So be it."

"Pardon?" He sank down into his chair and with his one hand began unbuckling the straps that held his peg in place.

"You are aware that we are out of morphine?" She waited for an answer but received only a studied glance. Laying the contraption aside, he rubbed the end of his leg encased in a footless stocking knit of the finest wool Louisa could find.

"So?"

"So I propose we go and obtain some."

"You what?" He stared at her openmouthed.

"You heard me. I thought to do this by myself, but I believe the two of us would be a lot more effective."

"And how are you planning to bring this commodity back?" He leaned back in his chair, feigning nonchalance.

She could tell he was acting because of the little finger twitching on his remaining hand. Always some portion of his body moved, especially when he was attempting to make her think otherwise.

"I don't know. I heard of a woman bringing something back tied to the inside of her hoops. I imagine I could do that."

"They shoot spies."

"We wouldn't be spies. We would be visiting our cousin. Perhaps we could call on other Southern sympathizers and seek their aid."

"Louisa, drop it."

His tone set her teeth on edge. She leaned forward. "In a word, my dear brother, no. If you don't want to go with me, I will go alone." She arched an eyebrow. "I know the trip would be very hard on you." Her voice dripped with honey.

"Louisa, as the head of this family, I forbid you to even consider such an action."

"You know, perhaps we could carve out your peg and store morphine in there. And in the handle of your crutch."

"Louisa!"

"I heard tell of a false bottom in a carpetbag, and some people store their jewelry in a book, hollowed out for just that purpose. Why, if we used the family Bible, no one would question—"

"Louisa Marie Highwood, you are beyond the realms of possibility."

"Now, what could we take Cousin Arlington that he might not be able to get in that big city? Something of home?"

"Louisa, I swear I will lock you in your room."

"Zachary James Highwood, those ideas went out with the dark ages. Now, when do you think would be a good time to leave? Are the trains running north, or is there fighting between here and there? If there is, perhaps we should go by sea or head west and come into Washington from the North. Surely you would know the best route, since you traveled up there that summer during college." She waited a moment. "Or, if you won't go, perhaps I'll ask Carrie Mae. Two sisters traveling together . . ."

Zachary groaned.

"If only Jefferson would let her go without him. He is so solicitous of her."

Zachary leaned back and closed his eye.

The new lines on his face made her almost stop her planning, but not quite. She had her brother home safe, albeit much the worse for wear. Other mothers and sisters were far less fortunate.

"We must do this, Zachary. If there is any way to alleviate the suffering of our men, we must."

# CHAPTER THIRTEEN

## Springfield, Missouri

"Hey, young Highwood, that black of your'n still lookin' for work?"

"Yes, suh. But he's a free man, not mine."

"He works for you, don't he?" Dummont leaned on his arms. "Jules needs a blacksmith. His man took sick and died. The influenza, it be bad this year."

"I'll tell him." *And Meshach can ride Roman in now, so that will be easier. Don't think he'd take it otherwise.* She let her thoughts range as she browsed the aisles of the store that had merchandise up the walls and hanging from the ceiling. So much to do to get ready.

With her horse and mule loaded, she rode over to the house where Aunt Agatha now lived. Knocking at the door, she glanced around. Daffodils were sprouting, their green spears breaking through the leaves blanketing the flower beds. Crocus, purple and white, bloomed around the base of a redbud whose stems bore fat buds, promising blossoms soon.

"Ah, Jesse, how good to see you." Aunt Agatha opened the door wide. "Can you stay for a cup of tea?"

Jesselynn's mouth craved a cup of tea as a drowning victim craved air. "I wish I could, but look how late it is. I need to be back by dark." She handed her gifts to her aunt and gave her a hug. "Are you managing here?"

"Yes, the poor dears. They are so happy to have me here, and I feel at home. This ..." She paused, indicating with a sweep of her arm the cheery kitchen with blue-and-white plates on a rail below the ceiling and blue-and-white checked curtains at the windows. A black-and-white cat lay curled asleep on a chair cushion. "This is more like my home. I wish you had seen Oakfield." She shook herself and set the packet of food in the dry sink. "Thank you, my dear. You are so thoughtful. We shall have rabbit fricassee for supper."

Jesselynn watched her aunt. She appeared to have gained some of her weight back, and the sparkle had returned to her eyes. Maybe she would do fine here and not need to go west with them. For one so used to ordering her own home, with slaves waiting on her, she didn't seem to mind being the one who cared for the two old people.

"I'll tell cook. She's off to the market right now."

"Ah." That answered many questions. "I'll be on the road, then." She kissed her aunt's papery cheek. She smelled of rose water and happiness.

Jesselynn left town feeling more hopeful than she had for days.

Until the rain started again. Cold, wet, the dark cloud over her soul returned with a vengeance. Would she ever know simple joy again?

———

March 15, 1863

Three weeks later they were on the road west.

Jesselynn slapped the reins over the backs of Chess and the mule. "Giddyup there." She looked over her shoulder to see Aunt Agatha sitting in her rocking chair, knitting as long as the light lasted. Ophelia had the two boys singing with their feet waving over the tailgate of the wagon. Their sweet voices carried over the undulating grass of the prairie. The sun had just set, so the sky changed from vermilion to cerise and faded to lavender and finally gray. The evening star shone like a crystal against the deepening blue of the heavens.

"Come on, Jesselynn, make a wish upon a star." It was her brother Adam's voice, as familiar as if they were playing on the closely clipped lawns of Twin Oaks. Adam, the first of the Highwood men to fall to enemy fire. But so real. She tried to ignore the star that pulled her gaze like a magnet. I wish . . . I wish for a safe journey and a home at the end . . . for all of us. So two wishes. After all, she hadn't wished on that particular star for a very long time.

The jingle of the harness, the clop, clop of trotting horses' feet, and the singing reminded her more of a picnic than the long journey ahead. But here there were no rolling, bluegrass-waving hills of Kentucky, only flat prairie, broken by scattered farms like toys tossed out by children at play. They not only had a full wagon but two horses bearing packs and a new member, who sat rocking. Aunt Agatha, without a home since the old people she cared for had died from the flu, came along only out of sheer desperation and Jesselynn's threatening everything but force.

*Daddy, you'd better be appreciating this.*

Ophelia sat beside Jesselynn on the wagon seat, her stomach barely rounding in the first months of growing a baby. Both mares bred again, hopefully settled, but with their foals cavorting at their sides. Daniel, as the lightest, rode the filly, and Meshach and Benjamin the stallions.

If only they didn't have so far to go. The things she'd heard of the journey ahead made her long to remain in Missouri, or return to Twin Oaks. The last letter from Louisa told of the devastation of their home, according to a letter from the Marshes, their nearest neighbors. But the land was still there. And perhaps the silver and other treasures they'd buried in the rose garden. The land would still grow tobacco and feed Thoroughbred horses.

Meshach pulled back to ride alongside the wagon. The smile he gave Ophelia spoke of love and adoration, two things surely lacking in Jesselynn's life. When the letter came from Barnabas White, she'd waited for her heart to beat a bit faster, but even at his pledge to find them, she could only stir dead embers. Surely there was a man somewhere who would make her heart leap with joy at the sound of his voice—as it had for John's. Surely there was joy—somewhere.

She glanced down at the boots and britches she wore. *Humph.* That is, if anyone could ever get close enough to figure out there was a woman under this garb. Longing to wear a soft cotton dress caught her by surprise. To feel the swish of silk against her legs, soft shoes on her feet, hair falling down her back, inviting the fingers of the man she . . .

"Good grief!"

Her mutter gave Ophelia a start. "What dat?"

"Nothing. Just dreaming, I guess." She hupped the horses again. They had to make good time while they could. Who knew what tomorrow would bring? Right now they had the cover of darkness. All they had to do was get to the safety of Independence, Missouri, and sign on with a wagon train. Before the end of April.

They should have started earlier, but the land just now had dried out enough to travel after an unusually wet winter and spring.

"We got to slow down for de little'uns," Meshach said after they'd been riding several hours. So long about midnight they stopped for a breather. Meshach checked the straps and girths on the pack animals. Both foals started to nurse as soon as the mares stopped; then they collapsed on the grass, stick legs straight out. The horses immediately put their heads down to graze, the new grass already knee-deep.

"Milk. We'll buy milk for breakfast." Jesselynn had dreamed one night of buying a cow and taking her with them. Could they take a crate of chickens clear to Oregon? They had to have livestock if they were going to farm. She caught herself dozing before they started out again.

Benjamin, riding point, returned before the dawn made itself known.

"Good place up ahead." He rode beside Jesselynn. "Dere's a small creek. We can camp over de edge of de ridge, so be out of sight of de road."

"How'd you find it?" Jesselynn covered a yawn with her hand.

"Ahab tell me. Him thirsty." Benjamin slapped the shoulder of his mount. "Him better'n a hound dog for findin' water."

"Good. You tell ol' Ahab thank you for all of us." She pulled the wagon to a stop and staggered to the ground. One foot had gone to sleep and was letting her know about it in no uncertain terms, threatening to collapse at the slightest weight. She wiggled her toes and waited until she could hobble.

By that time Meshach had unhooked the traces and was leading the team out to graze.

They all went about their work silently, hoping those sleeping in the wagon would stay asleep. When Meshach volunteered to take the first watch, Jesselynn only nodded, took her deer hide and her quilt, and crawled underneath the wagon just as she had those months before they sheltered in the caves around Springfield. The thick grass formed a soft pallet, and the songs of peeper frogs composed her lullaby.

A rifle shot yanked her awake.

"Mercy sakes. What was that?" Aunt Agatha didn't sound particularly happy, but then she hadn't ever since she arrived at their cave.

If the couple she'd cared for had not succumbed to the influenza, she would still be in their lovely home in Springfield. *If* could be a mighty big word.

"Sounds like Meshach shot somethin—maybe our breakfast." Ophelia passed by Jesselynn's bed without checking to make sure she was awake. Birdsong replaced rifle song, and the fragrance of boiling coffee convinced Jesselynn it was indeed time to get up. This wasn't the first time she'd been awakened by rifle fire, and it most likely wouldn't be the last. Gratitude that it wasn't an enemy rifle flooded her as she pulled on her boots. She could hear the boys jabbering. They had their own language when they played, Thaddeus often translating for Sammy when the little one didn't have words for what he needed.

Jesselynn and the others had gotten used to that.

"Bring me a pan of warm water."

Jesselynn spun around in time to see Ophelia doing just that. The tone of Agatha's voice screamed mistress and slave.

"Put it there."

Jesselynn felt the anger swelling hot in her middle. When Ophelia returned to the fire, Jesselynn went on the attack. Only her mother's voice counseling patience kept her from dragging Agatha off behind the two trees and lambasting her good. Instead, she stopped beside her aunt and said in the calmest voice possible with ricocheting insides, "Please, Aunt Agatha, may I speak with you for a minute?"

Agatha, bending over the washbasin with a wet cloth applied to her face, turned her head with a frown. "Can it not wait? As you see, I am in—"

"No, it cannot!"

Jesselynn's clipped voice and tense jaw must have communicated the message to the older woman, for she straightened and dropped her cloth back in the water.

"Yes, dear, what is it?"

*Dear? I am not your dear, and when we finish this tête-à-tête, you will most likely wish you had stayed in Springfield.* Jesselynn strode the ten paces to the tree line, her heels digging into the tender grasses. She spun and barely kept from crossing her arms over her chest. *What do I do with her? "Patience is a virtue well worth cultivating."* Her mother's voice again.

Jesselynn sucked in a deep breath and let it all out as she waited for her aunt to approach. Keeping her voice low so that Ophelia wouldn't hear, she began. "I know this trip was not of your making, mine either, but we need to get a couple of things clear."

"Really?" Her aunt's chin rose a fraction, and her shoulders straightened.

"Really. First off, Ophelia is *not* a slave to be ordered around, nor even a servant. She is a free black woman who chooses to go west with us. She and Meshach are married, by a minister, and are doing their part to help us all get safely where we need to go." She could tell her aunt was digesting these words by the expressions that flitted across her face.

"Besides that, in *our* family, we did not order the slaves about but rather asked them, said please and thank you, and treated them as civilly as we treated others."

"But—"

Jesselynn held up a hand. "I understand that is not the way of most slaveholders, but that *will* be the way here." Her words were coming faster and more clipped, if possible. "Also, for us to all be safe, I am Marse Jesse, not dear or Jesselynn."

"I know that."

"Yes, but you slip sometimes, and that very slip could cost someone their life."

"Well, I never!" Agatha drew her huff up around her ears. "If your daddy could hear you now, he would turn right over in his grave." She clenched her hands at her sides and leaned slightly forward. "You say your mama treated the slaves"—she gave the word a twist with a sneer—"so proper, well, she surely failed with her eldest daughter."

"Yes, I am sure she feels she did. But failed or not, whether I wanted this or not, I am in charge, and until we get to Independence, we all have to live with that." She let the silence lengthen, sure at any moment that Agatha was going to stalk off. Maybe even head back to Springfield. It would be easy to follow the road.

The boys' laughing made her want to join the circle around the fire, eat her breakfast in peace, and then do the chores of the day. She did not want to stand nose to nose with her aunt and create an enmity that could last forever.

"We will discuss this again later." Agatha turned on her heel and returned to her washbasin as if nothing had been said.

Jesselynn stared after her. So was this win, lose, or draw? Did it matter?

# CHAPTER FOURTEEN

## Heading West

Jesselynn felt as though a cloud hung over her, no matter how bright the sun.

While the boys laughed at the antics of the foals in the morning before they began to tire, she saw it all but couldn't drum up any joy from it. Even Aunt Agatha chuckled.

Every hoofprint carried them farther from Twin Oaks, her sisters, her brother. *I'll never see them again, nor the rebuilding of the big house.* Morbid thoughts dogged her, burrowed under her skin, and refused to let go. Worse than a tick head sunk under the skin that itched and festered, these thoughts poisoned her spirit and added the crack of a whip to her voice.

She felt Meshach watching her and waiting. Waiting for she knew not what.

Spring broke forth in all its glory, blossoming flowers, leaf buds unfurling, giving a wash of green to dark tree branches. Dogwood bloomed creamy white in the draws, and the redbud lived up to its name. When they stopped in the morning, Sammy and Thaddeus picked dandelions till their hands were milk sticky. Daniel showed them how to roll down a gentle hill, and from then on, every hill, of which there were many, needed a roll down.

"Come." Thaddeus tugged on her hand when she woke one afternoon.

"No, Thaddy."

"Joshwa." He said it as if he was fed up with reminding her. "You come see."

"See what?" All she wanted was a cup of coffee strong enough to hold her upright. Last night she'd fallen asleep on the wagon seat. Good thing she didn't topple over under a wheel. Or was it a good thing? Then there wouldn't be so many people to take care of.

Not that she was doing such a good job of that either. Aunt Agatha still said no more to her than absolutely necessary, but she didn't order the others around either. She and Jane Ellen seemed to have hit it off, or at least Agatha had a new lamb to shepherd now. She brought out one of her skirts and together they ripped the seams, cut it up, and made one for Jane Ellen. Then using some of the white cotton Jesselynn had bought, they made her a full-sleeved waist. Meshach carved buttons for it out of deer antlers and painstakingly drilled the holes.

Jane Ellen glowed. Agatha brushed and braided the girl's hair, and with some meat finally attaching itself to her bones, Jane Ellen was actually pretty.

The transformation made Jesselynn feel like an old worn-out rag. Once she had had long, thick hair that curled about her face when she let it. But she'd cut it off to become Jesse. Most days she wondered if it had all been worth it.

One night Benjamin found a large pond for them to camp by, so when Jesselynn fell asleep she could hear ducks quacking and the piping trill of the redwing blackbirds. When she woke, Ophelia dragged back into camp, her skirt speckled with the same mud that covered her arms and legs. But they had cattail roots boiled with onion for supper, along with a mess of crappies Daniel and Thaddeus caught. Fried fish had never tasted so good.

After they ate, Jesselynn wanted to sneak off for another nap. She just couldn't get enough sleep. Meshach beckoned her to follow him. Thinking something needed doing with the horses, she did as asked. But when they followed a track partway around the pond to a log, he sat down and patted the log beside him.

"You ready to tell me what's wrong?" He pulled a stalk of grass and chewed on the tender inner stem.

"Nothin's wrong." She could hear the growl in her voice, but doing something about it went far beyond her capabilities. *If that's so, why are you crying?* She gritted her teeth and stepped on a black beetle crossing in front of her. The crack of its shell pierced her to the marrow. What a wanton, cruel thing to do. Her insides felt as though they might choke her. Her eyes watered so she could barely discern the outlines of the pond and the cattails pushing up green alongside the winter-withered stalks of the year before. Peepers sang their own song, and somewhere a bullfrog chugged.

Her own misery sang louder, obliterating the spring orchestra.

Meshach spread his feet wide and rested his elbows on his knees. "You can't run. He find you all de time."

"He?" But she'd no sooner asked the question than she knew.

"God himself be after you."

Jesselynn snorted. "Naw, He don't care." She started to rise, but Meshach's gentle hand on her arm kept her in place.

"I know He care. And deep down you know dat too."

Jesselynn spun on him. "If that God of yours cares so much, why did He let this war go on? Why have so many men died? So many families been destroyed?" The weight bore her down, even into the wooden log. "All gone. They're all gone." Her voice rose. "Why, Meshach? You tell me why. I hate your God, and I hate what He's done." She shook her fist in heaven's face and crumpled into a ball of misery, her arms gripping her knees tightly, as if she would shatter into a million pieces if she let go. "Answer me, Meshach."

"Don' got no answers. Just got love. De love of de Father far beyond all dat. He keep us safe. He bring Marse Zachary back from de dead, He keep Lucinda from slave traders, we . . ."

"But Father is dead, the South is destroyed, Adam, John—"

"But dey in heaven wid de Lawd."

Digging out another answer took far more than she could muster. Heaven—her mother dreamed of heaven. Her father saw her and Jesus, or an angel, before he died. The joy that lit his face was beyond anything she'd ever seen.

"Dis here not our home. Our home be in heaven wid de Father and de Son."

Jesselynn sighed. Why would He want her back? All the hateful things she'd said, the terrible anger and hatred, the wicked thoughts.

"He waitin', Him and all de angels waitin' to shout joy and hallelujah over de lamb dat be found."

She looked over to see his eyes closed and his lips moving. She knew he was praying for her. One of her responsibilities as mistress

LAURAINE SNELLING

was to instruct her people in the ways of the Lord and to live her life as an example to them. *Oh, Mother, I have failed you so terribly.* The tears she'd been fighting so hard spilled over and trickled down her cheeks.

The boot was on the other foot. Meshach took his Lord very seriously to heart.

"He say to lay your burdens at Him feet. 'Take my yoke,' he say, 'for my yoke is easy and my burden is light.'" Meshach laid a hand on her shoulder. "De burdens too heavy for you. Let dem go."

"I can't." *I can't, God. I can't do this any longer. I'm dying inside. If you really are the God my mother loved and the Bible says, forgive me, deliver me, let me loose.* The tears that washed her eyes now bathed her soul and broke through the barriers to let the light back into her darkest corners.

Sometime later she pulled her shirttail loose to wipe her eyes.

Meshach still sat beside her, staring out over the ripples of the pond where several ducks had just landed. "God's Word say it all. Psalm ninety-one is for us headin' west. We like dat little ducklin' out dere who hide under him mama's wing. Only God's our mama and daddy all to once."

Jesselynn had to smile at the mallard hen, trailed by six bits of yellow, riding the ripples and following where their mother led. She sighed and let her head hang forward, like a sunflower too heavy for the stalk. "I think I owe some apologies."

"Mebbe. Mebbe not. But dey worries 'bout you."

She sighed—a long exhalation that dug up from her toes and the ends of her hair. She coughed, clearing her throat of the leftover tears. "We'd better be gettin' back."

"You ready?"

She nodded, chewing one side of her lower lip. "Thank you—I guess."

His smile warmed clear to her heart. "We thanks God."

"I did, and I do." She stood and stretched, feeling lighter than she had for months. She walked off, glancing over her shoulder to see if an old skin was lying on the ground behind her.

That night when Meshach read Psalm ninety-one, she listened instead of blocking his voice from her mind. "'He that dwelleth in the secret place of the most high shall abide under the shadow of the Almighty. I will say of the Lord, He is my refuge and my fortress; my

God; in him will I trust.'" A refuge is what He promised. A secret refuge in time of trouble. She thought back to the times they'd by-passed towns and army encampments as if they couldn't be seen. *A secret refuge? Have I just been too blind to see?*

---

They neared Carthage on the morning of the third day and stopped in a draw before they could be seen by the townspeople. When Jesselynn woke up after another restorative sleep without the nightmares that had plagued her for so long, she lay under the wagon listening to the private chatter of Sammy and Thaddeus. She heard Meshach reading the Bible to Ophelia and anyone else who wanted to listen. A squirrel scolded from a tree, a crow added to the dressing down, and the other birds ignored them, so she knew the fussing wasn't because of someone coming. Besides, Ahab was better than any watchdog if strangers came near.

She stretched and rolled over to her side to see Aunt Agatha's legs and feet not quite reaching the ground while she sat on the tailgate. *How do I go about making my peace with her?* All previous over-tures had been coldly rebuffed. The others had just smiled and nod-ded when she seemed to be her old self again. Thaddeus and Sammy now came to play about her feet and ask to be put up on the horses. Jane Ellen often watched to see when she woke up and brought her coffee if they had it or brought whatever kind of hot drink Ophelia made when they didn't. She knew she'd been forgiven.

Wasn't it too easy? she wondered, her head propped on her arm. She'd read the verses on forgiveness, needing only a reminder, since she memorized them as a child. All the Scriptures said was to ask, and God did the rest. Repent—now that was a word to get hung up on. Had she repented? She believed so. So now, as Meshach had re-minded her, don't let Satan get a foothold by telling you you weren't forgiven. Jesus said it was so.

"Thank you, Father," she whispered. "Now to live it." She threw back the covers and pulled on her boots before folding the quilt and the deerskin that kept the damp from seeping into her quilt.

"Next time we find running water, we *have* to do the wash." She strolled over to the campfire where Ophelia poured her a cup of cof-fee. "Where's Jane Ellen this morning?"

"She be lookin' for herbs and such."

"By herself?"

"She say she be in hearing distance." Ophelia used her apron as a hot pad to move the kettle back to the coals. "Turkey for supper." She nodded to where Daniel lay soundly sleeping. "Daniel bag it. Cook on spit."

Jesselynn's mouth watered at the mention of the delicacy. Turkeys were wily birds and hard to find. "We still have potatoes?"

"Um. Carrots and rutabaga too. Have a feast tonight."

"I'm goin' to ride into town to see what I can learn."

Meshach looked up from his reading. "Take Benjamin wid."

"No, he can sleep."

"Jesse?"

Jesselynn turned in surprise. Aunt Agatha was actually initiating a conversation—amazing. "Yes?"

"If a store has . . ." She lowered her voice and raised her head to glance around the camp.

Jesselynn stepped closer to hear better. "Has what?"

"Some finer cotton. I would like to make Jane Ellen some drawers and a camisole." She dug in a leather purse she kept on a chain at her waist. "Here is the money."

"Aunt Agatha, you keep your money. I'll gladly buy the material. Is there anything else?"

"No." She paused. "Unless you could maybe find some lace or ribbon." She leaned closer. "I don't think that girl has had anythin' nice in her entire life." She shook her head, *tsking*. "And she's such a good-hearted little soul."

"That she is." Jesselynn leaned forward and kissed her aunt on the cheek. "You are too." She left before Agatha could say a word.

Long before she got to Carthage, she remembered why she hated riding Roman. His trot tore loose every muscle in her body, at least it felt like it. She dismounted near what looked like a general store and ambled along the boardwalk. Touching the brim of her hat when she met a woman with a market basket, she paused and leaned against a wall to eavesdrop on two elderly men sitting on a bench, one smoking a pipe, the other chewing and spitting.

"Sad, ain't it? That Ben sure was a good man." *Hawk. Spit.*

"How he lived that long, I swain."

"You reckon they hung the guy that did it?"

"One of Quantrill's Raiders? They never hang 'em. Can't catch 'em. Strike and they're gone, just like a water moccasin I see'd down in Arkansas. Now that critter come right up over the gunwale of the boat. Beat him off with m' oar, I did."

Jesselynn wanted to beat them with an oar. What about the dead man? What about the Raiders? They *had* to get out of town. And quickly.

# CHAPTER FIFTEEN

## Richmond, Virginia

"Are you comfortable, Zachary dear?"

"As well as can be possible." The glare he gave her said more than words could have said about what he thought of her plan. He propped his leg along the crutch he braced on the facing seat of the railroad car.

The engine whistled. The train lurched forward, coal smoke blowing by their window. Louisa dug in her satchel and withdrew her knitting just as if they were sitting in the parlor at Aunt Sylvania's instead of on a train carrying them north to God only knew what peril.

The thought made Zachary clench his teeth. "If we ever get back home, I swear I am goin' to—"

"Yes, dear." Louisa played the wifely roll to the hilt, all sweetness and acquiescence now that she had her own way. But to tell the truth, once Zachary agreed to the outrageous plan of traveling north to get morphine and smuggle it back home, he'd begun preparations with a typical Highwood intensity. Gold for the purchases now filled the cavities hollowed out to hold the precious medicine, including the middle of the Bible she had lying on the seat beside her.

Anyone looking would only see a gallant young couple, she caring for a badly incapacitated husband, he a bit cantankerous, which anyone would hardly blame him for, seeing the residuals of his wounds and all. She waited on him hand and foot, even to fetching a coal to light his cigar and seeking a pillow to put under his leg.

Louisa received approving nods from an elderly couple seated across the aisle from them. While she tried to act as if traveling like this were an everyday occurrence, she wanted to plaster her nose to the window and not miss a single sight. *My land, to be rushing across the country at such speeds. Oh, if only Jesselynn were here. She would be near inebriated with joy.*

When the tracks ended at Fredericksburg, they transferred to a buggy for the ride to the Potomac River. Louisa nearly fell asleep but popped wide awake when the driver stopped. While she had a million questions, the look on Zachary's face warned her that silence was a better plan.

"Easy now," the man in black whispered as he helped them alight, traverse a small dock, and settle into a boat with high gunwales and a slender mast. Two men at the oars leaned into the pull.

At the far shore in Union territory, they entered a carriage for the drive into the capital. A basket of bread, cheese, and boiled eggs stilled the rumblings of their bellies. Louisa fell asleep before folding her napkin away.

----------

Gawking was not polite; she knew that. Her mother had made frequent admonishments of such when they were little. But this was the capital of the United States, of which she had heard so much.

"Can we drive by the White House?" she asked once they had secured a hansom cab.

"Whatever for? This is no longer *our* capital, or have you forgotten?"

"You needn't speak cruelly like that. Not all of us believe there will be two separate countries."

The glare he gave her should have melted her bones, let alone her spirit, but she ignored him and turned to watch out the window instead. The streets were a quagmire of conveyances of all types. Blue uniforms, women in finer dress than any she'd seen for a long time strolled the boardwalks or rode at a frantic pace, as if the speed with which they arrived made any eternal difference.

"Do you know where we are going?"

"I gave the driver Cousin Arlington's address, or at least the address we have for him. His family might be there, even if he is off with the army somewhere."

"Oh, I hadn't thought of that. Of course, if he is a physician . . ." Her heart felt as though it had gained ten pounds of pure lead.

"If they do not invite us to stay, we will find a hotel, and you will remain there while I see to the availability of our supplies." He kept his voice so low she had to lean close to hear him.

Louisa devoutly hoped they would be invited to stay with their relatives. Surely the bonds of Southern hospitality still held true, even if . . . she couldn't bring herself to say they were on opposite sides. All she longed for was the end of the war. But then, the war hadn't held the allure for all the Highwood women as it had for the men.

What she really wanted was an end to the injured and the dying. Sometime earlier she had ceased to pray for either side, but only for the war to cease. Never would she entrust her brother with her feelings. He'd think her a traitor.

Deep inside she wished she could talk with President Lincoln and entreat him to stop the war. He seemed like a man with a concern for men dying, unlike the Southern firebrands. Again, unbeknownst to those around her, she prayed for wisdom for the two men in charge—Abraham Lincoln and Jefferson Davis—that they would end the fighting.

The cab stopped in front of a narrow three-story house that fronted directly on the cobblestone street, three polished steps from the sidewalk to the door with a shiny brass knocker. An urn with a boxwood topiary sat to either side of the steps, lending a touch of green to the brick face. A sign that read *Physician* hung from an ornate iron bar attached to the wall.

"Dis de place," the black driver announced as he stepped to the street and reached up for their one small trunk. Louisa handed out her carpetbag and accepted his hand to help her step down, turning to offer her assistance to Zachary. Getting in and out of conveyances had not become much easier, even with practice. With the driver's hand under his right arm and the crutch under his left, Zachary led with his good foot, staggering but for the bracing of his two helpers.

"Thank you." Once steady, he dug in his pocket for the coins, paid the man, and stared up at the windows with green shutters on the sides.

"Yo' trunk, suh?"

"On the steps, if you will." He nodded to Louisa. "You want to ply the knocker?"

Her heart felt as though it might knock its way right out of her chest. The moment of decision. What if they were turned away? She swallowed, glanced over her shoulder at the sound of the departing cab, took in a deep breath, and mounted the stairs. With a shaking hand, she let the knocker fall, then tapped it again.

# CHAPTER SIXTEEN

## Heading to Independence

Circumventing Blytheville took some planning.

Jesselynn stared at the map Benjamin had drawn in the dirt with a stick. Carthage lay behind them, Blytheville ahead. If there weren't regular Union army located in the area, the dreaded Quantrill Raiders could show up anywhere, anytime. They specialized in night travel too. Only their purpose wasn't a new life of freedom. Theirs was to bring destruction everywhere and plant fear into every heart within reach. They were supposed to be Confederate cavalry, but most people described them as the devil's cavalry.

"But if we go this way . . ." She pointed to a road that ran northwest from the one they were taking to meet the main road between Kansas City and points south. That road used by the armies and freight haulers, besides ordinary citizens, cut a line through Kansas farmland, rich when enough rain fell. Lakes and swamps dotted the Missouri side of the border, so travel could not be as direct. Jesselynn studied the drawing some more. The war! Always the war. Soldiers to hide from, no matter which side they fought for, since they all needed horses.

"We got dis far. We can make it." Meshach held Sammy up on his shoulders and jiggled him every once in a while, eliciting giggles from above and frowns from below. Thaddeus had yet to have a turn. "De good Lawd see us through."

"Which way do you think we should go?" She looked up in time to see Sammy clamp his little hands over Meshach's eyes.

"I think Benjamin should go on into Blytheville and ask around. Or you, like you done planned before." Meshach removed the hands from his eyes and jiggled his rider. More giggles.

Jesselynn sighed. Instead of getting easier to play the part of a young man, it was getting harder. *I should be used to it by now,* she told herself. *I can be a woman again when we reach Oregon.* In Oregon they would be safely away from the war. Away from slavery, armies, and bushwhackers. Away from traveling at night and worrying that they may be found during the day.

She'd heard the land there was free for homesteading, just as Meshach dreamed of. There were mountains and lush valleys where, folks said, you could stick a fence post in the ground and a tree would sprout. Fruit trees, tall trees to cut for cabins, wheat, cattle—everything seemed to do well in Oregon, just like in the Garden of Eden. Only the lazy would starve in Oregon Territory. Folks could eat off the land, they said, with enough wild things to feed anyone willing to pick, dig, or shoot. If the stories were half true, the land would be worth the trip.

But first they had to get to Independence.

She sighed and, ignoring her dreams of possibilities, turned her attention back to the matter at hand. *Lord, which way do you want us to go? Your Word says you'll guide us and keep us, and we need that now, as much as ever.* Daily she gave thanks that she'd turned back to her Lord. Even though at times the darkness would try to sneak in again, she remembered how she loved the light and wanted—needed it, like she needed air to breathe.

She took in a deep breath and let it out. "All right, much as I hate to, I'll take Roman and go explore a bit of the town. Daniel, you want to come with me?"

The youngest of their group, Daniel, roused from his dozing against a log and leaped to his feet. "Shore do, Marse Jesse. I gets Roman for us."

———

Both riding the mule, they entered the town by the back streets, only to find it full of people, all heading toward the town square. They caught the whispers. A hanging was about to happen. Jesselynn had no desire to see a hanging, but wandering through the crowd could most likely fill her in on all the news and the gossip too. They dismounted and tied the mule to a hitching post behind a store. With a pat on Roman's rump that raised a cloud of dust, she pointed Daniel down one street, and she took the other.

"Be back here before the sun goes past that church spire."

He nodded after following her pointing finger. "I be back."

Jesselynn could see the gallows looming black in the westering sun. A rope dangled from the high beam, but while the crowd continued to gather, no one mounted the stairs yet.

A woman pushed by, dragging a young child by the hand. "Hurry up, now. We want to be there when they put the rope over his head."

Jesselynn felt her stomach turn. She ambled from group to group, pausing now and then to listen. She stopped by a couple of townspeople when she overheard mention of the raiders.

"They come like thieves in the night, take what they want, and burn the rest." The speaker hawked and spit, nearly hitting Jesselynn's boot toe. "Sorry." The man glanced at her and turned back to his companion. "I heard tell that they are recruiting again, but you got to have your own horse to join up. Ya'd think the army would supply the horses."

"Shoot, the army ain't got siccum. They's pulling all the troops back to Virginny, I heard."

"Leavin' Quantrill in charge out here?" His look of shock sent shivers up Jesselynn's back.

"No. An army will remain at Fort Scott. They know the rebs will be right back here if there's no troops. Arkansas is too close for that."

When they started jawing about the local sheriff, Jesselynn slipped on to the next group. Who could she ask about the roads north? Who were they hanging and why? As more people poured into the square, Jesselynn almost resorted to pushing to get by a group of five women. Why was a hanging more like celebrating the Fourth of July?

"'Scuse me. Pardon me." One well-rounded matron stepped backward, right on Jesselynn's foot.

"Ouch." But her voice drowned in the laughter.

"Here now, son. Up on my shoulders, you'll be able to see everything." The man swung his boy up, barely catching Jesselynn with his elbows.

Drawing a breath of relief at escaping the horde, Jesselynn stepped up onto the porch of the bank building and leaned against the post, scanning the crowd while she drew her knife from her pocket and, opening the blade, began to clean her fingernails. Studying the impacted dirt, she listened to the men behind her.

"Hangin' is too good for 'im."

At that comment, she angled herself so she could see them out the corner of her eye.

"Shoulda just shot him. That's what I say. Anyone who'd rob the store and shoot ol' Avery through the heart deserves shootin'. Why, he gave away more food than he sold when times were really tough. Don't care how desperate the man was." He shook his head, then lifted his hat with one hand and smoothed his hair back with the other before settling the slouch-brimmed thing back securely on his head. "I went on the posse, ya know. If the sheriff hadn't threatened to shoot any man who took matters into his own hands, we'da been saved the work on the scaffold and all."

"But the 'portant thing is, he's goin' to swing."

"I just wished he'd been one of them raiders, that's all. Let me get my hands on those thievin' skunks, and I'd—"

"Just pray they don't come out your way."

"Ain't got nothin' for them anyways."

"You got chickens, 'n hogs 'n such, ain't ya? That's what they're lookin' for. And hay left in your barn or grain in the bin? They gotta eat and feed their horses. They don't offer no pay neither."

When a man shouted for their attention, Jesselynn's attention swung back to the raised platform. A quick glance told her the black-coated man boasted a star, so he must be the sheriff. As the crowd roared and pressed forward, the better to hear, she closed her pocketknife and, sliding it back in her pocket, stepped off the porch. All her listening had done was put the fear of night travel back at the top of her list.

*What do I do to keep the horses safe? I'll take regular army, gray or blue, any day over this.* At least she knew there was a garrison at Fort Scott. They'd have to swing west to miss that. Her mind made up, she strode on back to the general store and entered through two swinging doors, making her wonder if she'd found the saloon by mistake. A man in an apron nearly ran over her in his rush to get out the door.

"You'll have to come back later, boy. I ain't missin' the show."

"The show?"

"You know. The hangin'."

"Oh, could you cut me some cheese first and maybe weigh out a pound of coffee? I got to be on my way. Some of those peppermint sticks too."

The man rolled his eyes and shook his head. "Cain't it wait?"

"Nope."

The man groaned and stomped his way back to the counter. The way he slapped the cheese on the scale told her of his resentment. But when she paid him with a gold piece, his scowl lightened. He shoved her packets across the counter and almost beat her to the door, flipping the *CLOSED* sign as he left.

Jesselynn paused outside the store and studied those around her. Noticing a man who appeared content to stay where he was leaning against the railing of the store, she stopped beside him. "Mister, can I ask you a question?"

"Sure 'nough, boy. What can I do for you?"

"Well, my daddy sent me into town to ask about the best way to Independence. Ya see, we's goin' on west to Oregon." *Why'd you have to tell him all that?*

"Where's your daddy now?"

"Oh, camped some east of here. He's ailin', or he woulda come hisself."

"From what I hear, it takes a powerful lot of strength to go to Oregon."

"Ah, he'll be on his feet again soon." Jesselynn rammed her hands in her pockets and glanced up at the stranger from under her hat brim. "You been to Independence?"

"Many times. If'n it were me, I'd take the road that runs north of town. Cut off a few miles thataway. Road's good again now that the rain let up."

"Thankee, sir. I'll tell my daddy what you said. We be grateful." She started to back away.

"Where you all from?"

Just then a shout from the area of the platform snagged his attention and let Jesselynn slip away without answering. That was the way of folks, always asking questions. Ignoring the spectacle going on behind her, she made her way back to the mule.

"Why are folks so confounded enamored with watchin' some man die?" But asking Roman anything never had gotten her very far.

Daniel was nowhere in sight.

She checked out the church steeple. Sure enough, the sun had passed it some time earlier.

*I should just leave him, let him walk back to camp.* As the minutes passed, the thought took on more possibilities. Besides, if she thought about leaving him, the fear that something had happened couldn't take over.

A shout went up from the crowd on the other side of the building. The deed must have been done. Her stomach rolled. People would be disbursing now. "Daniel, you good for nothing young pup, I could—"

"*Psst!*"

She looked around.

"*Psst.* Over here, Marse Jesse."

She turned in time to see a dark brown hand beckoning from the other side of the alley and two doors down. She jerked the knot loose that bound the mule and, flinging herself on his back, had him moving before she sat upright. She slowed to a walk. Like a shadow Daniel leaped from his hiding place and had himself up behind her, scarcely touching her foot and extended hand.

"Hey! Hey, you. Stop!"

The shout propelled them into a canter, and within moments they were beyond accosting.

"What on earth did you do this time?" Jesselynn wanted to turn and look into his eyes so he wouldn't lie to her. *Takes a liar to know a liar.* The thought made her slap the reins on Roman's shoulder.

# CHAPTER SEVENTEEN

### Blytheville, Missouri

"Who was that?"

"I don' know. Just ride." The terror in his voice fueled her own fear. She kicked Roman to a dead-out gallop. The clatter of horses' hooves sounded behind them. Was someone following them?

No trees, nothing to lose them in. Nowhere to hide.

"Turn off here," Daniel yelled in her ear, the wind nearly snatching the words and flinging them back before she could hear. She pulled back on the reins, and Roman slowed quickly enough to send her up on his neck. When he turned, they fought to stay mounted, even though they felt as if they were at the wrong end of a catapult.

"How far?"

"Dat barn up ahead."

Ignoring the dog barking at their heels, they veered around behind the gable-roofed barn and plowed to a stop. Roman sounded like a bellows in full operation, and Jesselynn knew she sounded about the same.

"What in heaven's name was that all about?" While she tried to quiet her breathing so she could hear if they were still being followed, the growling dog did nothing to help.

"Who's that out there?" The bellow came from the direction of the house.

The dog upped the volume, as if calling his master to come help.

"Daniel!"

"Some white man said I was with the man they done hanged."

Between his terror and the barking dog, Jesselynn wanted to clap her hands over her ears.

"You were with what man? We just got to town."

"I knows dat, but he started comin' after me, and dat's when I hid under dat house to wait for you."

The dog raised the pitch on his bark.

"Shaddup, you mangy cur." The owner of the voice rolled around the corner of the barn, rifle at the ready across his broad chest and broader belly. He pointed the rifle at the two on the mule. "Well, let's y'all jist get on down off'n that there mule and answer me some questions. Me 'n the deputy, that is."

The man coming around the other side of the barn wore a shiny star on the lapel of his leather vest and a smile that sent shivers up and down Jesselynn's back.

"Now, boys, just ease on down to the ground so's we can talk all friendly like."

"Where I come from, we don't call pointin' a rifle at a stranger very friendly."

"Well, now, you might if'n one of the strangers was wanted for murder." The deputy used one finger to tip his felt hat farther back on his head.

Jesselynn shook her head as she slid off the mule, shielding Daniel by taking a step forward right in front of him. "No way could Daniel here be wanted for murder. We just rode into town this afternoon, been on the road from Springfield for three days. We're lookin' for to find the best way to pick up the road to Independence."

"Now, boy, why in the world should I believe what you say? A man back in Blytheville says yer slave was with the man who shot poor ol' Avery. Shot 'im in cold blood, he did."

"I'm right sorry to hear that, but first of all, Daniel is not my slave but a freedman, and according to what I heard, the shooting happened over a week ago. We weren't anywhere near here then." Jesselynn made sure she sounded as Kentucky as possible and educated to boot. While she sounded as self-possessed as she was able to, her teeth had a heart-stopping desire to clack together. She hid her hands in her pockets to disguise their shaking.

"Well, son, I think we'll let the judge decide that." The deputy strode forward and grabbed Daniel by the upper arm. "Come along, boy."

"No!" Jesselynn tried to step between them but got shoved out of the way for her efforts. When she reeled back against the mule's shoulder, the dog growled and bumped her leg with his nose, teeth bared and hair raised along his back and shoulders. The urge to kick him made her foot twitch. "Call off your dog, mister, before I—"

"Before you what?" The man's voice rumbled with laughter.

When Daniel hung back and sent her a terrified look over his shoulder, the deputy jerked him hard enough to make him stumble. For that he got a clout with the rifle stock.

"Marse Jesse! Don' let dem take me!"

His cry nearly broke her heart. She started after the pair, but the dog grabbed hold of her pants leg, taking some skin with it.

Jesselynn turned and gave the dog a vicious chop with the side of her hand, right on his nose. The dog yipped and let go. Ignoring the burning in her calf, she started after the deputy, who was now tying a rope around Daniel's chest, binding his arms straight down to his body.

"Hold 'im there, Jason."

The calm command brought the owner's rifle to hand, and a bullet puffed the dirt a couple of feet in front of her.

"He's done nothing wrong. He wasn't even here." But talking did no good as the deputy shook out a few lengths of rope and mounted his horse.

"Give me any more lip, and I drag 'im to town. Take your pick." He settled his hat down on his head and stared at Jesselynn.

*God, help us. What do I do now?*

"How 'bout I ride into town with you and straighten this all out?" She fought to keep the tremor out of her voice.

"Suit yourself. Perhaps the judge'll want to talk to you too." The veiled threat worked. Her mouth went dry as a creek bed in August.

She swallowed and cleared her throat. "No more than I want to talk with him." With a glare at the dog owner, she swung aboard Roman and followed the deputy around the barn and back out to the road. By now the sun had dipped appreciably lower, and all Jesselynn wanted to do was hightail it for their camp and get out of the area. But leaving Daniel was not even a thought. He would be with them when they hit the road north.

Two men met them on the road and fell in beside the deputy. Daniel trotted to keep up with the trotting horses, but the men in front of him paid him no more attention than if he'd been a cow. In fact, less.

Jesselynn brought Roman up beside Daniel. "Do you have your manumission papers?"

He shook his head. "Back at de camp. Put de papers in Meshach's Bible."

How many times had she told them they needed the papers on their person at all times? Slave traders wouldn't let them go back to anywhere for their papers. But scolding him would do no good now. Most likely he'd been doing a good enough job of that himself.

"I'm heading back to camp then, but I'll be in town as soon as I can get there. Just do what they tell you so they have no call to whip you."

"Dey don' need no call, Marse. Dey gonna whip dis poor nigger sure as de sun rise."

*Lord, let it only be a whipping. Please, God, not a hanging.*

"We'll pray that not be so."

"Hey, you, leave that boy alone."

At the jerk on the rope that caused Daniel to stumble and nearly go down, Jesselynn dropped back. When they reached the main road, she turned east as they turned west. Digging her heels into the mule's ribs, she slapped him with the reins too. "Hup, Roman, come on."

A few minutes that seemed like hours later, she tore into camp and threw herself off the mule's back before he came to a skidding stop. "They've got Daniel." She tried to draw a breath and speak at the same time but only succeeded in making herself cough.

"Who got Daniel?" Meshach thumped her on the back to help her breathe.

"A deputy. Someone said Daniel was with a man who shot the owner of the store. They hung that man this afternoon in the center of town." Jesselynn took the cup of water Jane Ellen handed her and guzzled it, water dripping unnoticed down her chin. She wiped her mouth with the back of her hand and handed the cup back. "Thanks." Turning to Meshach, she closed her eyes for a moment to get the facts straight. "They'll hang him for certain if we don't do something and do it fast." She sucked in a deep breath and let it out. If she didn't calm down, she'd be worthless. "He says his papers are in your Bible. You get those, and I'll get Daddy's journal. That should prove who we are."

"We take de wagon? Dey see we be travelin'."

"Lawd, keep our Daniel safe." Ophelia clasped her hands to her bosom and looked heavenward. Sammy, clinging to her skirt, set to whimpering, which brought out a quivering lower lip on Thaddeus.

"Here, let me take them babies." Jane Ellen reached for Sammy and, after settling him on her hip, took Thaddeus's hand. "We'll go look for the ducks."

"You want I should go too?" Aunt Agatha looked over her spectacles. "Might lend a note of propriety. I can show letters and things from Springfield. There are dates and such on them."

Jesselynn wrinkled her brow in thought. "I think not at the moment." The last thing she wanted to do was subject the rest of the family to any fracas in town. "Just pray that most of the folks have already gone home. There surely was a crowd there for the hangin'. You'da thought a circus came to town, such an air of jollity." The thought still made her stomach clench. Even worse, she knew there wouldn't be a trial and a formal hanging for a black boy like Daniel. Some group of men would just take him out to a tree or use the beam at the livery and string him up.

"All right, let's harness up Roman and Chess. Benjamin, you make sure the rest of the horses are well grazed and watered. We might be leavin' in a hurry. Ophelia, have supper ready and everything else packed up." She glanced around the camp. No matter what, they were pushing out as soon as they had Daniel in tow.

She glanced over her shoulder as they left the camp. Aunt Agatha was sitting in her rocker, both boys in her lap while Jane Ellen and Ophelia were making biscuits for supper and some to harden for eating later on the trail. They looked so peaceful, as if no one was worried sick about Daniel, but she knew they were. Ophelia might be singing, but her songs were always prayers for the good Lord's intervention in their lives.

Once in town she directed Meshach to the jail, where they tied up the team in the rear so no one would get too interested in the horse. Stepping down, they heard a *psst*.

"Marse Jesse, over here." Daniel, one eye swollen closed and lower lip thick and split, waved at them from the barred window of the jail.

"How bad off are you?" Jesselynn stepped close so they could whisper.

"Dey ask me 'bout dat man dey hung, and I don know nothin' 'bout him. Dey says I lyin' and den dey hit me. Not too bad. Sheriff come in and make dem stop."

Jesselynn breathed a sigh of relief. While the deputy had already made up his mind, perhaps the sheriff was a man of integrity. And the judge, if they could meet with him.

"I'm sorry, Daniel, I should never have brought you to town with me."

"You don't know 'bout dis here man either."

"I know, but—" Jesselynn stopped. Crying over spilt milk never did anyone any good. "You just sit down and rest. We'll take care of this." She caught a nod from Meshach, and the two of them headed for the front door of the building. A sign above the heavy wooden door read *SHERIFF* in letters large enough to be seen from a distance. When they pushed it open, the deputy she'd encountered earlier sat behind the wooden desk drinking a cup of coffee and smoking a cigar.

"I'd like to speak with the sheriff." Jesselynn kept her voice even and polite, in spite of an urge to have Meshach pick the man up and throw him through the window, bars and all.

"He ain't here."

"I can see that. Where can I find him?"

"At home. He don't like to be disturbed when he's eatin' his supper." He waved the cigar for emphasis.

Jesselynn counted to five. Ten would take too much time and effort. "And where might his home be?"

"He'll be back in an hour or so. Thataway I can go eat."

Meshach shifted from one foot to the other. Jesselynn could feel his anger like something alive in the room.

The deputy could sense it too. Eyes slit, he shifted his gaze from one guest to the other. "I wouldn't want to hurry him meself." Slowly he lowered his boots to the floor and sat up straight, his elbows resting on the desk as if to prove his nonchalance.

"Since I heard the dead man had a trial, is there a judge in town?"

"Left on the stage yesterday."

Jesselynn counted again. Why did everything seem to be against them?

The gleam in the deputy's eye said he was enjoying their frustration. *He's most likely the kind of man who pulled legs off live frogs when he was young. Thinks no more of treating black boys the same.*

"Thank you for your information. Now where did you say the sheriff lived?"

"I din't."

Meshach took a step forward and leaned toward the desk. His fists looked powerful enough to drop a horse with one blow.

"Ah, the sheriff lives two blocks over and three down, on Hawthorne. White house with green shutters." The deputy pointed toward the west.

As they turned to leave, he added, "Don't you go worryin' 'bout that nigger back there. After tomorrow there won't be no more problem."

Meshach pulled the door closed behind him with a thud big enough to shake the boards beneath their feet. "I surely do hopes the sheriff be a better man than that 'un."

"Me too, Meshach, me too. Tryin' to figure out what he meant about no more problem scares me clear to Sunday."

"Dis 'bout as bad as Daniel in de lions' den."

"Worse. Men can be meaner than lions any day." Together they followed the directions to the sheriff's house, then sat down to wait, leaning against the picket fence that fronted the street.

Meshach pulled up a blade of grass and chewed the tender stem.

Jesselynn knew from his quiet that he was praying. While she tried to put the entire mess into the Lord's strong hands, pictures of the deputy dragging Daniel at the end of the rope intruded. And fears of Daniel dangling from the end of a rope made her stomach roil and her blood boil. *Lord, surely you wouldn't let him come so far to be strung up for something he didn't do. We have so far to go, yet we're close to being free too.*

She glanced sideways to see Meshach with his head back against the fence, his eyes closed, and wearing a slight smile as though he was lost in a pleasant dream. Surely he was praying, not sleeping. She watched for any sign of awareness. A bee buzzed over his head and was gone. Children shouted from a yard somewhere nearby. A baby cried and stopped in that instant that said someone had come for him.

Jesselynn wished someone would come for her. All this was just too much. *God, what do you expect of me? I can't keep on taking care of all these people, and short of breaking Daniel out of the jail, I don't know what to do.*

She felt like shaking her fist. "He's innocent," she whispered.

"I know dat, and you know dat. Now we just wait 'till de sheriff know dat too." Meshach's gentle answer smoothed over her restlessness like a loving hand.

Jesselynn sighed. "I sure hope that sheriff is enjoying his supper."

When they heard the front door click closed behind them, they both got to their feet and turned to greet a man, nearly as tall as Meshach, settling his hat over a bald spot pushing up through wisps of gray hair. Furry eyebrows nearly met over the bridge of a nose that had encountered one too many fists.

"Good evening, Sheriff."

"Sorry, I didn't know anyone was waiting. Why didn't you come to the door?"

"Ah, your deputy said you didn't like to be disturbed during supper."

The sheriff shook his head. "That Rudy, I'd soon as fire him as keep him." He stopped at the gate. "So what can I do for you?"

"You can release my friend, Daniel, who looks plenty worse than the last time I saw him. I am Jesse Highwood from Midway, Kentucky, and Daniel used to be one of my father's slaves until he was given his manumission papers before we started west."

"What is bringing you this way?"

"We got burned out, so decided that Oregon might be a good place to start over."

"And your father?"

"Killed in the war. I'm the oldest remaining son, and all I want is to get my people west. Daniel was with us in Springfield up until three days ago when we started out. No way could he have been here."

"You got any papers to back all this up?"

Jesselynn pulled Daniel's manumission papers from her pocket. "This here and more in the wagon."

"Come on, then. Let's go on back and study this situation. We have a man who swears your Daniel was with Gardner when he shot and killed Avery Hopkins."

"When was he killed?"

" 'Bout dusk a week ago Friday."

"And this man has seen Daniel today?"

"Yup. Says he's the one."

Jesselynn walked between the two men back to the jail. Surely he believed her. It certainly seemed so.

After he dismissed the deputy, the sheriff took the chair. "I have one question for you, young man. Why did your boy run today?"

"Because someone shouted at him and came after him. If you were young and black, and the white crowd was in a hangin' mood, wouldn't you run?"

"Guess I'd have to say that I would."

Jesselynn let him think for a moment. The silence hung heavy in the room. "So how about if we take Daniel on back to camp with us and get on the road?"

"Sorry, I can't do that."

She saw Meshach's hands clench at his side. "Why not, sir?"

"Because I'm going to have to defer to the judge on this. I've heard both sides, and while what you say makes good sense, the man who identified Daniel is a highly respected citizen of our town. If I just let this boy go, there'll be all kinds of devil to pay. I have to follow the law, and the law says suspects have to be proven guilty."

"But we weren't anywhere near here a week ago."

"So you say. It don't have to take that long to get here from Springfield." He looked up at her, his gaze penetrating. "Can you prove your boy was in Springfield with you at that time?"

Jesselynn turned to look up at Meshach, who gave a barely perceptible shrug. *How, how can I prove he was there?* The question ricocheted through her mind. She felt like melting into a puddle on the floor. "No, I don't guess that I can. I have three other adults that will swear he was with us, but no concrete proof." She thought of her journal. Had she written Daniel's name in during the Springfield stay? Again a no dragged her down further.

"So what happens now?"

"I keep him here in jail until the judge returns in two days, and then we go before him with all the information. He hears both sides and will make a decision. I abide by whatever decision he makes."

"And if he goes with your man's opinion?"

"Then most likely your boy will hang."

# CHAPTER EIGHTEEN

## Washington

"Yes, suh." The maid standing in the doorway failed to smile.

*Do we look that disreputable?* Louisa thought about checking her clothing to make sure no rents showed. But she knew that wasn't so. She'd brushed and ironed her blue traveling outfit herself.

"Is my cousin, Dr. Logan, at home?" Zachary's voice carried just the correct amount of arrogance, in spite of the all-too-visible scars.

"Yes, suh. Who shall I say is callin'?" The woman didn't move from her position as doorkeeper.

"Zachary Highwood and Miss Louisa Highwood." He flashed her a smile that made the eye patch look only more dashing.

She started to shut the door, paused, and added. "I be right back."

"And leave us standin' on the street?" The shock in his voice apparently made her rethink her dilemma. With a frown, she stepped back and indicated they should enter.

"I send a man for your trunk." She pointed through a narrow archway. "You may wait in there." With that and a flurry of her skirt, she hastened down a walnut-lined hall.

The room they entered looked more like the waiting room of a doctor's office than a front parlor. Chairs and sofas lined the walls, and creamy camellias dropped petals on a hexagonal table with feet swept up in a curl. Oil paintings of rivers and trees, a house and field, horses and hounds hung on the walls. A closed door bore a gold sign reading *OFFICE*.

They had not been shown to the family quarters.

Louisa picked up a magazine and flipped through it, grimacing at the political cartoons. If this was any indication of their cousin's views on the war, she knew he and Zachary would most likely come to radical disagreement.

The maid returned. "This way."

Louisa and Zachary exchanged a look of raised eyebrows and slight shrugs.

*We got beyond the first gatekeeper,* she thought. *What will be the next?*

A woman with fashionably styled gray hair greeted them with outstretched hands. "Oh, my dears, please forgive Becca's caution. We've had some unsavory visitors in the last months. I am your cousin Annabelle, and I know Arlington will be so sorry to have missed you. He was required at the hospital again, you see. With all our boys—" She stopped and blinked. "Oh, forgive me, here I go rattling off like some ninny when you must be thirsty, and hungry too, for that matter. Have a seat there. Becca, take his cape and have cook bring us some coffee. Doesn't that sound good on a chill afternoon like today?" She bustled as she spoke, settling her guests in two chairs by the fire and pulling up another for herself. "Now, you must tell me all about yourselves as I only know hearsay about my husband's Southern kin." Even her hands fluttered as she raced on. "You're from where now?"

"Richmond, Virginia." Louisa answered quickly before her cousin's rushing flow of words continued.

"Ah, yes, such a lovely city."

"I'm sure it has changed since you last saw it." Visions of the freedmen's shanties down the streets from stately homes flew through her mind. Even though Richmond was the capital of the South and had never been shelled, the war showed itself in homes falling into disrepair due to the menfolk off fighting and no money to be had for upkeep. The frenzy of government had Richmond by the throat.

"As has Washington. Soldiers everywhere, and if not men, then supplies. Why, we have the hardest time getting tobacco."

*Shame we don't still have Twin Oaks. We could have brought you some.*

Becca entered and set a silver tray with a silver coffeepot and dainty china cups on the table next to her mistress. A silver salver held a variety of cookies and small cakes.

"Do you take cream or sugar?" Annabelle poured a cup and glanced over at Zachary. At the shake of his head and polite "No thank you," she handed the cup on the saucer to Becca along with the platter of cookies to take to Zachary. "And you, Louisa?"

"Yes, please." Louisa refrained from looking at her brother. She could read his mind. *What a waste. What a total and absolute waste.*

"Do you have any idea when Arlington will be home?" Zachary asked after a sip of coffee.

"Goodness me, no. I never do. We were supposed to attend a ball tonight, but his men always come first." The last was said with just enough twist to let Louisa know the woman would much rather be at the ball with her husband in tow. The nerve of him, putting wounded and dying soldiers before the enjoyment of his wife!

Since they were not part of the society in Richmond, they were not subjected to routs and parties, to balls and afternoons filled with calling on friends and gossiping. Louisa had watched Carrie Mae and Jefferson pursue a place in the Southern political theater, wanting no part of it herself. She'd rather work at the hospital any day. At least there she could be doing some good.

Now she sipped her coffee and listened to her cousin's wife rattle on.

"Have you been to Washington before?" Before Zachary could answer, Annabelle continued. "Our city was so beautiful before all those contraband camps sprang up. All those slaves who run away and come up here expectin' *us* to support them."

Zachary set his cup and saucer on the whatnot table next to his chair. "Thank you so much for the delicious coffee, Cousin Annabelle, but we must be going." He pushed himself erect and tucked his crutch under his arm. "Louisa?"

"Oh, I am so sorry to hear that. Becca, bring their things, please. I'll be sure and tell Arlington that you visited. Is there someplace he can reach you?"

"I'll send a message around in the morning." Zachary stooped to let Becca settle his cape about his shoulders.

Louisa kept a smile on her face while inside she seethed. If cousin Arlington was anything like his wife, the less they saw of him the better. As a Union army doctor, there was no way he would make sure they had access to the supplies they so desperately needed anyway.

"Oh, dear, I must call you a cab. Becca, send Harry out for one." Annabelle turned back to her guests. "Won't take but a moment or two. Wouldn't you rather sit down again?"

"No, thank you. As you can tell, it takes me a little longer than most to—"

"Ah, yes." She turned to Louisa. "Do greet your dear aunt for me. Arlington has spoken so highly of her."

"Oh, you mean Aunt Sophia?"

"Yes, indeed, the dear woman."

Louisa smiled so sweetly her jaw ached. "I shall most certainly do that. Thank you again for the pleasant repast." She nodded and, reaching into her bag, took out her gloves and pulled them on. "If you are ever in Richmond, do come to call." *Dear Cousin Annabelle doesn't even know Aunt Sylvania's name.*

Zachary led the way to the front door, smiled at Becca, who stood without moving, and stepped outside. "I'll have the driver get our trunk. Wouldn't want to be a bother or anything."

If the woman understood his sarcasm, she ignored it.

The arrival of the black hansom cab, even with the same driver, caught their attention.

"You wants yo' trunk, suh?"

"Yes, thank you." Zachary waited for Louisa to settle in the carriage while the driver fetched their trunk and put it up on his seat. Then he handed Zachary in and, with a slight bow, shut the door.

Zachary leaned back against the cushions. "Well, I never."

"Me either. Mother would have had us horsewhipped for treating guests so carelessly. And family, at that." She shook her head. "I do pray that this is not a portend of things to come." If Zachary were as angry as she, he was hiding it well. She mentally counted to ten and then to thirty. Still, the seething in her mind set her stomach to lurching, just like the carriage as it hit a pothole. She took another deep breath.

"Well, we know one thing," Zachary said.

"What's that?" Louisa turned from glaring out the window.

"We can't count on Cousin Arlington for anything."

"Perhaps he is different than his wife."

"You always were one to hope for the good." He rubbed his leg to ease the straps. "But I'll believe it when I see it. I shall send around a message of where we are stayin', but that is as far as I go. After all, I wouldn't want to keep them from a *ball*, for pity's sake."

*I won't let pride get in my way, brother dear. If there's morphine to be had, I'll walk on my knees for it.*

# CHAPTER NINETEEN

## Blytheville, Missouri

"So where do we go from here?"

Meshach leaned against the wagon wheel. "I don't know, but God knows."

"I'm sure He does, but right now it doesn't look like He's talking."

"You been askin'?"

Jesselynn sighed. "Of sorts. I ask, then I wait." *For nothing. I don't hear anything. Why, right now when we need answers immediately, does God go silent? Father, what are we to do?*

"Psst."

They both turned to see Daniel back at the window. He glanced over his shoulder, then beckoned them closer. When they stood within whispering distance, he gripped the bars and pressed his face against them.

"What he say?"

"We have to wait for the judge to return in two days. He has to hear the evidence."

"But we weren't nowhere near here a week ago."

"I know." If a black face could be gray with fear, Daniel's was. Jesselynn figured she didn't look much better.

"What dey gonna do, Marse Jesse?"

"Don' matter what *dey* gonna do. We's prayin' for de Lawd's deliverance." Meshach spoke with such intensity that Jesselynn felt sure if she turned around, she'd see a heavenly vision right behind them.

"Dat deputy, he say dey gonna hang me like dey done de robber."

"Daniel . . ."

"He say niggers like me good for nothin' but hangin'."

"Easy, boy."

"He say hangin' too good for what I done. I should be shot." Tears streamed down Daniel's cheek from his good eye, leaving tracks in the dirt and blood from the beating. One drop leaked from the eye swollen shut. "Marse Jesse, I din't do nothin'." His voice cracked.

Jesselynn's heart did the same.

"Hey, you, get away from that window!" The deputy's voice came from down the alley.

"We'll be back in the mornin'." Jesselynn pressed Daniel's fingers clamped around the bars. "You eat your supper and sleep well. You're safe in there at least."

"Spend the night on your knees, boy. We all be poundin' the gates of heaven. God says He listen when Him chilluns cry. He say He be our protector, our shield. He never leave us nor forsake us. Think on Him words."

"I try." Daniel rubbed his nose with the back of his hand and flinched.

"I said, git on outa there." The voice was slightly slurred and nearer.

Jesselynn and Meshach climbed up on the wagon, and Meshach backed the team so he could turn around. Jesselynn glanced over her shoulder to see the deputy and two other men making their way toward the jail.

"Just a minute." She leaped to the ground and trotted around the brick building to the front entrance. Stepping inside, she waited for the sheriff to look up from his bookwork. "Sir, I hate to bother you, but I got me a real bad feelin'. You *will* keep Daniel safe tonight, won't you?"

The man stared at her through squinted eyes. "That's my job, boy." The steel in his tone impaled her to the floor.

"I . . . I know that, but anybody could stick a gun in that window, shoot him, and be gone before you could get there."

"You think I didn't know you were out there talkin' with him?"

"No, sir. I mean, yes, sir." *But did you hear your deputy threaten to kill an innocent black man?* Jesselynn wished she were anywhere but trapped in the sheriff's gaze.

"I think you don't quite understand, Mr. Jesse Highwood. This here's a good town. Folks abide by the law here. We won't have any funny business goin' on."

"Thank you, sir. Sorry to have bothered you." She turned for the door but stopped one more time.

"I'll move him to another cell without a window."

With that she touched the brim of her hat and headed back out the door. *Just wish I felt as confident as he does, but that deputy reminds me of Dunlivey—mean ugly as sin clear through.*

Back in camp, they told the others, and for a change Ophelia didn't carry on with her moaning and crying. Instead, she drew herself up to her full height and looked Meshach in the eye.

"You better git on back to town and make sure nothin' happen to dat boy."

"Now, Ophelia . . ." Jesselynn started to interrupt but shut her mouth when she saw the look that passed between husband and wife.

"I takes Roman soon as I eat supper. Benjamin, take him to graze for me, will you?"

"Better take the rifle too." Jesselynn fetched it from under the wagon seat.

Man and mule disappeared into the darkness less than an hour later, the thud of cantering hooves their last contact.

"My land, what is this world comin' to?" Aunt Agatha shook her head and kept on shaking it as she sat back down in her chair by the fire and picked up her sewing. "Lord preserve us, this surely does test my faith. I was so certain the Lord would deliver that boy right into your hands."

"I thought so too." Jesselynn slumped against a tree trunk. "I should have gone with Meshach."

"He hide better at night." Ophelia settled Sammy into the quilt next to Thaddeus, who was already asleep. "Now, you be good boy and go to sleep." She sank down on the tailgate so she could pat his back and picked up the words of her song as if she'd been singing it all along. "Our home is over Jordan. Deep river, Lord, I want to cross over into campground." Her rich voice soothed both ear and soul.

*Lord, keep them safe, as it seems there's nothing I can do to help. Hurry the judge back and make him listen to the truth. If you would make the man who says he saw Daniel realize the error of his claim, that would most likely be the best way out.*

*"The Lord shall preserve thy going out and thy coming in."* The words seemed to hover on the air.

Tears sprang instantly to water her eyes. Too long. It had been too long since she had felt His presence, had heard His voice.

Ophelia moved on to another one of her songs, and Benjamin, who had just brought in the horses, hummed along with her. Aunt Agatha leaned forward in her rocker to catch the firelight on her stitching. Thanks to her, Jane Ellen had new undergarments to go with her new skirt and waist, Sammy had two new shifts, and Thaddeus had graduated to pants, leaving his worn shift for Sammy to grow into. Aunt Agatha wanted to sew a skirt for Jesselynn but suggested it only once, since the lecture she received on safety had sent Sammy hiding behind Ophelia's skirt.

Jesselynn laid her cheek against her knees, arms clasped around her shins. The music softened to a murmur, like a summer creek whispering over stones.

A stick burned through in the fire and settled into the ashes with a spray of sparks. The *whoo-whoo* of an owl sounded from somewhere above them, and a dog barked in the distance.

Comforting sounds, if she could think of anything besides town and the jail. One by one the others headed for bed, whispering their good-nights as if afraid to break a spell. Her eyes grew heavier until she stood to keep awake. First watch was always hard, but then so were the others. And tonight with only three of them to share the load, it would be a long night.

Around midnight she woke Benjamin and crawled into her own quilt. One good thing about watch, she had plenty of time to pray, and staring at the star-studded sky continually reminded her that God, who'd created the universe, cared about this ragtag band of sojourners.

It seemed she'd just fallen asleep when her eyes flew open. With one motion she grabbed her boots and rolled out of bed. "I'm going to town," she whispered to Benjamin. "Get Chess for me, please." While he did that, she retrieved the pistol from its box, along with shells to fill her pockets.

Benjamin led Chess up to the fire and fetched the saddle. Within minutes she was cantering down the road, leaving him with reminders that he was in charge and if they didn't return by dawn, he should get everyone up and ready to ride, just in case they needed a quick getaway. The sense she was needed in town spurred her to a gallop.

Coming around the back instead of down Main Street, she could see torches flared and hear shouting voices before she reached the rear of the jail. She stopped several houses away and tied Chess to a fence, then ran, staying in the shadows until she could hide in the corner near the window.

"Daniel!" She hissed his name, trying to keep her voice lost in the shouting.

No answer came. She edged to the window but could see nothing inside. Light outlined a closed door toward the front of the building. Either the sheriff had moved Daniel as he promised or . . .

The *or* didn't bear thinking.

Gun at the ready, she edged closer to the street that ran in front of the building.

"Now, folks, let's calm down and talk about this like the sensible folks that you are." The sheriff sounded as if he were at a church social, his voice so calm and reasonable.

"Just let us have that nigger pup, and you can go on back home to bed." The shout sounded like a half-bottle one.

Someone else cheered. Several shouted their agreement. Others laughed.

The hairs stood up on the back of Jesselynn's neck. Where was Meshach?

"Now, you know I can't do that. The lad is innocent until the judge says he's guilty. You elected me to—"

"And we can un-elect you too. Keep that in mind."

"I'm right aware of that, but y'all go on home now, and we'll discuss this in the mornin'."

*Please, God, make them listen to him. Make them go home.* She shivered both from the brisk wind picking at her jacket and the menace of the voices.

"Marse Jesse, dat you?" Meshach's voice from behind her sounded as welcome as coffee on a cold day.

"Yes. Is there another way into the building?"

"No, suh. I tried pryin' at the window, but nothin' gave."

"Where is Daniel?"

"In another cell. I asked the sheriff."

"So he knows you're here?"

"He knows I *was* here. He think I go on back to camp."

A shout jerked their attention to the street.

"You ain't goin' in there!" The sheriff sounded harried now.

Meshach tapped Jesselynn on the shoulder. "You go dis way, and I go round de other. Dat man need backup."

Jesselynn edged her way to the front corner of the building, counted to ten, and stepped into the torchlight. With everyone's attention on the sheriff, she stepped up on the stone stair before anyone noticed her. Meshach did the same, both of them with their guns raised.

"Well, I'll be . . ." The sheriff muttered as the mob quieted.

"Just some friendly help, sir." Jesselynn aimed her pistol at the man in front who seemed to be the ringleader. She glanced around in the flickering torchlight, fully expecting to see the deputy leading the charge.

"Now, as I said before, y'all go on home. Your wives are waitin' for you, and if I know the ladies of this town, they're goin' to be a little huffy over the shenanigans out here tonight. And, George, see you in church tomorrow?"

The hefty fellow in front growled something, spun on his heel, and pushed his way through the ranks behind him. Within a minute the crowd had faded away like clouds blown on the wind.

"I could have handled them myself." The sheriff let out a breath and turned to the two behind him.

"I know. But we didn't want anyone hurt." *Least of all Daniel.*

"Thank you." The sheriff shook hands with each of them in turn. "There won't be any more trouble tonight. Too close to daylight. And tomorrow night, the women won't let their men out of the house without a fight. Besides, the saloon is closed on Sunday. These men needed a keg of liquid courage to make them brave enough tonight to cause a ruckus. At heart, this is a good town, like I told you before."

"A good town maybe, but a hangin' brings out the worst in folks. Leastwise that's what I been told." Jesselynn stuck the pistol in her waistband and looked up at the sheriff. "Now, can we take our boy and go?"

"Nope. Like I told them out there. The judge will be sittin' on

Monday, and he'll make the decision."

"Was the man who mistook Daniel out in the crowd?"

"I believe so."

*Meaning yes. How can we prove Daniel wasn't the one?*

# CHAPTER TWENTY

"We're goin' to church," Jesselynn announced Sunday morning.

"Now?" Jane Ellen nearly dropped Sammy, grabbing him before he took a head dive off the tailgate. "All of us?"

"We better get on the road pretty quick, or we might be too late." Jesselynn looked down at her britches and shirtfront. Never had she gone to church in such filthy clothes. Of course, she'd never gone in britches either, but that made no difference at the moment. She turned to the wagon and dug in her box for a clean pair of pants and a shirt. The shirt had a rip on the right-side front.

"Here, hand me that. I can stitch it up while we ride in the wagon." Aunt Agatha *tsked* as she studied the tear. " 'Pears to me I should be sewing you a shirt along with the others."

"Thank you." Jesselynn turned to Thaddeus. "Come on, little brother, let's get your face washed. You can wear your new pants."

"What's church?" Thaddeus looked up at her, a wrinkle between his eyebrows.

"Don't you remember goin' to church at home? Where the organ music played, people sang hymns, and a man in a black robe preached the sermon?"

"What's a sermon?"

"The pastor teachin' about God's Word, you know, the Bible?" Jane Ellen looked up from searching for something in the wagon.

"Like Meshach?"

"Like Meshach. Come on, we need to hurry." But hurrying Thaddeus was like trying to hustle snails. The more she prodded, the slower he went. When they were all in the wagon but Benjamin, who needed to stay with the horses, Jesselynn looked them all over and smiled. "We look right presentable."

As the wagon rumbled along and Ophelia took up singing in the back, Meshach leaned closer to Jesselynn on the wagon seat. "Not that I mind goin' to church, but we doin' this to impress the sheriff?"

"Couldn't hurt. You know, I been thinkin'. Benjamin and Daniel are much the same size. What if I ask the sheriff or the judge to let Benjamin take Daniel's place and see if that man still says that's the boy he saw runnin' off. That would prove he didn't really recognize Daniel, wouldn't it?"

"But now Daniel all beat up."

"Hmm." She nodded, thinking so hard the horses picked up their trot, setting the harness to jingling and Thaddeus to giggling.

"More. Go faster."

"You set yourself right down, young man." Aunt Agatha snagged him by the back of his britches and plopped him back to sitting.

"So how do you think we could make it work?"

"Beat up Benjamin?"

Jesselynn jerked around to see if he was serious, then studied the horses' rumps. "Actually that might not be a bad idea. If it could save Daniel's life, I bet Benjamin would take a punch or two."

She let her thoughts roam as they trotted the road to town and on to the white painted church with a steeple and bell in the tower. They'd just tied the horses to a shade tree when the bell began to peal.

"Ah, I ain't heard a churchbell since we left home." Meshach paused in helping the women to the ground. "Sounds mighty pretty."

Jesselynn took Thaddeus's hand and leaned down to whisper. "Now, you have to sit still in church and no talking. You understand?"

His lower lip came out, and Jesselynn sighed. "Thaddeus Joshua Highwood, you don't want to embarrass us, do you?"

He cocked his head, question marks shooting from his eyes.

"What emb'rass mean?"

She swung him up to ride on her hip. "It means make us look bad. You can be such a good boy. Please?" She tickled his ribs with one finger.

"I be good." He squirmed and giggled, then gave her a hug and a kiss.

She hugged him back and set him down to walk up the three stairs. Aunt Agatha led the way, greeting the man at the door.

"We're travelin' through and so appreciate a house of worship. Your churchbell made me think of home." With the quaver on the end of her words, the man patted her hand and gestured toward the doors to the sanctuary. "Here, I think there's room enough for y'all in this back pew."

While some folks turned to see who was coming in, most kept their attention forward, where a man walked to the center and raised his black hymnbook. "Welcome, friends. We'll open this morning with hymn number 265, 'Holy, Holy, Holy.'" He nodded to the woman at the piano, and she commenced to play. "Let us stand."

As the music filled the church, Jesselynn gazed around the congregation, hoping to see the sheriff and wishing she knew what the judge looked like in case he was in attendance. How could she convince them to agree with her scheme?

*Lord, you know the desires of our hearts. We don't ask for anything but justice. Please set Daniel free. This is the only plan I could come up with, but if you have something better, so be it.*

When the minister stood behind the pulpit, Thaddeus shook her arm. "Sit on your lap?"

Jesselynn helped him up, and he snuggled against her chest. She stroked his back with one hand and tried to concentrate on what the preacher was saying. But all she could think of was Daniel.

Her mother would have been disappointed had she known of Jesselynn's worrying. *"Take it to the Lord, and leave it in His hands."* Jesselynn could hear her dead mother talking more easily than she could the preacher. *"Why, frettin' can't even change the color of one hair on your head. God has big hands and broad shoulders. Let Him carry your burdens."*

*You made it sound so easy, Mother, and it's not. Daniel is my responsibility, and he is in jail.*

She glanced over at Meshach. He was nodding in agreement with the preacher. Sammy slumbered in Ophelia's lap. Jane Ellen kept her fingers busy, pleating the fabric of her skirt. Aunt Agatha jerked, an obvious reaction to falling asleep.

The minister droned on. When he finally reached the amen, the congregation stirred and stood for the final hymn. Jesselynn saw the sheriff several pews ahead of them and off to the other side of the room, right on the aisle. She handed a sleepy-eyed boy to Jane Ellen, and as soon as the people began to move, she darted out the side aisle and headed for the back. She *had* to talk with the sheriff.

She caught up with him as he stepped down the last step and settled his hat back on his head. "Sheriff." When he didn't respond, she leaped the steps and raised her voice. "Sheriff!" She'd caught up with him by the time he turned. "Can I talk with you a minute?"

"I guess so. What do you need?"

"I need Daniel out of your jailhouse, but I'd like to talk with you about an idea I had."

"Well, son, I need to get over and relieve my deputy." He raised his hand to stop her before she got the words out. "No, it's not Rudy. I wouldn't leave him in charge again, not with your boy in there."

Jesselynn let out the breath she didn't realize she'd been holding. "Can we talk and walk?"

"Let's have it."

Jesselynn told him her idea of switching the two young black men. "It would show that he was mistaken, don't you see?"

"I'm not blind, son."

"Oh, sorry."

He rubbed his chin with one finger. "You know, that might work, but I'd have to talk it over with the judge first. We brought your boy a basin and water so he could wash. His eye is lookin' some better."

Jesselynn wished he would quit referring to Daniel as her "boy," but wisely she kept her mouth shut. She shoved her hands into her pockets and kept pace with the sheriff. "Thank you, sir. Would it be all right if I talked with Daniel some?"

"Don't know why not." He opened the door and led the way in. After dismissing the deputy, he took the keys and, unlocking Daniel's cell, stepped back to let her go in. "Call when you're ready."

Jesselynn stood at the bars watching Daniel, not saying anything. He seemed to be asleep on the cot. His face did look better, but overall he appeared to have lost twenty pounds and shrunk in inches, as if caving in on himself. Even if he hadn't eaten, she figured the look had nothing to do with his body but all with his mind. She'd seen a wild animal caught in a trap look the same back home.

If they didn't lynch him first, Daniel would die in here. He'd never have his freedom.

"Daniel?"

"Marse Jesse, you done come to set me free?" He rolled to his feet in one motion and flew to the bars.

"I wish." She wanted to catch his face before it hit the floor. "Now, Daniel, don't take on so. We got a good idea goin' if the judge will go along with us."

"Is de judge a good man?"

Jesselynn shrugged. "We've been prayin' so. The sheriff seems hopeful."

"Why don' he let me go?" Daniel gripped the bars till the tendons in his arms stood out. "I din't do nothin' wrong."

"I know that." If only she could take him in her arms and hug the life back into him. She touched the side of his face near his eye. "This is lookin' better."

"I can see outa it, leastways. Thought I was a goner for sure last night. I prayed de Lawd take me home, but I's still here."

"I know. But you go ahead and rest up, 'cause when we get you out of here, we'll be hittin' the trail hard. Benjamin said you just wanted a night without guard duty." She hoped this would bring a smile, but Daniel just shook his head. "I takes all de nights if'n I gets outa here. Why God do dis to me?"

"*And tribulation worketh patience*..." She could hear her mother's voice reciting the verses she'd committed to memory over the years. She repeated the verse for Daniel. "I don't know why God allowed this, but that's what the Word says, so we'll just get through this. And we'll all be more patient because of it." She kept herself from shuddering at the word *tribulation*. Even the sound of it dragged up bad feelings.

"I tries, Marse Jesse. I tries." A tear seeped from under the swollen eyelid.

"I better go so we can get back to camp. Everyone sends you love." She patted his shoulder. If only she could think of something really heartening to cheer him, but the snores of a drunk in the next cell drove all encouraging words right out of her mind. If she didn't get out of there pretty quick, she'd be crying right along with Daniel.

She sniffed and headed for the door. "I'm ready," she called and threw a smile over her shoulder to the young black man, who stood leaning his forehead against the bars, his hands clamped so tightly they looked as if they could bend iron.

*God, please help him. Help us. Please.* Her feet seemed to weigh twenty pounds each as she left the jailhouse. Meshach had driven the wagon up to the hitching post, so she had to summon an instant smile. Letting Thaddeus know how bad things were was unnecessary. She didn't need two crying little boys.

"Where's Daniel?" Thaddeus greeted her with a frown. "He go with us."

"Soon, Thaddeus, soon."

"Why not now?"

"Ah . . ." She looked to Meshach for an answer.

"Hey, Thaddeus, look what I got." From the rear of the wagon, Jane Ellen held out her closed fist.

When Thaddeus scrambled back to see what she held, Jesselynn breathed a sigh of relief. "Bless you, girl," she said only loud enough for Meshach's ears. He shot her a smile as he hupped the horses and headed the wagon out of town.

Now all they had to do was get through until tomorrow.

# CHAPTER TWENTY-ONE

Dawn came to eyes bleary from lack of sleep.

"Where's Meshach?" Jesselynn asked, stumbling over a rock on her way to the already leaping fire.

"Grazin' de horses." Ophelia used her apron to lift a boiling pot off the cast-iron tripod.

Jesselynn looked over to see that Benjamin still lay wrapped in his quilt and deerskin. He'd stood the last watch. The boys and Aunt Agatha had yet to make an appearance, for which Jesselynn was grateful. Let those who *could* sleep do so. Nightmares, the first in a while, had ridden her all night.

"Here." Ophelia handed her a cup of steaming coffee.

"Thank you. Reckon I don't know what I'd do without you."

"You make your own coffee, dat's what." Ophelia straightened and kneaded her back with both fists. "Breakfast ready soon as de biscuits done." Gravy bubbled gently in one frying pan, and smoked venison simmered in another.

What Jesselynn wouldn't give for two eggs fried till the centers ran only slightly when stabbed with a piece of toast or biscuit, bacon or ham or sausage fried just right, and syrup to drizzle over pancakes so light they could float right off the plate.

The kind of breakfast Lucinda served nearly every morning during their life at Twin Oaks.

Sometimes Jesselynn thought she'd lived another life back then, one with no connection to the one she was living now.

"Think I'll get a letter written while I wait. Anything you want me to tell Lucinda or the girls?"

Ophelia patted her rounding belly. "You can tell dem 'bout dis little one. Dat make Lucinda pleased as punch." Ophelia looked down, shaking her head ever so slightly. "Lucinda do love de babies. You think maybe when we gets to Oregon, we could write Lucinda to come too?"

"She'd never leave Twin Oaks, not when she stayed on after it burned to the ground."

"You never know."

"You just spoke a mouthful of truth. Who'd ever have thought we'd be in a wagon almost to Kansas on our way to Oregon?" Jesselynn stretched her arms over her head and yawned fit to crack her jaw. Since she didn't really expect an answer, she turned and approached the wagon, treading lightly so as not to wake those still sleeping. Once she had her writing case in hand, she returned to the fire, grateful for its warmth in the wind that teased her hat, the brim so limp it flopped in response. She drew her coat closer around her middle and took a seat on a hunk of oak trunk Meshach had carted along since they left the caves. Later on they might need it for firewood, but in the meantime it made for good sitting.

After sharpening her turkey-quill pen she wrote swiftly, first to Lucinda, then to Sergeant White, and finally to her sisters in Richmond. Once in a while she flipped back through her journal to keep track of what all had happened. She didn't mention to Lucinda that Daniel was in jail. No sense bringing her more worry, especially since the letters might be mailed before they knew the outcome.

Sergeant White would understand her consternation, however. When she thought of the Confederate soldier they'd nursed back to health, his smiling face came to mind. Especially the smile he reserved for her once he realized she was not the young man she portrayed. He'd seen behind the act, but had he touched her heart more deeply than a friend? While sometimes she thought so, other times she just wondered. Perhaps there would be a letter when they reached Independence. After all, he had said he'd catch up with them.

She sighed as she signed her name with a flourish. The one to her sisters took the longest.

*Why is it that God seems to allow more trials, in this case an actual one, with judge and all? He promised the Israelites that they would pass through to the Promised Land. I so thought He meant the same for us. While Meshach seems to have no doubt that we will journey on with all of our band intact, I am still struggling with trusting a God who has taken so many from me, and so much. I long for Twin Oaks and life as it used to be. Always and always, the war has destroyed the crops, the land, and the people. Are these the years of the locust? Will He really restore us as though this has never been?*

*My eternal thanks will be raised for Meshach, who took me in hand and made me see that life without our Lord is nothing but a long, dark, miserable existence. I am learning to walk with Him, keeping the picture of our mother always as my example. Sometimes, like now with Daniel in jail, I say with my teeth clenched, I will trust Him. I will praise His holy name. A sacrifice of praise, the psalmist calls it, and for me that truly describes what I must do. The black demon reaches out for me, but when I praise our God's holy name, the sun comes out and warms me again. Thank you, heavenly Father.*

She continued on with the news of how Thaddeus was talking and little Sammy was outgrowing his clothes. She told how Aunt Agatha sewed for one and all as she rocked her way across the countryside.

*You should see her. We have her rocking chair fitted just so between the boxes and supplies, and her needle flies while her chair rocks the miles away. She tells stories to the young'uns and is teaching Thaddeus his numbers and letters. Jane Ellen has appointed herself as Aunt Agatha's protégée and is learning womanly things as the wagon bumps along.*

*The two foals don't seem harmed by the travel, but we have to stop to let them graze and rest more often than we normally would. I long for the day when we can travel during daylight instead of darkness. As long as we make it to Independence without a brush with the Quantrill Raiders, I will—no I must—trust our God for His protection. I must. I must.*

> Your loving sister,
> Jesselynn

*P.S. As I said before, send any correspondence to the post office in Independence, Missouri. We will be waiting there to gather our sup-*

*plies and sign on with a wagon train going west to Oregon. I have a feeling we really have no idea what we will encounter on our journey, but I will make sure we are as prepared as humanly possible. May our God and Father bless and keep thee. JH*

"You wants breakfast now?" Ophelia held out a plate of steaming food.

"Thank you." Jesselynn closed her writing case and set it beside her. "That smells heavenly." She sniffed again and smiled at the fragrance. "Your biscuits give Lucinda's a real challenge. I'd hate to have to judge them in a contest."

Ophelia smiled and ducked her head. "Thank you, Marse." The glint in her eyes told far more than her smile. Comparing her biscuits was a compliment akin to the Father's "well done."

While she ate, Jesselynn ruminated on the plan to substitute Benjamin for Daniel and show that the man in town hadn't really seen either one of them. Something about it dug down in her soul like a tick on a feeding frenzy. But short of breaking Daniel out and streaking across the countryside, nothing came to mind. When she closed her eyes, she could remember one of the dreams that had plagued her the last two nights. She saw Daniel swinging at the end of a rope.

The stark fear in his eyes when she had visited him in the jail raised the hairs on the back of her neck.

No matter, she'd have to wait until she could ride into town and talk with the sheriff, hoping he'd been able to speak with the judge.

When Meshach sat down beside her with his full plate, she glanced at him in time to see the same weary look she felt.

"You didn't sleep either?"

He shook his head. "Prayin' more important den sleepin'." He cut into his gravy-laden biscuit with his fork. "I asked de Lawd for a sign, but I ain't seen nothin' yet. Dis here's one of de times we got to walk by faith."

Jesselynn felt a shiver race up her back. Talking about walking by faith and doing it were two entirely different things. Especially when a young man's life hung in the balance.

"Surely you don't believe it is God's will for Daniel to hang for something he didn't do?"

Meshach shook his head. "Not God's will, but sometimes He lets folks do bad things. Daniel know who his Savior be, and heaven be home for us all, 'specially poor black men and women."

"Meshach, don't talk that way. We got to get Daniel out of there."

"I knows, but I cain't say how. Be God's grace for sure."

Jesselynn felt like shaking the big man. *Don't you dare give up! We can't let them hang him.* But she kept the thoughts to herself, knowing that Ophelia might go into one of her rantings if she heard them. Jesselynn stared at the congealed gravy left on her plate. She'd thought of mopping it up with another biscuit, but her stomach rolled over at the notion. Instead, she scraped the remainder into the fire and dropped her utensils into the pot of simmering water and soap.

"I'll go on and wash up." Leastways then she could leave camp and be by herself. Somehow she argued with God better when it was just the two of them. But arguing and pleading seemed to do no good, and when she returned to camp, she was no nearer a solution than before.

"I believe we should all go into town with you for the trial." Aunt Agatha delivered her pronouncement as if she were the judge.

Jesselynn looked toward the two little boys with Jane Ellen as their overseer. She had taken to instructing them on table manners, having recently learned them herself from Aunt Agatha.

"No, Sammy, use your spoon." Thaddeus's command overrode Jesselynn's tangled thoughts. "See, like this." He demonstrated, ushering biscuit and gravy to his mouth without spilling, to the applause of Jane Ellen.

Sammy giggled, squirmed, and stuck his forefinger in his mouth—after swiping it through the gravy.

When Thaddeus rolled his eyes in perfect mimic of Aunt Agatha, Jesselynn choked on her swig of coffee, sending splatters to sizzle in the flames.

Jane Ellen took over ferrying food to Sammy's mouth, which opened and closed obediently. In the months he'd been with them, the grinning black baby had come a long way from a scrawny, squalling orphan found on a Kentucky hillside.

Aunt Agatha poked Jesselynn with the end of a stick. "Did you hear me?"

Jesselynn nodded. "Just trying to figure what is best."

"I, at least, will be going along. My thought was we look more respectable if we are all in attendance. No judge will think we are a gang of ruffians when he sees us."

*I wouldn't be too sure of that.* Jesselynn kept the thought to herself. But yet she had to admit that her aunt was right. They didn't look any worse than other families moving west and most likely better than a lot of them.

"Shame we don't have a buggy. That would make a better impression than the wagon."

"I don't know about that. People sure look twice when they see you sitting up there in your rocking chair, knitting or sewing as we go along." The few times they'd traveled in daylight, the reaction had been just that.

"Hmm." Agatha gave her a studying look, the kind that elicits fidgets, feet and hands that twitch, the urge to rub her hand across her mouth in case food remained on her face.

Jesselynn kept her gaze on her aunt's hands. If she looked into her eyes, she knew she'd see disapproval of what Jesse was wearing—a man's hat and britches. If she thought that donning women's clothes would save Daniel, she'd do it in an instant, but that might endanger all of the rest of them.

"We'll be ready to leave in a few minutes." Jesselynn turned to Meshach and spoke in a low voice. "Any suggestions?"

"I could stay with de horses in case you wants Benjamin to take Daniel's place. We can't take dem to town."

"I know. I'm beginning to think I should go by myself first and talk with the sheriff, then come back and get the rest."

"Might be de best idea." He stood and stretched. "I get de mule."

———

She kept Roman at a canter all the way to town, pulling him up at the hitching post in front of the jailhouse. Few people were out on the streets. The general store had yet to open its doors, but she could hear the school bell ringing the children in for class.

She paused in front of the jail door and took a deep breath, then pushed open the door and entered. "Good morning, Sheriff." Gratitude that the man behind the desk wasn't the deputy widened her smile.

"Mornin'. Your boy is lookin' some better. Hope you brought him some clean clothes for the trial. Judge said he'd commence with the proceedings at ten o'clock. The witness has already been notified."

"What did he say about our substitution idea?"

"Said if he caught any such shenanigans in his court, he'd hang 'em both."

The flat way he delivered his pronouncement made Jesselynn wonder which side the sheriff was on. Earlier he'd seemed sympathetic to Daniel. Now she wasn't so sure. But did it matter? "Okay if I see him?"

"Suit yourself. Just leave that firearm here on my desk."

Jesselynn removed the pistol from her waistband and, laying it on the desk corner, followed the sheriff through the door to the cells. While Daniel still occupied the cell away from the windows, two other men were snoring on the cots in the larger cell with an outside view.

"Hey, boy, you got company," the sheriff called out.

Daniel dropped his hand from over his eyes and rolled to a sitting position. He shook his head as he stood and crossed to the bars. "Dey gonna hang me, Marse Jesse. I jist knows it."

"Now, Daniel, don't talk such a way. They have no proof you were even here." She spoke low, for his ears alone as soon as she caught his horrified glance at the other cell. "Your face looks much better."

"Yes, suh." He rested his forehead against the cold bars.

"Did you have breakfast?"

He nodded. "Marse Jesse, I want to go home."

She knew what he meant. Back to Twin Oaks, back to a time before the war when the family all lived and laughed and the slaves had been as much family as anyone. "I know. I'm going back to the camp for the others and will bring you clean clothes. You wash up good."

"I bin prayin'."

"So have we, Daniel. So have we. Surely God hears and will execute His justice." *Surely He will. Father God, please don't let us down, not at the cost of this child's life.* She knew she sounded like the preacher from home, but did she really believe they worshiped a God of justice? At least justice in the here and now? Eternal justice was much easier to believe in, but the daily kind? The war and the resulting carnage caused faith to waver, especially newly recovered faith like hers.

"I'm going back to get the others."

"Who take care of de horses?"

"Benjamin. Ophelia and Jane Ellen will stay in camp with the little ones." She made that decision as she spoke. The courtroom was no place for children or for a keening black woman if the judgment went against them.

"You hurry back?" The stark fear in his eyes made her wrap her hands around his on the bars.

"Have faith, Daniel." She knew she was saying the words as much for herself as for him. As she left the jailhouse, she glanced up the street to the town square. The gallows still stood, a mute testimony to man's idea of justice. She swung atop the mule and cantered out of town, not daring to gallop or he would be too winded to hitch to the wagon. There was no way she'd harness up one of the stallions today, and the mares had to stay with their foals.

While it seemed like hours, they were on their way back to town within the hour, bearing a packet for Daniel and all wearing clean clothes. Ophelia waved them off, tears streaming down her cheeks.

"Bring dat boy back here. We needs him." Her words echoed on the breeze and reverberated in Jesselynn's heart.

They stopped at the jail, and Jesselynn took the packet in for the sheriff, but the deputy sat at the desk instead.

"Sheriff's gone over to the courthouse. Left me to bring your boy over."

"I brought some clean clothes for Daniel."

"That rope don't care he got clean clothes."

Jesselynn stepped up to the desk and slammed her palms down on the wood surface. She leaned slightly forward on rigid arms. "*Mister* Rudy! You will take these into him or I will. The sheriff told me to bring them, and I surely wouldn't want to have to tell him you refused his orders." The thought of her pistol hanging heavy at her side pulled at her stiff arms. But she kept her gaze locked on the deputy in the chair.

He dropped his gaze first. "Go on back." He motioned over his shoulder with his thumb. "But don't say I didn't warn you." His eyes glinted mean like those of a weasel she'd once caught raiding the hen house. At least she'd been able to shoot it. Her trigger finger twitched. She didn't want to kill him, just wound him a bit. Bullies like that deputy never could tolerate pain of their own, no matter how they tried to inflict it on those less fortunate.

Daniel slipped into the clean pants and shirt while Jesse turned her back, then handed his dirty things through the bars. His hands shook so badly he dropped his shirt and had to pick it up again.

"Don't you go minding that cruel creature out there. Men like him's the reason we need so many judges." She rolled his things and tucked them under her arm. "You look right presentable now, so we'll just go before the judge and tell him the truth, and we can be on our way west." She forced every smidgen of confidence she could dredge up into her voice and tightened the smile that threatened to quiver to death at any moment. If she showed her anxiety, she knew Daniel would melt into a whimpering black puddle on the floor. "The truth will out." That phrase had been one of her mother's favorites.

She turned at the sound of the opening door to see the sheriff enter the aisle between the cells. He started to say something, saw the gun in her waistband, and strode forward with his hand out-stretched.

"Just give me the gun, nice and peaceable-like, and we won't have any trouble."

"That deputy didn't ask for it, so I didn't offer." Jesselynn handed the gun over, butt first.

"Thank you." The sheriff stuck it in his waistband and shook his head.

From the look in his eyes, Jesselynn felt right grateful she wasn't walking in the deputy's shoes. "How long until we head for the court-house?"

"'Bout half an hour. If you want to go over and get a place to sit, I'll be bringin' your boy over after I shackle his hands." He looked at Daniel. "You wouldn't be tryin' to run on me, would you, boy?"

Daniel shook his head. "No, suh."

"You mind if Meshach comes in to stay with him until then?"

"No, I guess not."

"Good. Then my aunt and I will go over and reserve our places." Jesselynn touched the back of Daniel's fingers, gripped so tightly around the bars that his knuckles grayed. "Not long now and we'll be on our way back to camp, then on to Independence." She took two steps toward the door, but his whimper, like a pup about dead, stopped her. *Lord, what can I say? What more can I do?*

*"Trust me."* She turned to see who had spoken. Nothing looked

different. No one had said a word. She stepped back to the bars so she and Daniel were about nose to nose. "The Lord says we got to trust Him."

"I know. I do, but . . ." Daniel closed his eyes and shook his head. His sigh nearly ripped her heart out. "I'm tryin', Marse Jesse, I'm tryin'."

"I know. Soon now." This time she hustled out the door as though alligators were snapping at her heels. Sending Meshach back inside with orders to stay with Daniel, she backed the team and drove the two blocks to the courthouse. Tying up in the shade, she helped Aunt Agatha down from the wagon. Agatha kept her own counsel after one look at her niece's face on returning to the wagon. The older woman checked the adjustment of her hat, picked up her knitting bag, and let Jesselynn take her arm on their way into the building.

A line of townspeople barred the door until Jesselynn led Agatha forward and whispered to the man in charge. "I'm Master Jesse Highwood, and it is my . . ." What could she call him? He was no longer a slave, but would being a freedman cause more trouble?

Aunt Agatha took a step forward. "The young man in question is my slave, and I am here to see that he is returned to me at the earliest convenience." Her harrumph made her seem to grow a foot taller.

The man started to say something, then nodded and turned to point to a row of benches just this side of a wooden railing. "Right over there, ma'am. You can be seated at any time."

"I will need room for one more."

"You take as much space as you'd like. I'll be lettin' in these other folks in a few minutes."

Jesselynn could feel the dagger stares slamming into the middle of her back. Ignoring the temptation to glare back at them, she followed her aunt down the aisle. Agatha left enough space on the bench for Jesselynn and Meshach and sat herself down, spreading her skirts and sitting board straight as she picked up her knitting needles and commenced the soft clicking of the ivory as the yarn became the arm of a sweater. She glanced once around the room, ignoring the whispers from all around them as if they were not even there. She could have been ensconced in front of a parlor fire for all the peace that seemed to flow out of her.

When a hiss of "nigger lovers" reached her ears, Jesselynn tried to imitate her aunt. If only she had knitting or mending along. She was wondering how men managed situations like this when more murmurs from behind made the hair tingle on the back of her neck. Couldn't these people understand or at least entertain the notion that Daniel hadn't been anywhere near Blytheville? Had no one told them the truth of the matter? If she'd had any hope they'd listen to her, she would have stood and demanded their attention.

Agatha put her hand on Jesselynn's arm, apparently sensing her agitation, then continued with her knitting. Jesselynn got the point, the silent admonition.

The sheriff entered from a side door, one hand on Daniel's upper arm, nearly dragging him forward. They took two chairs behind a table in front of the railing.

Jesselynn didn't need to turn around to be sure the courtroom was full. The hate rolled against her back like surf against a rock, splashing up and dashing back down, sucking at her as if to pull her under. She wanted to turn and search out Meshach. She needed to. But after a comforting glance at Daniel, she kept her back straight and her eyes forward.

"All rise." The sheriff stood as he spoke, pulling Daniel up with him. "Judge Stuart McCutcheon presiding."

Dressed in black from beaver hat to shiny boots, the man compelled attention. Not that he was good-looking in a conventional way, but his face brought to mind granite, cut square and clean. His eyes, sheltered under wild black brows, seemed those of a man who had seen far and wide, both in country and into men's souls.

"Be seated." His words precise, his voice rang with authority.

Jesselynn felt she should stand and salute. Instead, she sat.

The sheriff read from a paper he held open with both hands. "The state of Missouri accuses Daniel Highwood, here seated, to be the accomplice of James Gardner, already convicted of the murder of Avery Dunbar and hanged."

The judge, now seated, leaned forward. "How do you plead?"

Daniel tried to speak, but the words refused to come.

"He says he is not guilty, Your Honor." The sheriff laid his paper on the table and took his chair.

"They all say that!" The growl from the back of the room snapped the judge's head up.

"Quiet! If you cannot be quiet in my courtroom, you will leave." He stared around the room, nailing everyone to their seats. Someone coughed, then silence reigned. "That's better." He looked at the sheriff. "Tell us, Sheriff, how he came to be in your custody."

The sheriff stood and cleared his throat. As if reciting a grocery list, he told of the accusation, the chase, the capture, and the jailing. "And so, Your Honor, this court has been called to determine the guilt of this man." He gestured to Daniel, who stared at his hands.

"What's this I hear about a near riot at your jail?"

"Just a few of the hotheads attempting their own form of justice."

"I see. Who is it that accused this man?"

"Jason Stillwater. Said he'd seen this young man trail James Gardner into the store when he shot ol' Avery. But he disappeared before we caught the killer."

The judge looked around the room. "Stillwater, you here?"

"Yes, sir." A man who appeared to have seen better days stood with his hat in his hand, his fingers crippling the brim.

"Get on up here where I can talk with you." The judge pointed to a chair off to his right.

The sheriff crossed the room and held out a black Bible. "Lay your hand on it. Now, do you swear to tell the truth?"

"I do."

"Then sit."

The judge waited a moment for the air to settle. "Now, Stillwater, tell me what you saw. Not what you thought you saw and with no addin' to it, you hear?"

"Yes, sir. The night ol' Avery was kilt, I was comin' down the street. I saw a man walk into the store, and this here nigger." He pointed at Daniel.

"Enough! I said to tell only what you saw!"

The bench Jesse sat on shuddered with the thunder.

"Ah, yes, sir. I saw a skinny black man follow Gardner into the store."

"How do you know they were together?"

"He was followin', sneakylike. Both was strangers to Blytheville. Leastways, I din't know them."

"How do you know this young man is the one you thought you saw?"

"Same kinky hair, same kinda clothes, same height. I knows he the same ni—ah—boy."

*Where is Meshach?* Surely this wasn't evidence enough to hang Daniel.

"I see." The judge glanced around the room. "Anyone else see a stranger in town that night?"

Jesselynn started to rise, but Aunt Agatha put a hand on her arm. Jesselynn settled back in her seat. Daniel glanced her way, his eyes rolling in terror.

*God, help us, please. For mercy's sake, help us.*

# CHAPTER TWENTY-TWO

## Washington

"Bored, that's what I am." Louisa paced to the window again.

Three days Zachary had been going to his mysterious meetings. Three days she'd been stuck in a hotel room, and now she was out of yarn. Three days and they hadn't heard from Cousin Arlington. She'd written three letters, requested three stamps that her dear brother had yet to provide, and thought of at least thirteen ways she could do away with him.

She'd memorized the newspaper, had found it amazing the different views this paper had, compared to the Richmond *Gazette*. Why, according to this paper, the North had already won the war, no matter how many battles it lost. But reading between the lines, she discovered the same illness on this side also—leaders who were afraid to lead. Men who would rather talk and let others do the fighting. "Daddy, it's probably a good thing you died when you did. Succumbing to a broken heart might be even worse."

There, now she was talking out loud to herself on a consistent basis. "Zachary Highwood, where in heaven's name are you?" Her stomach complained at the length of time since she'd fed it, but she was under strict orders not to leave the room until he returned.

She crossed back to the window again and peered down at the street two stories below. Rain and incessant traffic had turned the dirt street into a quagmire. While some streets were brick or cobblestone, the lesser ones weren't, hence the mudhole.

Louisa fetched her bag from the nightstand drawer and counted her meager cash. Enough for yarn, if she could locate a store, and for coffee and a biscuit or something light in the dining room downstairs. Calling her brother every name she could think of, she donned her traveling jacket, pinned her hat firmly in place, arranged the net over her face and threw a cape around her shoulders. Sometimes it was easier to ask forgiveness than permission.

Refreshed by her tea and coffee cake in the dining room, she stopped under the portico that extended beyond the front doors. Rain had turned from sprinkles to sheets. Not even for yarn would she brave that downpour. Sighing, she turned back. Perhaps they had a library, or at least a shelf of books, where she could borrow one.

But when she made her request at the desk, the clerk shook her head. "Sorry, ma'am, but books we ain't got."

"Yarn, then? I've run out."

"I'll ask cook. She always has her needles going for our soldiers who be needing wool stockings all the time."

*That too is the same as for the South. But did their yarn come in blue?*

The young woman returned in a few minutes with a ball of undyed yarn, the same as Louisa used. "Here you go, ma'am. Good way to spend such a rainy afternoon."

Louisa thanked her and turned to head back up the stairs.

"Oh, ma'am," the clerk called, "I have a message delivered for your husband. Might you take it up with you?"

"Of course." Her curiosity running rampant, Louisa took the envelope and returned to her room. It was good quality paper, no return address or stamp, so someone had dropped it off. Zachary's name stood out in bold script, most likely masculine. She tapped the edge of the sealed envelope on the side of her finger. If it hadn't been sealed with wax, she could have steamed it open. But there was no way to redo wax, at least without having wax at her disposal. A candle might have worked, but all the lights were gas.

With a sigh, she set the envelope on the mantel, took her chair, and resumed her knitting. And here she'd thought the trip would be exciting. Dusk parted the rain curtain and eased onto the stage, welcomed by gas streetlights and people hurrying home so quickly that the streets cleared in a short time.

Still no Zachary. When she dropped two stitches turning the heel, she had to admit it. Fear had become a real presence in the room and in her mind. Something could have happened to him. After all, he was seeking contraband to take back to the South. While he'd warned her more times than she cared to count that there was danger here, she'd put aside his admonitions with a light heart. After all, they were doing the will of the Lord in seeking to care for His hurting children. She had prayed for guidance, and the ease with which they'd traveled seemed to be a confirmation of divine intervention.

But where was Zachary?

If Zachary didn't return, what could she do? Best throw herself on the mercy of Cousin Arlington, she decided.

Her hands fell idle, and she closed her eyes. *Dear Lord, please help us. Bring Zachary back safe and sound and provide the morphine that we came for.* Her prayer degenerated into a succession of pleadings, and throughout she felt as though her petitions went no further than the ceiling. *Oh, Lord, have you forsaken us?* The thought made her stomach flutter and her hands shake. Surely not. Surely Zachary was just busy and forgot the time.

*What if I can't get home again until after the war is over?*

"You goose! Now stop that." She picked up her knitting again and made a choice. "'The Lord is my shepherd; I shall not want. He maketh me to lie in green pastures: he leadeth me beside the still waters. He restoreth my soul. . . .'" By the time she'd recited the Twenty-third Psalm, the Ninety-first Psalm, and the Sermon on the Mount, she knew whereof her help lay. God said He would never leave her but would be her protector, and so He would.

Whether proper or not, she descended the stairs to the dining room again, this time for supper, smiling at the man who showed her to a small table in the corner. "Thank you."

"You were almost too late," the waiter said with a smile. "The beef is gone, but cook made a good chicken pie. And the bread is fresh, as always."

"That sounds delicious."

"Will your husband be joining you?"

"I think not. He must be caught up in business. Could I have a cup of tea now, please?"

"Of course."

Sitting there sipping her tea, she caught the eye of a woman, also alone, at a nearby table. Louisa nodded and smiled politely. At least she wasn't the only one eating by herself. She glanced around the rest of the room, then coming back to the other woman realized she had tears running down her cheeks, in spite of an apparent effort to stem the flow.

Louisa beckoned to the waiter. "Could you please bring my supper to that table?" At his nod, she picked up her cup and crossed the short distance. When the woman nodded, Louisa took the other chair and leaned forward.

"Sometimes telling total strangers is easier than talking with our loved ones. I'm Louisa Highwood." She waited for another sniff.

"Mrs. John Hinklen, Joanna." The woman dabbed at her eyes again. "Forgive me for such blubbering, but you see, I received notice two days ago that my husband, Major Hinklen, died of his wounds while trying to cross the Rappahannock. No matter how prepared I tried to be, I cannot quit crying. I thought perhaps some supper might help."

"How long since you've eaten anything?"

Joanna shrugged.

"Have you family?"

A shake of the head. "Not here. We're from New York, and we have no children."

When the waiter set her supper in front of her, Louisa turned to him. "Have you any soup for Mrs. Hinklen? That might sit better than the chicken pie."

"Yes, surely."

"Oh, and a pot of tea, please. A large pot."

An hour later, Louisa knew all about the Hinklens and hated the war even more—if that were possible.

But Zachary had yet to make an appearance.

# CHAPTER TWENTY-THREE

## Blytheville Courtroom

Jesselynn rose and spoke. "Your Honor, may I—"

"No. You'll get your turn."

Jesselynn sank back down on the bench.

Someone stood up behind them. "Yer Honor, I think I saw what Stillwater saw."

"Were you with Stillwater?"

"Not exactly. I was over by the livery, just bringin' my horse out to head on home."

"And what exactly did you see?"

"Ya know how ya see somethin' out of the corner of yer eye, but when you turn quick, you don't see nothin'? Well, that's kinda the way it was, but right on the front stoop of the store."

"Did you see the killer go in?"

"Not exactly, but I heard the shots."

"Thank you. You may sit down."

The judge stared around the room again. "Anyone else?"

Jesselynn started to raise her hand but found it clamped by Aunt Agatha. She glared at her aunt, but the hand held. With a jerk she freed herself and stood.

"Your Honor, Daniel Highwood was with us and has been with us since we left home in Kentucky. We were still in Springfield." Her words tripped faster as she neared the end.

"And you are. . . ?"

"Jesse Highwood, last remaining son of Captain Thaddeus Highwood of Midway, Kentucky. Ah . . . he instructed me to . . . ah . . . join my aunt in Springfield after . . ." She paused. How to tell the tale and yet not all of the tale?

"Your Honor, may I clarify things for you?"

Jesselynn looked down to see her aunt with one genteel hand raised in the air, her voice rich and smooth like warm molasses.

The judge nodded. But when Agatha started to rise, he raised one hand as if in blessing. "No, you may remain seated."

Jesselynn sat down, closing her gaping mouth with a snap.

"I am a widow, Your Honor. My husband, Hiram Highwood, was one of the early casualties of this terrible war. He believed he was needed by our President Jefferson Davis, and nothing anyone said would keep him from servin' with the Confederate army." She lifted a bit of cambric to her nose and to the edge of her eye, cleared her throat and, at the judge's nod, continued. "Some bushwhackers burned our farm to the ground, and since I had no funds with which to pay our taxes, even our land is gone. But with my dear nephew and our few remainin' slaves, I have determined to start over again in Oregon country. But, Your Honor, I am getting on in years, and I desperately need every hand I can get. I lived in Springfield all my life, and if you want I can send for letters from our pastor, from the doctor, and from anyone else you need, sayin' that I was still in Springfield at that time and all my household with me."

Jesselynn schooled her face to not reveal her surprise. Her household? They'd argued fiercely for her to accompany them. And they'd been living in a cave.

"I would be livin' there still were it not for the passing on of my dear husband." The handkerchief fluttered again. "Surely you would want to come to the aid of an agin' widow, destitute due to the travesty of war."

"And you would swear on the good book that Daniel Highwood was with you all the time?"

"I would, Your Honor." She leaned forward. "I will do so right now if you so decree."

"That will not be necessary." The judge folded his hands on the desk top. He looked to the sheriff and then around the room.

Jesselynn held her breath.

The judge picked up a wooden gavel beside him and slammed it down.

She jumped, her air whooshing out.

"Free him. I find this young man innocent due to lack of sufficient evidence to convict him."

A groan rumbled through the room, and snarling could be heard, nearly covering an expletive or two from the direction of the witness.

"Silence!" The gavel thundered again. The judge was forced to slam wood on wood again, but the room quieted down. "Now, Sheriff, remove those shackles so these folks can be on their way." Glancing around the room, his face a study in stern lines and frown slashes, he continued. "And if I hear of disruption of any kind with the intent to harm anyone in my jurisdiction, I will personally nail that scumbag's hide to the nearest barn. Is that understood?"

Jesselynn felt extremely grateful he wasn't directing his diatribe at her. As soon as the sheriff had unshackled Daniel, she, her aunt, and the young man strode up the aisle, looking neither to the right nor to the left. Meshach met them at the door and closed it behind them.

"Where were you?" She kept up the pace even as she asked the big man. "We saved you a place."

"Didn't you see? No darkies down in the front, only in a bitty little section at de back. I stayed dere. Much better." He pushed open the door and ushered them out to where the sun caught them full in the face.

Daniel stopped and lifted his face to the warmth. "Thank de Lawd, I can feel the sun again."

"We need to thank Him for all He has done." Aunt Agatha stopped at the wagon and waited to be assisted to her chair. "I sure do wish we could leave that camp right now and, as the Lord's Word says, 'shake off the dust' of this place from our feet. You think it might be safe to travel during the day?"

Jesselynn took the reins and backed up the horses, since they were hemmed in on both sides with other teams and wagons, then headed them up the street and toward the camp. "All we need is for someone to see the horses, and then we'll have more trouble than a fox in a henhouse. Stealing them and selling them to the army would net someone better'n a year's wages. I sure do pray the sheriff keeps his deputy under lock and key for the next several days. He didn't look like he took too kindly to the judge's final speech."

"I heard the sheriff say somethin' 'bout one more misstep and he was fired." Daniel huddled right behind the wagon seat, casting fear-filled glances back down the road. "I surely do hope the sheriff keep him busy in town."

"What if you and Daniel take the horses and head out across country? Surely you could stay away from farms and such, and we'll go the roads with Benjamin as lookout. We could meet up the Kansas Road aways. Anything to get out of here safely."

Meshach sat, his elbows propped on his knees, and stared at the rumps of the team. He shook his head slowly, teeth worrying his lower lip. "I don't know. If we get stopped without you, we in bad trouble."

"I know. But if I take the horses, then you'd have Aunt Agatha to ward off any unwanted attention." She turned to her aunt. "You were magnificent in that courtroom."

Agatha looked up from her knitting. "Thank you. If you ask me, I think we need to travel on right now, and if you go with the horses, the rest of us will manage. If need be, I know how to use a firearm too. Hiram—may his soul rest in peace—taught me before he left for the war."

Jesselynn shook her head. "Aunt Agatha, you're just full of surprises today." She could feel the smile stretching cheeks that hadn't found a lot to smile about lately. "What do you think?" She glanced at Meshach.

"Don' seem like no best way. Just hope God's sendin' angels around us, 'cause we might be needin' dem."

"Hope doesn't do anything, young man. Prayer does it all." The word came from over their shoulders.

"Yes'm."

"Yes, ma'am." They spoke at the same time.

Jesselynn felt like whistling. Daniel was free, and so were they.

When they reached camp, Ophelia had a meal waiting and all the boxes packed. As soon as they ate, they loaded the wagon and hitched the team of Chess and Roman back in the traces. Standing in a circle, they bowed their heads while Meshach prayed.

"God in heaven, we thank you for saving Daniel from the hangman today. Thank you for watching over us so wise and good, for keepin' us safe. Thank you dat you are puttin' legions of angels all around us to protect us from de enemy. De Bible say you are our sure defense, and we thank you for dat. Keep us safe, Lawd, so we can praise yo' holy name. Amen."

They echoed his amen and helped Aunt Agatha up into the wagon, tossing the boys in after her. Daniel, with one of the guns at his side, took up a seat on a box in the rear with Meshach and Ophelia on the wagon seat. Every time they loaded, the wagon seemed heavier laden. Jesselynn had already decided they would need two wagons and four teams of oxen to transport all the needed supplies for the long march to Oregon. Nightly she stewed over where the money would come from. The stash from the sale of the horses dwindled every time she went to town.

Benjamin held the lead ropes to the mares and filly while Jesselynn mounted Ahab. *Lord, I sure do hope this is what you want us to do.* Jesselynn took the lead lines and watched the two foals galloping and kicking up their heels. They darted around their dams and then charged off again. "You two better save your energy. You're goin' to need it later."

"Dey feisty all right." Benjamin took one of the lead lines. "We might shoulda broke dem to halter. Keep 'em safer dat way."

"Tonight when we stop." She rode up beside the wagon. "Once we reach the road, we'll find a good place to camp and wait for you. Watch for a white rag on a branch."

Meshach nodded. "Go with God." He flapped the reins, and with a groan and screech the wagon eased forward. Chess and Roman pricked their ears forward and plodded on out of the camp.

"You too." Jesselynn and Benjamin waited for only a moment before heading north to go cross-country. She'd asked one of the shopkeepers where the other roads ran and had drawn Meshach a rough map for the best way to stay away from Blytheville. While it would take longer that way, she knew it was for the best. They should meet up by nightfall, but just in case, she and Benjamin had saddlebags of supplies and their quilts rolled in deer hides tied behind their saddles.

After a mile or two, Jesselynn took all the lead lines and let Benjamin travel a bit ahead to keep them out of some farmer's territory. When they crested one of the many rolling hills, he'd steer them away from the secret valleys where cattle grazed and wheat and hayfields glinted green in the dancing breeze. A dog or two barked at their passing as they bypassed swamps in the lowlands and ponds where blackbirds sang and bullfrogs bellowed their spring love songs.

"Fish taste mighty fine for suppah." Benjamin reined in his stallion and let him drink at a shoreline. Jesselynn let hers have a few mouthfuls before pulling Ahab and the mares back. One of the foals stuck a foot in the water and leaped backward as if he'd been bitten.

"That they would." Jesselynn studied the terrain ahead of them. The land glowed golden in the setting sun. They had yet to come across the Kansas Road, and since they'd been traveling more or less west by northwest, she was beginning to feel niggles of apprehension. Had the shopkeeper been less than honest with them? Or had they not made the time she thought they would?

Most of all, had they made a terrible mistake in splitting the family and going two separate ways?

She dismounted and, removing Ahab's bridle, let him graze along with the mares. Both foals now had turned to nursing, their brush tails flicking from side to side. "If you think you could catch some fish in a half hour or so, give it a try. Surely we'll find the road pretty soon, and we'll get a fire started right away."

Benjamin took his fishing line and hook from his saddlebag and made his way farther up the bank. She could hear him cutting a willow branch for a pole and knew he would look under rocks in the shallows for periwinkles for bait. She trapped a grasshopper with one hand but let it go. True, grasshoppers made good bait, but she dared not leave the grazing horses to go look for Benjamin. Both foals flopped over on their sides, ribs rising and falling with their sleeping breaths. Legs straight out, they looked worn-out, like toys a child dropped when tired of them.

Jesselynn propped her back against the trunk of a willow tree, knowing that if she lay down, she'd be out just like the foals. The contented crunching of the grazing horses worked like a lullaby, the blackbirds' trills drifting on the cooling air.

She jerked awake and forced herself to her feet. What was she doing nodding off when who knew how many miles they had left to go before reaching the Kansas Road? She whistled and waited for Benjamin to answer. When no answer came, she sighed. He'd probably found a good fishing hole beyond earshot. The thought of fried fish for supper made her forgive his carelessness.

She whistled again and listened.

Nothing but a blackbird answered. A swallow swooped by, its open beak catching bugs over the water. Ahab lifted his head, ears pricked to the north. She clamped a hand over his nose just before he whinnied.

# CHAPTER TWENTY-FOUR

"Marse Jesse?"

Jesselynn let her breath out on a sigh, not aware she'd been holding it until her shoulders sagged. "Over here." She stroked Ahab's soft nose and let him return to his grazing. She should have known that he recognized the person arriving even if she couldn't. He hadn't acted as if it were a stranger, come to think of it. *Silly goose*, she scolded herself, *to get in a bother like that.*

Benjamin swung into view, grinning wide as the Missouri sky with a string of perch over his shoulder. "Told you we have fish for supper."

"We should have left a while ago." She tightened the saddle girth and buckled the chin strap to Ahab's bridle.

"Sorry. Dem fishes bitin' so good, I din' want to stop." Benjamin handed her the lead lines and mounted Domino, tying the string of fish to his saddle. "Least de horses had a good rest."

The evening star hung in the western sky when they trotted out on the Kansas Road looking both north and south. No sight of Meshach and the wagon—not that she'd really expected any. Still, she'd been hoping. Could the wagon have gone by this point already? Not likely. While she and Benjamin had made many detours, still they'd followed a fairly straight route—she hoped. At least they found the road, but then any route west would have eventually done just that.

Another thing—how far south of Fort Scott were they, and

finally, where should they set up camp? The questions buzzed like angry yellow jackets in her mind.

"You think they've gone by?"

Benjamin, who'd been studying the surface of the road, shook his head. "Roman ain't. Can always tell his prints."

"Could another wagon or wagons have wiped those out?" She wished she'd been paying more attention to tracking, but then since Benjamin was so good at it, why did she have to? Questions, questions.

They could hear a dog barking off to the west. The road ran along the eastern edge of a gently rolling open prairie with a series of hills and draws, the likes of which they'd come through to the east. They'd crossed a creek a mile or so behind, but what could they hang a marker on out here?

Benjamin returned from a jaunt north. "Farms ahead, both sides of de road. We make camp back on de creek?"

"I suppose so."

Benjamin swung down from his horse and, with the reins looped over his arm, set about gathering stones.

"What are you doin'?"

"Makin' dem a marker." He piled the stones on the right-hand side of the road and then, a couple of feet due east, piled a few more. Wiping his hands on his pants, he mounted Domino again and headed east. A willow thicket both signaled the location of water and hid it from sight. Rotting stumps showed where settlers had taken out the larger trees for firewood or lumber.

The horses pushed through the willows to drink, Ahab raising his head and looking back the way they had come. When he dropped to drink again, Jesselynn felt her shoulders relax.

Within a short time, they had hobbled the horses to graze, the foals had nursed, and Jesselynn dug in her saddlebag for the flint to start the fire. She and Benjamin gathered dead branches from the thicket, and after clearing out a patch of grass down to the dirt to keep from starting a prairie fire, they laid the wood and soon had a fire blazing. Jesselynn hunkered down on one of the stumps and studied the flames. She should be scaling fish. She knew that, but the knowing and the doing were two different things.

What if someone had stopped the wagon? What if the deputy had come after them in spite of the sheriff's orders? She about gagged on the *what if*s and threw herself to her feet. Digging a hunt-ing knife out of her saddlebag, she set about the scaling, using the stump as a table. Work always held worrying at bay.

"How are they goin' to see those stones in the dark?" She turned to Benjamin, scale-covered hands on her hips.

"Dey won't. Meshach pull up someplace to wait till dawn. We wait here till dey find us."

"I wish we'd never split up like this." She dug down in her sad-dlebag for a tin of grease and dropped some in the frying pan. They'd be eating mush if it weren't for Benjamin and his fishing. She dusted cornmeal over the fish and laid them one by one in the sizzling pan. She had to add wood often, since the branches were so small, but the fire was hot enough to fry supper, and that was all that mattered.

"I'se gonna set me some snares. See what we kin get." Benjamin spoke from directly behind her, making her jump.

"Can't you warn me? You're quieter even than Meshach." She knew she sounded grumpy, but frying fish didn't keep her mind oc-cupied, and the worries crept back in. No wonder Ophelia sang a lot. Kept the mind busy so she couldn't worry.

"Sorry. I'll whistle when I come back so's you don' go and shoot me."

"Thanks." The quiet but for the grazing horses should have been peaceful. Frogs sang in the bulrushes. The fried fish smelled heavenly. She set her mind to thinking of how to keep the fried fish overnight so the others could have some when they arrived in the morning.

Supper seemed extra quiet without Sammy and Thaddeus with all their giggles and Thaddeus's eternal questions. She even missed Meshach's reading from the Bible, and since she'd left her writing case in the wagon, all she could do was stare into the fire until her eyes refused to stay open any longer. Since Benjamin said he'd take first watch, she wrapped herself in her quilt and tried to sleep.

Praying didn't help. She'd asked God's blessing and protection for every person she'd ever known and still she lay awake. Until Ben-jamin started singing to the horses. His rich voice singing the songs of his people, of glory by and by, overlaid the songs of the frogs and peepers, and she slept.

———

Ahab whinnied halfway through the morning. The answering

bray could only come from Roman. Jesselynn whooped and danced a shuffle step around the fire pit. She stirred what ashes remained, added thin twigs, and blew on the few glowing coals. A couple of dry willow leaves, an extra puff, and the embers came to life, sending up a tendril of smoke before bursting into flame. They'd have coffee before long.

"Jesse, we's here." Thaddeus, standing beside Meshach on the wagon seat, waved, his face one big smile.

Meshach stopped the team on the first level spot and set the brake. Thaddeus scrambled over the wheel and hit the ground running, straight into Jesselynn's outstretched arms.

"Why you left us?" He put one hand on either side of her face and stared into her eyes. "You don't do that no more."

She kissed his cheek and stood up with him in her arms. "You know we have to keep the horses hidden, and when the wagon is traveling during the day, what else could I do?"

His frown said he was thinking hard. When he shrugged and squirmed, she set him down and, after greeting the others, looked up at her aunt.

"Everything all right?"

"Right as rain. Help me down, please. I about rocked my legs to sleep." Once on the ground, she settled her skirts and looked around the camp, if it could be called that. "We drove until near dark before we found a good place to stop, but other than a wave from a couple of wagons passing by, we talked to no one. Meshach kept looking for a marker, but I never saw a thing when he pulled off the road. How did he know?"

"Two small piles of rocks off the right side of the road."

"Well, my lands." She reached back in the wagon for the coffeepot. "Is there fresh water here?"

"A small creek. Benjamin dug out a hole so we can dip clear water. I'll get it."

When she returned, Jane Ellen had the boys looking for wood, Benjamin was skinning the three rabbits he'd snared, and Meshach had the team hobbled and grazing. Since they'd eaten the remaining fish for breakfast, Ophelia set one rabbit to simmering and cut up the other two for frying. The fragrance of coffee and frying rabbit soon called to them all. Hard-dried biscuits tasted much better dunked in coffee.

They took turns napping in the afternoon heat and at dusk headed north toward Fort Scott, with Jesselynn wondering how they would circumvent the fort when they got there. Just before dawn Daniel returned from one of his scouting forays to wave them off on a track heading west.

"Onliest way to get by de fort," he reported.

They had to dry camp that night and ration the water barrel, letting only the mares get all they wanted so they would have enough milk for the foals.

"We better get another water barrel," Jesselynn said as they ate dried biscuits and leftover fried rabbit. "I'd hoped to wait until Independence, but . . ."

"What we got, four more days?"

"Maybe six." *I wish I could talk to someone about Independence. Is there a fort near there? How will I get enough money for two wagons and all we need? How long, oh, Lord, how long will I have to make all the decisions?*

She knew the answer to that. Until the war was over. Until she could bring the horses back to Twin Oaks. She'd kept the thought at bay, fighting to keep it from living full blown in her mind. If she made it to Oregon, how would she ever bring the horses back to Twin Oaks?

Three nights later they smelled smoke before they saw the orange glow in the sky.

"Somebody's barn burnin'." Meshach clucked the team into a hard trot. Perhaps they could help. Riding Ahab, Jesselynn leaned forward and let him out. Within three strides, he was running free, for the first time in months. The even beat of his hooves sang to her memory of mornings on the track at home, brought back the laughter of old Joseph when he punched down the stopwatch, the smell of horse sweat and good leather. She slowed her horse, swerving to follow Benjamin into a farmyard. Not only the barn was blazing but the house too, even though the distance between the two should not have set one from the other.

Ahab snorted and tried to turn and leave, but she kept him steady with a firm hand. When Benjamin called to her, she dismounted and led Ahab over to a tree where Benjamin knelt by a woman who appeared to have crawled there for safety. But she hadn't been safe. The blood from the gash on her head and another from a bullet wound in her right shoulder said as much.

"Who did this?" Jesselynn handed her reins to Benjamin and pillowed the woman's head on her knees.

"Quantrill's Raiders. They . . . took . . . our . . . cattle. When . . . John . . . my husband . . . shot one of them . . ." The pause lengthened. "Th-they . . ." Her voice grew fainter.

"Don't try to talk. We'll find a doctor." She'd have missed the shake of the woman's head had she not been watching her so closely.

As if she hadn't heard, the woman continued. "They . . . shot . . . John . . . and . . . fired . . . the . . . house. The . . . children . . ."

Jesselynn knew no one would have survived that blazing inferno. With a crash the beams of the barn collapsed. The woman sagged, gagged, and was gone.

Jesselynn laid her back in the dust. The house, too, fell in on itself. A dog howled, a mournful lament that sent shivers up her spine.

Benjamin went to the wagon that had just arrived. Meshach joined Jesselynn beside the body. "How come no neighbors come to help?"

"Quantrill's Raiders." As she said the words, an idea slugged her in the chest. "They must have left just before we got here. We could have run into them. Oh, Lord, our God." Tears gathered and broke. She wasn't sure if they were tears of sadness for the woman and her family or tears of gratefulness that they'd been spared. Surely the raiders would have killed them all to get such horses as theirs.

"He surround us wid angels, just like we asked." Meshach got to his feet. "You see any other bodies?"

"Ask Benjamin. I've been right here." The howl rose again, eerie. "Do you see the dog?"

"Over by de house." Benjamin joined them. "Onliest thing alive, far as I can see."

"Get de shovel. We bury her, den get outa here."

"No, we just leave. The neighbors will come by when they know it is safe." Jesselynn wiped her eyes with the back of her hand. "Come on, let's get out of here."

"But . . ."

She snatched her reins out of Benjamin's hand and threw herself into the saddle. All they needed was to be caught here and accused of killing the family and starting the fire. They'd all be hanged.

They pulled back to a slow trot after they'd covered enough distance from the burning to be safe. Jesselynn settled into her saddle, fighting to keep her mind from replaying the death scene. No wonder people spoke of *The Raiders* in hushed tones. Fear did that to a body.

When the sun rose, she hated to stop. The closer they were to Independence, the safer they'd be—at least from the Raiders. But as the area became more settled, a new danger arose.

"Hey, Marse Jesse, you see dat dog followin' us?" Benjamin motioned with his head.

Jesselynn looked back to see a black dog, part shepherd from the look of him, with a patch of white around one ear. "How long he been with us?"

"Saw him at first light."

"Where do you think he's from? Someone's goin' to be real sad, missing their dog."

"No, I think they all dead."

"Oh." What more could she say? Looked like another war victim had joined their journey.

Where could they hide the horses until they could purchase their supplies and head out with a wagon train? And for how long? The farther north they traveled, the less the grass had sprouted. For the horses it wasn't a problem; for oxen it would be.

# CHAPTER TWENTY-FIVE

## Independence, Missouri

Jesselynn rode past camps of staring sojourners before she found Independence proper.

"Hey, Chess, if all of these people are wantin' to go on to Oregon, there might not be room enough left over for us." The horse twitched his ears and trotted on. Riding Chess was immeasurably easier than riding Roman. Cows bellowed, horses whinnied, children ran screaming after one another, two men stood toe to toe slugging at each other while a crowd cheered them on. Wash hung from lines strung between wagons and tent poles. The smell that assaulted her nostrils could have used a stiff wind to blow it clear to the Mississippi. By then it might be bearable.

Two dogs ran in front of her horse, setting him to shying and her to paying better attention. Wouldn't that be wonderful to fall in the slop that Chess's hoofs clopped through?

The recent rain hadn't helped—that she knew for certain—but still, had no one dug latrines? Or if they had, didn't the people gathered here use them?

She stopped at the first store she came to and asked how to find a wagon train to join.

"Sorry, son, but most of the trains are already made up, just waitin' for the grass to grow."

"But surely there must be one that will take on two more wagons. We'll more than carry our own load."

"If'n there is such, you tell yer pa to come on in here and do the dealin'. Nobody's going to talk with a young boy like you." The bearded man behind the counter scratched his belly through a shirt that might once have been white.

"Like I said, my daddy is too sick to leave our camp. He sent me ahead to . . ."

"Sorry, can't help you. Next?"

Jesselynn turned away. It didn't help that this was the third time she'd heard those same words, or close to it. She thought of taking out the gold coins in her bag and dropping them on the counter, but from the looks of the crowd, that didn't seem to be a good idea either.

Besides, from what she could tell, supplies cost about twice what she'd heard before. Or more. Maybe they ought to set up an outfitting business of their own. Surely Meshach could get work here. There were enough wheels to fit and repair to keep a hundred blacksmiths busy.

At the end of the fruitless day, she asked directions for the post office. At least she ought to be able to find that. On the way she noticed another store, this one closed for the day. She'd try there tomorrow. She flipped Chess's reins around the hitching rail and took the two steps to the post office in one stride. The four letters the postman handed her when she said her name made up in part for the futility of the day. Two from Richmond, one from Sergeant White, and the last from Lucinda. She stuck them in her pocket to read back at camp and strode next door to an apothecary. She chose a peppermint stick for each of the boys and a packet of horehound drops and another of lemon drops. They'd all earned a treat. After studying the man's wares, she promised him she'd return to load up her simples box, then headed back to camp.

The heavy feeling persisted, just like the gray skies that hung low enough to snag with a fish pole. In spite of the gray she reminded herself that even though she hadn't found a wagon train, she'd learned plenty about getting ready.

And a possible way to make some money. She nudged Chess into a canter all the way back to the river bottom where they'd made camp.

"No wagon train, but we got letters." She dug them out of her pocket. "Which do you want to hear first? From Richmond or from Lucinda?" She'd keep Barnabas's letter to read by herself later.

"Lucinda." Her black members spoke as one.

Jesselynn opened the envelope and withdrew the ink-dotted sheet. While Lucinda could write well enough, she had a hard time keeping the quill from blobbing ink.

" 'Dear Marse Jesse and everyone,

We miss you so bad here. But thank the Lord we are alive and well. Joseph say to tell you he found some tobacco seeds, so we will have some crop in. Thanks to the garden and Joseph setting snares, we been eating well enough. Many have died of influenza, but we are safe so far. Black wagons carry bodies to the cemetery often. Men come home to die if they can.

I thank the Lord He keeping you safe. Tell Ophelia we are glad she and Meshach will have a baby. When will you come home? I got a letter from Miss Louisa. She working at the hospital. What her mother say about that, hmm? We digging the fields with a man pulling the plow. Goes slow.

Crocus come up, war or no war. Lord keep you in His care.

Lucinda' "

Jesselynn let the silence lengthen. She knew the others were thinking of home just as she was. Somehow she could not erase the picture of the big house. Twin Oaks still lived and flourished in her mind.

The letters from Louisa and Carrie Mae told of Christmas in Richmond, what was happening in the legislature, and the things they'd made for Christmas gifts. Zachary added a note of his own, barely legible with his left hand, but he had cared enough to write.

" 'You take good care of those horses, you hear? We need them to start over, but I know you know that and are doing all you can. If I could sneak back to Twin Oaks I would, but I am pretty hard to disguise, missing a foot and hand, let alone the eye.

Louisa is still grieving for her lieutenant, but I keep telling her he is dead, not just missing. She refuses to believe that, since there is no proof, but she must get on with her life. Carrie Mae tries to introduce her to young men, but you know our Louisa, stubborn to the hilt. I do not know where she gets that trait. Of course, none of the rest of us suffer from that affliction. May our God and Father keep you all safe. I trust that one day we shall see each other again—this side of heaven, I do hope.

Your loving brother,
Zachary' "

By the time she'd finished reading the letters, Sammy and Thaddeus had gone off to play, and the rest of them, other than Jane Ellen, were drying their eyes. Ophelia rocked gently, then hummed, and finally her song bathed the others in comfort. It was a deep river for sure, between them and home. How many more rivers would they cross before they found a new home, a free home, a safe home?

When the song died away, Jesselynn pulled herself back to the moment. "While I'm searching for a wagon master and train, you get Ahab back in condition," she instructed Benjamin.

His eyes rounded, along with his mouth. "For racin'?"

She nodded. "But you have to keep it a secret. No one can know about him."

Now he rolled his eyes, along with shaking his head. "Where we got space for dat?"

Jesselynn turned to Meshach. "I know the chance we're taking, but I can't figure any other way to get enough money to outfit us. We need two wagons and at least eight oxen, along with all the rest." She raised her hands and dropped them again. "Any other suggestions?"

"Like you said the other day, I could find work."

"I know. And you better do so. Daniel and Benjamin will have to guard the camp."

"I can graze the horses." Jane Ellen looked up from the willow basket she was weaving.

"And I can help guard the camp. No one expects an old woman to be able to shoot a gun." Aunt Agatha laid the shirt she was sewing for Jesselynn down in her lap. "Besides, with you off racing Ahab, Patch will let us know if anyone is comin'." They'd named the dog that had insisted on joining up.

The dog, lying beside the rocker, raised one ear, the tip of it flopping forward. For some reason he had adopted Aunt Agatha as his mistress, yet at the same time kept a watchful eye on the boys. If Sammy strayed too far from the fire by himself, Patch would go round him up and herd him back. He'd obviously been a cow or sheep dog.

Jesselynn half smiled and shook her head gently. All of them were learning that they could do things they never thought they could or would have to do.

And the dog, who'd shadowed them when they left the burning farm, adopted them so quickly it felt as if he'd always been part of the family.

When Jesselynn thought about the last week, she had to remind herself that God was in control and had a plan for all the goings-on. They'd rushed to get to Independence, and none of the wagon trains were heading out yet, though one wagon master had said "any day now." She still felt guilty for not burying the woman at the farm, even though she knew that staying there long enough to do the job right could have caused them all sorts of trouble. Ahab's throwing a shoe didn't help much either. Cost them a couple of hours. All the rush, and now they waited. And tried to find a wagon train.

For the next couple of days she rode on into Independence in the early morning, talked to as many people as she could, and came home to shake her head again. She had ordered two wagons, longer and sturdier than the one they were using now, and had brought back heavy canvas to make coverings for the hoops. Aunt Agatha, Jane Ellen, and Ophelia had been stitching on the covers ever since Jesselynn hauled it into camp. Meshach had fashioned leather hand-pieces like sailors used to help force the needles through the heavy fabric. Jesselynn planned to sell the present wagon when she sold Chess.

Ophelia and Jane Ellen dried fish and rabbit, whatever Daniel could bring in above what they ate every day.

One morning she and Meshach rode in to town together, he bareback on the mule, his sack of tools slung over one shoulder, his quilt rolled in a deerskin over the other.

"I'm not so sure I think this is a good idea." Jesselynn sighed and shook her head. She seemed to be doing a lot of that lately.

"Anythin' I can bring in'll buy more flour and beans. Could be I find us some oak for a barrel too. Wish now I made another back at de cave."

"Pray that I find us a wagon train today. With all the people gathered here, there has to be more trains being organized." She squeezed Chess into a faster trot. "Keep your eyes open for oxen. I heard there were more coming in."

"Got money enough to pay for dem?"

Jesselynn shrugged. "We will soon enough." Checking out the horse racing was another thing to watch and figure how best to win.

She left Meshach at the first blacksmith shop and returned to the store that had been closed the evening before. The proprietor smiled when she entered.

"Name's Robinson. How can I help you, son?"

"My family is here to head out on the trail, and we need supplies. And a wagon train."

"You came to the right place. Just this mornin' I heard of a new train formin' up under a man named Torstead."

"Really?" Her heart leaped at the news. "How can I, what do I—"

"Whoa." He held up both hands. "Got a bargain for ya. Buy what you need here—I got about the best prices around—and I give you a list of suppliers for what else you need. No one on my list cheats my customers, or I don't send them no more." He leaned on the counter, propped up by stiff elbows. "Now, what do ye need? Wagons, oxen, feed, flour—I got a list here that most wagon masters go by." He slapped a piece of paper on the counter.

"Already ordered the wagons. Need most everything else."

"How many folks in your party?"

Jesselynn mentally counted. "Nine. Two little ones." She didn't dare tell him about the horses.

"Hmm." The man scratched out some numbers on a slate and held it out for Jesselynn to read.

"Now, that is the amount for each person, you understand."

Jesselynn nodded and returned to her reading. Two hundred pounds of flour, seventy-five pounds of bacon, five pounds of coffee, two of tea, twenty-five pounds of sugar—brown the best—half a bushel of dried beans, one bushel of dried fruit, two pounds of saleratus, ten pounds of salt, half a bushel of cornmeal.

When she started multiplying by six—she counted Jane Ellen as a child—she felt her jaw begin to drop. A keg of vinegar, rope, tools, kitchen things, clothing, a small stove—where would they store all this? And she hadn't added grain for the mares yet.

"That thar list is mighty complete."

"I can see that." She read a section on taking milk cows. How she wished that were possible. "And you say you can supply all of this?" *And we've got the forge and Meshach's tools. Leastways we got our guns already, but we need more ammunition.*

"Either me or my list of suppliers." Robinson scratched his chin. "Goin' west takes all a man has and then some." He nodded as he spoke. "Better to take extra food and water than trinkets like furniture and things. You can always make your own once you get there."

"Well, sir, thank you for the advice." She rolled her lips together and, chewing on the bottom one, slit her eyes in thought. "Guess I better go find that Mr. Torstead, then."

"Wolf, he goes by Gray Wolf."

Jesselynn left the store with the name Gray Wolf Torstead branded on her mind and no idea where to find the man who owned the name.

He was a half-breed. What would Aunt Agatha have to say to that? And what if he wouldn't take them on? The fears hammered in time with Chess's easy trot. Robinson at the store thought the man was camped southeast of the square. All she had to go on was a name: Gray Wolf Torstead. Even the name intrigued her.

By late afternoon she felt as though she were chasing a will-o'-the-wisp or a swamp light. Many people she asked had seen him, but he'd gone somewhere else and they weren't sure where. When she finally located his simple camp, she dismounted and took up residence on a rock. Better to wait for the mountain to come to her than hightailing it after a mountain that moved around more than a hound hot on a rabbit trail.

———

If frustration had a name, today it was Wolf—Gray Wolf Torstead for a full name, but few called him anything other than Wolf. Instead of snarling as he wished, he stood silent, dark eyes blank, body still as his namesake on a hunt. He wanted to be wagon master of this forming train about as much as he wanted to dig an arrow out of his thigh, something he'd been forced to do some years in the past. The scar reminded him of that whenever he stripped to tribal dress.

He listened to the two men arguing and dreamed of home. Of the land of the Oglala Sioux, where the rivers ran clear, not the muddy brown of the Kansas, and the wind blew clean, not fetid as it did in this morass of an encampment. The smoke of cooking fires and blacksmith coals hung like that of a far-off forest fire, burning both nostrils and eyes.

He waited.

"So what do you think, Mr. Wolf?" The shorter of the two turned to the silent third of their party.

"Just Wolf. No mister."

"Ah, sorry." The man scrubbed a hairy hand across an equally hairy face. He reminded Wolf of a badger, pointed skinny nose, beady eyes, and scrabbling for a toehold where there might be none. When backed into a corner, as he was being now, he would fight to the finish.

"Can they join us or not?"

"Only if they have sufficient supplies and a wagon that will go the distance. I inspect everything. Anything less will slow the entire train." He knew from the glances they exchanged that when he spoke the language of his father, white men were surprised. He looked more Sioux than English. Before he died, his father had taught him well. To read, to write and do sums, to speak the good King's English, as Eviar Torstead called it. He also taught his son smatterings of Norwegian, Eviar's native tongue. His mother's people taught him to walk tall on the land and be one with horse and wind.

This would be his last train. The only reason he took the position of wagon master was for the gold it would bring. Gold that would buy guns for his people to hunt the buffalo, knives to skin them with, and blankets to warm them in the winter. Thanks to his father, he believed that whites and Indians could live in peace, learning from each other and sharing the riches of the land.

Everything always came back to the land.

While keeping his thoughts as his own, he waited for a response.

The taller man spat into the mud. "Ain't no breed goin' to inspect my provisions." He turned the last words into a sneer.

"Then you will not be joining my wagon train." Wolf heard the *my* and wondered when he had accepted responsibility. Up till then it had been *their*.

"You gonna let him talk like that?" The spitter spun on the badger.

"He's the boss. He promised to get us to Oregon, and I aim to follow his good sense. He's made the trip four times as a scout and knows whereof he speaks."

"Well, I ain't lettin' no breed tell me what to do." He spat again, this time within inches of Wolf's boot.

"That's your choice, mister." Badger nodded to Wolf and the two walked away, leaving the spitter sputtering.

"Sorry about that."

"Not your fault. We'll have enough trouble on the trail without someone like him along."

"Trouble? You don't mean Indian trouble—oh, pardon me, but do you?"

Wolf shook his head. "There's plenty else waitin' for the unwary. 'A wise man counts the cost before he begins to build his barn.' " Quoting from Scripture came easily to him. After all, he'd learned to read from that one book his father kept with him always.

"You said that right. I'm hopin' one day to do just that, build me a barn, but out in Oregon Territory. They say the trees are so big you only need one to build a house. That true?"

"Depends on if you saw up lumber or build a log house." Wolf paused, catching sight of a slim young boy sitting in his campsite. "Looks like I have someone waiting for me."

"I'll be goin' on, then. How soon you think we might be ready to head west?"

"When I'm certain everyone is ready."

"Oh, 'course." Badger sketched a nod and turned away, settling his hat more firmly on his head as he went.

Wolf kept track of the man out of the corner of his eye, all the while aware of his visitor. If someone had sent the boy, he had to know Wolf wasn't looking for any single young men to join his train. Singles, either male or female, spelled nothing but trouble on a wagon train.

# CHAPTER TWENTY-SIX

## Washington

"Miss, a box came for you."

Louisa turned at the clerk's call. "Thank you." She turned to Mrs. Hinklen, who appeared to have spent as sleepless a night as had Louisa. "You go on and order us coffee while I take this up to my room."

Surprised at the weight, she took the stairs as quickly as possible, what with trying to keep from stepping on the hem of her skirt and not drop the box. Only her name and room number identified the box tied with brown cord. Once inside with the door closed, she tried untying the knots, but when they didn't yield, she snatched up her scissors and cut them away. A note lay on top of a tightly woven bag of something.

"Dear Louisa, take this and do with it as we discussed. Do not count on seeing me again before you leave for Richmond." The Z told her whom it was from, even though the writing was difficult to read. And the message mind numbing.

"Zachary, where are you?" She covered the box again and slid it under her carpetbag in the chifforobe. "Oh, Lord, protect him, please. I almost lost him once. Don't let this be permanent." Knowing that Joanna waited for her, she tucked the note into her bag and, locking the door, descended to the dining room again.

"I have decided to go to Fredericksburg," Joanna announced as soon as Louisa had sat down. "I will not let them bury my husband in some nameless grave. I will take him home for a decent burial."

"Surely the army would ship his body home."

"I'm not counting on anything from the army any longer. They might have owned my husband, but they do not own me." She sniffed back incipient tears and straightened her spine. "I have cried enough. Would you help me get to Fredericksburg?"

"Ah, how do you . . . I mean . . ." *I've not told her I'm from the South. How does she know?*

"Dear Louisa, my husband and I lived in Kentucky for some years. I recognize your accent, and while you might be living here in Washington, I seriously doubt it." She kept her voice low and leaned forward, her hands clasped on the table. "I will have a pass enabling me to travel to Fredericksburg. Where do you live from there?"

"In . . . in Richmond, with my aunt. My older sister sent my sister and me to live with our aunt in Richmond, thinkin' we might be safer there."

"And you are—so far. No one has been able to take Richmond."

"Not for lack of trying, but you're right." Louisa thought of the box upstairs. Without Zachary's hollow leg and crutch, could she stash all of the powder?

"You could travel as my companion."

"Or, once we are in Southern control, you could travel as mine." The two women looked deep into each other's eyes. "And you could come on to Richmond if you like. We will always have a place for you."

"Thank you, my dear, and likewise. I'll contact those in charge and make the arrangements. Hopefully we can leave in the morning, depending on when the trains are running."

When Louisa returned to her room, she found a note on the floor. The simple message made her sigh in relief. "Do not be worried. *Z.*" She sank down on the bed and clutched the paper to her heart. "Thank you, Lord, for listening and caring, even when I don't feel like you are there. I know faith and feelings aren't the same. I believe. Help, thou, my unbelief."

By the time she went to bed that night, she had neat packets of white powder sewn into the lining of her traveling skirt and jacket, into the false bottom of her reticule, and into the false bottom of the carpetbag. She hadn't needed the pocket in her Bible.

———

While the sun returned the following day, the streets remained a quagmire. Louisa dashed off a note to Cousin Arlington, informing him that she was sorry they were unable to meet, but she was leaving for home within the hour. She kept her tongue firmly planted in her right cheek while she penned the letter and readied it for mailing. Every time she heard footsteps outside in the hall, she paused, hoping the doorknob would turn and Zachary would enter.

But he didn't.

Her carpetbag was packed and ready to go. As she scanned the room for anything she might have missed, her eyes fell on the envelope she had placed on the mantel—the letter that had arrived for Zachary. Should she take it with her or leave it at the hotel desk in case Zachary should return?

She made her way downstairs, thankful at least that she at least had her return ticket. What if that had been with Zachary too? The more she thought about it, the more she realized their preparations had been woefully inadequate. With her mind made up she walked over to the desk. "Could you please hold this for my husband?" At the clerk's nod she smiled. "Thank you."

Once on the porch, she glanced around, hoping against hope to see Zachary and his peculiar gait come to her. She didn't give up until she and Joanna were seated in their buggy and Union officers had checked their papers.

"I'm sorry you have to make such a trip," the sergeant said, touching a finger to his hat. Not until he left did Louisa dare to relax. As the buggy started, her air released, and she leaned against the buggy window.

Within minutes, they both had their knitting in hand and, between watching the scenery and sharing memories of happier days, the miles sped by.

Once they had crossed the river, a Southern officer gave Mrs. Hinklen stern looks until he read her pass and then saluted. "I'm right sorry, ma'am. You'll find the officers' bodies, those we have anyway, in a warehouse in Fredricksburg. He might already have been buried."

"I sent a telegram."

"I understand, but . . ."

"Whom do I need to see?"

"Captain Jefferson, ma'am." The look he sent Louisa made her increase her prayers. Surely this poor woman would be allowed to take her husband's body home for a decent burial. The wagon ride to Fredericksburg showed a land ravaged by war.

They said their good-byes at the warehouse as dusk rolled in. While Mrs. Hinklen still wore traces of the peculiar shade of green she'd turned when identifying the bloated body of her dead husband, she gave Louisa a hug and promised to write.

"One day, my dear, when this war is over, as it eventually must be, please know that there is a place for you in a lovely little town in the Adirondacks. People come from all over the world for the waters, and I will be greeting them on the steps of our small resort."

"Thank you. I know Aunt Sylvania will be sad you couldn't come farther. As I am."

"We helped each other, and that is the way life is to be lived, war or no war."

Louisa waved good-bye as a buggy carried her to the southbound train. Had she and Gilbert had a chance to marry, would she be a widow now too?

The closer to home she got, the more she wondered if there had been a message from him.

*What am I going to tell Aunt Sylvania about Zachary?*

# Chapter Twenty-Seven

Independence, Missouri
April 1863

"You lookin' for me?"

Jesselynn got to her feet. "If you're wagon master Gray Wolf Torstead, I am." Finding his eyes took some looking up. Straight gaze, straight mouth, straight dark hair caught back in a thong, cheekbones carved of mahogany, rich like the sideboard at Twin Oaks. His buckskin shirt, fringe missing in places but soft and fitting like glove leather, made broad shoulders look more so.

"I am."

Jesselynn swallowed. "My name is Jesse Highwood and my—" She caught herself. If she lied about her father now, she'd be found out much too soon and branded a liar. This man deserved a straight answer. *But what if he says no if I tell him the truth? If?* She caught herself again. *When?* Perhaps telling as much truth as she dared would be sufficient. "My family is lookin' to join a wagon train to Oregon. I heard you were still takin' on wagons."

"How many?"

"Many?" *Wagons or people?*

"Wagons, and do you have all your supplies yet?"

"I've ordered two wagons. They should be ready any day."

"Who from?"

"Jenkins Wagons. Folks said they were built to last."

A slight tip of the head may have meant he agreed, maybe not. "Where's your folks?"

The gold bullion question. "My aunt is back at our camp, along

197

with our freedmen and women. We all want to start new in Oregon." His eyes, they looked right through her.

"You're from the South." Not a question.

She nodded. "Kentucky."

"Confederate?"

She shrugged. Her political leanings were none of his business.

"How old are you, young Jesse?"

"What difference does it make? I can do the work of any man." His gaze locked with hers. He waited.

She kept from scuffing her boot in the dust only with a supreme effort. Chess nudged her in the back. "Nineteen, no twenty." She caught herself. Tomorrow was her birthday.

His eyebrows joined. "Which?"

"Does it matter?" Why not just tell him? Cat-and-mouse games had never been her forte.

"No. Either way, you're too young. We need men, strong men."

"I have three black men with me. Meshach is bigger'n you and stronger than two men. Benjamin is an expert horse wrangler, as am I, and Daniel can find fish and rabbits where none exist. We can all shoot straight and keep our mouths shut."

"But can you all follow orders?" His question came soft and pointed.

"When need be." She held his gaze only with an effort, finally blinking and looking to his chest. Her heart fluttered like a bird trapped by a window and throwing itself against the pane, seeing freedom on the other side and not understanding the glass between.

"What are you runnin' from?"

She caught her breath. Raising her chin, she stared back at his obsidian eyes. "The war. What are you runnin' from?"

A tiny flare flickered in the depths of black, then it was doused. He too had secrets to hide.

A long pause before he shook his head again.

"I have the money." She broke in before he could utter the final word. At least she spoke only half a lie. She would have the money as soon as she sold Chess and located a race or two.

"Come back to me when you have your wagons, and we'll see." While he still shook his head as he spoke, he hadn't said no.

Her heart settled back to a steady beat. "I will, but what guarantee do I have that there will be a place remainin' for us?"

SISTERS OF THE CONFEDERACY

"None."

She clamped her teeth on the words that threatened to spill out. Sucking in a deep breath, she spoke through gritted teeth. "I may not be a man full grown, but gentlemen do not do business this way. When I meet all your requirements, I expect to be allowed to join your train, sir."

"I am no gentleman."

"I can tell that, but Mr. Robinson at the store said you are a man of honor, that we could trust you, and you would be fair." She took a step closer.

Wolf kept from stepping back before the onslaught of this young rooster. Schooling his face took little effort, in spite of the grin that tickled his cheeks. And his insides. Grown men took his no for an answer. Why not this Jesse Highwood of Kentucky? He said he had freed black men, meaning he'd had slaves. Why was getting to Oregon so important to him? He looked far too young, hadn't even shaved yet, besides not having filled out. If Jesse Highwood was twenty, he, Wolf, was the south portion of a mule goin' north.

"Come to me when you have your wagons."

*I'll see you run over by my wagons!* Jesselynn flung herself on Chess's back and glared down at the mountain that refused to move. "I will be back."

Wolf dipped his chin in the briefest of nods and turned to answer a man who'd come up beside him.

Pure rage felt hot, but this time Jesselynn felt determination cold as a three-foot icicle on a January morning. Showing up Mr. Gray Wolf Torstead would be the utmost pleasure. Those wagons would be the toughest and tightest ever built. No way was that insufferably stubborn man going to keep them from going to Oregon.

He'd thrown down the gauntlet. She had picked it up.

---

"Three days? But you said they would be ready today." Jesselynn glared at Jenkins, who seemed oblivious to living up to his word.

"One of my men took off wi' dat last train. Can't build wagons widout good men."

"I will bring you a good man tomorrow." Mounting Chess with-

199

out using the stirrups was becoming a habit. Anger gave strength to her legs. "In fact, I'll bring you two. You can deduct their wages from the cost of my wagons." *If he thinks he can pull the wool over my eyes just because I'm young, he has another think coming.* The ride to the iron-mongers took less time than usual.

"What do you mean no horseshoes? You promised me six boxes, for both horse and oxen."

"Sorry. The barge ain't showed up. Spring slows down the river traffic. Maybe t'morrow."

"What about yokes for the oxen?" If they had any sense, she told herself, Meshach could have carved those back in the oak woods too. So many things they hadn't thought of. She shook her head and, turning, strode out the door, her bootheels clacking on the floor-boards in a satisfying enough manner. Stomping would have felt bet-ter, along with door slamming. But both would have said what she'd been accused of far too often lately—being young. If they figured out she was female . . . It was bad enough being a *young* man, or boy, as she was so often called. No wonder Meshach wanted to go to Oregon. He was far beyond *boy* status, yet so many referred to him that way, all because of his dark skin. On the way back to where she'd tied Chess, she added to her litany of frustrations. Their money would not stretch near far enough, she had yet to find a race for Ahab, and her curse was upon her.

She'd awakened that morning dreaming of Twin Oaks and her mother cosseting her during that time. Today she had no time for cramps or hot bricks. She had to get her people on the way to Oregon.

---

The first wagon train left the next morning.

On the way back from checking with Jenkins Wagons again, she saw a crowd gathered to the east of town. When a mass shout went up, she angled her horse in that direction and watched the action from his back.

Two horses, one black and one bay, drove across a makeshift fin-ish line, the black a winner by a head. Easing Chess forward, she made her way through the crowd of shouting men until they stopped just short of two men, one with a slate and chalk, the other handing out money.

The money man stepped up to the rider on the black horse and handed him a leather pouch that clanked when changing hands. The purse, and it had to contain gold.

Jesselynn dismounted and, with her reins looped over her arm, waited until the betters collected their winnings before approaching the man who seemed to be in charge.

"Pardon me, sir, but could I ask you a question?"

Porkpie hat tipped up, he turned. With a quick glance at her, he shifted the cigar in his mouth from one side to the other before speaking. "Yeah, boy, what do you want?"

"I want to know how this racin' is set up."

"Just the way you sees it. Two riders, two horses. One wins, one loses."

"And the others?"

"Others?" The cigar shifted again. This time he removed it between two fingers, spat a quid off to the side, and put the cigar back. He seemed to chew it more than smoke it.

Jesselynn stood her ground. "Those who placed the bets. The odds?"

"No odds. Just divvy up the take." He hawked and spat. "What's it to you? That horse don't look to have no speed."

Five days had not been enough to get Ahab in shape, but if the contenders ran no faster than the ones she'd seen, Ahab didn't need to be in condition. The trick would be getting him to run more slowly. So the bets would be more the second time.

Jesselynn headed for home without badgering the ironmonger again.

"He ain't ready." Benjamin shook his head.

"I know, not ready for a real race, but the horses I saw were just fast, not Thoroughbreds."

"What if someone steal him?"

"We won't let them. You and Meshach go with me. Daniel can stay here to guard the others."

Meshach sighed, shoulders slumping after a full day at Jenkins Wagons. "I don't like the bettin'. The purse be enough."

Jesselynn knew she'd made a mistake in mentioning that she planned to bet—on herself. She refused to entertain the thought that if she lost the sixty dollars, she lost a wagon. But Ahab wouldn't lose. She was sure of that.

"Betting makes perfect sense. We can only race one day, then Ahab has to disappear again. With each day, the danger increases, and we can't take that chance. He runs once, barely wins. . . ." She paused. Shook her head ever so gently, a smile, slight, barely moving her lips. Her head nodding only a bit, thinking, planning.

"I don't like dat look." Meshach studied her through narrowed eyes.

"I lose the first race." She held up a hand to stop their sputtering. "By only a nose."

Benjamin snorted. "You think you can hold him back?"

She nodded. "But then I demand a rematch. Give him an hour, and we run again. This time we bet. We win, and we buy the rest of our supplies."

"And pray de army don't get wind of de fast horse down in Independence."

"Who goin' lay de bets?" Meshach looked up from studying his clasped hands resting on his knees. He hadn't left off sitting on his chunk of wood since the discussion began.

Jesselynn froze. Meshach was right. She couldn't ask him or Benjamin. A black with sixty dollars in gold would be suspect immediately. And she couldn't bet herself.

"I will. Won't be the first time, and most likely not the last." Agatha set Thaddeus off her lap and stood. "Only thing, we'll have to take the wagon, then."

*Why can't anything ever be simple? I was just going to go race the horse and get out of there again. But what else can we do?*

That left Ophelia and Daniel alone with the horses and the camp and the young'uns, though Jane Ellen considered herself as grown as Daniel, at least. And she could shoot too.

Jesselynn looked to Meshach, who refused to look up at her. But she read disapproval in every line of his weary body.

"When will our wagons be ready?"

"Tomorrow or de next day."

"I heard another train is pullin' out in the mornin'."

"Yes, suh. Where you get de oxen?"

"I talked with a man today. He has nine, but not all are trained yet."

"Buyin' all nine?"

"Depends on the purse."

Before she fell asleep that night, Jesselynn wandered out to where Daniel had put Ahab to grazing on a long line. She leaned against the stallion's shoulder and stroked his neck on up to rub his ears. Ahab lowered his head and sighed, leaning into the ministering fingers.

"You want to run tomorrow, old son?" She ran her fingers through his mane, snagging on a burr. "Daddy would die again if he saw how bad you look." The mane and tail hadn't been combed since they left Twin Oaks, and a brush was used only on the places the harness or saddle might rub. She thought of the racing saddle tucked away in the trunk, underneath the two dresses she had brought along. She almost hadn't put it in.

She rubbed the stallion's nose and wandered back to camp. The men had insisted she not take a turn at watch tonight so she would be fresh for the race. Daniel and Benjamin both wore grins that clearly showed their excitement. Even Thaddeus caught the feeling, though no one told him they would be racing Ahab.

"You go to sleep now like a good boy." Jane Ellen's voice wore that patient tone that said she was repeating herself.

Jesselynn reached in the wagon for her bedroll and gave her little brother a poke. Giggles erupted, and Thaddeus rolled over to grab her hand.

"Kiss, Jesse."

Jesselynn kissed his cheek and stroked back his curly hair. If only his father could see him now. He would be so proud. She laid out her bedroll and glanced heavenward. "Daddy, if'n you're watchin', please do all you can to make sure we win that race tomorrow. Might be the most important race Ahab ever ran."

While she kept her voice to a whisper, she lay back on her bedroll and studied the stars, stars they'd be following west. Good thing the Lord said He'd guide their steps. She hoped and prayed that included both racing and westering the miles.

# CHAPTER TWENTY-EIGHT

"Now, you understand the rules?"

Jesselynn nodded. While she wore her stirrups shorter than usual, she tried to look like any normal rider, not a jockey.

"He's mighty light compared to Erskin there." One of the spectators hawked and spit, then squinted up at Jesselynn. "Might make a big difference."

"Erskin been at this long enough. He knows what that black can do."

Jesselynn fought to keep her concentration on the race, not on the gaping group of humanity that looked like bathing might be against their religion. At the Keeneland Track, where her father raced his Thoroughbreds, the crowd dressed for the day as a social event. Hats were *de rigueur,* and the loveliest of gowns the custom. Not the morass of pressing, stinking men who crowded Ahab, making him lay his ears back. He looked ready to bite the next man who came near.

"Hey, boy, you ready?" The owner and rider of the black spat off to the side of his horse. Did everyone chew tobacco here?

"Anytime, sir." She touched a finger to the brim of her slouch hat. The porkpie had a habit of blowing off in a stiff wind, and she planned on a stiff wind from release to the finish line.

The man in charge pointed to a man waving a red flag and waiting better than a quarter mile away. "You start there when he says, and the first one across this line is the winner. There'll be no striking a horse but your own, no jostling, bumping, or cutting off the other horse. I want a clean race. You hear?"

Jesselynn nodded, having a feeling that experience had necessitated the rules. She glanced at Erskin, who wore a smirk fit to rile the staunchest peacemaker. Wishing she had watched more races to see what kind of shenanigans he pulled, she glanced around the crowd to see Aunt Agatha sitting up in her rocking chair in the wagon bed, knitting away just as if she were back in camp. She caught Jesselynn's eye and winked.

Jesselynn acted as if she didn't know her, but the wink warmed her insides. She wished the race were longer. Lots of horses could go the short distance, but it was in the longer races where the Thoroughbreds excelled.

"Hey, Erskin, you not gonna let a young pup like that beat ya, are you?"

"Just put your money down, and let's get on with this. I got work to do."

At that, half the crowd burst into guffaws. Erskin was well known, obviously.

"Okay, now, easy canter up to the starter. Everyone stand back, clear the track."

Jesselynn glanced down. The mud had dried, but *the track*, as he so euphemistically called it, looked hard as a brick, none of the sand and well-dug surface of a real race track. She did as the man ordered and set Ahab at an easy canter to where they would start.

"Where'd you get that horse, boy?" Erskin pulled up beside her.

"Family horse. Just likes to run. Pulls a good plow too." She leaned forward slightly to stroke Ahab's neck. Not that he'd ever been hitched to a plow, but Erskin wouldn't know that.

"You ever raced 'im before?"

"Me? No. Daddy just thought it might be a fun idea." This at least was no lie. She herself had never ridden Ahab at the track in a real race. She had trained him at home. And her daddy, why, he had thought racing Thoroughbreds one of the chief delights of this life.

He'd be heartbroken to see his pride and joy in the condition he was in.

They reached the starter, who looked about as reputable as the man at the other end. "Y'all ready?" he asked.

Jesselynn wished she had goggles but only nodded after settling herself deeper in the saddle. Ahab shifted from one front foot to the other. "Easy, son."

The man pointed his pistol in the air, paused, and the shot rang out. Ahab leaped as if from a starting gate, but before he hit his stride, the black was three lengths ahead and extending his lead.

"Go, Ahab!" Jesselynn crouched over his withers, making herself as small as possible, urging him on with hands and reins.

They lost by a length, but toward the end they were gaining. If only they'd had more track to cover.

Ahab was blowing hard when she pulled him to a canter, then a trot, and turned back to where Erskin stood, accepting the congratulations of the crowd—and the purse.

"Sorry, boy. Someone shoulda warned ya." He turned and slapped his horse's shoulder. "Yes, sir, this old boy can run."

Losing the twenty-dollar gold piece she'd had to put up galled her hide. Losing the race made her see shades of red—bright red. "That he can." She forced the chosen words past teeth clamped together to keep the flood inside. The flood attacked her instead. Calling herself all kinds of names, none of them complimentary, she led Ahab off to walk him around and cool him down.

How stupid to think she could win so easily. Sure, let the other horse catch up and push ahead at the last moment. What was she thinking of?

She stayed away from Aunt Agatha and the wagon.

Leading his horse, Erskin caught up with her. "No bad feelings now, are there? After all, your horse there has a good heart. He didn't quit on ya."

Jesselynn just nodded and kept on walking.

"Tell ya what I'll do. How about you meet me back here again tomorrow morning, same time, and I'll let ya see if you can win yer money back? How's that?"

"You mean no money up front?"

"Right, that's what I mean. Outa the goodness of my heart." He clapped one hand on his chest, even though it was on the wrong side.

"So, what's the catch?" Jesselynn stopped walking and faced him square on.

"No catch. Just that if I win, I keep both horses. You win, you get 'em both—and the purse."

She kept her mouth closed and her eyes from widening through supreme willpower. All her mother's training on good manners and deportment came to the fore. She eyed the man, rock steady. "On one condition." *Oh, Lord, am I being a fool? Or am I just being my daddy's girl? Zachary wouldn't even hesitate. But I've got all these people to think of.* She sighed. That's what she was thinking of—getting her people to Oregon.

She shook her head, turned away. The stakes were too high.

"I'll throw in an extra hunnerd dollars."

*He thinks he's got us whupped and down.* "On one condition."

"What's that?"

"We double the length of the track."

He studied her through squinted eyes, looked up at the cotton-bole clouds and back at her. "Done."

While she hesitated to shake his dirt-engraved hand, she knew that gentlemen did so. Not that he was a gentleman, more like a conniving lowlife, but the race was set. She mounted Ahab. "Tomorrow then." And rode off.

She headed up the river in order to fool anyone following her, and when she was certain no one was on her trail, she angled back for their camp. As soon as Aunt Agatha arrived, Jesselynn unhitched Chess, saddled him, and cantered back to town, leaving instructions for Daniel and Jane Ellen on caring for Ahab.

Aunt Agatha had only shaken her head. She'd heard the buzz before she left the crowd.

Jesselynn put money down on the oxen, rode by to check on the wagons, which were promised for the morning, stopped at Robinson's store to finish ordering the supplies, including another oak water barrel, and listened again to the excuses from the ironmonger.

"But, Jehosaphat, he come up de river, say my barge be here tomorrow. Dey got stuck on a sandbar, but all right now."

She nodded and left. At least they hadn't thrown the boxes of shoes overboard.

If she kept busy enough, she couldn't think about the morning.

But back at camp, Daniel and Benjamin didn't even try to hide their fear—or was it sorrow? Meshach shook his head and returned to his Bible reading before it got too dark to decipher the pages. She didn't dare ask what the Good Book had to say about gambling—if anything.

"We're going to win," she promised the stars from her bedroll.

———————

Ahab pranced in the coolness of the early morning and ate his oats with ears pricked forward as if he knew what was coming. When Jesselynn lifted his front foot to pick the dirt out, he turned his head to nudge her seat, nearly sending her flying flat out.

"Ahab! Whatever is the matter with you?"

"He like dat racin' again." Meshach started to brush off the mud crusted on the horse's shoulder, then stopped. "One day we get to brush and polish this old son till him look like the granddaddy Thoroughbred he be."

"Did you pray for us to win?"

"Hmm." He nodded. "But more I pray for God to keep you both safe and for us all to get on de road before trouble happen. Just do yo' best. That all you can do."

Jesselynn nodded. Earlier that morning she had decided that none of them would place a bet. Winning the purse would be enough.

They hitched up the wagon and, with Aunt Agatha stitching away in her rocking throne, headed for town. Once she dropped Benjamin and Meshach off at Jenkins, Aunt Agatha would drive the wagon herself over to watch the race. Jesselynn made a detour and came toward the racing ground by another direction. When they won, everyone would be on the lookout for her and her horse. Keeping the camp safe was more important than anything.

The crowd was double the size of the day before, and the man with the slate was doing a brisk business. Erskin and his black were the center of an admiring group; a silver flask along with a long-necked bottle made the rounds, upping the hilarity that greeted every joke and sally.

"Come on over, boy, have a tote." Erskin waved to Jesselynn.

She shook her head but smiled to show she wasn't being uppity.

Suddenly she felt like throwing up. Right there in front of everyone. Right now! She wanted to call the whole thing off, but Erskin had signaled the time had come to mount up. Too late. Whether she felt relief or fear, she didn't know.

She sucked in a deep breath, held it, and nudged Ahab forward toward the starter, who was just a speck but for his red flag. Red flag, pistol shot, race. In that order.

*All right, calm down. This is just a race like any other, and this time the distance is on our side.*

*But how do you know the black can't run distance too? And you can lose Ahab!*

That was one of those thoughts she'd been refusing to acknowledge. She didn't know. But she would soon find out.

She squeezed Ahab into a canter and could feel him arch his back to take an extra jump or two—sheer energy. As her daddy always said, *"Poetry in motion. That's a good runnin' horse."*

"Well, Daddy, today our poetry had better sing loud and clear." She swept by the starter with a nod and turned in a gentle half circle to bring Ahab back to the starting line. Erskin trotted up and, with a tip of his head, took his place between her and the starter.

"Now, remember, if'n either of you start before the gun, you get one more chance, and after that it's a forfeit."

"You didn't mention that yesterday."

"What's that you say?" The man cupped his ear to hear better, the red flag dangling behind him.

Jesselynn shook her head to signify it didn't matter. Ahab settled on his haunches and stopped the restless shifting. Ready, like an arrow to be released from a bow.

"Ready."

The black jumped forward, eliciting a curse from his rider. Erskin rode him in a circle and came up from behind.

While he performed his move, Jesselynn stroked Ahab's neck. "That's all right, old son, you be ready now. He'll get off faster than we do, but we'll catch him flyin'." Looking neither to the right nor to the left, she concentrated on the gap between Ahab's pricked ears.

The shot! The leap! And they were pounding the dust one length behind the black. Jesselynn crouched forward. "Okay, now, let's get up about his stirrup." She loosened the reins, and Ahab leaped forward as if she'd been holding him back. They came up even with the black's streaming tail, then with his haunches, and then even with the stirrups.

Erskin went to the whip, and the black surged forward.

Wind sang in her ears, hooves thudded, and Ahab grunted as he pulled up head to neck.

Erskin beat the black, both on rump and shoulders, screaming at him for more.

Ahab surged by him, still picking up speed, and crossed the finish line with half a length to spare.

If she hadn't been the horsewoman her father had trained her to be, Jesselynn might have fallen off from sheer relief. Instead, she let Ahab run a bit before easing him back first to a hand gallop, then to a canter. She turned to trot back to where the crowd stood in silent grief. Jesselynn glanced over at Aunt Agatha, who wore a grin from here to Sunday. A brief sketch of a nod was her only answering motion.

Jesselynn stopped in front of the chalk man and leaned forward to pat Ahab's steaming shoulder.

"Here you go, boy. I never saw a horse run like that 'cept at a real honest-to-God track one time. That horse sure can run." He handed her the leather pouch, which she stuck in her pocket.

Erskin strode up and handed her his horse's reins. "I kept the saddle. That weren't part of the bet."

"I didn't bet. You set up the parameters."

He raised an eyebrow, but she didn't bother to explain. "Thank you. We will treat him well. What is it you call him?"

"Blackie."

Jesselynn looked around to see her aunt standing several feet distance.

"That was a fine race, son." Her eyes twinkled. "Your mother must be right proud of you."

"Thank you, ma'am." Jesselynn ducked her head, as was proper. It helped hide her almost smile. She mounted Ahab again and clucked the other horse to follow them. She trotted a ways and stopped. Clear as if someone sat on her shoulder, she heard a voice tell her to offer Blackie back to his former owner for a hundred dollars.

*That's crazy. Why, the army would pay two hundred . . . or more.* Ahab sighed and shook his head, setting the reins to flapping. Jesselynn looked around. No one nearby was paying any attention. Shaking her head and giving a heavy sigh, she turned the horses back toward the now thinning crowd. Aunt Agatha and the wagon were heading out the other way. When she found the chalk man, she stopped. "You seen Erskin?"

"Probably in the saloon drowning his sorrows. Losing Blackie hit him hard."

"Thanks. Which saloon?"

"Oh, most likely the Western Belle. Favorite place o' his."

Jesselynn found the place after a bit of searching, tied the horses to the hitching rail, and took the steps two at a time. She paused before the swinging doors. Saloons were no places for young women, but since she was a young man, it should be all right. But it wasn't. She stepped back when someone pushed the doors outward.

*Come on. Quit wasting time. Get on in there and find the man so you can get Ahab back under cover.* With that as a prod, she pushed the doors and followed them inward, blinking in the dim light. Even at this time of the morning, smoke hung like a shroud over the room. Two tables were set up for cards, but she found Erskin leaning against the bar, a bottle in front of him.

"Mr. Erskin?"

He turned with a snarl on his face that only intensified when he saw her. "What do you want now? You got my horse. Ain't got nothin' else."

She nearly coughed on the fumes flung her way by his words. "I have a proposition for you."

"Yeah?" He hoisted the bottle, his Adam's apple glugging several times before he handed the bottle in her direction. "Have some."

"No, thanks. My daddy don't hold with his son drinkin' liquor yet." She leaned against the bar and waited for him to repeat the chugging noise and smack his lips. "Now, I was wondering if you would like to buy Blackie back."

"Buy him back? Are you outa your ever-lovin' mind? 'Course I want him back."

"Good. How does a hundred and fifty dollars sound?"

"Ain't got that much."

"How much do you have?"

"A hunnerd."

"Gold?"

A nod.

"Sold. Come on out and get him." Jesselynn turned toward the door expecting him to follow, but halfway there she realized no sound of boot steps came behind her. She turned.

Erskin stood as if he'd been turned to salt. He blinked, the only part of his body that seemed to work other than his hand that clenched and relaxed before clenching the bottle again.

"Are you comin'?"

"Aye, boy, that I am."

Jesselynn hoped Blackie knew his way home, because the way Erskin swayed and stumbled, he wouldn't be doing much guiding.

She left with his blubbering thank-yous ringing in her ears. Maybe she could be called all kinds of fool, but right now a peace rode her shoulders, and it failed to evaporate on the roundabout ride back to camp.

————

Two days later she had the new wagons loaded and the oxen pulling them into Wolf's camp. "We're here for your inspection."

His eyes didn't look one mite more accommodating. After he went through all the boxes, bags, and barrels, he stopped next to her.

"All right. Much against my better judgment, you can join us. We leave day after tomorrow."

"Good. That'll give me time to sell my other wagon and the extra horse." She glanced up into his face, hoping for a smile, a nod, something that indicated he was pleased. Nothing.

"Now, you've told me everything else you are bringing, right?"

*Everything but seven Thoroughbreds, but they shouldn't cause any problem.*

"I don't like surprises."

Jesselynn shrugged. "I better get on back to camp." *God, forgive me, but I don't know what else to do.*

# CHAPTER TWENTY-NINE

## On the Oregon Trail

"Here come the wagons!" Thaddeus threw himself back against Jane Ellen's chest.

Her grunt spoke volumes for the strength the little boy gained daily.

Jesselynn released a deep breath she wasn't aware she'd been holding. Sitting high on the wagon seat, she let her thoughts and fears run rampant. What if Gray Wolf took another route? What if he refused them when he saw the other horses? Of course he wouldn't be seeing the horses until later. With the sun barely out of bed, the wagon train snaked along the trail, already raising a cloud of dust. The western sky, however, looked about ready to take care of the dust problem. A chill wind blew, precursor to the black, moisture-laden clouds.

But to the east, the sun shone, waking the diamonds that slept on the spring grass. Dandelions opened their golden faces to the morning and hid in the growing grass. With thirty wagons, this train was smaller than some of the others, and from what she'd heard, was better prepared.

Wolf had seen to that. He rode now at the head of the train, his spotted horse—she'd heard they were called Appaloosas—dancing with energy.

She wondered how far ahead their horses had gotten. Meshach, Daniel, and Benjamin had taken them south to meet with the wagon train later in the day. If she'd dared, she'd have sent them on ahead

Children waved from front porches as the caravan passed by, farmers from out in their fields. Their route took them down the streets of Olathe and Lawrence, heading them southwest until the Oregon Trail left the Santa Fe Trail. Then they'd turn north and cross the Kansas River at Topeka. The noon stop was short—no campfires allowed—but it gave the oxen and horses a rest, as well as those walking alongside the wagons. Since they stopped by a creek, the animals drank their fill, and the children waded in the water.

They were barely on the road again when the threatening storm hit with teacup-size raindrops. All the walkers scurried for the wagons, leaving the drivers and the animals to brave the elements. Jesselynn was soaked within seconds. *I shoulda had Jane Ellen take over for Aunt Agatha.* But it was too late now.

"Leastways the canvas ain't leakin'," Jane Ellen said from behind her shoulder. "That greasin' we did makes the water run off slicker'n off a duck's back." She lifted her face to the rain sheeting down. "Smells good, don'tcha think? All clean and fresh."

Jesselynn had to agree. The world always smelled better after a rain, and it wasn't like this one was so cold. Chilly yes, but not bone-deep freezing like earlier in the year.

"Rain like this makes the grass and flowers just leap outa the ground. I love springtime."

Jesselynn had to smile. Not often did Jane Ellen say this many words at one time without someone having asked her questions.

"Sure do hope Meshach and the boys got a place to stay dry. How soon you think we'll be meetin' up with 'em?"

"Long about sunset." Jesselynn flipped the reins to move the oxen along better. The gap had widened between them and the wagon in front. She touched the right rear oxen with the tip of the whip, and he lunged into the yoke. "You just stay up there too. No room for a lazy ox here."

"He's the purtiest one though, ain't he?"

"Isn't he."

"I think so."

"No. I mean, you don't say 'ain't.' The proper way is 'isn't he.'"

"Oh. That's right. He is right purty, ah . . . isn't he?"

"Guess so. But he's lazy." Jesselynn popped her whip over him again. "Got to keep on him all the time."

The sky lightened, and off to the west a band of light broke through just above the horizon. The rain changed to a drizzle, then stopped.

"You think we'll see a rainbow?"

"Good chance." Jesselynn was hoping she'd see Meshach. But the rider coming toward them was definitely not he. The horse's red chest and white-spotted rump were a surefire giveaway.

"You all right back here?" Wolf sat his horse as if born attached.

"Hey, Mr. Wolf." Jane Ellen leaned across the seat to wave.

"Just Wolf, no mister." He pulled up alongside the wagon.

"Is Wolf your whole name?" Jane Ellen slid one leg across the seat and, with a lithe twist, took up sitting beside Jesselynn.

"Nope. Between my father and my mother, they named me Gray Wolf Torstead."

"So you are Mr. Torstead."

"Guess so, but most folks call me Wolf." He nudged his horse into a trot and waved back at them.

"Ain't he beautiful?" The reverence in the words kept Jesselynn from making a smart retort. When she glanced at Jane Ellen, the thought hit her. Jane Ellen was becoming a young lady. One who showed an interest in the male of the species and whose heart could be trampled by a crush.

"Isn't."

"He is too." Like a fluffy hen defending her chicks, Jane Ellen went on the attack.

"No, I mean, remember I said not to use 'ain't.' Use 'isn't.' You asked me to teach you proper English, and that's what I'm tryin' to do."

"Oh, sorry." But the stars had left her eyes, and she wrapped her arms around her middle, leaning forward to check on the squeaky wagon tongue. "Meshach will want to know about that squeak. He said if it squeaks, grease it."

Thankful for the change in topic, Jesselynn breathed a sigh of relief. Far as she was concerned, Wolf might be a striking man, but all he did for her was make her mad. Overbearing, stubborn—she had a long list of words to describe him, not many of them complimentary.

"Speak of the devil," she muttered under her breath.

Wolf rode back into view, stopping at each wagon to speak to the driver. When he got to her, she waited a tick before looking up.

"We're stoppin' for the night about half a mile up the road. There's water there and plenty of pasture. Your wagon will be the last into the circle, so will be the most difficult. We'll be forming circles every night for safety's sake, even though right now there's nothing to fear."

She wanted to ask more about the circle but refrained. If he thought she couldn't maneuver this wagon, he had another think coming. But what about Aunt Agatha? After a long day on the wagon seat, she might be all stove-up. Besides, she hadn't driven four up before, let alone oxen.

"Thanks. We'll manage."

"I can get someone else to drive your aunt's wagon in."

"I said we'll manage." *Don't go doin' us any favors. We can handle things ourselves.*

The look he gave said clearly what he thought of her bad manners. Which wasn't anywhere close to what she thought about his. *My mother would have an attack of the vapors, and I never once saw her go into a spell like that. She didn't have the vapors.*

Jockeying the final wagon into place took several men giving conflicting advice, oxen more well trained in backing and, as Meshach would say, "a heavy dose of prayer." More than once she wished he were there, beginning to be concerned as the sun set fire to the western sky and gilded the edges of the remaining clouds. They'd just dropped the wagon tongue in place when the horsemen trotted up to the wagon.

"Coulda used you a few minutes ago," Jesselynn said by way of greeting.

"Sorry, thought you be farther up de road." Meshach dismounted, signaling for the others to do the same.

"These are *your* men?" Wolf nudged his horse closer to where she stood.

"Ah, yes."

"And *your* horses?"

"Yes."

He leaned over to say softly, "And why wasn't I informed that we would have seven horses along?"

Jesselynn squared her shoulders. If there was to be a fight, she was ready.

He waited.

So did she.

"I remember askin' if you had any other livestock."

"I know, but I've had to keep the horses hidden. They're all that's left of Twin Oaks breeding farm. We need good blood to start over." She knew she was talking too much and sounding breathy on top of it. But they *had* to be part of the train. Who knew when another would form up?

"They're Thoroughbreds."

"Yes, sir."

With eyes narrowed so his gaze was even more piercing, Wolf stared at her. "Does that big stallion have anything to do with winning a race a day or two ago?"

She couldn't think of a lie quick enough. "Yes, sir." Good. Telling the truth felt good.

"Remember when I said you had to be able to take orders?" At her nod, he continued. "One of my most important orders is that no one will tell me a lie. Only the truth."

*And I am living a lie.* "Yes, sir."

"I will decide by morning."

"Decide, sir?"

"Whether you and your horses will be continuing on with the wagon train." He turned and rode off before she could sputter an answer.

# CHAPTER THIRTY

"You can come on one condition."

Jesselynn stood straighter in the predawn gray light. "What is that?"

"If there is any trouble that can be laid at your door, you wait for another train."

"Trouble?"

"With your horses or your men."

"With *you*" was implied.

While dark eyes can become obsidian, green eyes turn to steel. Her jaw matched. "There will be no trouble."

"No racing."

"Do you take me for a fool? Of course there will be no racing. I wouldn't have done so then if we'd had the money for the supplies." She felt like adding a few well-chosen names but clamped her tongue between her teeth to keep it from further flapping.

"Thoroughbreds are too high-strung for a trip like this. You're going to lose them."

"Over my dead body." *He has no idea what we've gone through to get this far. I will not lose them. Thoroughbreds are far tougher than he thinks.* She refused to think about the foals. She'd carry them in the wagon if she had to.

"Suit yourself. I would recommend turning back now."

"We'll be ready when the others are. Thank you for your concern." She couldn't resist the sarcasm.

The look he gave her, other than finely honed anger, asked a question too. Only for the life of her, she couldn't figure out what it was. She was still puzzling on that when he rode off.

The wagon that had been first the day before fell in behind her as the circle straightened to a long line. Jesselynn waved to the driver, a woman wearing a sunbonnet dangling on a ribbon down her back. A black shawl hugged her shoulders and crossed in front.

"I'm Abigail Brundsford."

"Jesse Highwood. That's my aunt Agatha ahead." In spite of the three men now in attendance, Agatha had asked if she could drive again for a while. Since Jesselynn didn't want her walking, she agreed. She'd rather be riding but knew that after the noon break, Meshach could drive. Right now he kept the mares on lead lines and tied Roman and the spare ox behind the wagon. Once they were out of such civilized territory, Daniel would use Roman for hunting.

Daniel had snared two rabbits during the night, and Ophelia rose early to fry them for breakfast. The folks in the wagon in front of them had sniffed appreciatively as they ate their mush.

Throughout the day, other members of the party wandered back to introduce themselves, so that by noon Jesselynn's head was filled with a mishmash of names, trying to remember which went with what face. One family had enough children to start their own town.

When Wolf signaled the stop, Aunt Agatha's hands were blistered from holding the reins.

"Why didn't you put on gloves?" Jesselynn cupped her aunt's hands in her own.

"I don't have any gloves. That's why."

"Ophelia, please get out some of that salve that I bought in Independence."

Agatha tried to pull her hands away, but Jesselynn didn't release them until the salve was rubbed in and two strips of cloth bound the oozing sores.

"All we need is for this to go putrid on us."

"Pshaw, I've had blisters before. Paid them no nevermind, and they healed up just fine."

"Good. Let's hope these do too."

That night after supper, one of the men brought out a fiddle and another a harmonica. They started with music to sing by but moved on to dance tunes. Jesselynn and Agatha sat together on the wagon tongue, Jesselynn clapping while Meshach and Ophelia danced a jig.

"Hi, my name's Elizabeth." Suddenly appearing in front of Jesselynn, the no-longer-a-girl-but-not-yet-a-woman shifted from one foot to another after introducing herself. Her strawberry hair hung in a thick braid down her back, and the same color eyebrows shadowed her eyes so that the color was hidden. But her flaming cheeks matched the fire that now burned in embers.

Agatha prodded Jesselynn so that she turned to her aunt with a question that drowned in the laughter in her aunt's eyes. Jesselynn looked back to the visitor.

"Pleased to meet you. I'm Jesse Highwood."

"I know."

"She wants you to ask her to dance," Agatha whispered.

Jesselynn felt her face flame. She glanced down at her boots, wishing she were out with the horses where it was safer. "Ah, which wagon is yours?"

Elizabeth looked over her shoulder. "The one with the table and checkered cloth. My mama says even though we are on the way to Oregon, we don't have to give up all the comforts of home."

"Oh."

The fiddler changed to a reel, and all the dancers lined up, partners facing each other with some distance between them.

"Do you know how to dance the reel?" Her hands bunched the folds in her skirt.

"Ah, ah . . ."

"You could learn real fast. I taught my brother."

"'Scuse me. I better go check on the horses." Jesselynn got up so fast she nearly tripped over the wagon tongue in her hasty departure.

"He's just shy," she heard her aunt say before she was out of earshot. *Agatha Highwood, I swear I'm going to make you pay for this.* She didn't return to the circle until long after the fiddle had been put back in its case and most of the bedrolls been laid out under the wagons.

Dodging Elizabeth over the next few days took some doing. Jesselynn chose to ride Ahab as a line of defense. She didn't dare knit or help too much with the cooking. Even braiding rawhide might be thought of as women's work.

Wolf set up an order for night watches, and the men all took their turns, including Jesselynn.

By the time they turned off at Topeka, the train had fallen into the rhythm of the road. Up before daylight, a quick breakfast, hitch up, and move on out as the sun broke the horizon. Then a short noon stop without fires, stopping for the night where there was water and pasture for the cattle and horses. With the scarcity of wood, it became the job of those who walked along to pick up any wood they found, or dry cow pies. Dried cattle dung burned hot and slow.

They paused only long enough on Easter Sunday for one of the men to read the Easter story and everyone to sing a hymn, closing with the Lord's Prayer. For dinner they ate dry biscuits and dust. For grace at supper Meshach announced, "Christ is risen." The others answered, "He is risen indeed." Jesselynn went to bed murmuring those words again, adding, "Thank you, Jesus."

They'd been on the trail two weeks when they neared Alcove Springs.

"We'll do an extra day or two here," Wolf announced as he rode down the line that afternoon. "This place has a good spring, the folks who live here are friendly, and there's plenty of available pasture. There's even some shade, with the big oak trees they have."

"Ah, we can wash clothes." Aunt Agatha turned to Ophelia, who walked beside her wagon. "We have plenty of soap?"

"Yessum." Ophelia snagged Sammy up and set him on her shoulders. "Come on, baby, we got water ahead."

Thaddeus ran back to her. "Play in the water."

"And take a bath."

His smile disappeared. "No bath."

Jesselynn chuckled. "If that isn't just like a boy." Looping the reins around the brake handle, she leaped to the ground to pace alongside the slow-moving oxen. Even Buster, the lazy one, had learned to lean into the yoke and keep a steady, plodding pace. Since they were midway in the line of wagons, they just kept the pace unless something really unusual spooked the animals. And she could walk along beside. Some of the men used a goad and rarely rode the wagon seats. Anything to make the loads lighter.

With the ease born of practice, they circled the wagons downstream of the farmstead and set up camp. The women gathered all the dirty clothes together and headed for the creek. When Jesselynn started off with an armful, Aunt Agatha touched her arm.

"I don't think that is a good idea."

"What? Washing clothes?"

"No, *you* washing clothes. Do you see any of the other men or older boys helping?" Agatha kept her voice low and glanced around to see if anyone was close enough to listen.

"But..." She knew Agatha was right. Ophelia, Jane Ellen, and Agatha could go join the party at the creek, but not Jesselynn.

Meshach set up his forge, Daniel raced off with a fishing line, and Benjamin took the oxen and horses out to graze.

"If I graze the horses and oxen, Benjamin can go hunting."

"That's a fine idea."

Jesselynn retrieved her writing case, along with the rifle and ammunition from the wagon, and dogtrotted after Benjamin. *Ah, hours alone. Out on the prairie with no one but me and the animals.* The thought made her run faster. She stopped when she heard a yip behind her. Patch, tongue lolling, came running after her.

"You should be watching Sammy and Thaddeus."

The dog sat at her knee, white ear flopped forward, head tilted slightly to the side. He whined and looked toward the animals.

"You'd rather herd cattle. Can't say as I blame you." She turned and started after Benjamin again, but when Patch wasn't beside her, she looked back to see him still sitting in the same place. "What do you need, a special invitation?" She slapped her thigh. "Come on, then." The dog bounded across the already grazed grass to her side, running with her stride for stride.

Running yielded a pleasure so deep she felt like shouting. While guilt that she wasn't back helping with the wash tried to inveigle an entrance, she brushed it off like a pesky fly. Today she could be free.

"Benjamin, wait up."

He stopped Roman and turned to look over his shoulder. "What you want, Marse Jesse?"

"I'll do the grazing." She held the gun up. "You get to go hunting."

"Ah, fine idea." He slid to the ground and waited for her to catch up.

"How far out do I need to take them?"

"I keeps dem away from de other animals. Ol' Ahab get all excited around other mares. So maybe down de creek a mile or so, wherever de grass be good."

# LAURAINE SNELLING

"You take Roman then, and Patch will help me keep them in line. Think I should hobble the horses?"

He handed her the hide and braided hobbles, took the gun, and, mounting Roman, gave her a grin that she knew matched her own.

"Enjoy yourself."

"I do intend just dat. 'Sides, deer taste mighty good. We could dry some on top de wagon."

"Or share it with the others. If you can, get two."

"Marse Wolf, he say dey goin' form up huntin' parties when we get out more."

"Good. You can show 'em how." She watched him head for the hills to the east, then turned to follow the grazing animals. Once Ahab threw up his head and stared off to the south, but when whatever had gotten his attention left, he went back to grazing.

Jesselynn moved them out farther, hobbled the two stallions, and sat down in the grass to write her letters. Patch lay down beside her but leaped up when one of the oxen got too far away from the others and drove it back to the herd.

"You are one fine dog." She scratched his ears and his back when he lay back down beside her. The foals both stretched flat out on their sides, tired of playing. So far they were holding up well, but then, there had been plenty of water and grazing for the mares. The horror stories she'd heard started after Fort Laramie.

*Dear Sergeant White,*

She still had trouble calling him by his Christian name, even though he'd kissed her once.

> *I was so sorry to hear that you will be unable to join us like you had planned. I know how it is when family things get in the way of our own dreams. Camping at Alcove Springs in Kansas wasn't what I thought I would be doing, that is for certain. The only thing I knew about Kansas was John Brown's trying to free the slaves. So far, it seems a good place, with hills and valleys threaded with creeks. Right now the land is green and the sun warm but not hot. I have an idea I am seeing this land at its most idyllic. The farms seem fair prosperous, with many acres sown to wheat that is coming up nicely. Seems there's been enough rain for that. Not that rain is helpful to those of us who are traveling.*

She told him the events so far, sharing her rejoicing that Wolf, the wagon master, had found no cause to send them back.

> *In fact, he hardly says anything to me at all. He is more than polite to Aunt Agatha, who is an excellent drover. Whoever would have thought it? But traveling like this brings out the strengths of an individual—that I know for a fact.*
>
> *I am having some trouble keeping in the guise of a Jesse with all these people around. No wonder you were able to discern that I am a woman in man's clothes. Today Aunt decreed that I would not help with the washing in the creek, so I am the grazer, along with the dog who adopted us from a farm we saw burning on the way to Independence. He is a fine cattle dog and herds Sammy and Thaddeus just like calves.*

She knew he would get a chuckle out of that and planned to tell her sisters the same.

Her stomach rumbled, reminding her that she was missing dinner. Ah, well, too far to go back. She glanced around at her charges. Several of the oxen were lying down, chewing their cuds. One of the foals was up and nursing. The other mare lay down and rolled, scratching her back to get rid of the winter hair.

Jesselynn looked to the east, following Ahab's attention. Easy to recognize because of the spotted rump on his horse, Wolf rode with a fluid grace, he and the horse as one body. Seeing him like that brought up a thought. Why did he seem to ignore their wagon? She saw him visiting with the others as they plodded their way across the land, but other than to tip his hat to Aunt Agatha and give them instructions, he stayed away. Now he'd taken his hat off and untied the thong, letting his hair stream in the breeze, dark and thick. She'd heard two men talking about "the breed," as they called him. Not Wagon Master Torstead, or Mr. Wolf, but the derogatory term that set her teeth on edge. She'd felt like punching them. If all Indians looked like him, they were indeed a noble race.

Patch sat up and looked back toward the wagons, a whine catching her attention. Meshach came striding across the field as if he owned the land himself.

"Go get him." She whispered the command to Patch, and he took off as though someone had set fire to his tail.

Patch reached Meshach, ran around him yipping three times, then charged back to Jesselynn and lay panting at her side. He leaped to his feet, raced out after that same wandering ox, drove him back to the herd, and returned to drop in his place in Jesselynn's shade.

"Brung you some dinner." Meshach swung a sack to the ground and followed it down. "Got to shoe the red ox. Found his shoes loose dis mornin'."

"Did some others come to have any shoeing done?"

"Did two horse, one ox. Fixed a handle on a cast-iron kettle. De folks know I can do all dat."

"Good." Jesselynn watched as another of the oxen lay down with a grunt. "Guess they about had enough."

"Don't take long wid grass good as dis." He pulled a stalk and set to chewing the tender end. "I be gettin' on back. Sammy fell in de water, come up laughin', so Thaddy jump in after him. Jane Ellen haul dem out and take off dere clothes, handed dem soap." He shook his head in gentle laughter. "Dey some boys."

Jesselynn took two biscuits and a piece of fried rabbit out of the sack. Patch watched her every move.

"I be goin'." Meshach stood and removed a rawhide thong from his pocket. "Since tomorrow be Sunday, we goin' have a church service. Mr. Morgan be de preacher."

"They should ask you."

"A black man be de preacher?" He gave a short laugh and shook his head. "You been in de sun too long widout a hat."

"You know your Bible better than any of them."

He just waved and went on to tie the loop around the ox's neck, flipped another loop around the muzzle for a halter, then headed back to camp with the ox. "I bring him back when he done."

Jesselynn tossed the bone and half a biscuit to her watching companion and licked the grease off her fingers.

After finishing a letter to her sisters, she took out the journal and caught up the entries for the last couple of days. Describing the place where they camped made it sound like a bit of heaven. Trees along the creek, grass, cultivated fields, gentle hills bordering the wide flat valley, a creek that serpentined its way to the distant river. Sky so blue that the few puffy clouds looked painted on, and birdsong to thrill one's soul. She glanced down to find a tiny pink flower at her feet. Heaven indeed. But black folk weren't welcome here, and the land had a price, no longer free for the working as in Oregon.

She closed her journal with a clap and set it, along with the ink, back in the leather case. Time to work with the foals. The colt didn't like the idea of being led around at all. Time to get over that.

"Marse Jesse! Marse Jesse!"

Jesselynn looked up to see Jane Ellen running across the field, waving at the same time.

*What could be wrong now? Thaddeus?* Her heart leaped.

# Chapter Thirty-One

### Richmond, Virginia

"Worryin' sure does keep you on your knees," Louisa said to no one in particular.

"What's that you say, dear?" Aunt Sylvania looked up from her stitching. When no answer was forthcoming, she returned her attention to the wool jacket spread across her lap.

Louisa set her stitching off to the side and rose to wander to the window. Every day she prayed for Zachary to return. Every day for these four weeks she'd gone to bed fighting despair. Not hearing from either of the young men foremost in her life had begun to wear on her.

"Think I'll go work in the garden."

"That's a good idea." Sylvania held the jacket up, studying the sleeve cap.

Louisa wandered out the back door and across the flagstone verandah only to find two men already out there, one edging the pathways, the other tying up the sweet peas that refused to climb the trellis. There wasn't a weed in sight, nor a dying blossom to clip off, nor a bit of mulch to be spread. Short of transplanting something that did not need transplanting, there was nothing for her to do. The garden looked better than it ever had, even when Sylvania had had a gardener with helpers.

If only she could go over to the hospital.

If only she could find Gilbert . . . and Zachary.

*Lord, I'm caught in the* if only's, *and that's not a good place to be. How am I to be grateful for not knowing if my brother or my fiancé*—well, he wasn't quite, but she'd come to think of Lieutenant Lessling as that—*are alive. And my biggest problem is that I am not busy enough to keep from thinking.* She had to be honest. *From worrying. And I know worrying is a lack of faith. I know that. Lord, give me something to do.*

"*Go sew on the jacket.*"

"Is that all you can think of?" She glanced heavenward as she muttered her rejoinder.

"You need somethin', Miss Louisa?" The taller of the two men stood a couple feet away.

"No. No thank you. Would you and Private Daniels like something cold to drink?"

"Hot maybe. 'Specially if Abby has those molasses cookies I been smellin'. Sure makes me think of home."

"You sit down, and I'll bring them right out."

"No, you don't need to wait on us. 'Less o' course you might want to read while we eat?"

His hopeful look made her smile. At least here was something she could do to make someone else happy.

"Come on into the parlor, then, so the others can hear." Two of the newer men were still bedridden and might be for some time, since her team of herself, Abby, and Reuben were still fighting the putrefaction of their war wounds.

By the time she'd read them several psalms and one act of *The Merchant of Venice*, she'd gone hoarse, and two men in bed were soundly sleeping. Since sleep brought healing, she tiptoed out of the parlor and gently closed the door behind her.

"I don't think Corporal Downs looks very good. The fever must be back." She stopped at her aunt's side. "We don't have any morphine left, do we?"

Sylvania shook her head. "A bit of laudanum is all. I thought sure we had him on the road to recovery."

"When he wakes, I think I'll change the bandage on his stump. No sense waiting on the doctor to tell us what we can find out for ourselves."

But while the stump looked like only healthy healing flesh, the man had slipped into delirium. When they called the doctor, he listened to the man's chest and shook his head. "Pneumonia. I can take him back to the hospital, or you can fight it here."

Louisa knew their soldier had a much better chance at the house. "We'll keep him."

"Reuben, let's move Jacob to Zachary's bed. I'll get a mustard poultice started. Abby, you make up willow-bark tea. We've got to get his fever down."

They all headed for their duties, moving like a well-ordered machine, with each knowing what lay ahead. They'd been through this before—won one and lost one. Louisa hated to lose.

---

By the darkest hour before dawn on the second day, they had to admit defeat. The soldier's tortuous breathing had stilled.

Tears flowed down Louisa's face. "God, why? Didn't you hear our prayers? We tried so hard."

Reuben patted her shoulder. "God hear us, missy. He just say no. Dis boy now dancin' in heaven all whole again. You want him back to dis?" His hand gestured to the world around them. "You go on now. Get some sleep so you don't get sick."

"I should . . ." She could barely hold her head up.

"You should go to bed." Sylvania stood in the doorway, her dressing gown belted, her mobcap in place. "They will take care of the body."

"Yes, Aunt." But as Louisa pulled herself up the walnut stairs, her tired mind went to two other men. Where was Zachary? Was Gilbert still alive, and if so, where was he? *Why, God?* turned to *Where, God?* as she threw herself across the bed. "I'll undress in a few minutes, rest first." She wiped her tears on the pillow slip and knew no more.

Sometime later Abby came up and drew the covers over her, gently closing the door on the way out.

Dusk grayed the window when Louisa came fully awake. She lay cocooned in the warmth of her quilt and thought back to the battle. They'd done their best. She knew that. The enemy had been stronger, or their soldier had been weaker. How could he not be, with the septic wound?

"Oh, Lord, how long? How long must this war go on? Please, I beg of you, bring Zachary home again safe and sound. And if you can find it in your will, bring Gilbert also." A vision of Gilbert in the hospital contrasted to Gilbert admitting his love for her on the front porch made her smile. He had come so far. Loving him now was easy.

Jacob was back in his bed in what used to be the dining room, and the other bed was made ready for another soldier.

She sat down at the desk and wrote a letter to the boy's mother, telling her what a fine son she had and how he had fought hard both for the South and for his life.

> He said our cook's molasses cookies were good, but not up to those his mother made. He spoke of his home and family and how grateful he was that you raised him to know our living Lord. I know he is dancing with the angels in heaven now and wanting you to remember him strong and fine.
>
> In the name of our risen Lord,
> Louisa Highwood

She'd written to this mother before when her son first came to live with them. Return letters had been so appreciated.

She stared at the sheet of paper. If only she had Gilbert's home address so she could write her future mother-in-law and ask if they'd heard of their son. The harder she tried not to think of him, the more he came to mind. Was he suffering somewhere? Or had someone taken him in as they were doing? That is, if he were injured.

When Zachary returned, she would implore him to inquire again about Gilbert. Perhaps someone, somewhere, knew something. *When Zachary returned.* So much seemed to hinge on when Zachary would come back.

She refused to consider the threatening thought that surfaced when she least expected it. What if Zachary never returned?

# CHAPTER THIRTY-TWO

On the Oregon Trail
May 1863

"Some'uns been shot!"

"Who?"

"That man, Jones, with the big black beard." Jane Ellen put her hand to her side and struggled to catch her breath. "'Phelia said to get you. You the best healer around."

"You stay with the stock, then. Keep Patch with you." Jesselynn tore off across the field, her writing case clutched in one pumping arm. She hadn't thought to ask how bad, but at least she knew where her medical box was packed.

She shut her mind against any speculating and concentrated on breathing and not tripping on a gopher mound. "Where are they?" she asked as soon as she got to the wagon and could breathe.

Ophelia pointed to the right wagon and handed her the wooden box she'd stocked with supplies in Independence. "Dey got in a fight."

Jesselynn took the box and headed across the inner circle of wagons. She had to keep in mind that Ophelia had been the one to call her, not Wolf or one of the other families. But then, how would they know about her training? After all, healing was woman's work, unless there was a doctor around.

"Fools," muttered one of the men standing near the wagon.

"What happened?" Jesselynn paused beside him to figure out how to handle this.

"Got to drinking and got into an argument over something. Most likely too stupid to matter."

"But drinkin' is against the train's rules."

"I know, but when Wolf rode off, these two hit the bottle. You can bet there'll be a thorough inspection after this."

Jesselynn nodded. "I better see what I can do."

The wife of one of the men dabbed at a shoulder wound that still seeped, tears trickling down her thin cheeks. The other man sat with a makeshift bandage around his upper arm.

"I din't mean to hurt 'im, just scare him a mite." Tears rolled down Rufus Jones's cheeks.

Jesselynn dropped to her knees beside the woman. "Here, why don't you let me see what I can do."

"You a doctor?"

"No, but I've done quite a bit of treatin' wounds and such." She didn't say she'd learned it all from her mother.

The woman relinquished her place but moved back only a pace. Jesselynn examined the wound and felt under his shoulder, hoping for an exit wound. No such luck. That meant the bullet had to come out or he'd die of gangrene, not that he might not anyhow.

"I'm going to have to take the bullet out."

"I'se afeared of that." The woman wrung her hands. "He's not a bad man, but when he starts to drinkin', he . . ." Her voice trailed off.

Jesselynn knew that the Jones brothers had already built themselves a reputation as cantankerous and hard to get along with. But with most of the men out of the camp and the women washing clothes, the two had time to go at it.

"I'm going to need some help holding him down."

A snore from the wounded man released enough fumes to make her lean back. "Whew, maybe not. Go get Meshach. He's workin' at the forge."

"I'se here."

The deep voice from behind her made Jesselynn sigh with relief. Between the two of them—her cutting and Meshach holding and praying—they'd manage.

"Get us some water boiling, Mrs. Jones. We gotta get your husband cleaned up some. And is there any of that liquor left? We can use it to clean out this hole in his shoulder."

"Waste of good liquor," muttered the man she'd spoken with earlier.

"Be that as it may, I'll need you to hold down his legs. Anyone else around?"

"Only the womenfolk." His voice hardened. "And that other piece of worthless trash, his brother."

Jesselynn looked over her shoulder. "You can lie across his legs. That shouldn't hurt your arm any." *And it might be good if it did.* She looked again. The low-down dog was sound asleep. She and Meshach exchanged glances. They didn't need words. Wolf had almost turned *them* down, yet he'd taken on this heap of trouble?

Before Mrs. Jones could get the fire hot to boil the water, someone else brought a steaming kettle over and set it on the tripod. "Mrs. Jones, you found that liquor bottle yet?" She raised her voice to be heard over the snoring.

"Yes, but . . . but Tommy Joe, he might be . . ."

"Get the bottle or Tommy Joe might not live to drink anymore."

Mrs. Jones squeaked like a mouse trapped by a cat's paw, but the bottle showed up at Jesselynn's side.

"Sure would be easier if he was on a table."

"We can use the two planks from their wagon."

Jesselynn didn't need anyone to tell her who said that. Wolf's voice sounded flat, like a sharp piece of shale.

"Meshach, come help me set them up." The two men left, and Jesselynn sat back on her heels. The man she'd been working on stirred and blinked, then returned to snoring. She might have to give him a few more swigs, but, then, she'd seen men die, poisoned by the drink they craved. But other than the gaping hole in his shoulder, Tommy Joe—she shuddered at even the name—was in good shape. His color, what she could see under the matted black beard, looked good, and his breathing was steady. A belch made her blink. Her eyes watered.

When they had Jones on the makeshift table, Meshach handed her a freshly honed knife. Jesselynn washed her hands with soap and hot water, and after closing her eyes for a moment to ask for her Father's guidance, she stepped up to the table. Wolf stood across from her, Meshach beside her, and Jones's brother and another man at the hips.

"Ready?" They all nodded.

She barely flinched as she inserted the point of the knife into the wound to widen the hole for her fingers. Jones groaned.

"Hold him." Using her fingers as a probe, she felt around the tissue, searching for the bullet and any pieces of bone. She felt the sharp point of bone and with thumb and forefinger wiggled it free and dropped it on the ground.

*Oh, Lord, please help me.* Blood welled around her searching fingers. "Come on, come on." More prayer than mutter, she focused only on the sphere beneath her fingertips. Something hard.

Jones groaned, gagged, and vomited, splattering the wagon. "Turn his head." Meshach kept one hand on the man's arm and turned his head with the other.

"Hold him." Before she could say the words, all four men had thrown their bodies over the thrashing man on the table. In spite of the bucking, she probed and knew for sure she had the bullet. "Got it."

She held up the smashed bit of metal. Blood welled where her fingers had been. Jones gagged and wretched again, spewing foul-smelling vomitus all over Wolf's buckskin shirt.

The look of disgust on Wolf's face made Jesselynn want to smile. Instead, she grabbed the bottle of whiskey and, spreading the wound wider, poured the liquid in.

Jones let out a scream that could be heard for miles. He thrashed and bucked, sending his brother flying.

"Ow, my arm," Rufus cried.

"Pour some of that down his gullet." Wolf gave the order but didn't reach for the bottle. He left that to their other assistant, whose expression said what he thought of the whole thing. When their patient settled down again, Jesselynn looked to Meshach.

"You think we need to heat the knife?"

Meshach shrugged. "Might be de other enough. Him bleed good."

Jesselynn nodded and went ahead with the bandages, wishing she had some of the healing salve her mother used to use. While she had the recipe, she'd not had all the ingredients.

"Let's take him back to his own wagon. His wife can take care of him there." Wolf nodded to the three men, and they did just that.

Jesselynn washed her hands and glanced down at her clothes. "Looks like I been butchering hogs."

"Leastways with hogs, you got something good at the end." Aunt Agatha handed Jesselynn a towel to dry her hands. "You get those clothes off, and I'll wash the blood out before it sets up."

"Thanks." Jesselynn felt the quivering start in her toes and work its way up until she was shaking like she had the ague. Her knees turned to mush, and the world started to revolve.

"Sit and put your head down." Wolf grabbed her shoulder and plunked her down on a wagon tongue.

"Let go of me." She tried to flail at his restraining hand, but the action made her stomach roil. She kept her head down.

"Better?"

"Yes." She'd known what to do. He'd just beat her to it. She breathed in and out, deep breaths that brought her world back to standing still. His hand on her shoulder felt warm and comforting.

"Where did you learn to operate like that?"

"From my mother, but it's all a matter of sense." She slowly sat upright, ready to duck her head if the world tilted. When it stayed in place, so did she.

"Well, if he makes it through without gangrene, he'll owe you a debt."

Jesselynn shook her head. "No, no debt. I'd just as soon no one told him who did it. But the next time he punches his wife, you better do something about it, or I will."

"You take care of your business, and I'll take care of mine." The bite had returned to his voice.

So much for any moment of truce. Why couldn't she learn to keep her mouth shut, as her mother had always recommended? Jesselynn picked up her medical box and headed back to her own wagon, where Meshach had the forge back up hot and the iron ringing on the anvil. Two oxen were lined up waiting for his attention. He glanced up when she passed him, nodded and, after raising one eyebrow, went back to work. Didn't take much to read her thoughts, she knew. The thunder sitting on her forehead would be easy to see. Or maybe it was the lightning bolts shooting from her eyes. Shame the object of her frustration wasn't in reach of one.

Even though Tommy Joe Jones recovered with little problems, he never did come by to say thanks. Jesselynn wasn't surprised, but it sure sent Aunt Agatha off in a huff whenever she saw the man.

To the chagrin of the other hunting party, Benjamin returned with two deer and three prairie chickens, while the others had only a few ducks and a goose. Daniel brought back a string of catfish and bluegill, so they ate the fish and parceled the other out among the wagons.

"How'd you do that, boy?" Ambrose McPhereson, who was camped in front of them this night, asked. "I never saw nothin' out there."

Benjamin looked up from scaling fish with a smile that crinkled his eyes. "Think like a deer."

"Anytime you want to give me lessons in deer thinkin', I'll be ready."

"Thank you, suh."

"Name's Ambrose, not sir. What's your name?"

"Benjamin Highwood, suh."

"Well, Benjamin, how about I call you that and you call me Ambrose? Before this trip is over, we're all goin' to be family or foe, and I sure don't want to be any part of the latter."

Jesselynn watched the look on Benjamin's face as the man walked away. That alone made the trip worthwhile.

———

Just before they left the campsite at Vermilion Creek, a single wagon drawn by two teams of horses pulled into the area. The man who stepped down off the wagon seat appeared to have seen better days. When he lifted his hat, wiry gray hair flew in the breeze and matching brush covered his face. Gimping on one leg, he hitched across the packed dirt until he reached the nearest wagon, the one driven by Aunt Agatha.

"Howdy, ma'am." He touched the brim of a hat that was more slouch than firm. "Where's yer wagon master?" He coughed at the end, as if he hadn't done much talking of late.

Agatha nodded to where Wolf stood talking with two men. "The one in the buckskin shirt."

"Thankee."

Jesselynn looked back at his wagon in time to see an elder boy pop his head out and then retreat. Jane Ellen glanced at Jesselynn. "Bet that's his grandpap."

"You think so?" Jane Ellen had an uncanny way of picking up on things. Jesselynn had come to accept this as a gift, so she pretty much agreed.

"Looks like they come a long way."

"Most likely. All of us have."

"His horses need a good feedin'."

*Come on, let's get on the road.* Jesselynn felt as if she were all dressed up for a party and nowhere to go. First time in their traveling that Wolf didn't have them on the road by full light. She thumped a tattoo on the boot rest. "Hand me those strips of rawhide. Might as well make myself useful if we're going to be a while."

"They sure do be jawin'."

"They can do their jawing while we drive on, can't they?" Jesselynn knotted one end of the three thongs together and hooked that over a nail driven in the boot brace. Braiding rawhide was almost as good as knitting for keeping one's mouth from running off.

The new man limped back past their wagon and climbed up onto his own. When Wolf signaled the start, the new wagon fell in behind them.

"Well, I'll be."

Crossing the bridge over Vermilion Creek sure beat the fording they'd done on others. The hollow sound of hooves on plank, the creak of the gear and wheels was music to Jesselynn. While the rest had felt good, the need to get going again had returned. Besides, the farmer there had been making eyes at Ahab. And who was the man with the wagon? Would he be friend or trouble? Trouble or troubadour? She shook her head. Where had *that* come from?

# CHAPTER THIRTY-THREE

"Highwood, you're on second watch tonight."

"Yes, sir." Jesselynn fought to keep the snap from her voice. Why couldn't she just nod like most of the others?

The dissecting look she got from Wolf made her feel as if he was studying her, not quite sure how to take her.

"Jones, you too."

Jesselynn coughed to hide the groan she'd almost let slip. Rufus was about the last man she wanted to stand watch with. While the bullet hole in his arm was healing well, it hadn't helped his disposition any. He and his brother were weasel-mean clear through.

"Just you keep that fancy pants away from me," Jones muttered with a sneer in Jesselynn's direction.

Jesselynn could feel her right eyebrow arch. *What in the world is the matter with him? He got it in for me just 'cause I let someone else bandage his arm? We saved his brother after all. Wasn't my fault the two of them were fighting.*

Meshach shifted closer to where she sat on the wagon tongue. They'd had the bad luck to be camped right behind the Joneses in the circle of wagons. Not that anyone wanted to be on either side of them. In spite of Wolf having cautioned them, the language was enough to make a washerwoman blush.

Patch came and sat at her knee.

"That's enough." Like a rifle crack, Wolf's command split the air.

Jesselynn felt more than heard Patch's growl. Meshach cleared his throat. The two sounded much alike.

"Git 'im away from that nigger and then see—"

"I said *enough*." The whisper was far more intimidating than the bark.

Rufus shut up but rose from his seat and ambled off behind the wagon.

Jesselynn still wasn't sure what all the shouting was about, but she knew it had something to do with her.

"I switch wid Marse Jesse." Meshach didn't ask—he stated.

Wolf shrugged. "Suit yourself."

Jesselynn waited until the others had gone before hissing at Meshach. "What was that all about?"

Meshach shook his head. "Better dis way."

Across the circle Henry Bronson was tuning up his fiddle. Jesselynn breathed a sigh of relief. Since she had first watch, she wouldn't have to worry about young lady Elizabeth making doe eyes at her.

———

Wolf knew the urge to kick Rufus Jones out of camp was not to be acted upon. But the thought of knocking the meanness out of him had plenty of appeal. Why hadn't he seen what a passel of trouble those two brothers were? Young Highwood had done nothing but help the two, saved the life of one actually, but they still had it in for him.

Instead of joining the dancers around the fire, he saddled his horse and rode out to where the cattle and horses were grazing. The stars looked low enough that if he stood tall in his stirrups, he might pluck one out of the sky. A thin band of light still outlined the western horizon. Animals were better company than people anyway.

The thought of taking this wagon train clear to Oregon galled worse than a burr under a saddle. Especially after that crack tonight. There'd be more blood let on this train before the end of the trail, of that he was sure. Granted young Mr. Highwood was a trifle on the effeminate side, but he was still a boy, and some took longer to fill out than others. From what he heard and saw, the boy knew his medicine. Knew an awful lot for his age. Whatever his age was.

*If he was with my people, he would have gone on his vision quest by now and most likely been on a raid to another tribe's camp. Stealing horses was a step in growing to manhood.*

He sat listening to the crunch of animals grazing, the occasional snort of a horse, the stamp of a foot. The fiddle sang of love and loss from behind him, the notes holding on the slight breeze like smoke. He sorted the odors on the wind that carried the pleas of the fiddle. Fresh cow manure, spring grass, dried horse sweat, fire smoke, fried venison, again thanks to that young black of Highwood's. He'd said Benjamin could find deer and rabbit when others failed, and he'd proven himself repeatedly. But now that they were beyond the dense civilization of eastern Kansas, the game would be more plentiful.

He'd rather throw down his bedroll out here than in camp any day.

---

"That old goat," Agatha grumbled as she stirred the morning mush.

"What are you talkin' about?" Jesselynn stretched her arms above her head and yawned fit to crack her jaw.

"Brushface asked her to dance, and she din't take to it."

"Why not? Mr. Lyons seems like a very nice man." Jesselynn dropped forward to touch her hands to the ground, anything to stretch out her back. "And besides, you shouldn't call him that." She must have slept on a dirt clump or something. By the time she roused Meshach for his watch, she could have slept on solid rock—with thorns in it.

"Speak of the angels—"

"Devil, most likely."

"Aunt Agatha, he'll hear you," Jesselynn hissed under her breath.

"Morn'in." Nathan Lyons tipped his hat in greeting.

"Morning, Mr. Lyons. Fine day." Jesselynn watched her aunt out of the corner of her eye.

Agatha's *harrumph* could be heard several wagons away.

Jesselynn glanced at Ophelia, who rolled her eyes and shrugged. When Agatha turned to fetch something out of the wagon, Jesselynn sidled over to Ophelia. "What is goin' on here?"

"Mr. Lyons, he go out of him way to be nice to her, but she... oh, she get all riled up."

"I see." But she didn't see a thing. Life would be so much easier if she could just ride and not have to sort out all the people. Like that pile of worthless bones, Rufus Jones. Whatever had gone on last night was sure to come around and cause trouble again. If only she understood what it was all about.

Halfway to the noon rest stop, Mrs. Brundsford caught up to Jesselynn walking beside her lead ox. "Mr. Jesse, I hate to bother you, but could you come look at Mrs. Smith's littlest boy? He ain't been well for the last couple of days."

"The little guy with red curly hair?"

"That's the one—Roddy."

"What seems to be the trouble?"

"A'fore he was just listless, you know, wanting to be held all the time, whiney. But today he's burning up with fever."

Jesselynn called to Jane Ellen walking some ahead. "Come take my place for a while."

Jane Ellen dropped back and took the goad Meshach had fashioned. "Where you goin'?"

"Going to the Smith wagon."

The little boy lay on a pallet on a box in the rear of the wagon, where the rolled-up canvas side gave him a bit of breeze. His mother put another wet cloth on his forehead as Jesselynn and Mrs. Brundsford came around the end.

"I brung Mr. Jesse."

"Thank you for coming, but I don't see what you can do. He's just doing poorly."

Jesselynn laid a hand on the pale forehead. "He's burning up with fever. Get that blanket off him and soak it in water. Wet, it might do him some good."

"But he's got the shakes one minute—"

"I know, but we need to get that fever down." They'd just removed the blanket when the boy jerked so hard he almost fell off the box. He twitched all over and banged his head on the wood.

"Oh, he's goin' to die."

"Hold him in your arms." While she talked, Jesselynn dipped part of the blanket in the water and laid it on the child's body. Roddy jerked again.

"Has he had anything to eat? To drink?" His mother shook her head at both questions. "Here." Jesselynn handed a cup of water to Mrs. Smith. "See if you can spoon some into him when the fit is over." While she worked with the child, Jesselynn racked her brain trying to think what her mother did in cases like this.

*Willow tea.* But where could they get willow bark out here? And there was no fire to boil water with anyway. *Would laudanum help? But he's not in pain.* She tried to sort out the conflicting thoughts. *Dear God, help us. Please, you love the little children, and we do too. Help us in the name of Jesus.*

The boy lay limp, his chest rising only slightly with each slow breath. But he was cooler to the touch. And he wasn't shaking.

"Oh, dear God, thank you. Thank you, Mr. Jesse." Mrs. Smith kissed her child's little hand, tears trickling down her cheeks. "I already lost two babes, one born dead and another about this age. I sure do pray the Lord spares little Roddy here."

"We'll do what we can. Get as much water in him as possible. If Benjamin can bag some prairie chickens, we can make a broth tonight and get some nourishment in him." Jesselynn laid her hand on the child's chest, feeling the heartbeat only faintly. "Got any molasses or honey you could stir into the water? That might make him want more."

"That I do." Mabel Smith pointed to a box up behind her. "Get the jug out of there," she told her older daughter.

Jesselynn left them spooning honey water into the little boy. He had that look of death about him, like a blown-out candle.

––––––––

A woman's keening woke the dawn. Jesselynn knew Roddy had died in his sleep. While he'd seemed some better the night before, she wasn't surprised.

The men dug a hole while the women dressed the child in a pair of pants and shirt, both sewn by his mother for his upcoming birthday.

"He looks so nice. At least we had something proper to bury him in." Mabel Smith stroked her child's corn-silk hair. "Now, Roddy, you just play with all those children round Jesus' feet." Eyes streaming, she looked to Jesselynn. "Thank you for tryin' to help us. Guess God just wanted another child back in His kingdom."

" 'The Lord gave, and the Lord hath taken away,' " murmured one of the other women. " 'Blessed be the name of the Lord.' "

Jesselynn nodded and turned away. *Little children shouldn't have to die like that. Why, God, do you spare mean hunks of offal like the Jones brothers and take a child away from his loving mother's arms like this? I just don't understand, and it makes me angry—real angry. Roddy brought joy and delight to everyone. Those others bring nothing but misery.*

She heard the others gathering for the reading and forced herself to join them, standing back on the fringes. Two of the men laid the small body, now wrapped in a quilt, in the hole. Mr. Bronson opened his Bible and read the Twenty-third Psalm. " 'The Lord is my shepherd; I shall not want.... ' " Other voices joined in, and the ancient words drifted across the prairie. Jesselynn sighed, wiped the moisture from her eyes, and felt someone staring at her. She turned enough to see Rufus Jones snickering behind her and pantomiming wiping his eyes, then pointing at her.

The urge to use the oxen whip on the pair of them rose so strong she rammed her hands in her pockets to keep from attacking. Benjamin and Daniel appeared on either side of her, as if drawn by an unseen force. They kept their gaze straight forward, bowing their heads in prayer with the others. Jesselynn sneaked a peek over her shoulder, but the two lowlifes were gone.

"Dust to dust, ashes to ashes, blessed be the name of the Lord."

"Amen."

The wagon folks paid their respects to Mr. and Mrs. Smith, then all returned to their own wagons and prepared to leave. Mr. Smith pounded a wooden cross into the ground at the head of the small grave.

"I hate to tell you this." Wolf stopped at the Smith wagon. "But that cross won't do any good. We have to drive the wagons over the grave...."

"No, Lord, no. Don't let this happen." Mabel's voice rose on a sob.

"But that's the only way we can keep wild animals from digging it up."

"I see." Mr. Smith nodded and blew his nose. "There now, Mabel, we will do what we must." He patted his wife's hand.

Wolf mounted his horse and trotted to the lead wagon. "Roll 'em."

Since the sun was well up by then, Jesselynn knew they would push hard to make up for lost time. But when her wagon pulled up to the now obliterated grave, it was all she could do to stay in line. Her mind flew back to the graveyard off from the big house at home. Carved headstones, a winged angel, small stones close together marking the passing of babies, manicured grass, a sheltering weeping-willow tree, petals of blooming honeysuckle—all surrounded by a wrought-iron fence. A place to dream, to remember, to feel the love that passed from generation to generation. A gentle plot filled with beauty and birdsong.

No markers here, only dust and sky and a westering vision.

*Mother, can you hear me? I want to go home.*

The horizon shimmered and danced through the veil of her tears.

———

"How are you, ma'am?" Wolf paused at the Smith campfire that night.

"Tolerable." Mrs. Smith sighed. "He did look mighty peaceful, our Roddy. And so nice in his new clothes. I sewed them up special, just for him. First time he didn't wear hand-me-downs."

Jesselynn paused before stepping over the wagon tongue so she wouldn't interrupt the conversation.

"I just wanted you to know how sorry I am."

"Thank you, Wolf. That means a great deal coming from you."

Since she heard Wolf heading the other direction, Jesselynn continued on her way to her neighbors' camp. If only she could figure out why she worked so hard to stay out of his way, other than the way he had treated her in the beginning, of course. Had his attitude changed?

She paused to think for a moment. Surely since she'd taken to doctoring those in the wagon train, he had shown her a measure of respect. And he appreciated the extra meat Benjamin and Daniel brought in. That was for sure.

She set her full water bucket down by the fire. Agatha and Ophelia had biscuits baking, beans cooking, and rabbit frying. "Sure smells good."

"Oh, there you are, Marse Jesse. Dat Missy Elizabeth, she be lookin' for you."

Jesselynn groaned. "Which way did she go?"

Ophelia pointed to the west.

Jesselynn headed east. Surely she was needed out by the horses.

# CHAPTER THIRTY-FOUR

### The Platte River

"Talk about flat."

"Mebbe dat why dey calls it de River Road." Meshach stood in his stirrups. "Sure do be flat—and long." He and Jesselynn had ridden Ahab and Domino ahead of the wagon train and stopped at the last rise so they could see both ways. The Platte River stretched as far as they could see both east and west, while the northern view across the river looked about the same. Muddy and wet was about all Jesselynn could think of it. Other than that, Wolf had said the River Road to Fort Laramie was the easiest part of the trail. Knee-high grass waved in the wind, just begging their horses and cattle to eat and drink their fill.

"Some sight, isn't it?" Wolf rode up and stopped beside them. "Not much flooding this year, but I've seen times when this was hill-to-hill water."

"Is that the Indian encampment over there?" Jesselynn pointed to an area where spirals of campfire smoke lazed in the air.

"Could be. But there are settlers taking up land along here too, now that the forts are in place."

"And the Indians leave them alone?"

"For now." Wolf didn't look at her when he answered. He didn't want to tell them of the recent attacks he'd heard about. As the whites settled instead of just passing through, the Indians had become more aggressive. Settlers drove off the game or killed it. The buffalo were getting scarce this far east, so the Indians were losing their hunting grounds.

"We've been fortunate, I hear, in not being attacked." Jesselynn turned to Wolf for confirmation.

"True." Wolf pointed to the west. "Fort Kearney is a day's journey over there. We'll be stopping for supplies."

The land shimmered in a haze, the light seeming to dance before their eyes. Bluebells and daisies dotted the grasslands, and meadowlarks trilled their courtship arias, often on the wing, liquid joy in the morning.

The creak of wagon wheels, voices calling with laughter as they glimpsed the flatlands, the bellow of a cow, all the sounds of the wagon train on the move broke into her reverie. She should go back and drive the wagon, but the thought held no appeal. Daniel was doing just fine. And Aunt Agatha would much rather drive than walk, so no one had spelled her since the beginning of the trip.

"There's a good place to camp about five miles upriver. We'll stop there for the night." Wolf turned his horse and squeezed him into a lope, seemingly without signal of either leg or rein.

Jesselynn turned in her saddle just enough to watch them streaking across the land. Wolf snatched his hat off and let the wind carry his hair in a dark banner behind him. She knew she rode well, but whether the difference was in Thoroughbred versus Appaloosa pony or his growing up on horseback and she in the big house, there was indeed a difference. A big difference. She patted Ahab's shoulder. At least her horses were holding up beyond his predictions. As was she.

Jesselynn sat bareback on Ahab, letting him and the others drink out of the Platte River. Ankle-deep, the stallion blew in the water and started to paw with one front foot, splashing water everywhere. "I know, you want a bath or at least a roll, but not here and not now." Ahab kept on splashing.

"He goin' roll on you." Benjamin shook his head. "You watch it."

"No, he won't. I won't let him." Jesselynn raised her face to the breeze that kicked up ripples farther out in the sand-colored water. Today had been the warmest so far, a portent of the heat to come.

Ahab buckled his front legs, tipping her forward, and before she could even gasp, she lay flat out in the river, sucking water with her snort. She scrambled away from the stallion so she wouldn't get caught under him and got to her feet, soaking wet from hat to boot heel.

Benjamin about fell off Domino laughing.

Jesselynn looked from her horse, who wisely kept his nose out of the water, to Benjamin and then down at herself. A chuckle rose, fluttered past the muddy-water taste, and burst forth. She looked a sight, she could tell. Taking off her hat, she slapped it against her thigh and crammed it back on her head, laughing all the while.

"Hey, horse, you sure fooled me."

Ahab surged to his feet—one dripping, muddy-coated mass—and shook. Mud splattered five feet in all directions.

Benjamin buried his face in Domino's mane, laughing fit to burst. "You cotched de black spot disease."

Only the thought of her heavy boots kept Jesselynn from diving in and taking a real swim. As she plodded toward the shore, she glanced up to see Wolf staring at her, his dark eyes slit, likewise his mouth.

"The water feels great, not that I planned to ... take ... a—" *What is the matter with him? Looks like he's seen a ghost or something.* She looked down to make sure her shirt was buttoned and knew what he was seeing. The strips of cloth she used to bind her breasts to keep them flat. Sure proof she was not who she said she was.

"*Mister* Jesse Highwood?"

At his sarcastic tone, Jesselynn could feel her water-soaked clothing begin to steam. She raised her chin and stared him in the eyes. "For as long as necessary, yes."

"Hey, Wolf." Young Billy Bronson cantered up to pull to a stop beside the paint. "I'll be a jumpin' bullfrog. Hey, Jesse, how's the water?" He leaned his crossed arms on the saddlehorn and gave her a studying look, then shook his head. "Well, I'll be ... who'd a-guessed it?"

Jesselynn ignored the teasing and, gathering her reins and a hank of mane, swung atop the stallion, who had not the grace to look ashamed of all the trouble he'd caused. With his mud and her wet clothing, she barely made it but finally was able to sit erect without asking for help. *Ask him not to say anything.* She answered that voice with another. *That will only make the gossip more titillating.*

*She's—he's a woman. Not Mr. Jesse at all.* Fury warred with joy, and confusion defeated them both. Wolf swung his horse around without a word and headed west on the Great Platte River Road as if savages were screaming on his tail. He shut off all thought and left himself to the rhythm of his horse's pounding feet.

"He goin' ride dat horse right into de ground, he keep up like dat." Benjamin brought Domino to a standstill beside her. The mares had already left the water and were grazing on a patch of green grass. One foal lay flat out, the other had gone back to nursing.

"Did I say somethin' wrong?" Billy looked after the racing Wolf.

*Or is he fleeing?* Jesselynn wondered. She wasn't sure. As unobtrusively as possible she pulled her heavy shirt away from her body. She couldn't go back to camp like this, and with the setting sun, supper would soon be ready.

"No, just got a burr under his hide." At least that was as good an explanation as any. "Did someone need him?"

"My pa was lookin' for him."

*Good thing he didn't come out. The whole wagon train would know by now. Not that they wouldn't anyway if the glint in Billy's eye is any indication.* Should she ask him to keep the secret? Was the secret necessary any longer? Sure they'd have to keep the horses away from the fort, but would folks knowing about her being a woman cause a problem?

Other than those who felt they'd been hornswaggled.

Like Wolf.

He could refuse to let them travel with the train. But why would he? They'd proven their worth.

She tried to keep the inner war from showing on her face. "We better get on back. How about you go ask Aunt Agatha for a jacket or vest for me." After Benjamin trotted off, she rounded up their horses and let them graze their way back to camp.

From the looks she received when she rode into camp, she knew Billy had blabbed.

"Well, I never..." One of the women muttered just loud enough for Jesselynn to hear.

"So what do we do?" Jesselynn asked Aunt Agatha when they met at the rear of the wagon.

Agatha sighed. "Old busybodies must not have enough to do to find time for all the gossipin'." She arched her back and dug her fists into the middle of it. "Land sakes, but that wagon has a hard seat."

"If it would help to put a back on the seat, Meshach could do that for you." Glad to be thinking of something besides her own britches, Jesselynn studied her aunt. In spite of the sunbonnet Agatha always wore, the sun had found its way to turn her aunt's cheeks and chin the color of soft, tanned deerskin. Her eyes had a brightness formerly lacking, and her mouth no longer looked pinched, as though she'd sucked on a lemon.

*No wonder Brushface finds her appealing. She is.* She knew she'd better be careful in referring to Mr. Lyons that way, but the name was so fitting.

" 'Pears to me that we can handle this in one of two ways."

Jesselynn waited, knowing there was no hurrying Aunt Agatha when she was pondering.

"One, we can call a meeting and tell the whole group, or two, we can ignore them and go on as though nothing was different." She kneaded her back again. "Personally, it ain't none of their business."

*And this from the woman who had a conniption fit the first time she saw me in britches?* Jesselynn bit her lip to keep the astonishment from her face. But Agatha didn't know about one important fact—the look on Wolf's face when he discovered her secret.

They reached Fort Kearney late the next afternoon. The United States flag snapped in the breeze, blue uniforms swarmed all over the place, and Jesselynn wanted to run back out on the prairie even though they camped half a mile from the fort itself. Another wagon train pulled in after they did. It also came from the east but on the Nebraska Trail, they learned later. After they'd circled the wagons and set up camp, Wolf and several of the men rode on into the fort proper.

When Wolf assigned the watches for the night, Jesselynn stared at him. Tonight had been her turn, and he'd not called her name. Since they were running the Thoroughbreds with the other horses and livestock much of the time, she tried to take extra duty, she and her men, rather than less.

"What de matter?" Ophelia stopped beside her as she stared after the departing wagon master.

"I'm not sure, but I aim to find out." Jesselynn took off at a dogtrot to catch up with his long-legged stride. Wolf Torstead could cover more ground in less time than any man she knew.

"Wolf!"

He stopped and turned around. They were far enough from camp now for no one to overhear.

"Why did you leave me out of the watch?" No pleasantries, just go for the jugular.

"Women don't stand watch."

"Oh." Of course, how could she be so stupid? What to say? "But—"

"No," he interrupted. His eyes narrowed. "Keeping women and children safe is part of my job, and I will do so."

"But I—"

"You want to wear britches, that is your choice, but who stands watch is mine." He didn't have to finish. The "and you won't be" rang loud and clear.

If she'd thought there was any chance of them becoming friends, the look he gave her disabused her of that thought.

"What are you so mad about? I did what I had to do. Even you could tell that."

His face looked like a slate wiped clean, so devoid of expression was he.

"Is it just because I fooled you? Would you have let me bring my wagons had you known I was—am—a female?" She almost said a woman but changed her mind. He most likely thought her still a young girl. At twenty, she was way past marrying age, according to custom.

He crossed his arms over his chest. "Are you finished?"

*Looks like it.* "Yes."

"Good." He turned and strode off, leaving her with her teeth clenched and her hands clamped into fists.

The names she called him under her breath had plenty to do with his parentage, or lack thereof, along with a few choice epithets overheard on night watch. Being a woman in men's clothing had offered her a different view of life in general and of women in particular. Her ears had burned at times.

———

When she went into the fort to buy supplies, she went as Mr. Jesse Highwood. She'd taken Aunt Agatha's advice and gone on as if nothing had happened. Sooner or later the gossip would die out. If only it could be sooner so she didn't have to put up with the disapproving glances and muttered remonstrances from most of the women in the train, and a few of their husbands too.

She laid her list on the counter and wandered down the aisles, looking at the harnesses, the boots, the woolen blankets. Warm as it was getting, woolen blankets weren't needed for some time. When her turn came, she waited while the proprietor finished with the earlier customer and turned to her.

"Hello, son, what can I get for you?"

Jesselynn pushed her list forward. "All of that."

The man read the list, looked up at her, back down at the list. "Ah, this looks like a lot. You, ah . . ."

Jesselynn dug in her pocket, pulled out her leather pouch, and plunked it down on the counter with a satisfying clink. "That should cover it." *Along with a lot more. What difference does it make if I'm a young man or young woman? If I hear one more time 'Is your daddy here?' I shall personally sock 'em with this rather than be polite.*

"Oh, and add on a dozen peppermint sticks and a packet of horehound drops."

"Yes, sir."

"I'll take two bags of oats on the back of the mule and pick up the other supplies tomorrow, if that would be all right."

"Fine, fine. Anythin' else I can get for you?"

*Amazing how the clink of gold changed his attitude.*

Walking back to camp would be good for her. She'd let Daniel come in to pick up the rest. "Daniel is one of my range hands. He'll be by tomorrow. He's black. That won't be a problem, will it?"

"None 'tall." He waited while she counted out his money, then tried to give her paper in return.

"No, I pay in gold, I get silver in change." She held out her hand.

With a glare and a grunt, he took the paper back and laid out silver. "Paper's just as good as gold here at the fort."

"But it might not be at the next supply station. I'm sure you understand." She gave him stare for stare and strolled out of the store. "He ups the prices for us anyway, Roman. I hate doing business with thieves." Jesselynn checked to make sure the bags were tied and balanced before setting out for the east gate and camp.

Off to her left a platoon of what must be new recruits was drilling, the sergeant barking orders. An officer watched the proceedings from the shade of a porch, smoking a cigar and blowing smoke rings.

"Hey, boy, you want to join the Union army? You look old enough."

"No, thank you."

"Make a man outa you." The officer waved his cigar and leaned against the porch post.

*Not much chance.* "I'm goin' to Oregon."

"You're making a big mistake." He blew another smoke ring.

Jesselynn didn't bother to answer. The sooner they left the area, the better.

She didn't rest easy again until they were two days west of the fort. In less than two weeks they'd be at Fort Laramie.

Was it time for her to become a woman again—or not?

———

*Twelve days, and we'll be at Fort Laramie. Two days of hard riding, and I could be home.* Wolf didn't have to close his eyes to see the pine-covered mountains, the clear running streams, and the tepees of his people. Home in Wyoming Territory. Could he force himself to go on to Oregon from Laramie? Instead of going home?

Visions of a laughing Jesse Highwood, soaking wet, dogged him day and night. What was her *real* name?

# CHAPTER THIRTY-FIVE

## Richmond, Virginia

*Dearest Jesse.* Louisa dipped her quill again and continued.

> *How I wish you were here, but even more I wish we were all at Twin Oaks where we belong, not scattered about the country like now. I have strange news. When Zachary and I went to Washington for medical supplies, he disappeared, and we haven't seen him since. That was over four weeks ago. I keep praying God is keeping him safe, but lately God seems to be saying no to my requests.*

She continued with a description of her trip and the happenings at the house, including a description of Aunt Sylvania reading to their soldiers and actually turning pink at their teasing. She told about the high life their sister was living with her lawyer husband in the Richmond capital.

> *I'm just grateful I don't have to be part of that, but Carrie Mae seems to enjoy herself. Who would have ever dreamed growing up that the three of us would be living such different lives? Please, please, I beg of you, write and let us know how you are. Regarding my lieutenant, as you referred to him, we still have no news. I am having a hard time believing the old saw "no news is good news" in this case. Surely if he were able, he would have written by now.*

She stopped and set her pen down, struck by a new thought. What if he just didn't care any longer? What if he had met someone new, or someone he knew before the army?

She stoppered the ink bottle and rose to go look out the window.

Her heart surged, and she let out a shriek. By the time she reached the front door, the others had come running.

"What wrong?" Reuben caught his breath.

"Nothing. Zachary is here!" She flung open the door to see her dear brother negotiating the three front steps.

"Easy. Don't knock me over." He raised a cautious stump, hopped the final riser, and leaned against the porch post. "Now." He spread his arms wide and welcomed her hug.

"Ah, Marse Zachary, you done made it home *again*." The emphasis on the last word made Zachary laugh, the pure joy of it rising to the newly budding leaves of the stately elm trees.

"Yes, old man, I am home again, but this time there was no doubt as to *if* but only *when*. Coming the route I did was considerably slower than the train Louisa took." He gave her a questioning glance, and she nodded.

Yes, she had delivered the morphine to the surgeon general at the hospital and nearly cried at the look of gratitude in his eyes. While he admonished her to never do such a thing again, she knew she would. Her boys needed it.

She hadn't gone back to ask if they were out again; she knew the answer without the asking. Five pounds or so of morphine, even rationed, wouldn't last long.

Aunt Sylvania appeared in the doorway, tears streaming down her cheeks. "Ah, dear boy, you have returned. Thank you, Lord above. I was beginning to think He'd called you home."

"Now, Aunty, I'm too mean to die yet. God doesn't want me till I get old and gray and with no teeth to jaw at Him with." He hugged his aunt, accepting all the pats from the help and the congratulations from the one remaining soldier who'd been in the house when he left.

"Lots of new faces. That's good, right?" He sank down into an easy chair and propped his crutch under his thigh so he could rest his leg on it.

"Mostly." Louisa took the chair nearest him, knowing they wouldn't discuss the trip until they were alone.

"You heard from the lieutenant?" he asked in a moment's silence while Abby handed around the coffee cups and a platter of lemon cookies.

"I musta knowed you was comin' home. Baked dese just today." Abby pushed the plate back at him so he could take more than two.

To please her, Zachary bit into one and smiled wide, shaking his head at the same time. "You make the best lemon cookies in the whole world."

"Go on, now, you say dat to all de cooks."

"No, not at all. Yours are the best." To prove it, he took a handful and set them on the table beside his saucer. "Now, then, tell me all the news."

For the next half hour, that's just what they did. When he was all caught up and the coffeepot empty, Zachary sighed. "If y'all don't mind, I could do with a lie down. You'll wake me in time for supper?" He smiled at Louisa. "Then I reckon I'll be really awake for another of our all hours' chats."

----

Later that night the two of them retired to his room after the others had gone to bed. After telling his own tale at her insistence, Zachary turned to Louisa. "Now, tell me everything, and I mean everything, about your trip home."

Louisa complied, trying to remember every detail. When she finished, he nodded, fingertips templed, his elbows on the arms of the chair.

"We need to go again."

"I know, but they know me there. Pretty hard to disguise limbs and a face like mine. If it hadn't been for the Quakers, I'd be in prison or shot. I do have some good contacts now if we can dream up a way to do this."

"I'll go."

"You and what brigade?"

"Zachary, I made it home by myself."

"Yes, thanks to a Yankee army wife."

"There's that too." Louisa waited for him to continue and, when he didn't, decided to ask her own questions. "Zachary, I have a favor to ask." When he nodded, she continued. "Would you please ask whomever you can about Lieutenant Lessling? I *must* know what happened."

"But, Louisa, you know the report said that he died in that train explosion."

"I know about the report, but he might have lived through it. Others did."

"Yes, and to the best of our knowledge, they are all accounted for. When people are alive, they come forth to say so."

"*Please.*"

He nodded. "If it will make you happy."

———

Two days later he sat her down on the chaise lounge on the verandah and took her hand in his.

"You don't have good news, do you?"

"No. But there was finally proof. A watch bearing his father's name was found at the site."

"So, he could be a—"

"No, dearest Louisa, the watch was attached to . . ."

Louisa covered her face with her hands. "No, don't say it."

"I'm sorry, but you wanted to know for sure."

"Yes." Pain struck, not only her heart but her entire being. Lieutenant Lessling was gone, forever and for sure. There would be no wedding, no life together. Her first love, her only love. She sat stone still, letting the tears flow. Finally she wiped them away, steel returning to jaw and spine.

"When can I leave for another trip? I must do some good with my life." She could hear the reckless tone of her voice. The look Zachary gave her said he had heard it too.

"We'll see, little sister. We'll see."

"Now you sound just like Daddy."

"I'll take that as a compliment." He rubbed his leg, digging under the straps. "If only we had all listened to wisdom such as his, perhaps . . . perhaps . . . but that is water under the bridge. Now we must see it through."

She thought he'd forgotten she was there until he looked up with anguish-filled eyes. "Louisa, I cannot lose you too."

"We shall see. After all, maybe the war will end next week." But both of them knew she was only trying to put on a good face. Maybe the war would go on forever, or at least until every Southern male was dead.

*"I will never leave you."*

*I know that, but, God, you seem so far away. And so many no's. Can I bear it?*

Surely it was the breeze that whispered, *Yes.*

# CHAPTER THIRTY-SIX

## The Great Platte River Road
## May 1863

Why did the land of the Oglala people have such a pull this time? Wolf had been pondering that question for miles, days, and weeks. Eyes squinted against the sun that set the land to shimmering, he studied the land ahead of them. Sod houses had sprung up in the last year like dirt boxes tossed out by a fretful child. Would the Oglala tolerate the white man taking over the land? Especially if the railroad cut its way across the prairies, as he'd heard it would.

His thoughts shifted back to the wagon train plodding along behind him. Another fight the night before, this time between two families he'd have never thought would cause trouble. And Jesselynn Highwood again patched up the wounded. No wonder she—hard to remember that he was really a she—was so skilled at stitching up flesh. It still rankled that she'd fooled him for so long. Of course now that he knew Jesse was Jesselynn, he could see all the signs that should have told him that in the beginning—the way she cared for her little brother and her ease with cooking and things of the camp. Now that the word was out, he saw that she'd picked up her knitting and patching.

The image of her with an arm around little Thaddeus, head tipped to listen to his story, ate at him. How could he have been so duped? If this was a day for studying on hindsight, he had plenty of studying to do.

"Mr. Wolf!"

And not enough time to do it.

He turned in his saddle to watch young Billy Bronson come flying across the plain. Wolf waited, something he'd learned to do well.

"Benjamin says there's buffalo over the rise. Should we send out a hunting party?"

"Get Benjamin and Daniel. Did he say how far away?"

"Mile or two."

"Good. Tell your father to come out here. You can come too. I'll lead the party."

Billy galloped off again.

Within minutes they gathered on the north side of the rise. "Now listen to me and listen good. A bull buffalo can be one of God's meanest critters, so don't take any chances." He looked right at Billy. "There will be no shootin' for shootin's sake. Each one will hone in on one buffalo. Shoot it, and get out of the way. Unlike bows and arrows, the sound of the rifle shots will spook the herd and send it into a stampede, hopefully away from the wagon train. "We're goin' to ride up nice and easy, as if we were buffalo ourselves." He glanced up to see Daniel and Benjamin swap smiles of pure excitement. "Any questions?"

When they all shook their heads, he added, "Aim for the head. Between the eyes is best—lose less meat that way. Don't shoot a cow with a calf either. But above all, be careful."

They walked the horses over the crest. He heard someone suck in a breath and knew it was awe and delight combined. While the herd was not nearly the size of those he remembered as a boy, the sight of hundreds of buffalo roaming across the plain thrilled a man's heart.

Slowly they eased toward the herd, stopping when the animals grew restless, then proceeding again. When they were close enough for clean shots, Wolf raised his hand and let it fall.

Shots rang out and five animals sank to the ground. The hunters hung back as the rest of the herd broke into a run, heading south away from the hunters as Wolf had hoped.

"You want we should get another?" Benjamin trotted his horse up to Wolf.

"No. This is plenty. Get more and the meat will spoil before we can dry it." He rode up to one of the kills. "Make sure they're dead and then slit the throats so they bleed out. Bronson, go on back to camp and have them circle the wagons for the night, then bring as many as you can to help butcher these beasts. We've not a moment to waste."

Working in pairs, they moved from carcass to carcass, bleeding them out, then gutting. Meshach showed up next, then the others as they could come. Working together, they stripped the hide off one, cut it in quarters, and, laying the meat on the hide, tied the legs together over a pole and slung ropes around it to carry it back to camp between two horses.

A cheer went up when the first load of meat reached camp.

"Bring in the stomachs and intestines too."

Benjamin nodded. The hearts and livers had gone with the first load. Every skillet in camp would be frying fresh liver for supper. By dark the only trace of the hunt left on the prairie was blood-soaked ground and the remains from the stomachs and intestines. Even the hooves and horns had gone to camp to be used however Wolf suggested.

The hunters dragged in with the final load.

Soon every cooking pot was bubbling with fresh meat, and every knife in the train was being used to slice thin strips off haunch and shoulder to hang to dry over the fires to be transferred to the sides of the wagons in the morning. The white canvases reflected the heat of the sun enough to continue the process started over the cook fires. Since Benjamin had been the one to spot the herd, one hide had gone to the Highwood wagons. Wolf gave his to Nate Lyons, and while the Jones brothers shouted they should have the third, he gave it to the Smiths, where he knew the hide would be valued for its warmth and tended carefully. Bronson kept one and gave the other to another family.

"Would you care to join us for supper?" Aunt Agatha, as even he'd taken to calling her, asked Wolf when he walked past their wagon.

He started to say no, thank you, but out of the corner of his eye caught the look of total disgust on Jesselynn's face. "Thank you, it would be a privilege." He glanced down at a tug on his pants leg.

"Buff'lo for supper, Mist Wolf." Thaddeus smiled up at him, blue eyes sparkling. "Me shoot buff'lo too."

"Someday."

"Uh huh, someday. Jesse say when I get big."

"Thaddeus, don't bother Mr. Wolf."

The little boy stepped back at the sharp tone in his sister's voice.

"Oh, he's no bother." Wolf heard a burst of laughter from the school-age children gathered around Nate Lyons. Every evening as soon as they'd made camp, he taught ciphering, spelling, reading, and writing. His storytelling drew children and grown-ups alike. His ongoing story of the Jehosaphats had become a nightly ritual for most of the camp before bedding down. That and the singing led by Bronson, the fiddler, and son Billy on the harmonica.

Wolf leaned down and scooped Thaddeus up to sit on his shoulder. "Can he come with me?" He asked the question of Aunt Agatha while keeping an eye on Jesselynn.

"I don't know why not." Agatha patted Thaddeus's knee. "Now you be a good boy, hear?"

Thaddeus straightened his back. "I always good."

Wolf let out a roar of laughter. Jesselynn's mouth made a string look thick, but did he glimpse a twitch at one corner? Maybe he was seeing things. "Hang on, partner. We've got business to attend to." Off they went, with him fighting the urge to look back.

"Why did you let Thaddeus go like that? He could be in the way." Jesselynn darted another withering look Wolf's way but realized she might as well stop. He wouldn't pay any attention anyway.

"If Wolf asked him, I thought it would be fine. Thaddeus didn't ask." Agatha stuck her threaded needle into the material of her waist, between shoulder and bosom, where hopefully it wouldn't snag on anything—or anyone. She tucked the shirt she'd been working on for Sammy in her voluminous apron pocket and, using the lower portion of her apron for a potholder, lifted the lid on the stewing buffalo.

"My, don't that smell good?"

Jesselynn sliced off another strip with enough force to cut into something else. Or someone else. She draped the pile of strips over the iron rack Meshach had fashioned for just this purpose, crowding those that had been hanging long enough to shrink some. She could hear the anvil ringing as Meshach worked to provide racks for some of the others. Other people dried the meat the old-fashioned way, over green willow branches lashed together.

Patch lay watching her, and if a bit dropped to the ground, it was his, quicker than a striking rattler.

"You're furious because you didn't get to go on the hunt," Agatha said, shaking her head and watching Jesselynn glare at Wolf while he talked to someone at the next wagon. Even Benjamin and Daniel had subdued their high spirits when they saw her. "You're being unfair, you know."

Jesselynn snorted and kept on slicing meat.

"Sorry, my dear, but women just aren't invited on hunts like that, britches or no."

"It's not fair." The words were forced between teeth clamped tight.

"I know, but it's not like we had nothing to do." Agatha filled a bucket partway with water and added a cup of salt to soak more meat. "Jesse, take my advice. Let it go and let the men have their fun. Heaven knows, there ain't been much time for fun on this journey."

Jesselynn let out a pent-up sigh. "You're right, but..." *But I wanted to at least see the herd. And I'm a good shot. It's just not fair. I know, Mother; the Bible never promised us fairness.*

When she finished cutting the meat off the haunch, she dropped the bones into another kettle. They'd be making soup out of that. She glanced around at the stacks of bones, hide, and meat to tend to. However would they be ready to travel in the morning? Benjamin had promised to make spoons out of the bone, and Ophelia had asked for a comb to be carved out of one of the ribs. Nothing would be wasted. Soon as she had the rack full of strips, she began chopping the meat in fine pieces to mix with cornmeal and onions to stuff in the stomach. Once boiled, the whole made a savory dish that would keep a day or two at least. Sliced, it fried up well.

"You mad, Jesse?" Thaddeus leaned against her knee.

"No, why?"

"Sad?"

She shook her head and leaned over to touch her nose to his. "What makes you ask?"

"You not smilin'."

*Oh, Lord, save this child, who sees so far beyond the usual.* She glanced up to see Wolf watching them. He always seemed to be watching her. What had she done now? She knew what she needed to do—ask Daniel and Benjamin to forgive her for being such a mean-spirited woman. She'd surely quenched their joy.

She lifted Thaddeus to her lap and blew kisses on his neck to make him giggle. "You are right, little brother. I've been too serious lately." Laughing would be a lot easier if Wolf didn't thwart her at every turn. Not letting her go on the buffalo shoot had been the final offense.

*She needs to laugh more.* Wolf watched the play between brother and sister. He knew what the other women were saying, that she shouldn't be wearing britches and acting like a man. Several of them had taken to snubbing her, not that it seemed to bother her much. She'd taught several other women how to dry the meat, shared her box of simples as she called them, and never had a cross word for any of them—except him.

If they'd been through what she'd been through—

He cut off the thoughts and held his coffee cup up for a refill. Jane Ellen smiled at him as she filled it.

"Elizabeth speakin' to you yet?" He kept his voice low, for her ears only.

Jane Ellen shook her head. "She says I lied to her, that I shoulda told her Jesse was ... is ..." She pursed her mouth and rolled her eyes. "I couldn't. Not one of us ever told nobody."

"Don't you worry about it. Elizabeth just got her pride hurt a bit. 'Twon't kill her."

"Thank you, Mr. Wolf. You want a hunk of cinnamon cake?"

"I sure do. That Ophelia be one fine cook."

"I made the cake." She ducked her head before he could see the blush.

"Then I'd say you are becoming one fine cook also. This wagon is sure blessed with good cooks."

"Good save there." Agatha sat down beside him and held up her cup for Jane Ellen to fill also. Setting her cup down, she took out her knitting and picked up where she'd left off. "I've been wanting to ask you something."

Wolf nodded, at the same time wishing he were somewhere else. Anywhere else. Agatha had that look in her eye. "What?"

She knit a few stitches. "About Oregon country. Do we dare believe all that hoopla about living off the land and anything and everything growing there?"

Wolf let out a sigh of relief. Why had he thought she was going to be talking about her niece? "You can believe much of it. Like Kentucky, the land is rich, the seasons fairly mild. The Indian tribes live off the land and the water. White men will build towns. There will be shipbuilding on the rivers, farming. When the railroad crosses the country—"

"That's nothin' but a pipe dream."

"No. It will happen. And if you think many people have crossed the country on the Oregon Trail, you wait to see what happens when the trains travel."

"What makes you believe that?"

"I've ridden this trail four times now. I see sod houses sproutin' like weeds in the spring, cattle grazing where the buffalo roamed, wheat fields where the prairie grass reigned."

"And will you farm or—?"

"No, I will . . ." He stopped. The song of the fiddle caught his ear. "Let's go hear the next chapter in the story."

"No, I don't waste my time listening to that old reprobate spouting off like that."

"Why, Aunt Agatha, here Nate has had nothin' but good to say about you."

"He better not be saying nothing 'bout me, that old brushface."

Wolf looked up just in time to see Jesselynn roll her eyes. Had she been listening to the conversation all along? He stood and tossed the dregs of his coffee into the fire. "Thank you for a fine meal and a pleasant evening." He tipped his hat to Agatha, nodded to Jesselynn, and followed the stream of folks congregating in the center of the circle.

The legendary Jehosaphats were in rare form that night, with Nate Lyons playing one part of the family after the other, from the grandfather sitting in the rocking chair to the mother scrubbing clothes on the washboard and the children getting in trouble no matter what they did. The fiddler got into it, playing on the low notes in the dark parts and lively high notes on the happy.

Jesselynn took her knitting over to the circle, chuckling along with the rest of them until she sensed Wolf behind her. She dropped two stitches and had to stop because she couldn't see well enough in the near dark to pick them up again.

"What'd you go and do that for?" she hissed.

"What?" He leaned down to hear her better.

"Nothin'." She stabbed the needles back in the ball of yarn, not wanting to admit the desire to stab them into him. Where had all this violence come from? She who never wanted to hurt anyone, unless of course they were wearing a blue uniform—or any uniform, for that matter.

As the applause broke out, she knew she'd missed a good part of the story. That man. Not only would he not let her hunt buffalo, now he'd ruined a perfectly good evening as well. She turned and left, oblivious to the lack of good-nights directed her way.

Wolf, however, was not oblivious. He steamed instead, responding to a pleasant "Good night, Wolf" with a curt nod. *What a cluster of hypocrites.* His father had always said, *"Give me a straight-up Indian any day before a backbiting white."* Maybe there had been truth in that theory. Now that he could live comfortably in either world, all he could dream of was the life he'd lived as a child—before his mother died of the pox and his father took him back to civilization.

Meshach was still chuckling when he returned to their own fire. Sammy lay sleeping in Ophelia's arms, and Thaddeus clung to Meshach's hand. Ophelia put the two boys to bed while Meshach checked the meat hanging on the rack. He threw more chips on the fire to keep it smoldering all night to dry the meat. By the time the camp settled down, the moon had leaped from the horizon and floated like a silver disc in the heavens. After making sure everything was put away in their camp, Jesselynn rolled into her quilt on the ground under the wagon. Why had Wolf stood behind her like that? Silencing a yipping coyote would be easier than silencing her thoughts.

At a whine from Patch, Jesselynn rolled over, fully alert, listening with every nerve. She held still, wishing for Ahab, who was out with the remuda. Laying a hand on the quivering dog, she tried to see what he saw. A growl rumbled in his throat.

Could it be Indians?

# CHAPTER THIRTY-SEVEN

Early June 1863

Another dog barked.

Patch growled again, and the hair rose on the back of his neck.

Jesselynn slid out from the covers and to her feet as soundlessly as whoever or whatever was bothering the dogs. She stood at the end of the wagon, searching the flatlands around them. The grass wasn't deep enough to hide much.

A third dog barked. Patch, at her knee, growled again. This time the hair stood on her own neck. Something was out there, but what?

She knew Meshach was behind her without looking. "You think something's botherin' the horses?" She kept her voice soft so only he could hear it.

"I go see."

"Take Benjamin?"

"I'se here."

She strained, hoping to hear something, anything. Meshach and Benjamin looked like shadows flitting across the prairie. Patch streaked after them. She could hear others rustling. The dogs had sounded the alarm.

A shout! A rifle shot! All from the direction of the grazing animals.

Jesselynn grabbed her gun. If someone stole the horses, this long ordeal would have been for naught. "Stay here and guard!" she ordered Daniel and threw him a gun. A volley of shots and shouting made her run faster.

The hoofbeats of a running horse caught her attention, even above the thundering of her own heart. Another shot. Then a horse and rider in pursuit.

She met Meshach and Benjamin returning with the Thoroughbreds.

"Dey got Marse Wolf's Appaloosa and one other."

"Who?"

"Indians, we 'spect."

"Where was the guard?" She knew two men had been assigned to keep watch, as they always did. She swung atop one of the mares to ride back to camp.

Meshach's snort said what he thought of the guard. "Mos' likely sleepin'. He weren't on him horse, dat's for sure."

"Who?"

"Dat worthless Rufus Jones. He was mountin' when we got dere."

"Where was McPhereson?"

"Don' know. Got to look for 'im."

By now half the camp was awake and other men running out to join them.

"Where's Wolf?" several men asked at the same time. "What happened?"

"Indian raid. Got two horses, one Marse Wolf's."

*At least our horses are safe.* But guilt stabbed her as soon as the thought. Wolf and his horse were like one. She'd heard he'd raised the striking bay-and-white Appaloosa from a colt and never rode any other horse. But where was he?

She tied the mares to the wagon and waited for Meshach and Benjamin to return with the others. They'd gone to help round up the herd and bring it closer to camp. A shout said they'd found McPhereson. When they rode in with a body draped across the saddle, she knew.

Not only two horses, but they'd lost a good man. While Jones slept.

*You don't know that for sure,* she reminded herself.

A lantern flared and lit the circle where they lowered the body to the ground. The gash across his jugular glowed black in the light. His wife burst through the circle and dropped to her knees beside the body, her keening cry bringing tears to Jesselynn's eyes. Surely this was a death that could have been prevented.

"Where is Wolf?" one of the men growled.

"Mebbe gone after de horses?" Meshach dismounted and joined the circle.

"On foot?" The man snorted this time.

"Where's Benjamin?" Jesselynn spoke for Meshach's ears only.

"Out on guard."

"What about Jones?"

"Don' know. Just someone got to stand guard. I go back out. We bring dem all close to camp." Meshach headed back out to the herd.

The sound of galloping hoofbeats drew their attention to a rider, etched in the moonlight, coming into camp.

Jesselynn knew who it was as soon as she caught the white splashes on the lead horse. It was Wolf's horse, so Wolf must be the rider. A second horse raced beside them.

Silence greeted his halt at the edge of the camp.

"One brave—he won't steal horses again." He glanced around the circle. "Where's Jones?"

Several shrugged. The wife's keening continued, broken only by her gulps for air. Aunt Agatha knelt beside her, her murmurs of comfort lost in the sorrow.

"Shouldn'ta happened."

"High price."

The muttering caught Jesselynn's attention. Why were they blaming Wolf when Jones was to blame? If he'd been on watch like he was supposed to . . . but did they know that? Had her men kept that knowledge to themselves? Knowing Meshach, she was sure that's what had happened.

Edging closer so she could tell Wolf what had happened without announcing it to everyone, she caught her breath. His left arm wore a gash from shoulder to elbow, the blood dripping down over his hand. She turned to see Jane Ellen at her side.

"Get my medicine box, please." Still keeping her voice soft, she added, "And ask Daniel to build up the fire. We need hot water."

Her attention shifted back to the circle. Wolf stood at an angle so the men couldn't see his arm.

"I didn't sound an alarm because that was the job of the men on guard. If there had been more braves, more horses would have been stolen, but since I heard one set of hoofbeats, I knew . . ." His words wore the patient tone of a man explaining things to children.

"Didja know McPhereson was dead?"

Wolf shook his head. "No, but I suspected as much. What about Jones?"

"He was sleeping." Jesselynn raised her voice so everyone could hear. "Meshach found him just mounting his horse, his bedroll out by the fire."

"Ya sure about that?" A voice rose from the gathered men.

"Meshach never lies."

"That worthless—"

Jesselynn took a step forward, hands clenched at her sides.

"No, I don't mean your sla—er, man." The man with a full mink beard backed off, hands in front of him. "I mean that lowdown Jones."

"Good thing, Henry, he—er, she woulda dropped ya for sure." The air lightened at the general chuckle but for the keening that had now diminished to hiccupping sobs.

"Oughta just string those two brothers up. Save the woman a life o' trouble."

"There'll be no talk of stringing anyone up. We don't know the entire story yet."

Jesselynn took her box of medical supplies from Jane Ellen and, holding it with one hand, tapped Wolf's arm with the other. "How about I fix that arm of yours before you bleed to death?" Not that there was much danger of that. The bleeding had slowed, the dark river coagulating on the buckskin shirt.

Wolf glanced down at his arm, then at her. "It's fine."

"It will be after I get it bandaged. Once I see it in the light, I'll know better if you need stitches or not." She wasn't prepared for the tension that ran up her hand to her shoulder when she touched his arm. Like touching a hot stove, only in that case she was wise enough to pull back. Instead, she pointed to the hunk of oak they'd been toting across the plains. "Sit."

Jane Ellen held the lamp as she examined the wound.

"You need to take the shirt off, or I'll have to cut out the sleeve."

"You're givin' me a choice?"

She nodded.

Even in the lamplight, his face went white when he tried to raise his arm to pull his shirt over his head. Sweat broke out on his forehead and upper lip.

"Jane Ellen." Jesselynn nodded to her helper and between them they pulled off the shirt, cushioning the injured arm as best they could in the process. Firelight played over muscles that bunched when she touched a hot, wet cloth to the arm.

Trying to be gentle, she ordered her shaking hands to get the job done.

With the dried blood cleaned off, the slash started bleeding again.

"I'm going to have to stitch it." She paused, half expecting him to argue. But when he only nodded, she motioned for Jane Ellen to thread the needle.

The rest of the wagon-train folks faded away, heading back to their beds for what remained of a short night for sleeping. Jones had yet to enter camp.

"This is going to burn."

His grunt said only that he'd heard her.

She trickled the whiskey down from his shoulder, the length of the slash. The deepest section crossed the muscle from elbow to shoulder, but while it nicked the muscle, the cut didn't appear to have severed it.

"You're lucky."

Grunt or snort, she wasn't sure of his response, other than the white skin around his eyes and mouth.

"Had it severed this muscle, you'd have lost the use of the arm or hand." Holding the lips of the slash with one hand, she inserted the needle through the skin and drew the thread through, back and forth, until the gaping wound lay snugly shut. She knotted the thread, snipped it with the scissors, and stepped back with a sigh. At least somewhere in the stitching her hands had stopped shaking. She applied some of the salve from her medicinals and, taking a roll of two-inch-wide sheeting, bandaged the arm. "If you wear a sling for a few days, it will heal more quickly."

"Thank you." He didn't look at her.

"How is he?" Aunt Agatha returned from settling the new widow into her wagon.

"Good, if we can keep this from goin' putrid."

"Leastways, it wasn't your right." When he didn't answer, Aunt Agatha cocked an eyebrow at her niece, who shrugged.

*Lord, get me outa here.* Her hands burned him far worse than the whiskey or the wound itself. Her touch, firm but gentle, set him to twitching, which only the stiffest resolve kept him from succumbing to. What was happening? Ever since he'd realized she was a woman and the original rage wore off, he'd fought to keep his distance.

He tried working up that initial rage at her duplicity, but somewhere in the last few days he'd lost that as well. And now he was in her debt, all for a knife slashing that should never have happened. All he'd wanted was his horse back. Fool young buck, counting coup by stealing a horse. Cost him his life and the train a good man.

He clenched his teeth against the pain of the needle pulling the thread through his skin. Would she never be done? In spite of his steel resolve, his stomach roiled, and he blinked to clear the black spots from his eyes. Sure, all he needed to do was pass out now.

His arm might as well have been branded.

When she stepped back, the cool breeze of the coming dawn dried the sweat on his chest. He stared at the ground. Could he stand without making a fool of himself?

"Thank you." Never would she know what the two words cost him.

"You're welcome. Can you make it back to your bedroll all right?"

He glanced up at her to see her nod at Daniel, who had come to stand beside him.

Right now what he'd really like was a tote of that whiskey she had so carelessly poured down his arm. It might have done more good down his throat. Instead of answering, he lurched to his feet. Without a backward look he staggered once, then gained his equilibrium and strode off toward his simple camp. He could feel her gaze all the way. Calling himself all kinds of names did nothing to ease the holes she burned in his back.

"Well, if that don't beat all." Agatha planted her hands on her hips and stared after the retreating wagon master.

Jesselynn felt as if she had been horse whipped. Her shoulders ached, her hands ached too, but more for the touch of him than the weariness. She jerked her mind back from where it had wandered and began putting things to right in her box. Each stab of the needle through his flesh had been like piercing her own. *What in the world is the matter with me?*

"Good night," she said to Agatha, who was settling in the wagon.

She tucked the box back in its place, and after checking on the herd of oxen and horses that now grazed near the circle of wagons, she crawled back in her bedroll, wishing for sleep for her burning eyes. The warmth seeped into her flesh and bones but did nothing to shut down the rampaging thoughts. She listened for the night noises—cattle and horses chewing the grass, an owl hooting, the cry of a nighthawk. Either of those last two could be an Indian signal. But surely they wouldn't come this close to camp. Agatha turned over above her with a sigh. Snores could be heard from the wagon in front of them.

Patch raised his head, setting her heart to thundering immediately, and it didn't stop when he sighed and lay back down. Since he felt his place was next to hers, she sensed his every move. He leaned into her stroking fingers, giving her wrist a quick lick in appreciation.

If one Indian got that close undetected . . . the thought made her stomach flutter. But all he'd wanted was a horse. Was that one horse worth the death of two men, one white, one red? *And would this be the last?* What if they were attacked by Indians? Other wagon trains had been, or at least she'd heard tell of it. Had Wolf ever fought off an Indian attack? Or was his being half Sioux an added protection for them?

Thoughts raced through her mind, circled, and came back for another attack. She turned over on her other side, Patch snuggled up against her back, his sigh a strong comment on her restlessness. Surely they had prayed for God's protection on their journey. Surely others had too, yet look what happened to some of them. She'd seen a blackened wagon or what remained of it. Had that been the work of Indians?

When the rooster, carried in a crate attached to one of the wagons, crowed, her eyes felt like burning coals, so intensely had she been staring into the darkness. Slowly, gently, dawn stole across the land, turning black to gray and washing the land in silver. By the time the sun broke the horizon, they were all near to ready for the wagons to pull out.

Didn't look to her like some of the others had had much more sleep than she had.

The second burial of the journey took more time for the digging, but the end results were the same. The slight mound of dirt would disappear under the wheels of the train.

"You seen that scum Jones?" Agatha asked in an undertone as they set the cooking things in the wagon box.

Jesselynn shook her head. "Don't care to neither. I just feel sorry for that poor woman to be married into such a shiftless bunch."

"I know. Poor white trash through and through." Agatha heaved herself up over the wagon wheel and settled on the seat she had padded with a quilt, thanks to Jesselynn's insistence. "You riding or walking today?" she asked.

"Depends on what Ophelia would like. Walkin', I guess. Most likely I'd fall asleep on the wagon. Could fall under the wheels that-away." Jesselynn touched the brim of her hat with one finger. "You get to be first today, so enjoy."

While she'd rather watch out across the ever changing prairie, she took her knitting out instead. Since the boys were playing in the back of Ophelia's wagon, she and Jane Ellen strode companionably along, both with their needles clicking as they turned wool into socks and sweaters for the winter. The cold in Oregon was more intense than that of Kentucky, or so they'd been told.

Jesselynn mulled over the events of the night before, her thoughts always returning to the feel of Wolf's skin under her fingertips. Knowing such thoughts were decidedly unladylike was no deterrent. She had to admit he'd been sneaking into her thoughts more and more lately, in spite of her good intentions.

She forced herself to think on the verse Meshach had given them for the day. *"Not by might, nor by power, but by my spirit, saith the Lord..."* That's all the further she got from memory. If only she could sit down with the journal and catch up on the letters she'd started for the family. The Lord himself had promised to watch over them. With that thought came another. But what about poor Mr. McPhereson? And his wife and family now left to fend for themselves? The Lord had promised to watch over them too.

She glanced up at the screech of a hawk, lost to her sight in the blue of the sky.

"Hey, you seen what's ahead?" Billy asked her from the back of his horse.

She shook her head, then looked to where he was pointing.

Far in the distant shimmering haze two rocks rose from the floor of the plain, one like a huge round table.

"Wolf says that's Courthouse Rock to the north, Jail House to the left. Immigrants been cuttin' their names in the sandstone for years. Like to be a hunk o' history right there for all to see. Mr. Wolf says maybe the Whitmans even signed it on their way to Oregon."

Jesselynn glanced up at the young man riding beside her just in time to catch one of the looks he slanted at Jane Ellen. Ah, no wonder he was paying such close attention to her. Another young pup sniffing around the females. She turned her attention to Jane Ellen to see her studying on her yarn, studying so hard she missed a hillock of grass and stumbled, catching hold of Jesselynn's arm to keep from falling.

Jesselynn kept a giggle inside. Indeed it must be spring.

Wolf rode back, stopping to talk with Aunt Agatha on the wagon, then rode over to her, his left arm hanging straight at his side.

"Keep a watch out. There's Indians trailing the train."

Her heart took up the staccato beat from the night before, but now she knew fear to be the culprit. Fear wore the same metallic taste as blood.

# CHAPTER THIRTY-EIGHT

## Chimney Rock

The Indians trailing the wagon train kept everyone on edge.

"What do you s'pose they want?" Jane Ellen glanced over her shoulder, fear eating at the edge of her mouth.

"To drive us all stark ravin' mad." Aunt Agatha shuddered as she answered. "If a horse gets loose or an ox, they'll get it. They'll steal whatever we don't nail down."

"How can you say that?" Jesselynn stepped over the wagon tongue, carrying two buckets of water from Plum Creek that flowed into the Platte River. She hated skimming bugs off the Platte River water. Besides, many had come up with diarrhea from drinking from the South Platte. "What's come up stolen so far?"

Agatha *harrumphed* and shook her head again. "You mark my words." She wagged her finger for emphasis.

Jesselynn looked over to the Lyonses' wagon, where the children were gathered for their evening lessons. "I bet this is the only wagon train that carries a schoolmaster along with it."

Agatha harrumphed again, louder this time and, muttering under her breath, strode to the back of the wagon and stuck her head inside, ostensibly searching for something. Ophelia chuckled and shared a private glance with Meshach, who was repairing a piece of harness for one of the other wagons.

Sammy held a bug up for Ophelia to see, and Thaddeus brought one to Jesselynn.

"Grasshopper?"

"That's right. Daniel is using grasshoppers for fish bait."

"Dan'l catch fish for supper?"

"I sure do hope so. Buffalo and beans is getting a bit monotonous." At home the greens would be growing heartily in the gardens and the snap beans they started in the cold frames beginning to blossom. Here they didn't dare even go out looking for greens since the Indians began following them. Dandelions and poke would go far toward making the supper more palatable.

"We be thankful for good food. Leastways we get enough to eat." Meshach smiled up at her to take any sting out of his words.

"I know." She felt like snapping but refrained. The restrictions of camp made everyone restless, just knowing there was danger near and not being able to do anything about it. None of the women and children had been allowed out of camp for the last three days. Even picking buffalo and cow chips had been curtailed.

Wolf wasn't winning any popularity contest by the tighter rules. "Seems like they blame him." She said it without thinking.

"Who?"

"Wolf. Like the Indians following are his fault."

"Make no sense, do it?" Meshach hammered home the final rivet and slung the harness over his shoulder. "Be right back."

With the supper cooking, Jesselynn dug her writing case out of the storage box and made herself comfortable, or as comfortable as possible on the wagon tongue and the braces that bolted it to the wagon bed. Uncorking the ink, she made several entries in the journal before beginning a letter to her sisters. Since they would be in Fort Laramie in the next few days, she wanted the letters ready to go back east with the mail.

*My dearest sisters.* That part was easy, but how could she describe life on the trail so they would understand, when they had never done anything more exertive outdoors than go on picnics? Anytime the Highwood women traveled overnight, the carriage had stopped at inns and way stations with beds and hot meals, or they stayed with friends and relatives. Jesselynn looked up at the sky bowl above them, the sun edging toward the horizon, the flat shallow river over a mile wide, the valley, if one could call the slight depression of the Platte River Road a valley, and the wagons in their nightly circle with the herd grazing near enough to hear the oxen chewing their cud. Since the Indians had begun following them, Wolf ordered camp earlier at night because the herd couldn't graze out farther where the grass was better.

She stared at a heap of possessions that someone had dumped beside the trail—a trunk, a spinet piano, and a breakfront—apparently finding them too heavy to carry any longer. Furniture that had once graced someone's home now lay weathering in the prairie sun and rain. No one else had room to pick it all up. Thanks to the cave living they'd done all winter, they had no fine furniture to cart along. Just the bare necessities.

She read her opening words again. *Dearest sisters.* That sure covered it. She shook her head. *And brother.* How could she have forgotten Zachary? She brushed the feathered end of the quill pen across her chin. What was left of her dashing big brother? His wounds had sounded hideous. Missing his right foot, his right hand and right eye, along with a gash down the right side of his face. How he must be suffering.

She added his name in the salutation and continued.

*We are still following the Platte River. Platte is French for flat, and it most certainly is that. Must be like Daddy said Louisiana is but without the levies.*

She told them about the Indian trying to steal horses and about Wolf's injury, not that it had slowed him down for long.

*I am feeling hemmed in, which is hard to figure, since we can see forever. It took two days from the first sighting of Courthouse Rock until we drew near, and even though it looked close enough to touch, those who insisted on going out there took a day to get there and back. The air is so clear and the land so flat that distance is impossible to figure. Each day's journey looks pretty much like the day before. Never thought I'd be able to walk along, knitting and chatting, and not fall over my feet.*

*We've buried two so far, a man and a little boy. The boy's mother was so stoic, grateful she had a nice outfit to bury her baby in. I wanted to run screaming, since none of the herbs and such I used to help him did any good. Death came so fast. The mother said our Father must have wanted her son up in heaven, but I think He has plenty of babies there already. Burying anyone is hard, but burying children is especially hard. If I didn't know there was a heaven, I might go stark raving mad.*

*The horses are holding up well, much to everyone's surprise. I believe the real challenge will come when we get to the mountains. As Wolf says, "We are on the easy leg of the journey now."*

*I hope and pray there will be a letter from you when we reach Fort Laramie. Thaddeus no longer asks to go home, and I am beginning to think he has forgotten Twin Oaks. He thinks he is old enough to join the other children in school, which is conducted by Mr. Nate Lyons in the evenings. Don't ever let on to Aunt Agatha, but I think Mr. Lyons is sweet on her. He brought her some wildflowers he had picked the other day. She still calls him Brushface, but I hope she can look beyond the wild hair and whiskers to see the value of the man within.*

She almost wrote more about Wolf, but after rereading what she had written, she realized she had mentioned him too much already. The thought made her pause. Did she write about him because he was on her mind so much?

*May our God and Father keep you in his tender care and grant you peace.*

> *With all my love,*
> *Your sister Jesselynn*
> *and all the rest*

*P.S. I forgot to tell you that my secret is out. They all know I am a female in men's clothing, and many of the ladies will not forgive me for the deception. So be it. JH*

She let the ink dry and folded the paper. She'd have to use another sheet of paper to make an envelope, since she had run out of that nicety.

Aunt Agatha invited Wolf to join them for supper.

Jesselynn made her way to the Lyonses' wagon and asked him to come too. *Tit for tat.* The thought made her smile.

"Thankee, but we already got an invite fer tonight." His eyes twinkled under brushy eyebrows. "We could come tomorrow." One eyebrow arched.

"That would be fine." She stopped herself from making the invitation a permanent one. As much as he was helping all those with children, he shouldn't have to cook his own supper on top of that. Maybe she should mention that to Wolf, and he could bring it up at one of the meetings. Sure as shooting, if she offered the suggestion, it would be voted down on general principles. Unless, of course, she took to wearing dresses.

Dusk shadowed the camp when Wolf joined them for supper. After Meshach said the grace, Ophelia dished the fried fish onto tin plates, and they all found a place to sit, mostly cross-legged on the ground.

Seemingly without his volition, Wolf found himself between two women—Jane Ellen with adoring eyes and Jesselynn who refused to look at him. *Now what have I done, or not done, as the case may be?* He slanted a peek to his right and saw Jesselynn helping her little brother cut his meat. How could he ever have bought her story that she was Marse Jesse? Surely if he had paid more attention he would have seen her tenderness with the children, her caring for her aunt, and the young woman on the other side whose doe eyes made him want to squirm.

"Seen anythin' of Jones?" Meshach looked up from his plate.

Even the thought of the worthless Rufus made his jaw tighten. "No. He most likely hightailed it on to Fort Laramie." *If the Indians didn't get him first.* Any day he expected to come across a carcass, minus the scalp. It would be a fitting end.

"Good fish."

"Thanks to Daniel." Meshach nodded to the young man sitting beside him.

"I strung out a trotline. Why don't de others?"

"Perhaps you could teach 'em how."

Daniel shrugged. "Mebbe." But his look said far more.

"We'll come on Chimney Rock soon, then a couple days to cross-in' the South Fork of the Platte." *Because he's black, the others don't want to learn from him, then they mutter and grumble about how the Highwood wagons eat better than the rest. Yet they always share. I'm sick to death of this insane backbiting.* Visions of high country with cool winds singing through the pine trees, Indian tepees instead of white-sailed wagons, his people laughing and dancing after the day's hunt. Home. He could almost smell it on the air.

Could he leave the wagon train at Fort Laramie and head north? Who would take it on?

He looked up to see those around him staring at him. "Could you repeat that?"

"I asked how many days to Fort Laramie?" Aunt Agatha covered her hand with her apron and picked up the coffeepot. "Anyone else ready for this?"

Wolf held up his cup. "Should be there in four to six days, depending on how the river crossing goes. We'll be at the ford tomorrow. California Hill after that."

"I see to the caulkin' den."

"You have any grease left?"

"Yes, suh. We brought plenty like you said back to Independence."

*If only the others had listened as well.* He wouldn't ask anyone to share with the Joneses. But theirs was the wagon that would cause the most trouble. He was sure of it.

By late afternoon the sprinkles turned to heavy rain, so that by the time they circled the wagons near the ford, man and beast were sodden. With thunder rolling and lightning forking the sky, Wolf ordered everyone to bring in their own animals and tie them on long lines to keep them from stampeding.

Jesselynn clamped her legs to keep Ahab under control. Head high, the stallion snorted and shifted beneath her. "Easy, old son. You've been through a lightning storm before." The rain ran cold from the brim of her hat and down her neck. Could have been ice, the temperature had dropped so fast. She tied him to a rear wheel of their wagon and climbed inside to sit cross-legged on a box and eat dried biscuit and dried buffalo with the rest of them. There'd be no fires this night.

The rain continued through the night, raising the river a foot by morning. Brown froth rushed toward the east with the opposite shore shrouded in rain sheets.

Jesselynn rode up to the three men gathered on the bank.

"I vote we go on over. Two feet deep ain't much. We crossed deeper."

"I heard there could be holes runnin' deeper. Sure did pick up the pace some overnight." They both looked to Wolf.

Jesselynn tried to read some expression on either face or body, but Wolf stood still as a well-sunk fence post.

The sounds from the circled wagons were blurred just like her vision. Ahab snorted and dug in the mud with one front foot.

Wolf looked toward the west from where the storm blew in. He sniffed the air, turned slowly to study the sky in all four directions, then nodded. "Looks to be breakin' up. Give it an hour, and then we decide."

Two hours later the first wagon entered the rushing water. A whip cracked. The driver yelled orders to his four oxen. Two men rode by the lead team, one on either side.

Wolf gave last-minute orders. "Now, if your wagon starts to float, go easy with the current, but keep angling toward the shore. Just keep a steady hand on those reins. Your oxen can swim if they have to."

One by one, the wagons entered the river. Some floated, some angled upstream, some floated down. Jesselynn pulled up behind the Jones wagon. Benjamin on Ahab and Daniel on Domino rode point.

Wolf stopped his horse next to Jesselynn. "Wait until they get over that sandbar before you start in."

"Right." She watched the wagon ahead grow fainter in the mist. "Here we go." She flicked the reins when a shout went up from the wagon ahead. "Oh, God, no!" The wagon tipped and fell.

Wolf spun his horse and leaped into the river.

"Whoa!" Jesselynn pulled back on the reins. "Go help." She need not have said a word, for Daniel and Benjamin were already following Wolf.

"Oh, Lord above, much as I hate—no dislike—those folks, please protect them."

"Jesselynn, can you see anything?" Jane Ellen leaned on Jesselynn's shoulder.

"No." *Oh, Lord, this could be us. But it's not. There's justice, Lord. Jones is such a rotten man.* Guilt grabbed her by the throat and shook her. Such a thing to think. *Lord, forgive me, please. I'm sorry for even thinking such a thing. What kind of a Christian am I? Mother, what you would say to me?*

With all the ropes on the wagon, they had it righted and pulled it out of the river before Wolf came back to signal the next wagon.

With a prayer on her lips, Jesselynn started into the river.

"Swing to the upstream just across the sandbar. There's a hole off to the right."

"Are the Joneses all right?"

Wolf didn't answer.

With Daniel and Benjamin on either side of the lead team, the oxen pulled steady, up over the sandbar and back in the water. One bellowed. They drew closer to the shore. She popped the whip, her feet braced against the boot board. Throwing themselves against the yokes, the oxen hauled the wagon up the gentle incline and out of the river.

"We did it!" Jane Ellen threw her arms around Jesselynn. "Thank you, Lord. We made it."

Jesselynn wrapped the reins around the brake handle, stood on shaking legs, and climbed down over the wheel to stand on firm ground again. She went around the wagon and reached up to grab Thaddeus and squeezed him tight.

He patted her cheeks. "You good driver, Jesse." He looked over her shoulder. "Meshach comin'."

Jesselynn looked up at the sound of a keening wail from the Jones wagon. She glanced at Jane Ellen, who shook her head, eyes wide.

Meshach pulled up beside them and helped Aunt Agatha to the ground. "Never thought I'd be so grateful to stand on dry ground again." She stamped her foot to make the point. "Thank you, Lord above."

They stood and watched the crossing of the remaining wagons. Two men lassoed the ox horns to assist the next wagon, which was floundering, and the last one made it to the far shore without incident. They circled the wagons on the northern verge so some could hang things out to dry.

Jesselynn inspected their wagons and found no leaks, thanks to Meshach's careful caulking. She could hear others grumbling. The rain had let up somewhere during the crossing, and thanks to the sandy soil, the puddles had disappeared. Ophelia started a fire with the twigs Jane Ellen and the boys brought back from the brush along the river and added the cow and buffalo chips they'd collected during previous days' walks. With the kettle boiling, she added shaved dried buffalo meat, the last of the remaining vegetables, and the rice she'd been saving. The savory smell rose to tantalize while Ophelia mixed up dumplings.

Jesselynn made her way over to the Jones wagon, much against her better judgment. She wanted to leave them to their soaked fate, but the sobbing hadn't ceased. Everyone else seemed to be ignoring them.

Jesselynn drew even with the boxes stacked alongside the wagon. "Shut up, woman! Just shut up!"

Jesselynn stopped. The crack of hand against flesh made her flinch. She stepped around the wagon to see Tommy Joe, hands clenched, standing over his wife. Mrs. Jones cowered on the ground, her baby clenched in her arms.

Tommy Joe reached for the soaked blanket-wrapped bundle. "He's dead."

"Leave her be!" Jesselynn stepped forward.

"Get outa here, you . . . you . . . interfering wench." Fists raised, he came at her.

With a growl like an attacking bear, Wolf grabbed Jones by the shoulder, spun him around, and planted a fist in Jones's face. Tommy Joe staggered, slumped to his knees, and toppled to the ground. Blood ran from his smashed nose.

Jesselynn knelt by the sobbing woman. She wrapped her arms around the thin shoulders and held her close, the wet bundle between them. *Oh, Lord, what can I say?* No words came, so the two women rocked together.

———

After the tragedy of the river they took the steep climb up and over California Hill with extreme care. The men braced against the wheels of each wagon to keep it from rolling over the oxen. Though it was grueling, Jesselynn knew it was just a foretaste of what was ahead for them when they reached the mountains. By the time they reached Ash Hollow, an extra day of rest was more than needed.

The morning they forded the river to Fort Laramie should have been a celebration, but discontent simmered beneath the surface like a kettle on slow boil. More than one family muttered that leaving the Joneses at Fort Laramie would be the best possible way to settle things.

They circled the wagons just south of the fort and made camp.

"Leastwise we don't have to worry about those Indians any longer." Aunt Agatha said what the others were thinking now that they were within the protection of the fort.

Jesselynn nodded. "Think I'll ride on in to the quartermaster tonight and see about ordering our supplies."

"Me go?" Thaddeus looked up from where he was digging a hole in the dirt with a stick.

"No, I—" But at the way his face fell, she changed her mind. "Why not? Come on, let's go get Roman."

The smile he gave her as he took her hand reminded her what little it took to make him happy. Riding with his big sister was one of those things. After bridling the mule, she set Thaddeus up on the bony back and swung herself up behind him. Handing him the reins, she nudged Roman forward. "You make sure you keep him goin' straight now, you hear?"

"I hear." His shoulders straightened as if she'd just asked him to take over the family.

*At home he'd be riding a pony all by himself in the paddock by now.* All the Highwood children could ride nearly before they could run, or at least it seemed that way. All but Thaddeus, another casualty of the war. Jesselynn dropped a kiss on his soft hair. He should be wearing a hat already too, but she had neither the time nor materials to make him one. So many things left undone, her daddy must be rolling over in his grave. Thoughts of her father made her shoulders slump. Sometimes the burdens got so heavy she could barely breathe.

As Meshach would say, "Time to put dem all back in de Lawd's hands—and leave dem dere." The leaving them there was the hard part.

"Ugh, bluebellies." Thaddeus snapped her back to attention.

"No. Don't you call them that." She gave him a gentle shake.

"You do."

"Not anymore. We've gone beyond the war. They are United States soldiers, and we are United States citizens. That's what your daddy always said."

"Bluebellies kill my daddy."

*Oh, Lord, preserve us. What can I say? He is so right.* Jesselynn sucked in a deep breath in the hopes it would help her think better. "Daddy was a casualty of the war, just like so many others. We have to forgive and forget." *So we aren't destroyed too.*

Jesselynn glanced up in time to catch the sight of a man disappearing behind one of the whitewashed buildings. "Jones!" *That scum is still alive.*

To tell Wolf or not dogged her all the way back to the camp. Thaddeus leaned against her chest, blissfully sucking on his peppermint stick. The hunk of cheese would bring cries of delight from those at the wagons, and the molasses would taste wonderful on pancakes in the morning. But if the others found out about Jones, would they demand a lynching?

Keeping the news to herself for now seemed the better part of wisdom, she had decided by the time they rode into camp. She lowered Thaddeus and his sack of peppermint sticks to the ground. "Now you go share those, you hear?"

He nodded and ran off, little-boy legs pumping, calling for Sammy and Jane Ellen.

She stripped the bridle off Roman and, with a swat on the rump, sent him galloping back to the herd. With the sack of supplies swung over her shoulder, she made her way back to the wagons, with each step wishing she hadn't seen what she had.

"Thought a trip to the store would take away that thundercloud sittin' on your head, not make it worse." Agatha studied her niece and lowered her voice. "Now, what is it botherin' you? No mail?"

Jesselynn shook her head. Seeing Jones had plumb driven the mail out of her mind. Another thing to hold against him. "Forgot to ask." She handed the tow sack to her aunt.

"What, then? You look blacker'n a bog at night."

Jesselynn sighed. She should have known better than to think she could pull off carrying a secret like that. "I saw Jones at the hostelry."

Agatha sighed and shook her head at the same time. "I know it isn't Christian, but I sure was hopin' the prairie or the Indians got him. You goin' to tell Wolf?"

Jesselynn shook her head. "Not unless I have to. Maybe the scum will just stay clear if he has any sense at all."

"Sure." Agatha rolled her eyes and opened the sack. "Ah, cheese. We can have it on biscuits for supper."

---

The camp had settled for the night when Jesselynn heard a shout. Rolling to her feet, gun already in hand, she stood beside the wagon searching the blackness for the reason. She could feel the warmth from Meshach right beside her.

"Hold 'im. He ain't gonna get away this time!" came the shout.

"Let's go," Jesselynn said, and together the two of them headed across the circle at a run.

# CHAPTER THIRTY-NINE

Fort Laramie

"Drop your guns.'"

Jesselynn spun at the guttural command. Wolf stood slightly behind her and off to the right, rifle in one hand, Colt in the other. She lowered her gun, realizing he wasn't even looking at her and Meshach. The men holding Jones stepped back from their captive, and those with guns holstered them.

"You can't be sticking up for the scum, Wolf. You know McPhereson died because this lowlife was too tired to stand watch properlike."

"He deserves a chance to say his piece to the military. They're in charge of the peace around here."

"I say let's just string 'im up."

"I din't sleep on watch. He hit me." Rufus whined like the bully-turned-weakling he was.

One of the men gave him a shove. "Then why'd that Indian not slit your throat too?"

Jones shrugged. "How should I know? I was just coming to when Highwood and her nigger run up."

"Then why'd ya run?"

"Reckoned they'd think I kilt Mac, that's why."

Jesselynn about choked on her rage. Meshach said he'd been lying on his bedroll or in it. Either way . . . "Don't believe a word he says," she hissed loudly enough for Wolf to hear.

"How'd you know Mac was dead?"

Silence.

"He's lyin', the dirty cur."

"Enough." Wolf took two steps forward. "Get some rope and tie his hands behind his back, then to a wagon wheel. We'll take him into the fort in the morning."

The men muttered and grumbled, but they did as he ordered. As soon as Jones was tied to the wheel, they moved off. Thunder rumbled in the distance, the smell of rain sweet on the breeze.

Jesselynn turned to head back to her bedroll. So Jones might get a bit wet. Far as she could see, more than his clothes needed washing. And some starch in his backbone wouldn't hurt neither. "You know he was lying."

"I knows. But de officer be de one to say, not us."

"I didn't think he'd be stupid enough to try and sneak into camp. What if his brother lets him go?"

"With Wolf guardin' 'im?"

"Oh."

A shadow by their wagon revealed a man as they neared. "Your turn on watch, Meshach."

"I know. Be right dere."

"You better get a slicker." She lifted her face to feel the first drops of the coming rain. Thunder rumbled again. "You want some extra help in case the storm spooks the cattle?"

"I go wid 'im." Benjamin handed Meshach a slicker. "I got Roman cotched already."

"Be careful." When she closed her eyes she could still see the dark slash of death across McPhereson's throat.

"Indians not come dis close to de fort." Meshach settled his hat more firmly on his head.

"I wouldn't want to bet your lives on it." She handed Benjamin her gun and drew more bullets out of her pocket. "As I said, be careful."

By morning everything not under canvas in camp was soaked, with water standing in puddles and the rain still sheeting down. The thunder and lightning had passed in the darkest hours without doing more than making the herd restless.

Jesselynn had heard Meshach singing during the night. The oxen seemed as comforted by it as she was.

With morning those assigned to the herd drove them down to

water and then took them farther from camp for better grazing. Daniel made sure the Thoroughbreds stayed toward the center of the herd so as to be less visible to the officers at the fort.

Jesselynn had just finished washing Thaddeus's face when she heard a shout from the western rim of the camp where Jones had been tied the night before. "Go to Jane Ellen." She gave her little brother a push in the general direction, grabbed the gun she kept nearby, and headed for the fracas.

"Come any closer an' I drill 'im." Tommy Joe Jones stood with his gun barrel tight to Wolf's back.

Jesselynn could only guess at what happened. Wolf was going to take Rufus into the fort, and the good-for-nothing brother showed up.

"Now cut 'im loose like you thought to and let 'im go."

Wolf stood like a stone carving.

"You heard me!"

Jesselynn dropped back behind one of the wagons and, leaping the wagon tongue, circled from the outside. If she could get off a shot . . .

"Don't nobody move or he's dead."

"Come on, Jones, you won't make it outa here alive if you do that." Mr. Bronson spoke in an ordinary voice as if they were discussing the price of flour. "Ain't you had enough bad luck on this trip?"

Eyes wild, Tommy Joe pushed the gun more firmly into Wolf's back. "I'm warnin' ya."

*Why didn't I kill him when I had the chance?* Wolf refused to flinch. The barrel bit into his back. He could feel sweat trickling down from his armpits. He caught movement out of the corner of his eye but didn't dare shift to see who was the stalker.

"Now cut my brother loose, nice and easy." The rifle dug deeper with every word.

One of the men came forward, knife at hand. Keeping one eye on the rifle, he leaned down to release the bonds.

"See, told you I waren't gonna hang for somethin' I didn't do," Rufus hissed.

Holding steady took every ounce of determination Wolf owned. He stared burn holes in the man near his feet. One jab, one kick. Could he do it?

"Now help 'im up."

Bronson took Rufus's arm as if reaching for a rattler and pulled him to his feet.

Rufus swayed, then spat in Wolf's face. "Shoot 'im, brother. Dirty Injun like him ain't fit to live."

The gun barrel wavered. Wolf dropped. A gun went off. Men hollered. Someone screamed. A body hit the ground.

*God above . . .* Wolf never finished the thought as he rolled and surged to his feet.

Tommy Joe lay writhing on the ground. Rufus stood with his hands in the air. Jesselynn Highwood held a gun on the two brothers.

"Shoulda shot to kill." Jesselynn glanced at Wolf to make sure he was all right.

"My leg!" Tommy Joe stared at the blood welling from his thigh.

"Be glad that's all." One of the wagon men retied Rufus's hands. "You gonna stop the bleedin'?" He looked to Jesselynn, who shook her head.

"Take 'em both into the fort." She tucked her gun in the waistband of her pants. *Thank you, God, for a clean shot.* She knew that as soon as her heart quit racing, she might be able to move. This is if her knees held steady.

The men went about their business as if she weren't even there. Wolf nodded. Was that in gratitude? Or what? She sucked in a deep breath and swallowed hard. The burning at the back of her eyes warned her to get the blazes out of there. She spun on her heel and took the long way back to her own wagons. No way was she going to let anyone see her cry.

*I shot a man! I shot a man!* The words kept time with the beat of her feet. *Why didn't I aim for his head?* It had happened so fast. She tried to remember each move. By the time she got back to the wagon, her hands shook so hard that she about dropped the gun. Tears blurred her vision. Her teeth clicked together no matter how hard she clamped her jaw.

"Jesselynn."

She ignored Wolf, threw her gun in the wagon bed, and kept on going, breaking into a run when she cleared the wagons. Feet pounding the dirt, she tore across the prairie, heading for the willows that lined the river. Her breath tore at her sides, but she forced herself to keep on running. Was that someone behind her? She couldn't slow to look. Tears streamed. Breathe! Run!

Blood! She could see dark blood. Could hear again the rifle shot. *I shot a man!* She fell against the trunk of a tree and wrapped her arms around the rough bark to hold her up. Darkness covered the backs of her eyelids. Light-headed, she slumped forward as her whole body started shaking.

Suddenly solid arms held her from behind. Wolf gathered her to his chest when the shaking let up.

"Go away." She let her head drop to his chest. Holding it up was beyond her.

"No."

She could hear his heartbeat, thundering much like her own. "I . . . I . . . shot a man."

"I know. Thank you." The words rumbled in his chest. His breath teased her ear.

"You . . . could have . . . been . . . killed." Each word tore the lining on her throat.

"I know. Glad you had good aim."

She rested against him. He smelled of woodsmoke and man. She dug in her pocket. No handkerchief. Sniffing, she leaned back enough to look up into his face. Blood ran down the side of his head.

"You're hurt!"

"His bullet just grazed me. Might never hear right from this ear again."

With tender fingers she reached to touch his ear. The tip of it was gone and powder burns laced the side of his head. "Head wounds bleed bad."

He stripped some willow leaves from the branches and handed them to her. She compressed them in her hand and applied them to the wound along with pressure to stop the bleeding. All the while her eyes held steady on his.

"What are you lookin' at?" His breath fluttered her eyelashes.

"You." She took in a deep breath and let it out. His dark eyes shimmered, grew warm and warmer. Her heart took up a new rhythm. Heat pooled in her belly. Even with blood trailing down his neck, he took her breath away. *Is this what poetry means when it says "the heart sings"?* "I need to bandage you up."

"Not yet." *You are proud and strong, like a Sioux maiden.* He tightened his arms around her rib cage. *"Thou art beautiful, oh, my love . . .*

*thy hair is as a flock of goats that appear from Gilead . . . my dove, my unde-filed . . ."*

"Jesse! Jesse!"

Jesselynn swallowed again. "They're calling me."

"I know." Slowly, as though she was more precious than anything he'd ever held, he loosened his arms and, inch by inch, let his hands fall away from her until they stood separate once more.

A sound came from her throat. A whimper. She must stand alone again. Alone. The pain ripped through her. If she reached for him, would he hold her?

She blinked. Swallowed. And stepped back. Her legs trembled. Her belly quivered as if a cold wind nipped it. She took another deep breath. "Come." She reached for his hand, and together they turned and stepped out of the willow screen.

———

"I'm not going on with the wagon train." Three days later Wolf stood beside her again.

"What do you mean?" Jesselynn forced the words past the constriction in her throat.

"I have to go home."

"Home is going to be in Oregon."

"Not for me. I've already spoken with the men. They've agreed to go on with the train that arrived yesterday."

"Why wasn't I included in the meeting?"

"He's a good man—Jason Cobalt. He's led other trains west and plans on stayin' there himself this time. He'll get you all through." He kept his hands from clenching. And his teeth. *Don't look at me like that! You said you wanted to go to Oregon. I'm gettin' you there.*

"Why?"

"I must go home. To my people." *Come with me.*

She stared into his eyes, looking for the man who'd held her. Dark. Flat. Not even a flicker. Swallowing her tears, she took a step back. "Go with God."

———

Two days later, with the sun near to breaking the horizon, the order came. The wagons unwound from their circles and pulled into the long snake of white canvas and straining animals. Getting over the divide and into the South Pass lay before them.

Jesselynn drove one of her wagons, Meshach the other. She'd heard of the Rocky Mountains ahead. She didn't look back. She let the tears flow. *Lord, someday, some way, I will see him again. Surely you mean for that to happen. Surely.*

Off to the north, always on the opposite ridge, Wolf rode his bay Appaloosa, the white patches catching the sunlight. He didn't turn off until he saw they'd safely crossed South Pass. *Someday, my love— someday.*

# LOST IN PARADISE

## Are Her Wounds Too Deep to Ever Trust Again?

The beautiful, exotic landscape of Hawaii surrounds Maddy Hernandez but all she can see are heartache and disillusionment. After all, this is the place to which she swore she would never return.

Healing, however, comes in all forms, and this is a story of how determination and faith can couple with unexpected blessings. You will be touched and moved by this eloquent and tender novel written by the bestselling author of the RED RIVER OF THE NORTH series.

*Available from your nearest Christian bookstore (800) 991-7747 or from Bethany House Publishers.*

LAURAINE SNELLING

*a novel*

HAWAIIAN SUNRISE

Even with a future so full of promise, her past seemed determined to haunt her...

## The Leader in Christian Fiction!

BETHANY HOUSE PUBLISHERS

11400 Hampshire Ave. South
Minneapolis, MN 55438
www.bethanyhouse.com